"A gripping, funny, page-turning,
pretty much perfect
work of magical literature."

—NEIL GAIMAN, BESTSELLING AUTHOR OF *THE SANDMAN* AND *CORALINE*

"A luminous, entrancing novel with an
enthralling pair of characters at its heart."

—*BOOKLIST*

"Appealing...
Original..."

—JOANNE HARRIS, AUTHOR OF *CHOCOLAT*

"Magic in every word."

—SHERRILYN KENYON,
NEW YORK TIMES BESTSELLING AUTHOR OF *BORN OF ICE*

BOOKS BY ROBIN MCKINLEY

Beauty: A Retelling of the Story of Beauty and the Beast

The Door in the Hedge

The Blue Sword

The Hero and the Crown

The Outlaws of Sherwood

Deerskin

A Knot in the Grain and Other Stories

Rose Daughter

Spindle's End

Sunshine

Dragonhaven

Chalice

Water: Tales of Elemental Spirits
(with Peter Dickenson)

Fire: Tales of Elemental Spirits
(with Peter Dickenson)

SUNSHINE

SUNSHINE

ROBIN McKINLEY

speak

An Imprint of Penguin Group (USA) Inc.

SPEAK
Published by the Penguin Group
Penguin Group (USA) Inc., 345 Hudson Street, New York, New York 10014, U.S.A.
Penguin Group (Canada), 90 Eglinton Avenue East, Suite 700, Toronto, Ontario, Canada M4P 2Y3
(a division of Pearson Penguin Canada Inc.)
Penguin Books Ltd, 80 Strand, London WC2R 0RL, England
Penguin Ireland, 25 St Stephen's Green, Dublin 2, Ireland (a division of Penguin Books Ltd)
Penguin Group (Australia), 250 Camberwell Road, Camberwell, Victoria 3124, Australia
(a division of Pearson Australia Group Pty Ltd)
Penguin Books India Pvt Ltd, 11 Community Centre, Panchsheel Park, New Delhi - 110 017, India
Penguin Group (NZ), 67 Apollo Drive, Rosedale, North Shore 0632, New Zealand
(a division of Pearson New Zealand Ltd.)
Penguin Books (South Africa) (Pty) Ltd, 24 Sturdee Avenue,
Rosebank, Johannesburg 2196, South Africa

Registered Offices: Penguin Books Ltd, 80 Strand, London WC2R 0RL, England

First published in the United States of America by The Berkley Publishing Group,
a division of Penguin Group (USA) Inc., 2003
Published by Jove, The Berkley Publishing Group, a division of Penguin Group (USA), Inc., 2004
Published by The Berkley Publishing Group, a division of Penguin Group (USA) Inc., 2008

This edition published by Speak, an imprint of Penguin Group (USA) Inc., 2010

1 3 5 7 9 10 8 6 4 2

Copyright © Robin McKinley, 2003
Text design by Tiffany Estreicher
All rights reserved

THE LIBRARY OF CONGRESS HAS CATALOGED THE BERKLEY EDITION AS FOLLOWS:
McKinley, Robin.
Sunshine / Robin McKinley.
p. cm.
ISBN 0-425-19178-8
1. Vampires—Fiction. I. Title.
PS3563.C3816S86 2003
813'.54—dc21
2003052415

Speak ISBN 978-0-14-241110-0

Printed in the United States of America

To Peter,
my Mel and my Con wrapped up in one (slightly untidy) package.
Hey, am I lucky or what?

PART ONE

I T WAS A dumb thing to do but it wasn't that dumb. There hadn't been any trouble out at the lake in years. And it was so exquisitely far from the rest of my life.

Monday evening is our movie evening because we are celebrating having lived through another week. Sunday night we lock up at eleven or midnight and crawl home to die, and Monday (barring a few national holidays) is our day off. Ruby comes in on Mondays with her warrior cohort and attacks the coffeehouse with an assortment of high-tech blasting gear that would whack Godzilla into submission: those single-track military minds never think to ask their cleaning staff for help in giant lethal marauding creature matters. Thanks to Ruby, Charlie's Coffeehouse is probably the only place in Old Town where you are safe from the local cockroaches, which are approximately the size of chipmunks. You can hear them *clicking* when they canter across the cobblestones outside.

We'd begun the tradition of Monday evening movies seven years ago when I started slouching out of bed at four A.M. to get the bread going. Our first customers arrive at six-thirty and they want our Cinnamon Rolls as Big as Your Head and I am the one who makes them. I put the dough on to rise overnight and it is huge and puffy and waiting when I get there at four-thirty. By the time Charlie arrives at six to brew coffee and open the till (and, most of the year, start dragging the outdoor tables down the alley and out to the front), you can smell them baking. One of Ruby's lesser minions arrives at about five for the daily sweep- and mop-up. Except on Tuesdays, when the coffeehouse is gleaming and I am giving myself tendonitis trying to persuade stiff, surly, thirty-hour-refrigerated dough that it's time to loosen up.

Charlie is one of the big good guys in my universe. He gave me enough of a raise when I finished school (high school diploma by the skin of my teeth and the intercession of my subversive English teacher) and began working for him full time that I could afford my own place, and, even more important, he talked Mom into letting me have it.

But getting up at four A.M. six days a week does put a cramp on your social life (although as Mom pointed out every time she was in a bad mood, if I still lived at home I could get up at four-twenty). At first Monday evening was just us, Mom and Charlie and Billy and Kenny and me, and sometimes one or two of the stalwarts from the coffeehouse. But over the years Monday evenings had evolved, and now it was pretty much any of the coffeehouse staff who wanted to turn up, plus a few of the customers who had become friends. (As Billy and Kenny got older the standard of movies improved too. The first Monday evening that featured a movie that *wasn't* rated "suitable for all ages" we opened a bottle of champagne.)

Charlie, who doesn't know how to sit still and likes do-it-yourselfing at home on his days off, had gradually knocked most of the walls down on the ground floor, so the increasing mob could mill around comfortably. But that was just it—my entire life existed in relation to the coffeehouse. My only friends were staff and regulars. I started seeing Mel because he was single and not bad-looking and the weekday assistant cook at the coffeehouse, with that interesting bad-boy aura from driving a motorcycle and having a few too many tattoos, and no known serious drawbacks. (Baz had been single and not bad-looking too, but there'd always been something a little off about him, which resolved itself when Charlie found him with his hand in the till.) I was happy in the bakery. I just sometimes felt when I got out of it I would like to get a little *farther* out.

Mom had been in one of her bad moods that particular week, sharp and short with everyone but the customers, not that she saw them much any more, she was in the office doing the paperwork and giving hell to any of our suppliers who didn't behave. I'd been having car trouble and was complaining about the garage bill to anyone who'd listen. No doubt Mom heard the story more than once, but then I heard her weekly stories about her hairdresser more than once too (she and Mary and Liz all used Lina, I think so they could get together after and discuss her love life, which was pretty fascinating). But Sunday evening she overheard me telling Kyoko, who had been out sick and was catching up after five days away, and Mom lost it. She shouted that if I lived at home I wouldn't need a car at all, and she was worried about me because I looked tired all the time, and when was I going to stop dreaming my life away and marry Mel and have some kids? Supposing that Mel and I wanted to get married, which hadn't been discussed. I wondered how Mom would take the appearance at the wedding of the remnants of Mel's old motorcycle gang—which is to say the ones that were still alive—with their hair and their Rocs and Griffins (even Mel still had an old Griffin for special occasions, although it *hemorrhaged* oil) and their attitude problems. They never showed up in force at the coffeehouse, but she'd notice them at the kind of wedding she'd expect me to have.

The obvious answer to the question of children was, who was going to look after the baby while I got up at four A.M. to make cinnamon rolls? Mel worked as appalling hours as I did, especially since he'd been promoted to head cook when Charlie had been forced—by a mutiny of all hands—to accept that he could either delegate something or drop dead of exhaustion. So househusbandry wasn't the answer. But in fact I knew my family would have got round this. When one of our waitresses got pregnant and the boyfriend left town and her own family threw her out, Mom and Charlie took her in and we all babysat in shifts, in and out of the coffeehouse. (We'd only just got rid of Mom's sister Evie and her four kids, who'd stayed for almost two years, and one mom and one baby seemed like pie in the sky in comparison. Especially after Evie, who is professionally helpless.) Barry was in second grade now, and Emmy was married to Henry. Henry was one of our regulars, and Emmy still waitressed for us. The coffeehouse is like that.

I *liked* living alone. I liked the *silence*—and nothing moving but me. I lived upstairs in a big old ex-farmhouse at the edge of a federal park, with my landlady on the ground floor. When I'd gone round to look at the place the old lady—very tall, very straight, and a level stare that went right through you—had looked at me and said she didn't like renting to Young People (she said this like you might say Dog Vomit) because they kept bad hours and made noise. I liked her immediately. I explained humbly that indeed I did keep bad hours because I had to get up at four A.M. to make cinnamon rolls for Charlie's Coffeehouse, whereupon she stopped scowling magisterially and invited me in.

It had taken three months after graduation for Mom to begin to consider my moving out, and that was with Charlie working on her. I was still reading the apartments-for-rent ads in the paper surreptitiously and making the phone calls when Mom was out of earshot. Most of them in my price range were dire. This apartment, up on the third floor at the barn end of the long rambling house, was perfect, and the old lady must have seen I meant it when I said so. I could feel my face light up when she opened the door at the top of the second flight of stairs, and the sunshine seemed to pour in from every direction. The living room balcony, cut down from the old hayloft platform but now overlooking the garden, still has no curtains.

By the time we signed the lease my future landlady and I were on our way to becoming fast friends, if you can be fast friends with someone who merely by the way she carries herself makes you feel like a troll. Maybe I was just curious: there was so obviously some mystery about her; even her name was odd. I wrote the check to *Miss Yolande.* No Smith or Jones or Fitzalan-Howard or anything. Just Miss Yolande. But she was always pleasant to me, and she wasn't wholly without human weakness: I brought her stuff from the coffeehouse and she ate it. I have that dominant feed-people gene that I think you have to have to survive in the small-restaurant business.

You sure aren't doing it for the money or the hours. At first it was now and then—I didn't want her to notice I was trying to feed her up—but she was always so pleased it got to be a regular thing. Whereupon she lowered the rent—which I have to admit was a godssend, since by then I'd found out what running a car was going to cost—and told me to lose the "Miss."

Yolande had said soon after I moved in that I was welcome in the garden any time I liked too, it was just her and me (and the peanut-butter-baited electric deer fence), and occasionally her niece and the niece's three little girls. The little girls and I got along because they were good eaters and they thought it was the most exciting thing in the world to come in to the coffeehouse and be *allowed behind the counter*. Well, I could remember what that felt like, when Mom was first working for Charlie. But that's the coffeehouse in action again: it tends to sweep out and engulf people. I think only Yolande has ever held out against this irresistible force, but then I do bring her white bakery bags almost every day.

Usually I could let Mom's temper roll off me. But there'd been too much of it lately. Coffeehouse disasters are often hardest on Mom, because she does the money and the admin, and for example actually follows up people's references when they apply for jobs, which Charlie never bothers with, but she isn't one for bearing trials quietly. That spring there'd been expensive repairs when it turned out the roof had been leaking for months and a whole corner of the ceiling in the main kitchen fell down one afternoon, one of our baking-goods suppliers went bust and we hadn't found another one we liked as well, and two of our wait staff and another one of the kitchen staff quit without warning. Plus Kenny had entered high school the previous autumn and he was goofing off and getting high instead of studying. He wasn't goofing off and getting high any more than I had done, but he had no gift for keeping a low profile. He was also very bright—both my half brothers were—and Mom and Charlie had high hopes for them. I'd always suspected that Charlie had pulled me off waitressing, which had bored me silly, and given me a real function in the kitchen to straighten me out. I had been only sixteen, so I was young for it, but he'd been letting me help him from time to time out back so he knew I could do it, the question was whether I would. Sudden scary responsibility had worked with me. But Kenny wasn't going to get a law degree by learning to make cinnamon rolls, and he didn't *need* to feed people the way Charlie or I did either.

Anyway Kenny hadn't come home till dawn that Sunday morning— his curfew was midnight on Saturday nights—and there had been hell to pay. There had been hell to pay all that day for all of us, and I went home that night smarting and cranky and my one night a week of twelve hours' sleep hadn't worked its usual rehabilitation. I took my tea and toast and *Immortal Death* (a favorite comfort book since under-the-covers-with-flashlight reading at the age of eleven or twelve) back to bed when I finally woke up at nearly noon, and even that really spartan scene when the heroine escapes the Dark Other who's been pursuing her for three hundred pages by calling on her demon heritage (finally) and turning herself into a waterfall didn't cheer me up. I spent most of the afternoon housecleaning, which is my other standard answer to a bad mood, and that didn't work either. Maybe I was worried about Kenny too. I'd been lucky during my brief tearaway spell; he might not be. Also I take the quality of my flour very seriously, and I didn't think much of our latest trial baking-supply company.

When I arrived at Charlie and Mom's house that evening for Monday movies the tension was so thick it was like walking into a blanket. Charlie was popping corn and trying to pretend everything was fine. Kenny was sulking, which probably meant he was still hung over, because Kenny didn't sulk, and Billy was being hyper to make up for it, which of course didn't. Mary and Danny and Liz and Mel were there, and Consuela, Mom's latest assistant, who was beginning to look like the best piece of luck we'd had all year, and about half a dozen of our local regulars. Emmy and Barry were there too, as they often were when Henry was away, and Mel was playing with Barry, which gave Mom a chance to roll her eyes at me and glare, which I knew meant "see how good he is with children—it's time he had some of his own." Yes. And in another fourteen years this hypothetical kid would be starting high school and learning better, more advanced, adolescent ways of how to screw up and make grown-ups crazy.

I loved every one of these people. And I couldn't take another minute of their company. Popcorn and a movie would make us all feel better, and it was a working day tomorrow, and you have only so much brain left over to worry with if you run a family restaurant. The Kenny crisis would go away like every other crisis had always gone away, worn down and eventually buried by an accumulation of order slips, till receipts, and shared stories of the amazing things the public gets up to.

But the thought of sitting for two hours—even with Mel's arm around me—and a bottomless supply of excellent popcorn (Charlie couldn't stop feeding people just because it was his day off) wasn't enough on that particular Monday. So I said I'd had a headache all day (which was true) and on second thought I would go home to bed, and I was sorry. I was out the door again not five minutes after I'd gone in.

Mel followed me. One of the things we'd had almost from the beginning was an ability *not* to talk about everything. These people who want to talk about their *feelings* all the time, and want you to talk about yours, make me *nuts*. Besides, Mel knows my mother. There's nothing to discuss. If my mom is the lightning bolt, I'm the tallest tree on the plain. That's the way it is.

There are two very distinct sides to Mel. There's the wild-boy side, the motorcycle tough. He's cleaned up his act, but it's still there. And then there's this strange vast serenity that seems to come from the fact that he doesn't feel he has to prove anything. The blend of anarchic thug and tranquil self-possession makes him curiously restful to be around, like walking proof that oil and water can mix. It's also great on those days that everyone else in the coffeehouse is screaming.

It was Monday, so he smelled of gasoline and paint rather than garlic and onions. He was absentmindedly rubbing the oak tree tattoo on his shoulder. He was a tattoo-rubber when he was thinking about something else, which meant that whatever he was cooking or working on could get pretty liberally dispersed about his person on ruminative days.

"She'll sheer, day or so," he said. "I was thinking, maybe I'll talk to Kenny."

"Do it," I said. "It would be nice if he lived long enough to find out he doesn't want to be a lawyer." Kenny wanted to get into Other law, which is the dancing-on-the-edge-of-the-muttering-volcano branch of law, but a lawyer is still a lawyer.

Mel grunted. He probably had more reason than me to believe that lawyers are large botulism bacteria in three-piece suits.

"Enjoy the movie," I said.

"I know the real reason you're blowing, sweetheart," Mel said.

"Billy's turn to rent the movie," I said. "And I hate westerns."

Mel laughed, kissed me, and went back indoors, closing the door gently behind him.

I stood restlessly on the sidewalk. I might have tried the library's new-novels shelf, a dependable recourse in times of trouble, but Monday evening was early closing. Alternatively I could go for a walk. I didn't feel like reading: I didn't feel like looking at other people's imaginary lives in flat black and white from out here in my only too unimaginary life. It was getting a little late for solitary walking, even around Old Town, and besides, I didn't want a walk either. I just didn't know what I did want.

I wandered down the block and climbed into my fresh-from-the-mechanics car and turned the key. I listened to the nice healthy purr of the engine and out of nowhere decided it might be fun to go for a drive. I wasn't a going for a drive sort of person usually. But I thought of the lake.

When my mother had still been married to my father we'd had a summer cabin out there, along with hundreds of other people. After my parents split up I used to take the bus out there occasionally to see my gran. I didn't know where my gran lived—it wasn't at the cabin—but I would get a note or a phone call now and then suggesting that she hadn't seen me for a while, and we could meet at the lake. My mother, who would have loved to forbid these visits—

when Mom goes off someone, she goes off comprehensively, and when she went off my dad she went off his entire family, excepting me, whom she equally passionately demanded to keep— didn't, but the result of her not-very-successfully restrained unease and disapproval made those trips out to the lake more of an adventure than they might otherwise have been, at least in the beginning. In the beginning I had kept hoping that my gran would do something really *dramatic*, which I was sure she was capable of, but she never did. It wasn't till after I'd stopped hoping . . . but that was later, and not at all what I had had in mind. And then when I was ten she disappeared.

When I was ten the Voodoo Wars started. They were of course nothing about voodoo, but they were about a lot of bad stuff, and some of the worst of them in our area happened around the lake. A lot of the cabins got burned down or leveled one way or another, and there were a few places around the lake where you still didn't go if you didn't want to have bad dreams or worse for months afterward. Mostly because of those bad spots (although also because there simply weren't as many people to have vacation homes anywhere any more) after the Wars were over and most of the mess cleared up, the lake never really caught on again. The wilderness was taking over—which was a good thing because it meant that it *could*. There were a lot of places now where nothing was ever going to grow again.

It was pretty funny really, the only people who ever went out there regularly were the Supergreens, to see how the wilderness was getting on, and if as the urban populations of things like raccoons and foxes and rabbits and deer moved back out of town again, they started to look and behave like raccoons and foxes and rabbits and deer had used to look and behave. Supergreens also counted things like osprey and pine marten and some weird marsh grass that was another endangered species although not so interesting to look at, none of which seemed to care about bad human magic, or maybe the bad spots didn't give ospreys and pine martens and marsh grass bad dreams. I went out there occasionally with Mel—we saw ospreys pretty often and pine martens once or twice, but all marsh grass looks like all other marsh grass to me—but I hadn't been there after dark since I was a kid.

The road that went to what had been my parents' cabin was passable, if only just. I got out there and went and sat on the porch and looked at the lake. My parents' cabin was the only one still standing in this area, possibly because it had belonged to my father, whose name meant something even during the Voodoo Wars. There was a bad spot off to the east, but it was far enough away not to trouble me, though I could feel it was there.

I sat on the sagging porch, swinging my legs and feeling the troubles of the day draining out of me like water. The lake was beautiful: almost flat calm, the gentlest lapping against the shore, and silver with moonlight. I'd had many good times here: first with my parents, when they were still happy together, and later on with my gran. As I sat there I began to feel that if I sat there long enough I could get to the bottom of what was making me so cranky lately, find out if it was anything worse than poor-quality flour and a somewhat errant little brother.

I never heard them coming. Of course you don't, when they're vampires.

I HAD KIND of a lot of theoretical knowledge about the Others, from reading what I could pull off the globenet about them—fabulously, I have to say, embellished by my addiction to novels like *Immortal Death* and *Blood Chalice*—but I didn't have much practical 'fo. After the Voodoo Wars, New Arcadia went from being a parochial backwater to number eight on the national top ten of cities to live in, simply because most of it was still standing. Our new rank brought its own problems. One of these was an increased sucker population. We were still pretty clean. But no place on this planet is truly free of Others, including those Darkest Others, vampires.

It is technically illegal to be a vampire. Every now and then some poor stupid or unlucky person gets made a sucker as part of some kind of warning or revenge, and rather than being taken in by the vampire community (if *community* is the right word) that created him or her, they are dumped somewhere that they will be found by ordinary humans before the sun gets them the next morning. And then they have to spend the rest of their, so to speak, lives, in a kind of half prison, half asylum, under doctors' orders—and of course under guard. I'd heard, although I had no idea if it was true, that these miserable ex-people are executed—drugged senseless and then staked, beheaded, and burned—when they reached what would have been their normal life expectancy if they'd been alive in the usual way.

One of the origins of the Voodoo Wars was that the vampires, tired of being the only ones of the Big Three, major-league Other Folk coherently and comprehensively legislated against, created a lot of vampires that they left for us humans to look after, and then organized them—somehow—into a wide-scale breakout. Vampirism doesn't generally do a lot for your personality—that is, a lot of good—and the vampires had chosen as many really nice people as possible to turn, to emphasize their disenchantment with the present system. Membership in the Supergreens, for example, plummeted by something like forty percent during the Voodoo Wars, and a couple of big national charities had to shut down for a few years.

It's not that any of the Others are really popular, or that it had only been the vampires against us during the Wars. But a big point about vampires is that they are the only ones that can't hide what they are: let a little sunlight touch them and they burst into flames. Very final flames. Exposure and destruction in one neat package. Weres are only in danger once a month, and there are drugs that will hold the Change from happening. The drugs are illegal, but then so are coke and horse and hypes and rats'-brains and trippers. If you want the anti-Change drugs you can get them. (And most Weres do. Being a Were isn't as bad as being a vampire, but it's bad enough.) And a lot of demons look perfectly normal. Most demons have some funny habit or other but unless you live with one and catch it eating garden fertilizer or old combox components or growing scaly wings and floating six inches above the bed after it falls asleep, you'd never know. And some demons are pretty nice, although it's not something you want to count on. (I'm talking about the Big Three, which everyone does, but "demon" is a pretty catch-all term really, and it can often turn out to mean what the law enforcement official on the other end of it wants it to mean at the time.)

The rest of the Others don't cause much trouble, at least not officially. It is pretty cool to be suspected of being a fallen angel, and everyone knows someone with sprite or peri blood. Mary, at the coffeehouse, for example. Everyone wants her to pour their coffee because coffee poured by Mary is always hot. She doesn't know where this comes from, but she doesn't deny it's some kind of Other blood. So long as Mary sticks to being a waitress at a coffeehouse, the government turns a blind eye to this sort of thing.

But if anyone ever manages to distill a drug that lets a vampire go out in daylight they'll be worth more money in a month than the present total of all bank balances held by everyone on the global council. There are a lot of scientists and backyard bozos out there trying for that jackpot—on both sides of the line. The smart money is on the black-market guys, but it's conceivable that the guys in the white hats will get there first. It's a more and more open secret that the suckers in the asylums are being experimented on—for their own good, of course. That's another result of the Voodoo Wars. The global council claims to want to "cure" vampirism. The legit scientists probably aren't starting with autopyrocy, however. (At least I don't think they are. Our June holiday Monday is for Hiroshi Gutterman who managed to destroy a lot of vampires single-handedly, but probably *not* by being a Naga demon and closing his sun-proof hood at an opportune moment, because aside from not wanting to think about even a full-blood Naga having a hood big enough, there are no plausible rumors that either the suckers or the scientists are raising cobras for experiments with their skins.)

There are a lot of vampires out there. Nobody knows how many, but a lot. And the clever ones—at least the clever and lucky ones—tend to wind up wealthy. Really old suckers are almost always really wealthy suckers. Any time there isn't any other news for a while you can pretty well count on another big article all over the globenet debating how much of the world's money is really in sucker hands, and those articles are an automatic pickup for every national and

local paper. Maybe we're all just paranoid. But there's another pecu-
liarity about vampires. They don't, you know, *breed*. Oh, they make
new vampires—but they make them out of pre-existing people.
Weres and demons and so on can have kids with ordinary humans
as well as with each other, and often do. At least some of the time
it's because the parents love each other, and love softens the edges
of xenophobia. There are amazing stories about vampire sex and
vampire orgies (there would be) but there's never been even a half-
believable myth about the birth of a vampire or half-vampire baby.

(Speaking of sucker sex, the most popular story concerns the fact
that since vampires aren't alive, all their lifelike activities are under
their voluntary control. This includes the obvious ones like walking, talking, and biting people, but it also includes the ones that are
involuntary in the living: like the flow of their blood. One of the first
stories that any teenager just waking up to carnal possibilities hears
about male vampires is that *they can keep it up indefinitely*. I personally stopped blushing after I had my first lover, and discovered
that absolutely the last thing I would want in a boyfriend is a permanent hard-on.)

So the suckers are right, humans *do* hate them in a single-mindedly
committed way that is unlike our attitude to any of the other major
categories of Others. But it's hardly surprising. Vampires hold maybe
one-fifth of the world's capital *and* they're a race incontestably apart.
Humans don't like ghouls and lamias either, but the rest of the undead don't last long, they're not very bright, and if one bites you, every city hospital emergency room has the antidote (supposing there's
enough of you left for you to run away with). The global council periodically tries to set up "talks" with vampire leaders in which they
offer an end to persecution and legal restriction and an inexhaustible
supply of pigs' blood in exchange for a promise that the vampires
will stop preying on people. In the first place this doesn't work because while vampires tend to hunt in packs, the vampire population
as a whole is a series of little fiefdoms, and alliances are brief and rare
and usually only exist for the purpose of destroying some mutually
intolerable other sucker fiefdom. In the second place the bigger the
gang and the more powerful the master vampire, the less he or she

moves around, and leaving headquarters to sit on bogus human global council "talks" is just not sheer. And third, pigs' blood isn't too popular with vampires. It's probably like being offered Cava when you've been drinking Veuve Clicquot Ponsardin all your life. (The coffeehouse has a beer and wine license, but Charlie has a soft spot for champagne. Charlie's was once on a globenet survey of restaurants, listed as the only coffeehouse anybody had ever heard of that serves champagne by the glass. You might be surprised how many people like bubbly with their meatloaf or even their cream cheese on pumpernickel.)

Okay, so I'm a little obsessed. Some people adore soap operas. Some people are neurotic about sports. I follow stories about the Others. Also, we know more about the Others at the coffeehouse—if we want to—because several of our regulars work for SOF—Special Other Forces. Also known as sucker cops, since, as I say, it's chiefly the suckers they worry about. Mom shuts them up when she catches them talking shop on our premises, but they know they always have an audience in me. I wouldn't trust *any* cop any farther than I could throw our Prometheus, the shining black monster that dominates the kitchen at Charlie's and is the apple of Mel's eye (you understand the connection between motorcycles and cooking when you've seen an industrial-strength stove at full blast), but I liked Pat and Jesse.

Our SOFs say that nobody and nothing will ever enable suckers to go out in daylight, and a good thing too, because daylight is the only thing that is preventing them from taking over the other four-fifths of the world economy and starting human ranching as the next hot growth area for venture capitalists. But then SOFs are professionally paranoid, and they don't have a lot of faith in the guys in lab coats, whether they're wearing black hats or white ones.

There are stories about "good" vampires like there are stories about the loathly lady who after a hearty meal of raw horse and hunting hound and maybe the odd huntsman or archer, followed by an exciting night in the arms of her chosen knight, turns into the kindest and most beautiful lady the world has ever seen; but according to our SOFs no human has ever met a good vampire, or at least has never returned to say so, which kind of tells its own tale, doesn't it?

And the way I see it, the horse and the hounds and the huntsman are still dead, and you have to wonder about the psychology of the chosen knight who goes along with all the carnage *and* the fun and frolic in bed on some dubious grounds of "honor."

Vampires kill people and suck their blood. Or rather the other way around. They like their meat alive and frightened, and they like to play with it a while before they finish it off. Another story about vampires is that the one domestic pet a vampire may keep is a cat, because vampires understand the way cats' minds work. During the worst of the Voodoo Wars anyone who lived alone with a cat was under suspicion of being a vampire. There were stories that in a few places where the Wars were the worst, solitary people with cats who didn't burst into flames in daylight were torched. I hoped it wasn't true, but it might have been. There are always cats around Charlie's, but they are usually refugees seeking asylum from the local rat population, and rather desperately friendly. There are always more of them at the full moon too, which goes to show that not every Were chooses—or, more likely in Old Town, can afford—to go the drug route.

So when I swam back to consciousness, the fact that I was still alive and in one piece wasn't reassuring. I was propped against something at the edge of a ring of firelight. Vampires can see in the dark and they don't cook their food, but they seem to like playing with fire, maybe the way some humans get off on joyriding stolen cars or playing last-across on a busy railtrack.

I came out of it feeling wretchedly sick and shaky, and of course scared out of my mind. They'd put some kind of Breath over me. I knew that vampires don't have to stoop to blunt instruments or something on a handkerchief clapped over your face. They can just breathe on you and you are out cold. It isn't something they can all do, but nearly all vampires hunt in packs since the Wars, and being the Breather to a gang had become an important sign of status (according to globenet reports). They can *all* move utterly silently, however, and, over short distances, faster than anything—well, faster than anything *alive*—as well. So even if the Breath went wrong somehow they'd catch you anyway, if they wanted to catch you.

"She's coming out of it," said a voice.

I'd never met a vampire before, nor heard one speak, except on TV, where they run the voice through some kind of antiglamor technology so no one listening will march out of their house and start looking for the speaker. I can't imagine that a vampire would want everyone listening to its voice to leap out of their chairs and start seeking it, but I don't know how vampires (or cats, or loathly ladies) think, and maybe it would want to do this. And there is, of course, a story, because there is always a story, that a master vampire can tune its voice so that maybe only one specific person of all the possibly millions of people who hear a broadcast (and a sucker interview is always a big draw) will jump out of their chair, etc. I don't think I believe this, but I'm just as glad of the antiglamor tech. But whatever else it does, it makes their voices sound funny. Not human, but not human in a clattery, mechanical, microchip way.

So in theory I suppose I shouldn't have known these guys were vampires. But I did. If you've been kidnapped by the Darkest Others, you know it.

In the first place, there's the smell. It's not at all a butcher-shop smell, as you might expect, although it does have that metallic blood tang to it. But meat in a butcher's shop is dead. I know this is a contradiction in terms, but vampires smell of *live* blood. And something else. I don't know what the something else is; it's not any animal, vegetable, or mineral in my experience. It's not attractive or disgusting, although it does make your heart race. That's in the genes, I suppose. Your body knows it's prey even if your brain is fuddled by the Breath or trying not to pay attention. It's the smell of vampire, and your fight-or-flight instincts take over.

There aren't many stories of those instincts actually getting you away though. At that moment I couldn't think of any.

And vampires don't move like humans. I'm told that young ones can "pass" (after dark) if they want to, and a popular way of playing chicken among humans is to go somewhere there's a rumor of vampires and see if you can spot one. I knew Kenny and his buddies had done this a few times. I did it when I was their age. It's not enormously dangerous if you stay in a group and don't go into the no-man's-land around the big cities. We're a medium-sized city and, as I say, we're pretty clean. It's still a dumb and dangerous thing to do—dumber than my driving out to the lake should have been.

The vampires around the bonfire weren't bothering not to move like vampires.

Also, I said that the antiglam tech makes sucker voices sound funny on TV and radio and the globenet. They sound even funnier in person. Funny peculiar. Funny awful.

Maybe there's something about the Breath. I woke up, as I say, sick and wretched and *scared*, but I should have been freaked completely past thought and I wasn't. I knew this was the end of the road. Suckers don't snatch people and then decide they're not very hungry after all and let them go. I was dinner, and when I was finished being dinner, I was dead. But it was like: okay, that's the way it goes, bad luck, damn. Like the way you might feel if your vacation got canceled at the last minute, or you'd spent all day making a fabulous birthday cake for your boyfriend and tripped over the threshold bringing it in and it landed upside down on the dog. *Damn.* But that's all.

I lay there, breathing, listening to my heart race, but feeling this weird numb composure. We were still by the lake. From where I half-lay I could see it through the trees. It was still a beautiful serene moonlit evening.

"Do we take her over immediately?" This was the one who had noticed I was awake. It was a little apart from the others, and was sitting up straight on a tree stump or a rock—I couldn't see which—as if keeping watch.

"Yeah. Bo says so. But he says we have to dress her up first." This one sounded as if it was in charge. Maybe it was the Breather.

"Dress her *up*? What is this, a party?"

"I thought *we* had the party while . . ." said a third one. Several of them laughed. Their laughter made the hair on my arms stand on end. I couldn't distinguish any individual shapes but that of the watcher. I couldn't see how many of them there were. I thought I was listening to male voices but I wasn't sure. That's how weird sucker voices are.

"Bo says our . . . *guest* is old-fashioned. Ladies should wear dresses."

I could feel them looking at me, feel the glint of their eyes in the firelight. I didn't look back. Even when you already know you're toast you don't look in vampires' eyes.

"She's a lady, huh."

"Don't matter. She'll look enough like one in a dress." They all laughed again at this. I may have whimpered. One of the vampires separated itself from the boneless dark slithery blur of vampires and came toward me. My heart was going to lunge out of my mouth but I lay still. I was, strangely, beginning to feel my way into the numbness—as if, if I could, I would find the center of *me* again. As if being able to think clearly and calmly held any possibility of doing me any good. I wondered if this was how it felt when you woke up in the morning on the day you knew you were going to be executed.

One of the things you need to understand is that I'm not a brave person. I don't put up with being messed around, and I don't suffer fools gladly. The short version of that is that I'm a bitch. Trust me, I can produce character references. But that's something else. I'm not *brave*. Mel is brave. His oldest friend told me some stories about him once I could barely stand to *listen* to, about dispatch riding during the Wars, and Mel'd been pissed off when he found out, although he hadn't denied they happened. Mom is brave: she left my dad with no money, no job, no prospects—her own parents had dumped her when she married my dad, and her younger sisters didn't find her again till she resurfaced years later at Charlie's—and a six-year-old daughter. Charlie is brave: he started a coffeehouse by talking his bank into giving him a loan on his house back in the days when you only saw rats, cockroaches, derelicts, and Charlie himself on the streets of Old Town.

I'm not brave. I make cinnamon rolls. I read a lot. My idea of excitement is Mel popping a wheelie driving away from a stoplight with me on pillion.

The vampire was standing right next to me. I didn't think I'd seen it walk that far. I'd seen it stand up and become one vampire out of a group of vampires. Then it was standing next to me. It. He.

I looked at his hand as he held something out to me. "Put it on." I reluctantly extended my own hand and accepted what it was. He didn't seem any more eager to touch me than I was to touch him; the thing he was offering glided from his hand to mine. He moved away. I tried to watch, but I couldn't differentiate him from the shadows. He was just *not there*.

I stood up slowly and turned my back on all of them. You might not think you could turn your back on a lot of vampires, but do you want to watch while they check the rope for kinks and the security of the noose and the lever on the trap door or do you maybe want to close your eyes? I turned my back. I pulled my T-shirt off over my head and dropped the dress down over me. The shoulder straps barely covered my bra straps and my neck and shoulders and most of my back and breast were left bare. Buffet dining. Very funny. I took my jeans off underneath the long loose skirt. I still had my back to them. I was hoping that vampires weren't very interested in a meal that was apparently going to someone else. I didn't like having my back to them but I kept telling myself it didn't matter (there are guards to grab you if the lever still jams on the first attempt and you try to dive off the scaffold). I was very carefully clumsy and awkward about taking my jeans off, and in the process tucked my little jackknife up under my bra. It was only something to do to make me feel I hadn't just given up. What are you going to do with a two-and-a-half-inch folding blade against a lot of vampires?

I'd had to take my sneakers off to get out of my jeans, and I looked at them dubiously. The dress was silky and slinky and it didn't go with sneakers, but I didn't like going barefoot either.

"That'll do," said the one who had given me the dress. He reappeared from the shadows. "Let's go."

And he reached out and took my arm.

Physically I only flinched; internally it was revolution. The numbness faltered and the panic broke through. My head throbbed and swam; if it hadn't been for those tight, terrifying fingers around my upper arms I would have fallen. A second vampire had me by the other arm. I hadn't seen it approach, but at that moment I couldn't see anything, feel anything but panic. It didn't matter that they had to have touched me before—when they caught me, when they put me under the dark, when they brought me to wherever we were—I hadn't been conscious for that. I was conscious *now*.

But the numbness—the weird detached composure, whatever it was—pulled itself together. It was the oddest sensation. The numbness and the panic crashed through my spasming body, and the numbness won. My brain stuttered like a cold engine and reluctantly fired again.

The vampires had dragged me several blind steps while this was going on. The numbness now noted dispassionately that they were wearing gloves. As if this suddenly made it all right the panic subsided. One of my feet hurt; I'd already managed to stub it on something, invisible in the dark.

The material of the gloves felt rather like leather. The skin of what animal, I thought.

"You sure are a quiet one," the second vampire said to me. "Aren't you going to beg for your life or anything?" It laughed. He laughed.

"Shut up," said the first vampire.

I didn't know why I knew this, since I couldn't see or hear them, but I knew the other vampires were following, except for one or two who were flitting through the trees ahead of us. Maybe I didn't know it. Maybe I was imagining things.

We didn't go far, and we went slowly. For whatever reason the two vampires holding me let me pick my shaky, barefoot, human way across bad ground in the dark. It must have seemed slower than a crawl to them. There was still a moon, but that light through the leaves only confused matters further for me. I didn't think this was an area I was familiar with, even if I could see it. I thought I could feel a bad spot not too far away, farther into the trees. I wondered if vampires felt bad spots the way humans did. Everyone wondered if vampires had anything to do with the presence of bad spots, but bad spots were mysterious; the Voodoo Wars had produced bad spots, and vampires had been the chief enemy in the Wars, but even the globenet didn't seem to know any more. Everyone in the area knew about the presence of bad spots around the lake, whether they went hiking out there or not, but there's never any gossip about sucker activity. Vampires tend to prefer cities: the higher density of human population, presumably.

The only noises were the ones I made, and a little *hush* of water, and the stirring of the leaves in the air off the lake. The shoreline was more rock than marsh, and when we crossed a ragged little stream the cold water against my feet was a shock: *I'm alive*, it said.

The rational numbness now pointed out that vampires could, apparently, cross running water under at least some circumstances. Perhaps the size of the stream was important. I observed that my two guards had stepped across it bank to bank. Perhaps they didn't want to get their shoes wet, as they had the luxury of shoes. It would be bad business for the electric moat companies if it became known that running water didn't stop suckers.

I could feel the . . . what? . . . increasing. Oppression, tension, suspense, foreboding. I of course was feeling all these things. But we were coming closer to wherever we were going, and my escorts didn't like the situation either. I told myself I was imagining this, but the impression remained.

We came out of the trees and paused. There was enough moonlight to make me blink; or perhaps it was the surprise of coming to a clear area. Somehow you don't think of suckers coming out under the sky in a big open space, even at night.

There had been a few really grand houses on the lake. I'd seen pictures of them in magazines but I'd never visited one. They had been abandoned with the rest during the Wars and were presumably either burned or blasted or derelict now. But I was looking up a long, once-landscaped slope to an enormous mansion at the head of it. Even in the moonlight I could see how shabby it was; it was missing some of its shingles and shutters, and I could see at least one broken window. But it was still standing. Where we were would once have been a lawn of smooth perfect green, and I could see scars in the earth near the house that must have been garden paths and flower beds. There was a boathouse whose roof had fallen in near us where we stood at the shore. The bad spot was near here; behind the house, not far. I was surprised there was a building still relatively in one piece this close to a bad spot; there was a lot I didn't know about the Wars.

I felt I would have been content to go on not knowing.

"Time to get it over with," said Bo's lieutenant.

They started walking up the slope toward the house. The others had melted out of the trees (wherever they'd been meanwhile) and were straggling behind the three of us, my two jailers and me. My sense that none of them was happy became stronger. I wondered if their willingness to walk through the woods at fumbling human speed had anything to do with this. I looked up at the sky, wondering, almost calmly, if this was the last time I would see it. I glanced down and to either side. The footing was nearly as bad here as it had been among the trees. There was something odd . . . I thought about my parents' old cabin and the cabins and cottages (or rather the remains of them) around it. In the ten years since the Wars had been officially ended saplings and scrub had grown up pretty thoroughly around all of them. They should have done the same around this house. I thought: it's been *cleared*. Recently. That's why the ground is so uneven. I looked again to either side: now that I was looking it was obvious that the forest had been hacked back too. The big house was sitting, all by itself, in the middle of a wide expanse of land that had been roughly but thoroughly stripped of anything that might cause a shadow.

This shouldn't have made my situation any worse, but I was suddenly shuddering, and I hadn't been before.

The house was plainly our destination. I stumbled, and stumbled again. I was not doing it deliberately as some kind of hopeless delaying tactic; I was merely losing my ability to hold myself together. Something about that cleared space, about what this meant about . . . whatever was waiting for me. Something about the reluctance of my escort. About the fact that therefore whatever it was that waited was more terrible than they were.

My jailers merely tightened their hold and frog-marched me when I wobbled. Suckers are very strong; they may not have noticed that they were now bearing nearly all my weight as my knees gave and my feet lost their purchase on the ragged ground.

They dragged me up the last few stairs to the wide, once-elegant porch; the treads creaked under *my* weight as I missed my footing,

while the vampires flowed up on either side of us with no more
sound than they had made ranging through the woods. One of them
opened the front door and stood aside for the prisoner and her guards
to go in first. We entered a big, dark, empty hall; some moonlight
spilled in through open doors on either side of us, enough that my
eyes could vaguely make out the extent of it. It was probably bigger
than the whole ground floor of Mom and Charlie's house. At the far
end a staircase swirled up in a semicircle, disappearing into the
murk overhead.

We turned left and went through a half-open door.

This had to be a ballroom; it was even bigger than the front hall
had been. There was no furniture that I could see, but there was a
muddle overhead—its shadow had wrenched my panicky attention
toward it—that looked rather like a vast chandelier, although I would
have expected anything like that to have been looted years ago. It
seemed like acres of floor as we crossed it. There was another muddle
leaning up against the wall in front of us—a possibly human-body-
shaped muddle, I thought, confused. Another prisoner? Another live
dinner? Was waiting to be eaten in company going to be any less
horrible than waiting alone? Where was the "old-fashioned guest"
who liked dresses rather than jeans and sneakers? Oh, dear gods and
angels, let this be over *quickly*, I cannot bear much more. . . .

The muddle was someone sitting cross-legged, head bowed, forearms on knees. I didn't realize till it raised its head with a liquid, inhuman motion that it was another vampire.

I jerked backward. I didn't mean to; I knew I wasn't going to get
away: I couldn't help it. The vampire on my left—the one who had
asked me why I didn't beg for my life—laughed again. "There's some
life in you after all, girlie. I was wondering. Bo wouldn't like it if it
turned out we caught a blanker. He wants his guest in a good mood."

Bo's lieutenant said again, "Shut up."

One of the other vampires drifted up to us and handed its lieutenant something. They passed it between them as if it had been no
more than a handkerchief, but it . . . clanked.

Bo's lieutenant said, "Hold her." He dropped my arm and picked
up my foot, as casually as a carpenter picking up a hammer. I would

have fallen, but the other vampire held me fast. Something cold closed around my ankle, and when he dropped my foot again it fell to the floor hard enough to bruise the sole, because of the new weight. I was wearing a metal shackle, and trailing a chain. The vampire who had brought the thing to Bo's lieutenant stretched out the end of the chain and clipped it into a ring in the wall.

"How many days has it been, Connie?" said Bo's lieutenant softly. "Ten? Twelve? Twenty? She's young and smooth and warm. Totally flash. Bo told us to bring you a nice one. She's all for you. We haven't touched her."

I thought of the gloves.

He was backing away slowly as he spoke, as if the cross-legged vampire might jump at *him*. The vampire holding me seemed to be idly watching Bo's lieutenant, and then with a sudden, spine-unhinging *hisssss* let go of me and sprang after him and the others, who were dissolving back into the shadows, as if afraid to be left behind.

I fell down, and, for a moment, half-stunned, couldn't move.

The vampire gang was, in the sudden way of vampires, now on the other side of the big room, by the door. I thought it was Bo's lieutenant who—I didn't see how—made some sort of gesture, and the chandelier burst alight. "You'll want to check out what you're getting," he said, and now that he was leaving his voice sounded strong and scornful. "Bo didn't want you to think we'd try anything nomad. And, so okay, so you don't need the light. But it's more fun if she can see you too, isn't it?"

The vampire who had dropped me said, "Hey, her feet are already bleeding—if you like feet." He giggled, a high-pitched goblin screech.

Then they were gone.

I THINK I must have fainted again. When I came to myself I was stiff all over, as if I had been lying on the floor for a long time. I both remembered and tried not to let myself quite remember what had happened. This lasted for maybe ten seconds. I was still alive, so I wasn't dead yet. If it wanted me awake and struggling, to continue to appear to be unconscious was a good idea. I lay facing the door the gang had left by; which meant that the cross-legged vampire was behind me. . . . *Don't think about it.*

I was up on my knees, halfway to my feet, and scrambling for the door before I finished thinking this, even though I knew you couldn't run away from a vampire. I had forgotten that I was chained to the wall. I hit the end of my chain and fell again. I cried out, as much from fear as pain. I lay sprawled where I struck, waiting for it to be over.

Nothing happened.

Again I thought, *Please, gods and angels, let it be over.*

Nothing happened.

Despairingly I sat up, hitched myself around to face what was behind me.

It was looking at me. He was looking at me.

The chandelier was set with candles, not electric bulbs, so the light it shed was softer and less definite. Even so he looked bad. His eyes *(no: don't look in their eyes)* were a kind of gray-green, like stagnant bog water, and his skin was the color of old mushrooms—the sort of mushrooms you find screwed up in a paper bag in the back of the fridge and try to decide if they're worth saving or if you should throw them out now and get it over with. His hair was black, but lank and dull. He would have been tall if he stood up. His shoulders were broad, and his hands and wrists, drooping over his knees, looked huge. He wore no shirt, and his feet, like mine, were bare. This seemed curiously indecent, that he should be half naked. I didn't like it. . . . Oh, right, I thought, good one. The train is roaring toward you and the villain is twirling his moustache and you're fussing that he's tied you to the track with the wrong kind of rope. There was a long angry weal across one of the vampire's forearms. Overall he looked . . . spidery. Predatory. *Alien.* Nothing human except that he was more or less the right shape.

He was *thin*, thin to emaciated, the cheekbones and ribs looking like they were about to split the old-mushroom skin. It didn't matter. The still-burning vitality in that body was visible even to my eyes. He would be fine again once he'd had dinner.

My teeth chattered. I pulled my knees up under my chin and

wrapped my arms around them. We sat like this for several minutes, the vampire motionless, while I chattered and trembled and tried not to moan. Tried not to beg uselessly for my life. Watched him watching me. I didn't look into his eyes again. At first I looked at his left ear, but that was too close to those eyes—how could something the color of swamp water be that *compelling?*—so I looked at his bony left shoulder instead. I could still see him staring at me. Or feel him staring.

"Speak," he said at last. "Remind me that you are a rational crea-ture." The words had long pauses between them, as if he found it difficult to speak, or as if he had to recall the words one at a time; and his voice was rough, as if some time recently he had damaged it by prolonged shouting. Perhaps he found it awkward to speak to his dinner. If he wasn't careful he'd go off me, like Alice after she'd been introduced to the pudding. I should be so lucky.

I flinched at the first sound of his voice, both because he had spo-ken at all, and also because his voice sounded as alien as the rest of him looked, as if the chest that produced it was made out of some strange material that did not reflect sound the same way that ordi-nary—that is to say, live—flesh did. His voice sounded much odder—eerier, direr—than the voices of the vampires who had brought me here. You could half-imagine that Bo's gang had once been human. You couldn't imagine that this one ever had.

As I flinched I squeaked—a kind of *unh?* First I thought rather deliriously about Alice and her pudding, and then the meaning of his words began to penetrate. Remind him I was a rational creature! I wasn't at all sure I still was one. I tried to pull my scattered wits to-gether, come up with a topic other than Lewis Carroll. . . . "I—oh—they called you Connie," I said at random, after I had been silent too long. "Is that your name?"

He made a noise like a cough or a growl, or something else I didn't have a name for, some vampire thing. "You know enough not to look in my eyes," he said. "But you do not know not to ask me my name?" The words came closer together this time, and there was definitely a question mark at the end. He was *asking* me.

"Oh—no—oh—I don't know—I don't know that much about

vam—er," I gabbled, remembering halfway through the word he had not himself used the word *vampire*. He'd said "me" and "my." Perhaps you didn't say *vampire* like you didn't ask one's name. I tried to think of everything Pat and Jesse and the others had told me over the years, and considered the likelihood that the SOF view of vampires was probably rather different from the vampires' own view and of limited use to me now. And that having *Immortal Death* very nearly memorized was no use at all. "Pardon me," I said, with as much dignity as I could pretend to, which wasn't much. "I—er—what would you like me to talk about?"

There was another of his pauses, and then he said, "Tell me who you are. You need not tell me your name. Names have power—even human names. Tell me where you live and what you do with your living."

My mouth dropped open. "Tell you—" Who am I, Scheherazade? I felt a sudden hysterical rush of outrage. It was bad enough that I was going to be eaten (or rather, drunk—my mind would revert to Alice), but I had to *talk* first? "I—I am the baker at Charlie's Coffeehouse, in town. Charlie married my mom when I was ten, just before the—er." I managed not to say "before the Voodoo Wars," which I thought might be a sensitive subject. "They have two sons, Kenny and Billy. They're nice kids." Well, Billy was still a nice kid. Kenny was a teenager. Oh, hell. I wasn't supposed to be using names. Oh, too bad. There are more than one Charlie and Kenny and Billy in the world. "We all work at the coffeehouse although my brothers are still in school. My boyfriend works there too. He rules the kitchen now that Charlie has kind of become the maitre d' and the wine steward, if you want to talk about a coffeehouse having a maitre d' and a wine steward." Okay, I thought, I remembered not to say Mel's name.

But it was hard to remember what my life was. It seemed a very long time ago, all of it, now, tonight, chained to a wall in a deserted ballroom on the far side of the lake, talking to a vampire. "I live in an apartment across town from the coffeehouse, upstairs from Y—from the old lady who owns the house. I love it there, there are all these trees, but my windows get a lot of—er." This time what

I wasn't saying was "sunlight," which I thought might also be a touchy topic. "I've always liked fooling around in the kitchen. One of my first memories is holding a wooden spoon and crying till my mom let me stir something. Before she married Charlie, my mom used to tease me, say I was going to grow up to be a cook, other kids played softball and joined the drama club, all I ever did was hang around the coffeehouse kitchen, so, she said, she might as well marry one, a cook, since he kept asking—Charlie kept asking—she said she was finally saying yes, because she wanted to make it easy for me. That was our joke. She met him by working for him. She was a waitress. She likes feeding people—like Charlie and me and M— like Charlie and me and the cook. She thinks the answer to just about everything is a good nourishing meal, but she doesn't much like cooking, and now she mostly manages the rest of us, works out the schedule so everyone gets enough hours and nobody gets too many very often, which is sort of the Olympic triathalon version of rubbing your stomach and patting your head at the same time, only she has to do it every week, and she also does the books and the ordering. Um. It's just as well she's back there because a lot of people don't come to us for nourishing meals, they come for a slab of something chocolate and a glass of champagne, or M—er, or our all-day breakfast which is eggs and bacon and sausages and baked beans and pancakes and hash browns and toast, and a cinnamon roll till they run out, which they usually do by about nine, but there are muffins all day, and then a free wheelbarrow ride to the bus stop after. Er. That's a joke. A wheelbarrow ride over our cobblestones would be no favor anyway.

"I have to get up at four A.M. to start the cinnamon rolls—cinnamon rolls as big as your head, it's a Charlie's specialty—but I don't mind. I love working with yeast and flour and sugar and I love the smell of bread baking. M—I mean, my boyfriend, says he wanted to ask me out because he saw me the first time when I was up to my elbows in bread dough and covered with flour. He says that for most guys it's supposed to be great legs or a girl being a great dancer—I can't dance at all—or at least a good personality or something high-minded like that, but for him it was definitely watching me thump into that bread dough. . . ."

I hadn't realized I'd started crying. My long-ago, lost life. The tears were running—pouring—down my cheeks.

And suddenly the vampire moved toward me. I froze, thinking, *Oh no,* and *at last,* and *okay, at least my last thoughts are about everybody at the coffeehouse,* but all he did was hold one of his big hands under my chin, so the tears would fall into his palm. I cried now from fear and anticipation as well as loss and sorrow, and my tears had made quite a little pool before I stopped. I stopped because I was too tired to go on, and my whole head felt *squashy.* I suppose I should have been flipping out. He was *right next to me.* He hadn't moved again. When I stopped crying he lowered his hand and said calmly, "May I have your tears?" I nodded, bemused, and, very precisely and carefully, he touched my face with the forefinger of his other hand, wiping up the last drips. I was so braced for worse I barely noticed that this time a vampire really had touched me.

He moved back against the wall before he licked the wet finger and then drank the little palmful of salt water. I didn't mean to stare but I couldn't help it.

He wouldn't have had to say anything. Maybe he'd liked the story of my life. "Tears," he said. "Not as good as . . ." a really *ugly* ominous pause here ". . . but better than nothing."

"Oh, gods," I said, and buried my face in my knees once more. I had begun to shiver again too. I was exhausted past exhaustion, and I was also, it occurred to me, hungry and thirsty. And, of course, still waiting to die. Gruesomely.

I couldn't bear not to keep an eye on him for long, however, and I raised my now sticky face from my knees soon enough. I wiped my face on a corner of my ridiculous dress. I hadn't really noticed what I was wearing—there had been other things on my mind since I had been obliged to put it on—in other circumstances I would have found it very beautiful, but an absurd thing for a coffeehouse baker to be wearing, even a coffeehouse baker in a ballroom with a ball going on in it. If I were attending a ball I would be there as one of the caterers, I certainly wouldn't be there for the dancing. . . . I'm raving, I thought. The dress was a dark cranberry red. Heart's-blood red, I thought. It was put together slyly, in panels cut on the bias, so it clung to me round the top and swung out into what felt like yards of skirt at the hem. It draped over my awkward knees in drifts like something out of a Renaissance painting. I supposed it was silk; I hadn't had a lot of close-up experience with silk. It was soft like a clean baby's skin. I knew quite a lot about babies, clean and otherwise.

I glanced at him—at his left shoulder. He was still watching me. I let my gaze drift down, over his ragged black trousers, to his bare feet. He too had a shackle around one ankle. . . .

What?

He was shackled and pinned to the wall just as I was.

He must have seen me working it out. "Yes," he said.

"Wh-why?"

"No honor among thieves, you are thinking? Indeed. Bo and I are old enemies."

"But—" The reason for the wasteland around the house was suddenly apparent. No shelter from daylight except inside the house. Whoever it was—Bo—thought the shackle itself might not be enough. The chain that held him was many times heavier than mine, and both the shackle and—I could see it, now that I was looking—the plate in the wall that held the ring were stamped with . . . well, to start with, with the old, most basic ward symbol: a cross and a six-pointed star inside a circle. The standard warding against inhuman harm that ten percent of parents still had tattooed over their babies' hearts at birth, or so the current statistics said. It was illegal to tattoo a minor, because of the possible side effects, and you nearly had to have a dispensation from a god to be granted a license for a home birth since the Wars because the government assumed that the opportunity for an illegal tattoo was the only reason anyone would want a home birth. Warding tattoos didn't happen in hospitals. Theoretically. Jesse and Pat said that no fiddling tattoo would stop a vampire, but the real reason for its being illegal is that the stiff fines levied against parents who had it done anyway was a nice little annual nest egg for the government.

There was some evidence that a tempered metal ward spelled by an accredited wardsmith and worn next to the skin would discourage a vampire that unexpectedly came in contact with it, long enough for you to make a run for it—maybe. The problem with that scenario is as I said, most suckers run in packs. One of the friends of the one that let go of you would grab you, and the second one would know where not to grab.

I didn't want to peer too closely, but there were rather a lot of other symbols keeping the standard one company: the staked heart (I hated this one, however simple and coolly nonspecific the design), the perfect triangle, the oak tree, the unfallen angel, true grief, the singing lizard, the sun and moon. There were more too. Under other circumstances I might have thought the effect was a little frantic. As if whoever had planned it was throwing the book at a problem they didn't know how to solve.

The wardings did seem to be having some effect. The ankle the shackle encircled was swollen and a funny color (although what counted as a funny color for a vampire I wasn't sure) and looked pretty sore. The skin looked almost . . . *grated*. Ugh. But if the metal ward did protect—or in this case debilitate—who had belled the cat—fixed the shackle? Leaving aside for the moment who had done the smithwork. I daresay a wardsmith wouldn't argue if a gang of vampires showed up and put their case persuasively enough. Which is to say good wardsmiths can't provide perfect protection, even for themselves.

But . . . did Bo have nonvampires available also? That standard ward was supposed to prevent harm from the rest of the Others too . . . which would mean that this Bo creature had human servants. Not a nice thought.

Again he seemed to read my mind. "They wore . . . gloves."

That had been another of those really nasty pauses. I stared at him. So, I thought, the wards do work, but a vampire can handle them so long as the vampire and, or possibly or, the wards are properly insulated? I wonder what the insulation is? No, I'm sure I don't want to know. There's a blow for all the wardcrafters if word gets out though. But then again maybe it would improve their business if it was known for certain that the wards worked at all. What a lot I am learning. Perhaps that was why Bo's gang had used gloves to touch me—in case of hidden ward signs. Now that I knew their attitude toward their guest a little better I thought perhaps they were hoping I was wearing a good one. And since I was chained up, making a run for it while he blew on his burned fingers or whatever wasn't an option for me.

Or maybe they just hadn't wanted to leave fingerprints on me. Perhaps it's not polite to handle another person's food even when you're a vampire.

There was a sputter and crackle behind me. I turned sharply around: one of the candles in the chandelier was guttering. They were all burning low, casting less light than they had. But the room seemed no darker; if anything the contrary. I looked out the nearest window. Grayness.

"Dawn," I said. I looked back at him. He was sitting as he had been sitting since I had come into that room, cross-legged, leaning—no, not quite leaning, straight-backed, only his head a little bowed—against the wall, arms on knees. The one time he had moved was when I'd wept. I looked at the windows in the big room. They were big too, and curtainless, and on three sides. I wondered about the weal on his arm.

Daylight increased. The sun was coming up over the lake, on my left. So we were on the north side of the lake; my family's old cabin was on the southeast, and the city on the south. Even in the desolation where I sat it was impossible for my heart *not* to lift at the coming of daylight. Dawn was usually my favorite time of day: end of darkness, beginning of light. I was kind of a light freak. I sighed. It occurred to me again that I was very hungry, and even thirstier than that. And so tired that if he didn't eat me soon I might die anyway. Joke. I didn't feel like laughing. I glanced at him. He looked even worse than he had by candlelight. *How long has it been?* Bo's lieutenant had said. So presumably he'd lived—if *lived* was the word—through some days here already. Ugh.

As the light grew stronger I could see the room more clearly. Near the corner to my left there was a heap of something I hadn't seen before. Too small to be another vampire. No comfort. It was something lumpy, in a cloth sack. For something to do I stood shakily up—watching him over my shoulder the whole time—and edged over toward it. I could just reach it, at the fullest extent of my chain, almost lying along the floor to do it. The vampire was tethered in the center of the wall of the room, while my staple was a little more toward this end. If our chains were the same length, then I could reach this corner, and he could not. More vampire humor? If it was me he wanted, of course, he could just pull on the chain. I stood up again. I opened the sack. A loaf of bread—two loaves of bread—a bottle of water, and a blanket. Without thinking I broke off an end of one of the loaves: standard store bread, fluffy, without real substance, spongy texture, dry crumb, almost no aroma. Not as good as what I made. It was carthaginian pig swill compared to what I made. But it was bread. Food. I raised the end I had broken off, and sniffed it more carefully. Why would they leave me food? Was it poisoned? Was it drugged, would it sedate me, so I wouldn't see him coming? Maybe I should want to be sedated.

I was so hungry that standing there with bread in my hands made my legs tremble, and I had to keep swallowing.

"It is food for you," he said. "There is nothing wrong with it. It is just food."

"Why?" I said again. My continuing total-immersion course in vampire mores.

Something like a grimace moved momentarily across his too-still face. "Bo knows me well."

"Knows . . ." I said thoughtfully. "Knows that you wouldn't . . . right away. The bale of hay to keep the goat happy while the hunters in the trees wait for the tiger."

"Not quite," he said. "Humans can survive several days, perhaps a week, without food, I believe. But you won't remain . . . attractive for that long."

Attractive. I looked down at the cranberry-red dress. It had had a hard night. It was creased, and there was more than one smudge of dirt at the hem as well as the spots that wiping a teary face make, and my feet, sticking out from underneath, were scratched and filthy. I would have looked no less a lady in my T-shirt and jeans. I ate the bread in my hand, and then I broke off more, and ate that. It tasted no better than it looked, and while it had a funny aftertaste I assumed that was just flour improvers and phony flavoring garbage and nothing worse. It also might be my mouth, which tasted pretty funny anyway after the night I'd just had. I ate most of the first loaf. How long were these supplies supposed to last? I opened the bottle of water and drank a third of it. It was a standard two-quart plastic bottle of brand-name spring water and the ring-seal on the lid had been intact when I twisted it loose.

I looked at him again. His eyes were only half open, but still watching me. He was well in shadow but while he sat as unmoving as ever, he looked smaller now. Under siege.

I moved into the sunlight streaming through the window. Food and water had helped and the touch of the sun on my skin helped even more. I set the sack down again, with the rest of the bread in it, and sighed and stretched, as if I were getting out of bed on a Monday morning, the one morning a week I got up after the sun did. I felt tired but . . . alive. I clung to this tiny moment of comparative peace because most of me knew it was false. I wondered how much worse the crash would be when the rest of me remembered, than if I hadn't had it at all.

As I say, I am a light freak. My mom found this out the first year after we left my dad. She'd got this ugly cheap dark little apartment in the basement of an old townhouse—she wouldn't take any of my dad's money so we were *really* poor at first—and I spent eight months crying and being sick all the time. She thought this was about losing my dad, and the doctors she took me to agreed with her because they couldn't find anything wrong with me except listlessness and misery, but the minute she could afford it she got us into a better apartment, on the top floor of the house next door, with real windows. (This was when she started working for Charlie, and the minute he heard she had a sick kid he gave her a raise. He didn't find out till later how young I was, and that she was leaving me home alone while she worked, and that the reason she tried for a job at the coffeehouse in the first place was because it was so close she could run home and check on me during her breaks.) It was winter, and she said I spent three weeks moving around the new place lying in every scrap of sunlight that came indoors—including moving a table and a heavy chest of drawers that were in my way—and by the end of that time I was well again. I don't remember this, but I do remember that that eight months is the only time in my life I've ever been sick.

I stood there in the sunlight feeling the life and warmth of it and holding off the crash.

I was still clutching the bottle of water. I looked at the vampire again. His eyes were shut, perhaps because I was standing in the light. There seemed to be a thin sheen of sweat on his skin. Did vampires sweat? It didn't seem a very vampiry thing to do.

I stepped out of the sunlight, and his eyes half opened again. He didn't look around for me; his eyes opened on where I was. I almost stepped back into the sunlight again, but I didn't quite. I walked over to him, to within easy arm's reach. "You haven't . . . killed me yet because if you did, that would mean Bo had won."

"Yes," he said. His voice, inflectionless as it was, sounded exhausted.

Pretending to myself I didn't know what I was about to do, I held up the bottle of water. If vampires sweated, maybe they drank water . . . too. "Would you like some water?"

He opened his eyes the rest of the way. "Why?"

Involuntarily I smiled. His turn for the intensive course in human mores. "I don't like bullies." This wasn't quite the whole truth, but it was as much of the truth as I knew myself.

He made the cough-growl noise again. "Yes," he said.

I held out the bottle and he took it. He sat looking at it for a moment, looked at me again, then at the bottle. He unscrewed the plastic cap. All of this was happening at ordinary human speed, although all his movements had that creepy vampire fluency. But then . . . another third of the water disappeared. I didn't see him drink. I didn't see his throat move with swallowing. But there was only one-third of the water left in the bottle, and he was screwing the cap back on. And he looked a little better. The mushrooms he was the color of hadn't been in the back of the fridge quite so long, and they weren't quite so wizened. "Thank you," he said.

I couldn't quite bring myself to say, "You're welcome." I moved far enough away again that while I was still mostly in the shade, the sun was touching my back, and sat down. The band of sun-warmth was a little like having a friend's arm around me. "You could have just taken it."

"No," he said.

"Well. Ordered me to give you some."

"No," he said.

I sighed. I felt *irritated* with this treacherous, villainous, mortally dangerous creature. The weight of irony might smash what remained of my mind into pieces before he did, in fact, kill me.

He said slowly, "I can take nothing from you. I can only accept what you offer. I can at most . . . ask."

"Oh, please!" I said. "I can refuse to let you kill me! Vampires have never killed anyone who hasn't said 'oh yes please I want to die, I want to die now, I want you to drink all my blood and whatever else it is that vampires do so that even my corpse is so horrible that after the police are done with it I will be burned instantly and the ashes sterilized before they're turned over to the next of kin!'" I would never have said such a thing while it was dark. Daylight was my time. For a few more hours I could forget that the nightmare would come again too soon. I was tired, and half-crazy with what I had already been through, and at some level I didn't care any more. I had seen the sun once more—it was a beautiful day—and if I was going to go out now, I was going to go out still *me*.

"If you have the strength of will you can stop me or any vampire," he said. Again the words came slowly, as they had when he had first spoken to me in the night. The curious thing was that he seemed to want to speak. He'd also used the word *vampire*. Well, so had I. "These signs," and he gestured briefly at his ankle. "They are . . . effective signs. They will do what they are made for. They will—contain. As Bo arranged for them to do here. They will also prevent inhuman harm to a human. But they can only do that if the human who bears the warding holds against the will of the one who stands against. Vampires are stronger than humans. Rarely can any hold out against our will. Why do you think you should not look in our eyes? We can . . . persuade you anyway. But looking into a vampire's eyes is any human's doom."

In horror I said: "Then they *do* ask you to kill them. They *do* beg you to . . ."

"Yes," he said.

I whispered: "Then, is it . . . okay, at the very end? Do they . . . like it, at the end?"

There was a long pause. "No," he said.

There was a longer pause. I jerked away from him, stood up, stood in the sunlight again. I pulled the bodice of the dress away from my body so the sun could pour down inside. I pushed my hair back so the light could touch all of my face, and then I turned round and pulled my hair up on the top of my head so that it could warm the back of my neck and shoulders. I was not going to cry again. I was *not* going to cry again. I could look at it as practical water conservation.

I looked at him as I stood in the sunlight. His eyes were closed. I stepped out of the sunlight, still watching him. His eyes half-opened as soon as I was in shadow. "How long can you hold out?" I said sharply, my voice too loud. "How long?"

Again his words were slow. "It is not hunger that will break me," he said. "It is the daylight. The daylight is driving me mad. Some sunset soon I will no longer be myself." His eyes flicked fully open, his face tipped back to stare at me. I averted my eyes, looked at the weal on his forearm. "I may . . . kill you then. I may kill myself. I don't know. The history of vampires is a long one, but I do not know of anyone who has had . . . quite this experience."

I sat down. I heard myself saying, "Can I do anything?"

"You are doing it. You are talking to me."

"I . . ." I said. "I'm not much of a talker. Our wait staff are the ones who know how to talk, and listen. I'm out back, most of the time, getting on with the baking." Although several of our regulars hung around out back, if they felt like it. There was also a tiny patio area behind the coffeehouse that Charlie always meant to get done up so we could use it for more seating, but he never did, maybe partly because it had become a kind of private clubhouse for some of the regulars. When the fan wasn't going but the bakery doors were open I listened to the conversations, and people came and leaned on the threshold so I could listen more easily. Pat and Jesse's more interesting stories got told out back.

"The worst time is the hours around noon," he said. "My mind is full of . . ." He paused. "My mind feels as if it is disintegrating, as if the rays of your sun are prizing me apart."

Silence fell again, and the sun rose higher.

"I don't suppose you'd be interested in recipes," I said, a little wildly. "My bran and corn and oatmeal muffins are second only to cinnamon rolls in the numbers we sell. And then there's all the other stuff, lots more muffins—I can make spartan muffins out of *anything*—and tea bread and yeast bread and cookies and brownies and cakes and stuff. On Friday and Saturday I make pies. Even Charlie doesn't know the secret of my apple pie. I suppose the secret would be safe with you." Charlie didn't know the secret of my Bitter Chocolate Death, either, but I didn't feel like mentioning death in the present circumstances, even chocolate ones.

The vampire's eyes were half open, watching me.

"I haven't got much more life to tell you about. I'm not a deep thinker. I only just made it through high school. I was a rotten student. I hated learning stuff for tests only because someone told me I had to. The only thing I was ever any good at was literature and writing with Miss Yanovsky." June Yanovsky had tangled with the school board because she chose to teach a section of classic vampire literature to her junior elective. She said that denying kids the opportunity to discuss *Dracula* and *Carmilla* and *Immortal Death* was in the same category of muddleheaded misguided protectiveness that left them to believe that they couldn't get pregnant if they did it standing up with their shoes on. She won her case. "I'd've dropped out if it wasn't for her, and also Charlie really laid into me about how much my mom would hate it if I did. He was right, he usually is, especially about my mom. I'd been working at the coffeehouse since I was twelve, and I went straight from part time to full time after I graduated. I've never *done* anything. The farthest I've been from New

Arcadia is the ocean a few times on vacation when the boys were little and the coffeehouse smaller and Charlie could still be dragged away occasionally. I like to read. My best girlfriend is a librarian. But I don't have time to do much except work and sleep. Sometimes I feel like there ought to be something. . . ." An image of my gran formed in my memory: an image from the last time I had seen her. I had never decided whether or not it was only hindsight that made me feel she had known I would not see her again, that she was going away. Superficially she had seemed as she always had. She had said good-bye as she always had. There was nothing different about that meeting except that it had been the last. "Sometimes I feel like there should be something else, but I don't know what it is." Slowly I added, "That's why I drove out to the lake last night."

I couldn't let the silence after that linger. "You could tell me about your life," I said. "Er." Life? What did you call it? "Your . . . whatever. You must have done lots of stuff besides . . . er."

"No," he said.

That was clear enough. I looked over my shoulder. The sun was getting up there. I looked at him again. The old-mushroom color was very bad again, and there was definitely sweat on his skin. He looked like he was dying, or he would have if he was human. He only didn't look like he was dying because he didn't look human.

"You could tell me a story," he said. The words were almost gasps. Did vampires breathe?

"A—what?" I said stupidly.

"A story," he said. Pause. "You have . . . little brothers. You told them . . . stories?"

Scheherazade had it *easy*, I thought. All she was risking was a nice clean beheading from some human with a cleaver. And while her husband was off his rocker at least he was *human*. "Oh—um— yes—I guess. But, you know, Puss in Boots. Paul Bunyan. Mike Mulligan and His Steam Shovel. The Knight in the Oak Tree. And they were always wanting stories about spacemen and laser guns. I read all of Burroughs's *Mars* books and all of Quatermain's *Alpha Centauri* books to give me ideas, except the women in my stories weren't so hopeless. Nothing very—er—riveting."

"Puss in Boots," he said.

"Yeah. You know, fairy tales. That's the one when the cat does all this clever stuff to help his master out, so his master winds up really important and wealthy and marries the princess, even though he was only the miller's son."

"Fairy tales," he said.

"Yes." I wanted to ask him if he hadn't been a child once, that surely he remembered fairy tales. Surely every child got told fairy tales. Or if it had been that long ago that he couldn't remember. Or maybe you forgot everything about being human once you were a vampire. Maybe you had to. In that case how did he know I would've told my brothers stories? "There are lots of them. Snow White. Cinderella. Sleeping Beauty. The Twelve Dancing Princesses. The Frog Prince. The Brave Little Tailor. Jack the Giant Killer. Tom Thumb. My brothers liked the ones best that had the least kissing in them. So they liked Puss in Boots and Jack the Giant Killer rather than Cinderella and Snow White, who they thought were all glang. I agreed with them actually."

"What is your favorite fairy tale?"

I made a noise that under other circumstances might have been a laugh. "Beauty and the Beast," I said.

"Tell me that one," he said.

"What?"

"Tell me the fairy tale of Beauty and the Beast," he said.

"Oh. Yes. Um." I'd learned to tell this one myself almost first of all, because the pictures of the Beast in the storybooks always annoyed me, and I didn't want any kids under my influence to get the wrong idea about him. I wondered if any even-more-than-usually-misguided illustrator had ever tried to make him look like a vampire. "Well, there was this merchant," I began obediently. "He was very wealthy, and he had three daughters. . . ."

How to tell a story—how to make it go on and on to fill the time—how to get interested in it yourself so it would be interesting to your listeners, or listener—all that came back to me, I think. It was impossible to know, and presumably vampires have different tastes in stories than little boys. I thought of a few car journeys we'd had on those holidays to the ocean, when I would tell stories till I was hoarse. There was a lot you could do with the story of Beauty and the Beast, and I had done most of it, and I did it again now. I watched the arc of the sun over my left shoulder. The light crept across the floor, and the vampire had to move to stay out of it. First he had to move in one direction, sliding along the floor as if all his joints pained him (how could he both look as if every movement were agony, and still retain that curious fluid agility?), and then he had to slide back again—back again and farther still, nearer to me. I moved to stay in the sun as he moved to stay out of it. I went on telling the story. There was no spot on the floor that he could have stayed in all day, and stayed out of the light. Vampires, according both to myth and SOF, did something like sleep during the day, just as humans sleep at night. Do vampires need their sleep as we do? So it wasn't only food and freedom Bo was depriving this one of?

He'd said it wasn't hunger that would break him. It was daylight.

I wondered dispassionately if I might be getting a sunburn, but I rarely burned anyway, and the idea in the present state of affairs, like worrying about a hangnail while you are being chased by an axe murderer, seemed so ludicrous I couldn't be bothered.

The sun was sinking toward the end of day, and my voice was giving out. I had drunk several more mouthfuls of water in the course of the story. (If you haven't seen a vampire's lips touch the mouth of your bottle, do you have to wipe it off first?) I concluded in a vivid—not to say lurid—scene of all-inclusive rejoicing, and fell silent.

"Thank you," he said.

My tiredness was back, tenfold, a hundredfold. I couldn't keep my eyes open. I *had* to keep my eyes open—this was a *vampire*. Was this one of the ways to—persuade a victim? Had he been killing two birds with one stone—so to speak? Make the day pass, make the victim amenable to handling? But didn't they *like* them *un*amenable? I couldn't help it. My eyes kept falling shut, my head would drop forward, and I would wake myself up when my neck cracked as my chin fell to my breastbone.

"Go to sleep," said his voice. "The worst is over . . . for me . . . today. There are five hours till sunset. I am . . . harmless till then. No vampire can . . . kill in daylight. Sleep. You will want to be awake . . . tonight."

I remembered there had been a blanket in the sack. I crawled over to it, pulled it out, put my head on the sack and the remaining loaf of bread, and was asleep before I had time to argue with myself about whether he was telling the truth or not.

I DREAMED. I dreamed as if the dream was *waiting* for me, waiting for the moment I fell asleep. I dreamed of my grandmother. I dreamed of walking by the lake with her. At first the dream was more like a memory. I was little again, and she was holding my hand, and I had to skip occasionally to keep up with her. I had been proud of having her for a grandmother, and was sorry that I only ever saw her alone, at the lake. I would have liked my school friends to meet her. Their grandmothers were all so ordinary. Some of them were nice and some of them were not so nice, but they were all sort of . . . soft-edged. I didn't know how to put it even to myself. My grandmother wasn't hard or sharp, but there wasn't anything *uncertain* about her. She was unambiguously herself. I admired her hugely. She had long hair and when the wind was blowing off the lake it would get into a tremendous tangle, and sometimes she would let me brush it afterward, at the cottage. She usually wore long full skirts, and soft shoes that made no sound, whatever she was walking on.

My parents split up when I was six. I didn't see my grandmother for the first year after. It turned out that my mother had gone so far as to hire some wardcrafters—smiths, scribes, spooks, the usual range—and on what money I don't know—to prevent anyone in my dad's family from finding us. My father hadn't wanted to let us go, and while his family are supposed to be some of the good guys, it's very hard not to do something you can do when you're angry and it will get you what you want. After the first year and a day he had probably cooled off, and my mom let the fancy wards lapse. My grandmother located us almost at once, and my mother, who can drive herself nuts sometimes by her own sense of fairness, agreed to let me see her. At first I didn't want to see her, because it had been a whole year *and* I'd been sick for a lot of it, and my mother had to tell me—that sense of fairness again—what she'd done, and a little bit, scaled down to my age, of why. I was only seven, but it had been a bad year. That conversation with my mother was one of those moments when my world really changed. I realized that I was going to be a grown-up myself some day and have to make horrible decisions like this too. So I agreed to see my gran again. And then I was glad I did. I was so happy to have her back.

She and I had been meeting at the lake every few weeks for a little over a year when one afternoon she said, "I don't like what I am about to do, but I can't think of anything better. My dear, I have to ask if you will keep a secret from your mother for me."

I looked at her in astonishment. This wasn't the sort of thing grown-ups did. They went around having secrets behind your back all the time about things that were horribly important to you (like my mom not telling me she'd hired the wardcrafters), and then pretended they didn't. There'd been a lot of that that nobody explained to me before my parents broke up, and I hadn't forgotten. Even at six or seven I knew that my mom's wardcrafters were the tip of an iceberg, but I still didn't know much about the iceberg. I didn't know, for example, that my father might have been a sorcerer, till years later. And sometimes grown-ups said things like "Oh, maybe you'd better not tell your parents about this," which either meant get out of there *fast, now*, or that they knew you would tell anyway because you were only a kid, but then they could get mad at you when you did. (That this had happened several times with some of my dad's business associates is one of the reasons my mom left.) But I knew my gran loved me and I knew she was *safe*. I knew she'd never ask me anything bad. And I knew that she really, really meant it, that I had to keep this secret from my mother.

"Okay," I said.

My gran sighed. "I know that your mother means the best for you and in many ways she's right. I'm very glad she got custody of you, and not your dad, although he was very bitter about it at the time."

I scowled. I never saw my dad. Once my gran had found me he started writing me a lot of postcards but I never saw him. And the postmarks on the cards were always blurry so you couldn't see where they'd been sent from. *All* the postmarks were blurry. Two or three a week sometimes.

"But she's wrong that simply keeping you ignorant of your father's heritage will make it as if that heritage doesn't exist. It does exist. You can choose to be your mother's daughter in all things, but it must be a choice. I am going to provide you with the means for making that choice. Otherwise, some day, that heritage you know nothing about may get you in a lot of trouble."

I must have looked frightened, because she took my hands in hers and gave them a squeeze. "Or, perhaps, some day you will be in a lot of trouble and it will get you out of it."

We were sitting on the porch of the cabin by the lake. We'd been walking earlier, and had picked a little posy of wildflowers. She'd fetched a mug from the kitchen and filled it with water, and the flowers were standing in that, on the rickety little table that still sat on the porch. We'd been walking in the sun, which was very warm, and were now sitting in the shade of the trees, which was pleasingly cool. I could feel the sweat on my face drying in the breeze. My gran pulled one of the flowers out of the mug, put it between my two hands, closed my hands together over it so it was invisible, and put her hands over mine. "Now, what have you got in your hands?" she said.

This was a funny sort of game. I said, smiling, "A flower."

"What else could you have inside your hands instead? What else is so small you can hide it completely, doesn't weigh very much, doesn't itch or tickle, is so soft you can barely feel it's there?"

"Um—a feather?" I said.

"A feather. Good. Now, think feather."

I thought feather. I thought a small, gray-brown-white feather. A sparrow, something like that. There was an odd, slightly buzzy sensation in my hands, under her hands. It was a little bit sick-making, but not very much.

"Now open your hands."

She took hers away from mine, and I opened them. There was a feather, a little gray-brown-white feather there. No flower. I looked up at her. I knew that one of the reasons my mom had left my dad was because he wouldn't stop doing spellworking, and doing business with other spellworkers. I knew he came from a big magic-handling family, but not everybody in it did magic. I had never done any. "You did that," I said.

"No. I helped, but you did it. It's in your blood, child. If it weren't, that feather would still be a flower. It was your hands that touched it, your hands that carried the charm."

I held up the feather. It looked and felt like a real feather. "Would you like to try again?" she said. I nodded.

She told me that we only wanted to do little things this first time, so we turned the feather into a different kind of feather, and then we turned it into several kinds of flower, and then several kinds of leaf, and then we turned it into three unburned matchsticks, and then we turned it into a tiny swatch of fabric—yellow, with blue dots—and then we turned it back into the flower it had been to begin with. "First rule: return everything to its proper shape if you can, unless there is some compelling reason not to. Now we've done enough for one afternoon, and we want to say thank you, and we also want to sweep up any rubbish we've left—like sweeping the floor and wiping the counters after you've been making cookies." She taught me three words to say, and lit a small bar of incense, and we sat silently till it had burned itself out.

"There," she said. "Are you tired?"

"A little," I said. I thought about it. "Not a lot."

"Are you not? That is interesting. Then I was right that I had to show you." She smiled. It was a kind, but not a reassuring smile. She was also right that I couldn't tell my mother.

My mother had stopped bringing me out and taking me back after the first few visits, although she made me wear a homecoming charm. I realized later that this might have looked like the most colossal insult to my gran, but my mother wouldn't have meant it that

way and my gran didn't take it that way. I hung it on a tree when I
arrived and only took it down again when I was leaving. My gran
walked me out to the road and waited till the bus came into sight,
made sure the bus driver knew where I was going (the charm
wouldn't have stopped the bus for me if I'd forgotten to pull the cord,
and I was still only a kid), kissed me, and watched me climb aboard.
"Till next time," she said, which is what she always said.

We played that game many times. I was soon doing it without her
hands on mine, and she showed me how to do certain other things too,
some of which I could do easily, some of which I couldn't do at all.

One afternoon she pulled a ring off her finger, and gave it to me.
"I'm tired of that red stone," she said. "Give me a green stone."

There were, of course, rules to what I had at first thought was a
game. The more dense the material, the harder to shift, so stone or
gem is more difficult than flower or feather. Anything that has been
altered by human interference is harder than anything that hasn't
been, so a polished, faceted stone is more difficult than a rough piece
of ore. Worked metal is the worst. It is both heavy and dense *and* the
least decisively itself. Something that is handled and used is harder
than something that isn't, so a tool would be harder to shift than a
plaque that hung on the wall, and a stone worn in a ring is going to
be harder than a decorative bit of rock that stood on a shelf. It is easier to change a thing into something like itself: a feather into another
feather, a flower into another flower. A flower into a leaf is easier than
a flower into a feather. But worked metal is always hard. Even a safety
pin into several straight pins is difficult. Even a 1968 penny into a
1986 penny is difficult.

She hadn't told me any of the details, that first day, when I turned
a flower into a bit of fabric. It showed how good she was, that she
could create not just human-made fabric, but smooth yellow fabric
with blue dots, instantly, with no fuss, because that's what I was trying to do, and she wanted me to have a taste of what she was going
to teach me, without fluster or explanation. But that had been nearly
a year ago, and I knew more now.

The ring was warm from her finger. I closed my hands and concentrated. I didn't have to do anything to the setting, to the worked metal. Changing the stone was going to be big enough. I had only ever tackled lake pebbles before, and they were pretty onerous. I'd never tried a faceted stone. And this was a ring she wore all the time, and she was a practicing magic handler. Objects that have a lot of contact with magic, however peripherally, tend to get a bit *steeped*. But I should still be able to do it, I thought.

But I couldn't. I knew before I opened my hands that I hadn't done it. I tried three times, and all I got was a heavy ache in my neck and shoulders from trying too hard. I felt like crying. It was the first time I had failed to change something: transmuting was the thing I was best at. And she wouldn't have asked me to do something I shouldn't have been able to do.

We were sitting on the porch again, in the shade of the trees. "Let us try once more," she said. "But not here. Come." We stood up—I still had the ring in one hand—and went down the steps to the ground, and then down to the shore, and into the sunlight. It was another hot, bright day, and the sky was as blue as a sapphire.

I wasn't ready for what happened. When I closed my hands around the ring again and put all my frustration into this final attempt, there was a *blast* of something—I shuddered as it shot through me—and for the merest moment my hands felt so hot it was as if they would burst into flame. Then it was all over and my hands *fell* apart because I was shaking so badly. My gran put her arm around me. I held up my unsteady hand and we both looked.

Her ring had a green stone, all right, and the setting, which had been thin plain gold, had erupted into a thick wild mess of curlicues, with several more tiny green stones nested in their centers. I thought it was hideous, and I could feel my eyes filling with tears—I was, after all, only nine years old—because this time I had done so much *worse* than nothing.

But she laughed in delight. "It's lovely! Oh my, it's so—*drastic*, isn't it? No, no, I'm truly pleased. You have done splendidly. I have wondered—listen, child, this is the important thing for you to remember—your element is sunlight. It's a little unusual, which is why I didn't spot it before. But you can probably do almost anything in bright sunshine."

She wouldn't let me try to shift it back. I thought she wouldn't let me because she knew I was too tired and shaken, that she'd do it herself after we parted. But she didn't. She was wearing it as I'd changed it the next time I saw her. We'd never left anything changed before, we'd always changed it back. I didn't know the words you said over something you weren't going to change back. Perhaps I should have asked her; but I thought of that ring as a mistake, a blunder, and I didn't want to call her attention to it, even though every time she moved that hand it called *my* attention to it. I couldn't even beg her to let me try to shift it back because I was afraid I'd only do something even uglier.

I might have asked her some day. But I only saw her a few more times after I changed her ring. We had been meeting nearly every month, sometimes oftener, through my tenth year. After my tenth birthday I only saw her once more. All the grown-ups knew the Wars were coming, and even us kids had some notion. But I never thought about the Wars coming to our lake, or that I might not see my grandmother again.

We didn't discuss sunlight again either. I didn't tell her that my nickname at the coffeehouse had been Sunshine since before Mom had married Charlie. I didn't know when I first met him that he said "Hey, Sunshine" to all little kids, and I thought he was making a joke about my name—well, what Mom had made of my name after she left my dad—Rae. Sun's rays, right? By the time I found out, Sunshine was *my* name. And then, because I was the only kid at that point that hung round the coffeehouse, the regulars started calling me Sunshine too. Pretty soon it *was* my name. It was so much my name that I didn't think of it when my gran first told me that sunlight was my element. Most people—even my mom—still call me Sunshine.

I dreamed all this—remembered and dreamed—lying on the ballroom floor, with my head on a sack with a loaf of bread in it, and a vampire leaning against the wall twenty feet away. All of it was as clear and vibrant as if I were living it all over again, complete with the strange feeling of being a child again when you know you're an adult.

Then the real dream began. I seemed to be back on the cottage porch with my grandmother, that first time, when we changed the flower, only this time we didn't sit in the shade but in strong sunlight. The flower was in my hands, and her hands were over mine, but I was the adult I was now, and neither of us spoke. I closed my hands, and opened them, and the flower was now a feather. I closed my hands, and opened them, and the feather was three matchsticks. I closed my hands and opened them, and the matchsticks were a leaf. I closed and opened them again, and now I was holding her plain gold ring with the red stone. The red stone flared in a sudden bright ray of the sun before I closed my hands again. Close, open, and there was the baroque monstrosity twinkling with green. Close open. My jackknife lay between my palms: the little jackknife that usually lived in the pocket of my jeans, that now lay hidden in my bra. Close open. A key. A key . . .

I WOKE UP. It was still daylight, but the sky was reddening with sunset. I was painfully stiff from sleeping on the floor. It was all still true: I was chained by the ankle, trapped in an empty house with a vampire. What I had dreamed was only a dream, and the sun was setting. I was also still horribly, murderously tired; I couldn't have had more than about four hours' sleep. If I'd had one of those hollow teeth that spies used to have in cheap thrillers, I'd have bitten down on it then. I didn't see how I could face another night. Bo's gang would be back, of course. To see how we were getting on. And my vampire—what a grotesque thought, *my* vampire—would have to decide all over again whether . . . however the question presented itself to him. Whether he was going to let Bo win or not.

I rolled over with a groan. He was sitting cross-legged in the precise center of the wall. Watching me. I pulled myself into a sitting position. My mouth tasted beyond foul. I'd left the water bottle within his reach, but he hadn't had any more. I made myself stand up—all my bones hurt—rather than crawl, and went toward him and picked it up. I was getting *used* to approaching him. It was true, what you've read, about how you can't maintain a pitch of terror for very long: your body just can't do it. I was sick with dread, I at least half wanted to die to get it over with, but I walked to within arm's length of a hungry vampire and picked up my bottle of water and drank out of it with no more hesitation than if he'd been Mel. "Do you want any more?"

He took it out of my hand, and disposed of half of what was left. Again I didn't see him drink. When he handed it back to me I stood there staring at it. I wanted to finish it—I was assuming Bo's gang would bring more, in the interests of keeping me "attractive"—but I felt curiously reluctant to wipe the top off under his eye.

He said, "You will contract no infection by sharing water with me."

There was a curious new quality in his hitherto expressionless voice. I thought about it for a while. To do with the tone. Something.

He sounded *amused*.

I forgot not to look in his eyes. "What if you've been—like, drinking bad blood?"

"What happens when you pour water into—alcohol? It mixes, it is no longer water, it is alcohol, and . . . clean of live things."

Clean of live things. I liked that. "It is *diluted* alcohol."

"This alcohol is still strong enough. And, as you might say . . . self-regenerating."

His eyes were not so murky as they had been last night. Presumably it was the water. Diluting something . . . else. "Please do not look in my eyes. It is coming night again, and . . . I still do not want Bo to win."

I jerked my gaze away. Bad sign that he'd had to tell me. Good sign that he still wanted Bo to lose. Good sign for what? Bo still had us. It's not as though this was some kind of trial, challenge, that when we got to the end if we'd survived they'd let us go free. This was it. It was only a question of really soon or slightly less soon. I wondered what Mom and Charlie and Mel and the rest were thinking; if Aimil knew yet. I hadn't not showed up on time to make cinnamon rolls in seven years. I'd never missed a morning till today. I never got around to taking holidays, and I was never ill. (Charlie, who never got sick either, used to say, "Clean living," which infuriated Mom, who had flu every winter.) Would they have told the police I was missing? Probably. But the police would have said that I was free and over twenty-one and to tell them again in a few days if I still hadn't turned up. Pat or Jesse might be able to make them look harder once they were looking at all, but I wasn't going to be alive in a few days. And our local cops were nice guys but not exactly rocket scientists. Not that rocket science would help me either.

There would be no reason to think SOF should get involved.

Who else would Mom or Mel ask? Yolande. But she wouldn't know anything either. They'd figure out that my car was missing. Would anyone think to go out to the lake and look at the old cabin? Not likely. Nobody else went out there but me, and I hadn't been there in years. I'd never even taken Mel there when we went hiking. I didn't think there were any regular patrols out there either; there wasn't any known reason the lake needed patrolling. And there were the bad spots. But if someone had gone out to the cabin and found my car, then what? I wasn't there, and I doubted vampires left clues. You heard about vampire trouble on the news when people started finding bloodless bodies with fang marks. And this house was very well guarded by the bad spot behind us.

I drank the rest of the water. I didn't wipe the mouth first. I thought, is my arm or my dress likely to be any more sanitary?

I turned toward the window. I felt the vampire watching me. "I have to pee," I said irritably. "I'm going to do it out the window. Will you please not watch? I will tell you when I'm done." Since I'd never heard him move before, he must have made a noise so I could hear it. I looked, and he'd turned his back. I had my pee, feeling ridiculous. "Okay," I said. He turned around and returned to watching me, his face as expressionless as before.

As he had seemed to grow smaller as the sun rose he seemed to grow larger as the sun set.

The last light waned and so did I. I was cold as well as sick and frightened, and my headache felt bigger than my head. I wrapped myself in the blanket and huddled as near to the corner as my chain would let me. I remembered the other loaf of bread, and pulled it out and began to eat it, thinking it might help, but it sat in my stomach like a lump of stone, and I didn't eat very much. Then I hunched down and curled up. And waited.

It was full dark. The moon would be up later but at the moment I could see almost nothing. On a clear night it is never quite dark outside, but we were inside. The windows left gray rectangles on the floor, but I could not see beyond them. I knew he could see in the dark; I knew vampires can smell live blood. . . . No, I thought. That hardly matters. He isn't going to forget about me any more than I am going to forget about him, even if I can't see or hear him—even if I've got so used to the vampire smell I'm not noticing it any more. Which just made it worse. I thought I would have to see him *cross* the gray rectangle between him and me—I was pretty sure his chain wasn't long enough to let him go round— I knew I wouldn't hear him. But . . . I hadn't seen him drink either. I bit down on my lips. I wasn't going to cry, and I wasn't going to scream. . . .

I almost screamed when I heard his voice out of the darkness. "They are coming now. Listen. Stand up. Fold your blanket and lay it neatly down. Shake your dress out. Comb your hair with your fingers. Sit again if you wish, but sit a little distance from the corner—yes, nearer me. Remember that three feet more or less makes no difference to me: you might as well. Sit up straight. Perhaps cross your ankles. Do you understand?"

"Yes," I croaked, or squeaked. I folded the blanket and laid it down. I wrapped the sack tidily around the remains of the bread. I put the empty water bottle with it. I shook my dress out. It was probably a mess, but there was nothing I could do about it. My hair actually looks a bit better if it doesn't get combed too often, so I tried to pull my fingers through it the way I would have if I were in front of the mirror at home. I wiped my face on my hem again. I felt unspeakably grubby and grimy—ironically perhaps, since I was still whole, I felt defiled. I certainly did not feel attractive. But I smoothed my skirt before I sat down again, just inside the darkness on my side of the gray rectangle, a good six feet from my corner. My chain lay slack, lazily curved.

"Good," he said from the darkness.

A for effort, I thought. June Yanovsky would be proud of me.

"They are coming" is perhaps a relative term. It seemed to me, my nerves shrieking with strain, that it was a very long time before the chandelier suddenly rattled ferociously—and then burst into light. The candles were all new and tall again. My gran had told me that setting fire to things from a distance was a comparatively easy trick, which helped explain why so many houses got burned down during the Wars; but the houses were already there, you didn't build them first. That two-second rattle had given me enough warning to swallow any cry, to force myself to remain as I was, ankles crossed, hands lying loosely one in the other, palms upturned and open. I doubted I was fooling anyone, but at least I was trying.

There were a dozen of them. I hadn't counted last night, so I didn't know if there had been more or less. I recognized Bo's lieutenant, and the one who had been my other guard. There are some people who say that all vampires look alike, but they don't, any more than all humans look alike. How many live people outside the staff in those asylums have seen a lot of vampires anyway? These twelve were all thin and whippy-looking and that was about the only clear similarity among them. And of course that they were vampires, and they moved like vampires, and smelled like vampires, and were motionless like vampires when they weren't moving.

"Bo said you'd hold out just to be annoying," said Bo's lieutenant. "Bo understands you."

I thought, he's *frightened*. That was supposed to be an insult, Bo's understanding, and he can't pull it off. And then I thought, I must be imagining things. Vampire voices are as weird as vampire motion and as unreadable as vampire faces. Hell, I can't even tell the boy vampires from the girl vampires. How do I know what vampire fear sounds like? If vampires feel fear. But the thought repeated: he's frightened. I remembered how reluctant they'd seemed last night, bringing me here. "Let's get it over with," Bo's lieutenant had said.

I remembered how they didn't want to get too close to their "guest," and how they did most of their talking from near the door, farther than his chain would stretch; how the vampire who'd held me had dropped me and run, when he realized his friends were leaving him behind.

"Is she still sane, though, Connie? It's harder if you keep them till they've gone mad, you know, and the blood's not as sweet. Bo finds this very disappointing as I'm sure you do, but that's the way humans are. You wouldn't want to waste what we brought you, would you?"

They were all standing just beyond the chandelier, so not quite halfway across the room. They had fanned out into a ragged semicircle. As Bo's lieutenant spoke, he took an ambling step toward us. The others fanned out a little more. My poor weary heart was beating desperately, hopelessly, in my throat again. This reminded me of any human gang cornering its victim; and however wary they were of Bo's "guest," they were still twelve to one, and the one was chained to the wall with ward signs stamped all over the shackle. I couldn't help myself. I curled my stretched-out legs under me. I wanted to cross my arms in front of my breast, but I reminded myself that this was useless—just as curling my legs up was useless— so I compromised, and leaned on one hand, and left the other one in my lap. I managed not to squeeze it into a fist, although this wasn't easy. The vampires—all except the one sitting against the wall next to me—took another slow, floating, apparently aimless step forward. I was pressing my back so hard against the wall my spine hurt.

I wished I knew what was going on—why were Bo and his guest old enemies? But then, even if I did know what was going on, how would that help me? What I wanted—to get out alive—didn't seem one of the options. So I might as well distract myself with wanting to know what was going on.

They didn't want to get too close, but they were still moving closer. I couldn't think of any reason this could be good news.

I never saw it coming this time either. They were vampires. I heard

Bo's lieutenant saying, as if his words were coming from some other universe, "Perhaps you just need a little encouragement, Connie." The words happened—seemed to happen—at human speed. Presumably that was because he wanted me to hear them. In the universe where my body was, I was picked up, and something sharp sliced high across my breast, just below the collarbones, above the neckline of my dress, and I was then thrown down, and my face banged into something hard, and I felt my lip split.

I heard: "Since you don't seem to like feet," and the goblin giggle from last night.

And then they were gone.

And I was lying across my fellow captive's lap. The cut in my breast had been so quick that it was only starting to hurt. The *cut* . . . I was bleeding, bleeding, fresh warm red blood, all over a half-starved vampire. I felt his hands on my bare shoulders. . . .

I snatched myself away, at what was no doubt good speed for a human. He let me go. I slid backward on my knees, skidding on my slippery red skirt, clutching at my front, feeling the blood sliding through my fingers, dripping on the floor, leaving a blood trail, a pool; more blood oozing from my lip, leaking down my chin.

He still hadn't *moved*. But this time, when I felt him looking at me, I had to look back. I had to look into his eyes, into eyes green as emeralds, as green as the stones in my grandmother's awful ring. . . .

You can stop me or any vampire if your will is strong enough.

I felt my hands fall—tumble—from my breast. I leaned forward. I was going to crawl toward him. I was kneeling in my own blood, smearing it across the floor as I crept toward him. My blood was spattered on his naked chest, across one arm, the arm with the weal on it. Don't look. Look. Look into his eyes. Vampire eyes.

. . . *if your will is strong enough.*

Desperately I tried to think of anything—anything—my grandmother's ring, which was the color of these eyes. My grandmother. *Sunlight is your element.* But it was darkness here, darkness barely lessened by candlelight. The candlelight was only there so that my weak human eyes could be more easily drawn by mesmeric vampire eyes. But I remember light, real light, daylight, sunlight. *Hey, Sunshine.* I am Sunshine. Sunshine is my name.

I remembered a song Charlie used to sing:

> *You are my sunshine*
> *My only sunshine*

I heard him singing it. No, I heard *me* singing it. Thin, wavering, with no discernable tune. But it was my voice.

The light in the green eyes snapped off, and I *fell* backward as if I'd been dropped. I turned, and scuttled for my corner. I burrowed under my blanket, and I stayed there.

I MUST HAVE slept again. Silly thing to do. Was there a sensible thing to do? Perhaps I fainted. I woke suddenly, knowing it was four A.M., and time to go make cinnamon rolls. But this time when I woke I knew at once where I was. I was still in that ballroom, still chained to that wall.

I was still alive.

I was so tired.

I sat up. It would be dawn soon. The candles had burned out while I slept, but there was dim gray light coming through the windows. I could see some pink starting on the horizon. I sighed. I didn't want to turn around and look at him. I knew he was still sitting in the middle of the wall; I knew he hadn't moved. I knew it as I knew that Bo's gang had been frightened. The blood from my split lip had stuck my mouth together and when I licked it unstuck and yawned it split again, with a sharp rip of pain that made my eyes water. Damn. I touched my breast dubiously. It was clotted and sticky. The slash had been high, where it was only skin over bone; I hadn't, after all, lost much blood, although it was a long gash, and messy. I didn't want to turn around. He had let me go, last night. He had remembered that he didn't want Bo to win. Perhaps my singing had sounded like the singing of a "rational creature." But the sight of my blood had almost been too much for him. I didn't want to show him my front again; maybe the scab would be too much of a come-on. I sucked at my lip.

With my back to him, wrapped in my blanket, I watched the sun rise. It was going to be another brilliant day. Good. I needed sunlight now, but I also needed as many hours as possible before sunset. How long could I afford to wait?

Charlie would be brewing the coffee by now. The sun was bright on the water of the lake. This would have to do.

I stood up and dropped my blanket. If the vampire had been telling the truth, I was safe from him now till sunset. I turned around and looked at the sunlight coming in the two windows I had to choose from. For no explicable reason I preferred the window nearer him. I avoided looking at him. I stepped into the block of friendly sunlight, and knelt down. I pulled my little jackknife from my bra, and held it between my two hands, fingers extended, palms together as if I was praying. I suppose I was.

I hadn't tried to change anything in fifteen years. I'd only ever done it with my grandmother, and after she'd gone, I stopped. Perhaps I was unsettled by what I had done to her ring. Perhaps I was angry with her for leaving, even though the Wars had started and lots of people were being separated from members of their families as travel and communication became increasing erratic and in some areas broke down completely. The postcards from my father stopped during the Wars. But I *knew* my gran loved me, knew that she wouldn't have left me again if she hadn't had to. I still stopped trying to do the things she taught me.

It was as if our time by the lake was a different life. My life away from the lake, away from my gran, was the life my mother had chosen for me, in which my father's heritage did not exist. Although I went to school with several kids from important magic-handling families, and some of them liked to show off what they could do, I was never really tempted. I oohed and aahed with the ordinary kids; and my last name, Charlie's last name, gave nothing away.

By the time the Wars ended, I was a teenager, and perhaps I'd convinced myself that the games by the lake with my gran had only been children's games, and if I remembered anything else I was dreaming. (Or the hypes or trippers I'd had had been unusually good.) It's not as though my gran ever came back and reminded me otherwise.

But my gran was right about my heritage not going away because everyone was pretending it didn't exist. I hadn't been near that place, that *somewhere* inside me, for fifteen years, but when I went back there that morning, kneeling in the sunshine, it wasn't just there, it had changed. Grown. It was as if what my gran had done—what we had done together—was plant a sapling. It didn't matter to the sapling that we'd then gone away and left it. It went on with becoming a tree. My heritage was the soil it had grown in.

But I had never done anything this difficult, and I hadn't done anything at all in fifteen years. Did you really never forget how to ride a bicycle? If you could ride a bicycle, could you ride a super-mega-thor-turbo-charged several million something-or-other motorcycle, the kind you can hear from six blocks away that you'd have to stand on tiptoe to straddle, the first time you tried?

I felt the power gathering below the nape of my neck, between my shoulder blades. That place on my back burned, as if the sunlight I knelt in was too strong. There was an unpleasant sense of pressure building, like the worst case of heartburn you can imagine, and then it *exploded*, and shot down my arms in fiery threads, and there was an almost audible *clunk*. Or maybe it was audible. I opened my hands. My arms felt as weak as if I'd lifted a boulder. There was a key lying in my right palm.

"You're a magic handler—a transmuter," said the vampire in that strange voice I no longer always found expressionless. I heard him being surprised.

"Not much of one," I said. "A small stuff-changer only." The kids from the magic-handling families taught the rest of us some of the slang. Calling a transmuter a stuff-changer was pretty insulting. Almost as bad as calling a sorcerer a charm-twister. "I thought you couldn't look at me in sunlight."

"The sound and smell of magic were too strong to ignore, and your body is shading your hands," he said.

I extended the foot with the shackle on it. This was the real moment. My heart was beating as if . . . there was a vampire in the room. Ha ha ha. My hand was shaking badly, but I found the odd little keyhole, fumbled my new key in it, and turned it.

Click.

"Well done," he whispered.

I looked out the window. It was maybe seven o'clock. I had about twelve hours. I was already exhausted, but I would be running for my life. How far could adrenaline get me? I had a vague but practical idea where I was; the lake itself was a great orienter. All I had to do was keep it on my right, and I would come to where I'd left my car eventually . . . probably twenty miles, if I remembered the shape of the shore correctly. If I stayed close to the lake I could avoid the bad spot behind the house, and I would have to hope there weren't any other bad spots between me and my car that I couldn't get around. Would I be able to change my shackle key into a car key? I doubted the vampires would have folded up my discarded clothing with the key in the jeans pocket and left it for me on the driver's seat.

Surely I could do twenty-odd miles in twelve hours, even after the two nights and a day I'd just had.

I turned to the vampire. I looked at him for the first time that day. For the first time since I'd bled on him. He had shut his eyes again. I stepped out of the sunlight and his eyes opened. I stepped toward him, knelt down beside him. I felt his eyes drop to my bloody breast. My blood on his chest had crusted; he hadn't tried to wipe it off. Or lick it up.

"Give me your ankle," I said.

There was a long pause.

"Why?" he said at last.

"I don't like bullies," I said. "Honor among thieves. Take your pick."

He shook his head, slowly. "It is—" There was an even longer pause. "It is a kind thought." I wondered what depths he'd had to plumb to come up with the word *kind*. "But it is no use. Bo's folk encircle this place. The size of the clear area around this house is precisely the size of the area Bo thinks can be kept close-guarded. He will not be wrong about this. You will be able to pass that ring now, in daylight, while all sane vampires are shielded and in repose, but the moment I can move out of this place, so will my guards be moving."

And you aren't, of course, at your best and brightest, I added silently.

I stood up and stepped back into the sunlight and felt it on my skin, and thought about the big tree where a tiny sapling used to be. There are a lot of trees and tree symbolism in the magic done to ward or contain the Others, because trees are impervious to dark magic. And then I thought about traps, and trapped things, and about when the evil of the dark was clearly evil, and when it was not quite so clearly evil.

There was a very long pause, while I felt the sunlight soaking through my skin, soaking into the tree that up till a few minutes ago I hadn't known was there, felt the leaves of my tree unfurl, stretch like tiny hands, to take it in. I was tired, I was scared, I was stupefied, I'd just done an important piece of magic, I was tranced out. I thought I heard a wind in the leaves of my tree, and the wind had a voice, and it said *yessssssssss.*

"Then you'll have to come with me," I said.

There was another silence, but when he spoke his voice struck at me as if it might itself draw blood. "Do not torment me," he said. "As I have been merciful to you—as merciful as I can be—do not tease me now. Go and live. Go."

I looked down at him. He was not looking at me, but then I was standing in the sunlight again. I stepped out of the sunlight but he still did not look at me. "I'm sorry," I said. "I am not teasing you. If you will not let me try the shackle on your ankle, give me your hand instead." I held my hand out—down—toward him, still sitting cross-legged on the floor.

More priceless sunlit moments passed.

"Would you rather die—er—whatever—like a rat in a trap?" I said, more harshly than I meant. "I haven't noticed you getting any better offers."

I didn't see him move, of course. He was just standing there, standing beside me, his hand in my hand. It was the first time I had seen him standing. His hand felt as inhuman as the rest of him looked: the right shape and everything, but all *wrong*. Wrong in some fathomless, indefinable, turning-the-world-on-its-end way. Also there was the smell. Standing beside him it was almost overwhelming. Mind you, he smelled a lot better than I did, I needed a bath like you don't want to imagine—there isn't much that stinks worse than fear—but he didn't smell human. He didn't smell animal or vegetable or mineral. He smelled vampire.

I took a deep breath anyway. Then I stepped back into the sunlight, still holding his hand, drawing it after me. His arm unbent and let me do it.

The sunlight struck his hand, halfway up the wealed forearm. Some subtle change occurred—subtle but profound. The feeling of his hand in mine was no longer a—a threat to everything that made me human. The hand became a—an undertaking, an enterprise, a piece of work. Maybe not that much different from flour and water and yeast and a rapidly approaching deadline of hungry, focused customers.

I felt the power moving through me. It did not come in fiery threads this time, but in slow, fat, curly ripples. The ripples made me feel a little peculiar, as if there was an actual *thing*, or things, moving around in my insides, shouldering my liver and stomach aside, twisting among my bowels. I tried to relax and let the ripples wiggle and squirm as they wished. I had to know if I could do this, do what I was offering to do, for a long time. Possibly till sunset. Possibly twelve hours or more. Could I bear this invasion that long, even though I was inviting it? What if I overestimated my strength, like a diver overestimating how long she could hold her breath?

I was *demented*. The most impressive thing I had ever done before today was turn a very pretty ring into an ugly botch. And I would have this vampire's . . . er . . . *life* totally in my hands.

I was trying to save the life of a *vampire*.

The ripples spread through me, first balancing themselves cautiously like kids standing on a teeter-totter, then slowly, gently, finding spaces where they could settle themselves down on various bits of my inner anatomy, like the last customers during the early breakfast rush finding the last available seats. Most of me was already full of things like heart and spleen and kidneys, but there were gaps where the power could fit itself in, attach itself to its surroundings. Tap into *me*. I felt very . . . full. As the connections were made—as the power made itself at home—the ripples began to change. Now they felt like the straps of a harness being settled in place, buckles let out a little here, taken in a little there. When they were done, it felt like a good fit.

I thought I could do it.

I sighed. I could no longer see my tree, because I had become it, embodied it, it grew in me, its sap my blood, its branches my limbs. The power wrapped round it like ropes and cables, flew from its boughs like banners and streamers. Perhaps the next time there was wind in my hair, it would rustle like leaves. *Yessssssss.* I held out my right hand, and he put his left hand into it. I drew him—all the rest of him—into the bright rectangle in front of the window.

Vampire skin looks like hell in sunlight, by the way. Maybe bursting into flames is to be preferred.

Anyway.

I felt my harness take its load. The pull was steady and even, the weight heavy but bearable. I hoped. "Okay," I said. "Back up again. I want both hands free to get that shackle off, and—um—we'll need to stay in contact while we—um—do this sunlight thing."

I didn't know vampires were ever clumsy. I thought grace came with the territory, like fangs and a complexion that looks really bad in daylight. They're always oilily supple in the books. But he *staggered* back into the shadow, leaned against the wall with a thump, dropped my hands, dropped his own hands to thud against the wall next to him. "What in creation *are* you?" he said. "That is no small stuff-changer trick. It is not possible. *It is not possible.* I have been standing in sunlight and *I know it is not possible.*"

It was nice to know I wasn't the only one of us feeling demented. I knelt to get at his shackle. I was relieved when the key worked for his cuff too; I guessed I was going to have to be pretty careful of my strength to be a successful sun-parasol for the undead for the next twelve hours. I was not thinking about any more of the implications of my offer than I had to. The main thing—the only thing—was: I couldn't leave him behind. I didn't care who or what he was. I couldn't walk out of this cage and leave some caged thing behind me. If I could help it. And, for better or worse, I could. Apparently.

The skin of his ankle looked terrible. I couldn't tell if the . . . peeling . . . was anything more than just chafing. I was careful not to touch it. My ankle didn't seem any the worse for wear, but there hadn't been any antihuman wards on my shackle that I'd noticed. Oh yes: they exist. They're not a lot talked about among humans, but they exist.

"What are you? Who are you?" he repeated. "What family are you from?"

I broke the cuff open. "My name is Rae Seddon, but what you're looking for is Raven Blaise. Seddon is Charlie's name—my stepfather's name—but my mother stopped me using Raven or Blaise as soon as we left my dad."

"You're a Blaise," he said, still leaning against the wall, but staring down at me as I knelt at his feet. "Which Blaise?"

"My father is Onyx Blaise," I said.

"Onyx Blaise had no children," barked the vampire.

"*Had?*" I said, just as sharply. "Do you know he is dead?"

The vampire shook his head, impatiently, but then went on shaking it again and again, as if bothered by gnats. Gnats might like vampires: they go for blood. But I didn't think that was the problem here. "I don't know. I don't know. He disappeared—"

"Fifteen years ago," I said.

The vampire looked at me. "Onyx Blaise had—has—no children."

How do *you* know? I wanted to say. Is my dad another of your old enemies? Or . . . your old friends? No. No. I hadn't seen him since I was six, but I couldn't believe that of my gran's son. "He has at least one," I said.

The vampire slid slowly down the wall to sit on the floor next to me. He started to laugh. Vampires don't laugh very well, or at least this one didn't. He half looked—sounded—like something out of a bad horror film—the sort of horror film that isn't scary because you don't believe it, it's so crude, where was their special effects budget?—and half didn't. The second half was like the worst horror film you'd ever seen, the one that made you think about things you'd never imagined, the one that scared you so much you threw up. This was worse than the goblin giggler, my second guard, from Bo's gang. I clamped my hands around the empty shackle and waited for him to stop.

"A Blaise," he said. "Bo's lot brought me a *Blaise*. And not just a third cousin who can do card tricks and maybe write a ward sign that almost works, but Onyx Blaise's daughter." He stopped laughing. Then I decided maybe silence was worse after all, at least when it followed that laughter.

"Your father didn't educate you very well. If I had killed you and had your blood, the blood of Onyx Blaise's daughter, the blood of someone who can do what you just did, I could have snapped that shackle as if the steel were paper and the marks on it no more than a—a recipe for cinnamon rolls, and taken the odds against me with Bo's gang, even after the weeks I've been here, even against all the others you haven't seen, silent in the woods, watching. *And I would have won.* That's what the blood of someone from one of the families can do, and a Blaise. . . . The effect doesn't last—a week at the most—but a lot can be done in a few nights." He sounded almost dreamy. "On Onyx Blaise's daughter's blood I could get rid of Bo for good. I still could. All I would have to do is keep you here one more day, and wait till sunset. I'm weak and sick and I see double in this damned daylight, but I'm still stronger than a human. All I would have to do is keep you here. . . ." His voice trailed off.

I didn't move. There was a small wispy thought in the back of my mind. It seemed to be something like: oh, well. A little closer to consciousness there was a slightly more definite thought, and it said, well, we've been here before, several times, in the last couple of days. We're either going to lose for good now, or we aren't.

I sat very still, as if I were trying to discourage a cobra from striking.

More minutes of sunlight streamed past us toward nightfall.

At last he said: "But I am not going to. I suppose I am not going to for some reason similar to whatever insane reason has made you decide to free me and take me with you. What happens when your power comes to its end, in five minutes or five hours? Well, I know that the fire is swift."

I moved. Slowly. Distracted, in spite of everything, by that *I know*. Not *I believe* or *I guess* but *I know*. Something else not to think about. I continued to move very slowly. Took my hands off the empty shackle. Slid the key into my bra again. It could stay a shackle key for now.

I was not, perhaps, fully convinced that the cobra had lowered its hood. I felt his eyes on me again.

"I did warn you that names have power," he said. "Even human names, although this was not what I was thinking of when I said it."

"I'll remember not to tell any vampires my father's name in the future," I said. I glanced out the window. We'd lost about half an hour since I'd made the key. I shivered. My glance fell on my corner; the sack looked plumper than it had when I last looked—before Bo's gang had come the second time. More supplies, presumably. I would need feeding to get me through this day, although I didn't at all feel like eating now, and neither of us had pockets to carry anything in. I went over to the sack and picked it up. Another loaf of bread, another bottle of water, and something heavy in a plastic bag. I pulled the heavy thing out . . . heavy and *squishy*. A big lump of red, bleeding meat.

I gave a squeak and dropped it on the floor, where it obligingly went *splat*.

The vampire said, "It is beast. Cow. Beef. I believe they have forgotten to cook it for you."

"I don't like cooked meat either," I said, backing away from it. "I—I—no thanks. Er—would it do you any good?"

Another of his pauses. "Yes," he said.

"It's all yours," I said. "I'll stick to bread."

I saw him, this time. Did he mean for me to be able to see him, was it hard for him to move in daylight even early in the morning and in shade, or was he merely luxuriating in being free from the chain? Or had he moved so little in the last . . . however many days and nights that even he felt a little stiff? He walked as slowly as a weary human might walk around the big rectangle of light on the floor, around it to my corner, although he still walked with a sinuousness no human had. He bent and picked up the drippy parcel. I thought, is he going to suck it dry or what?

I didn't see. It was like when he drank water. One moment there was water, the next moment there was not. One moment there was a big piece of bloody meat in a white plastic bag, and the next moment the white plastic bag, ripped open, was drifting toward the floor, and the meat had disappeared. Vampires sometimes like their blood with a few solids, I guess. Maybe it was like having rice with your curry or pasta with your sauce.

I decided against trying to tie the sack round me somehow, and ate most of the new loaf instead, although it tasted like dust and ashes, not wholly because it was more store bread. (I spared a brief thought about how vampires might go shopping for human groceries. Groceries *for* humans, that is.) Then I picked up the water bottle. It would come with us.

We had to get going.

We were leaving. We were on our way. We were going *now*. And I was scared out of my *mind*. What had I let myself in for? The mere thought of remaining in constant physical contact with a vampire was abhorrent, and he was right, what about when whatever-it-was ran out? But I couldn't force him to come with me. He had decided it was worth the risk. So how fast was the fire, anyway? Supposing it came to that. I didn't need an answer to that: not fast enough. Nothing like as fast as a nice clean beheading.

And if you're touching a vampire when he catches fire . . .

Okay, okay, wait, said a little voice in my head. How did you get here? You got here by making the best of a whole carthaginian hell of a series of bad choices. And remember he doesn't feel horrible when you're doing your sun-parasol trick. He feels more like . . . helping Charlie do the books when Mom's sick. Or dealing with Mr. Cagney.

Mr. Cagney was one of our regulars at the coffeehouse, and he was convinced that the rest of the world existed to give him a bad time. He was the only one of our regulars who couldn't manage to say anything nice about my cinnamon rolls. That didn't stop him from eating them, however, and listening to him complain on a day he had arrived too late and they were sold out had resulted in our always having one set aside for him. Dealing with Mr. Cagney was an effort. A big, tiring, thankless effort. On the whole I thought I preferred the vampire.

He was watching me. "You can change your mind." Then he said something that sounded almost human for the first time: "I half wish you would."

I shook my head mournfully. "No. I can't."

"Then there is one more thing," he said.

I was beginning to learn that I probably wouldn't like anything he said after one of his pauses. I waited.

"You will have to let me carry you till we are well away from here."

"*What?*"

"Blood spoor. Your feet will be bleeding again before we are halfway across the open area." Was there the faintest tremor in his oddly echo-y voice when he said that? "Mine will not. And Bo's folk will not be at all happy about our escape, tonight, when they discover it. They will find the trail at once if they have blood spoor to follow."

I laid on a pause of my own. "Are you telling me that if I had decided to leave you behind, I wouldn't have made it anyway?"

"I do not know. There might conceivably have been some reason you were able to escape—a faulty lock on the shackle, for example. Bo would have someone's . . . someone would pay severely for this, but it might end there. That we are both gone will mean that something truly extraordinary has happened. And it almost certainly has something to do with you—as it does, does it not?—and that therefore something important about you was overlooked. And Bo will like that even less than he would have liked the straightforward escape of an ordinary human prisoner. He will order his folk to follow. We must not make it easy for them."

This was the longest speech I had heard from him. It edged out his description of the supersucker he would have become on the blood of Onyx Blaise's daughter. "For a ma—a creature who is driven mad by daylight, you are making very good sense."

"Having an accomplice is . . . reviving. Any hope after no hope. Even in these somewhat daunting circumstances."

Daunting. I liked that too. That was as good as "clean of live things."

He moved toward me and held out his arms, slowly, as if trying not to scare me. There was a sudden, ghastly rush of adrenaline—my body was having some trouble keeping up with my mind's mercurial decisions—and I twitched myself sideways like I was moving a puppet. I put one arm round his neck—carefully, so I didn't stretch the dubiously clotted scab on my breast—and held the water bottle in my other hand. He bent and picked me up more easily than I pick up a tray of cinnamon rolls.

It was not going to be a comfortable ride. It was rather like sitting on the stripped frame of a chair that has had all the chair bits taken away—there are just a few nasty pieces of iron railing left, and they start digging railing-shaped holes into you at once. Also, if this was a chair, it was made for some other species to sit in. Vampires do breathe, by the way, but their chests don't move like humans'. Have you ever lain in the arms of your sweetheart and tried to match your breathing to his, or hers? You do it automatically. Your brain only gets involved if your body is having trouble. Fortunately there was nothing about this situation that was like being in the arms of a sweetheart except that I was leaning against someone's naked chest. I could no more have breathed with him than I could have ignited gasoline and shot exhaust out my butt because I was sitting in the passenger seat of a car.

I also had the weird sensation that he'd been several degrees *cooler* when he picked me up, and he'd matched his body temperature to mine. Speaking of matching.

We left by the door Bo's gang had brought me through, across the ghostly hall, and out through the front door, which had been conveniently left ajar. What did I know about vampire deliberateness? I could barely recognize my vampire's breathing as breathing. But I had a notion that he walked not merely without hesitation but *very* deliberately into the blast of sunshine at the foot of the porch, and turned left, toward the trees on that side. I felt my harness take the strain. If there had been real straps involved, they would have creaked. It was a long way to the edge of the wood. It was perhaps just as well he was carrying me; the heat of the sun seemed to be making me woozy.

Heat doesn't usually trouble me. One of the reasons Charlie had first let me help him with the baking when I was still small was because I was the only one of any of us who could stand the heat of it in the summer, including the rest of the staff. That was when Charlie's was still fairly small itself, and Charlie was doing most of the cooking, before he opened up the front so we could have tables as well as the counter and the booths along the wall, and before he built my bakery. The bakery now is its own room next to the main kitchen, and there are windows and an outside door and industrial-strength fans, but in July and August pretty much everyone but me has to get out of there and splash water on themselves and have a sit-down.

But this was something else. The big curly ripples of power I'd felt when we stood in front of the window seemed bigger and curlier than ever, and were slowing the rest of me down, taking up too much space themselves, squeezing the usual bits of me into corners, till I felt squashed, like someone in a commuter train at six P.M. Even my brain felt compressed. That sense of wearing some kind of harness that had also managed to nail itself into my major organ systems was still there, but I began to feel that it wasn't so much carrying the burden as holding me together, so that the power ripples knew where the edges—the edges of *me*—were, and didn't break anything. I didn't feel frightened, although I wondered if I should.

We reached the edge of the trees at last, and it was better at once in their shadow. I felt more alert, and *lighter* somehow, although I wouldn't have described the effect of the ripples as heavy. But that feeling of having all my gaps filled a little too full eased somewhat. I remembered what he'd said about daylight: *I feel as if the rays of your sun are prizing me apart.* The tree-shadow wasn't thick or reliable enough to protect us from the sun so the power was still moving through me, but I didn't feel I was about to overflow, or crack. I thought: okay. I can guard one vampire from the effects of bright direct daylight. I wouldn't be able to guard two. Not that this was a piece of information I was planning on needing often in the future.

"We've crossed their line," said the vampire. "The guard ring is behind us."

"They'll know we have, won't they?"

"They'll know tonight. We—do not pay attention to the daylit world."

"Will they know where?"

"Perhaps. But I am following the traces from when they brought me here—and, so far, it is the same way they brought you—and without fresh blood they will have trouble deciding what is old and what is new."

"Uh . . ." This wasn't a topic I was looking forward to bringing up. "You know you and I are both, uh, wearing quite a lot of my, uh, blood already. Uh. Crusted. From last night."

"That matters very little," said the vampire. "It is only blood hot from a live body when it touches the earth that leaves a clear sign."

I reminded myself this was good news.

He was silent for a while, and then he said, dispassionately as ever, "I had feared that even if you could, as you claimed, protect my body from the fire as we crossed the open space, that the sun would blind me. This did not happen. I am relieved."

"Oh, *gods*," I said.

"As you say. But as you said earlier, I did not see myself receiving any better offers either. It seemed to me worth even that price against the almost certain likelihood of annihilation at Bo's hands."

I said, fascinated against my better judgment, "You thought I could navigate you through the trees somehow?"

"Yes. I would not have been totally helpless. I can—detect the presence of solid objects. But it would not have been easy."

I laughed. It was the first time I had laughed since I had driven out to the lake alone. "No. I'm sure it wouldn't have been."

We went on some time then in silence. We had to stop once for me to have another pee. Gods. Vampires didn't seem to *have* bodily functions. I squatted behind him, holding one of his legs. While I was on the spot, so to speak, I had a look at his sore ankle. It still looked disgusting but I didn't think it looked any worse.

It occurred to me several times that we were making much better speed than we would have with me walking barefoot. And while the iron-railing effect was pretty painful I have ridden in cars with worse suspension than being carried by a striding vampire. That liquid motion thing they do is no joke, and one-hundred-twenty (give or take) pound burdens don't dent it either. If the ankle was troubling him it didn't show.

The cut on my breast hurt quite a lot but I had more important things to worry about. He carried me so smoothly that it didn't crack open anyway. Thankful for small favors. I felt that even our present momentous alliance might have been put under strain if I started bleeding on him again.

I was keeping a vague watch on the sun through the trees over the lake, and also, with the power alive and working, I seemed able to sense it in some way other than seeing or feeling the touch of its light, and I knew when noon had come and gone. I had had a drink out of the water bottle a couple of times, and had offered it to my chauffeur, but he said, "No, thank you, it is not necessary." He sure was polite after he'd decided not to have you for dinner.

It was much farther back to my car than I'd guessed. Thirty miles, probably more. Maybe I still could have made it by myself before sunset, even barefoot. Maybe.

But I wouldn't have made it much farther, and the car wasn't there.

I'D EXPLAINED WHERE we were going when we had started out. The vampire had said nothing, but then he often said nothing, and he hadn't disagreed. I had the knife-key in my bra; we'd either find him a nice deep patch of shadow while I did my trick again, or he could keep his hands on my shoulders to maintain the Sun Screen Factor: Absolute Plus. I hadn't thought a lot beyond that. I guess what I was thinking was that a car equaled normal life. Once I got in my car and stuck the key in the little hole and the ignition caught, everything that had happened would be over like it had never happened, and I could just go back to my life again. I wasn't thinking clearly, of course, but who would be? I was still alive, and that was pretty amazing under the circumstances.

I hadn't thought about what I would do with the vampire after we got to the car either. As much as had occurred to me was that he could keep one hand on my knee while I drove, or something. Nobody put his hand on my knee except Mel, but just how "somebody" was a vampire? I didn't think I could shut even a vampire in the trunk, although the shade in there ought to be pretty total, and I wasn't sure what the parameters were anyway. I knew that a heavy coat and a broad-brimmed hat weren't fireproof enough and historians had long ago declared that the famous stories of knights in heavy armor turning out to be vampires weren't true either, so probably one layer of plastic car wasn't enough. But then what? Where do you drop off a vampire whom you've given a lift? The nearest mausoleum? Ha ha. The whole business of vampires hanging out in graveyards is bogus—vampires don't want anything to do with *dead* people, and the people they turn don't get buried in the first place. But old nursery tales die hard. (So much for Bram Stoker et al., Miss Yablonsky's point exactly.)

So I hadn't made any contingency plans. When we got to the old cottage I said, "Okay, here we are," and the vampire set me down, and I was standing on my own feet, and trying not to step on anything that would make me bleed. He was hovering, however, and it wasn't only because of the sun; I'm sure he would have picked me up again faster than blood could drip if it had come to that. He had one hand tactfully on my elbow. The light was no more than dappled where we stood. Funny how the claustrophobic regrowth of wilderness scrub can suddenly seem treacherously open and sporadic when you're thinking in terms of your companion's fatal allergy to sunlight.

I knew where I'd left the car. It was a small cabin and the place you parked was right behind it. "It's not here," I said stupidly. For the first time I felt the ripples of power *lurch*, as if they might knock me over, as if they might . . . spill over the lip of me somehow, and be lost. I couldn't risk, no, I *wouldn't* risk . . . I turned round and *seized* him, wrapped my arms around him, as if he were a seawall and could turn back any vagrant tide, contain any unexpected breaker. His arms, hesitantly, slid behind me, and it occurred to me that our prolonged physical contact was probably no more pleasant for him than it was for me, if perhaps for different reasons.

I took a few deep breaths, and the ripples steadied. I steadied. He was a good wall. Really very wall-like in some ways. Solid. Immobile. I realized I had my face pressed against what I knew from experience was an ambulatory body . . . that had no heart beating. Funny. And yet there was a buzz of . . . something going on in there. Life, you might call it, for want of a better term. I had never met a wall that buzzed.

I let go. He let go, except for one hand on my shoulder. "Sorry," I said. "I thought I was losing it."

"Yes," he said.

"If I had lost it, you'd have die—fried, you know," I said, to see what he would say.

"Yes," he said.

I shook my head.

"My kind does not surprise easily," he said. "You surprised me, this morning. I have thus used up my full quota of shock and consternation for some interval."

I stared at him. "You made a *joke*."

"I have heard this kind of thing may happen, to vampires who linger in the company of humans," he said, looking and sounding particularly vampirish. "It is not a situation that has provoked much interest. And . . . I am not myself after a day spent in daylight."

I'm not feeling a whole lot like myself either, I thought. I was carefully not thinking about the *instinct* that had thrown me at him just now. Wouldn't grabbing a tree have steadied me at least as well? So what if maybe he fried? "So you are not surprised by the disappearance of my car. That makes one of us."

"I had thought it unlikely that Bo would allow so obvious a loose end to remain dangling."

"I'm sorry. Yes. That is—sense. But I don't know what to do now."

"We go on," said the vampire. "We must be well away from the lake before dark."

I was trying to bring my brain back into balance. Settling the ripples down seemed to have cost me a lot, and my brain didn't want to produce coherent thoughts. I was also, of course, so far beyond tired that I didn't dare look in that direction at all. "The lake?" I said.

He paused again, so I was pretty sure I wasn't going to like what followed. "Vampire senses are different from human in a number of ways. The one that is relevant in this case is that landscape which is all one sort of thing is . . . more penetrable to our awareness to the extent of its homogeneity. It is not the distance that is crucial, but the uniformity. Bo will be able to find us too easily within any of the woods of the lake because they are all the woods of the lake, even without blood spoor to follow. Once we are out of those woods . . . in some ways Bo will have more difficulty in tracing us than a human might."

A tiny piece of good news, if we lived long enough. Okay. The nearest way out of the woods was still the way we had been going—which must have been why the vampire agreed to it in the first place. The woods around the lake spilled into more woods and smaller lakes and some mostly deserted farmland before it came to any more towns. New Arcadia was the only city for some distance, and then there were a lot of smaller towns and villages spreading out from us, eventually themselves getting larger and closer together again till they became another city. But that was a hundred miles away.

"Where are you going?" I said.

"I am going where you are going till sunset," said the vampire. "Then you are going where you are going, and I am going where I am going."

I sighed. "Yes. No. I didn't mean to pry. Look, it is all very well that we have to get away from the woods, but that means going into at least the outskirts of the town. And while I can keep the sun off you, I can't make you look human. And let me tell you your skin

color is strictly incredible, and you're not even wearing a shirt. And
we don't have a car."

The vampire took this without a tremor. "What do you suggest?"

"The only thing I can think of is to plaster ourselves with
mud—especially you—stagger a little, and hit town at the tip of the
north end, where the druggies hang out. You do look a little like a
junkie, or you look a little more like a junkie than you look like anything else. Human. With any luck any junkies that have eyes left to
see you with will be so creeped out by how much worse it can get
than they realized that nobody will say anything to us." I paused.
"Then there's the poor but fairly respectable area, and they won't
like us, but if we keep moving they *probably* won't call the suck—the
cops. What worries me most is that some bright spark might guess
you're a demon. You manifestly can't be a vampire because you're
out in daylight. But you aren't, as I say, at all persuasive as human.
You *could* be a rather dim demon who doesn't realize how bad your
passing for human is—and since we have to keep hold of each other
someone might think you were kidnapping me—hell. And there's at
least one highway we have to cross too. Double carthaginian hell. I
don't suppose you know that part of town at all?"

"No."

"No. I don't either, much. Well, if they don't call SOF, we should
be able to find the nature preserve my landlady's house is on the
other side of. . . . I have no idea how far all of this is though. A ways.
We could have gone directly through town in my car." I looked ap-
prehensively at the sun, which was nearing midafternoon, and there
were still a lot of trees between us and pavement.

"Indeed you would not have been best advised to go directly
through town in your car, not with me in it with you. Your family
will have given the—the identification number to the police."

"What? License plate. Oh. Oh. I'm sorry. I hadn't thought of that
either."

"I had not supposed you had brought me all this way to betray
me at the last," he said.

No. "But . . . it's likely to be well past sunset before we get to my apartment," I said, trying not to sound desolate. I am *not* too tired to go on, I was telling myself. Not finding the car is only a *setback*. It's not the end of the story.

"I will see you home," said the vampire courteously, like a nice, well-brought-up boy seeing his date back to her house after dinner at the local pizza place.

There was no reason that this should make my eyes fill with tears. I was just tired. "I didn't mean—oh—thanks," I said. I should have wanted him gone as soon as possible. I should have been longing for the sight of the sun touching the horizon—at least once we got out of the trees. But I wasn't. I was grateful that he was going to see me to my front door. Standing by the cabin and looking at the place my car should have been and wasn't, I didn't think I could do it without him.

I was glad he hadn't fried.

We went down to the lake in our little connected duo. I had grown sort of used to being carried, and because it was such an odd thing to be doing at all, the crucial, fundamental oddness of our necessary proximity was less noticeable. Walking side by side with my hand tucked under his arm was much odder and more uncomfortable. I also found that it made me feel more lopsided. It was probably only a function of being so tired, but having the power exchange, or whatever it was, only going on through one hand made me feel dizzy. I leaned on him not very voluntarily.

The ground here was mostly dirt and moss with a little struggling grass or grasslike weeds, so my bare feet were not in much danger. When we got to the shore I chose the marshiest place I could find—I knew where to look, there was a little inlet just east of the cabin—and made him sit down in it, and then rubbed bog slime and mud all over him, including his hair. He was so skinny my hands went *thump thump thump* down his ribs. He put up with all of this with perfect stoicism. He put one hand round my ankle—so I would have both hands free—but I told him to use both ankles for balance. My balance.

I was a little more artistic about my own ornamentation. I only had to look like someone who might be jiving with this freak in a nonmandatory way. So I rubbed mud into my hair and let it drip down one side of my face and over that shoulder. I primly kept the mud away from the cut on my breast. My mother's rules of hygiene were very clear about preventing dirt from entering an open wound, and I didn't have a Band-Aid to hand. It would have had to be several very large Band-Aids anyway. (I hoped mud on the vampire's injured ankle wasn't going to cause him any problems: that the clean-of-live-things trick was a general defense.) Besides, the slash was probably good added verisimilitude and we could use all the help we could get. Verisimilitude of what? My lip was still swollen but it had stopped bleeding hours ago, and the metal tang of blood was no longer in my mouth. Hooray. I wanted to feel as little like a vampire as possible. I didn't like the sensation that the boundaries were getting a little blurry.

I had spent a lot of time sitting by this same inlet with my grandmother. In the fifteen years since then it had changed its course and silted up. When we had sat here you could hear the small pattering stream that had created the inlet, but it was silent now. All I could hear was my own breathing, and the splat of my handiwork. There weren't even any birds.

The vampire insisted, if you could call it insisting, that he would carry me the last stretch of woods to the first streets of the town. Homogeneity, he reminded me, and blood spoor. And I remembered how much faster we went when it was only him walking—and that it was another twelve or fifteen miles to the edge of town—and made no protest.

He carried me right up to the crumbling cement of the end of the last street, and let my legs drop down gently on the disintegrating curb. I didn't have to pretend to lean on him to keep contact; I needed him to keep me upright. I put my arm through his and my hand on his wrist. We bumped gently at shoulder and hip. The power ripples sloshed a little as I adjusted to walking on my own feet again, but there was none of the sudden danger of losing my balance that there had been when I'd discovered the disappearance of my car. In fact the ripples now seemed to be slightly altering their shape and pattern to help me. The dizziness I'd felt when we walked down the inlet subsided.

I had just enough sense left to put the now-empty bottle of water in a city litter bin.

I don't ever want to have another journey like those last fifteen or so miles across town. I know I keep going on about how tired I was, but that last exhaustion was like a mortal illness, and I felt I could see my death a few hundred feet down the street ahead of us. I'm a pretty good walker, but I'm talking about normal life: Mel and I might hike fifteen miles around the lake looking for animals and trying to stay out of the way of Supergreens, but we would take all day at it, have several rest stops and a long halt for lunch, and go home tired and pleased with ourselves. We would also be wearing shoes. This was fifteen miles on top of all that had gone before, and I'd been running on empty for a long time already. It wasn't only my death I was seeing; I was beginning to hallucinate pretty badly. Lots of people get sort of gray, ferny, cobwebby mirages around the edges of their vision when they get overtired—and I'd had them before occasionally when we were shorthanded at the coffeehouse because everyone was sick but Charlie and me, and we were working sixteen-, eighteen-hour days day after day—but this was the first time the ferns and cobwebs had things moving around in them, not to mention the new, full-color palette. It was not an enjoyable experience. I did recognize what was going on, and went on peering through the fringes of my private picture show, and making out which way we should be going out there in the real world. I knew the layout of my city pretty well even if I didn't know all its details, and even at this final personal frontier I kept my sense of direction. It was, however, just as well that I was so numb I was barely aware of my poor feet. And it was a good thing that blood spoor was no longer an issue.

The sun was by now moving quickly toward setting, which should have been a good thing; the pair of us were going to be less grisly-looking in twilight. No one accosted us. We saw a few people, but either they were already totally lit and away and having much better private screenings than mine (which several of them were animatedly discussing with themselves) and couldn't care less about us, or they took one look and crossed to the other side of whichever street we were on, and kept their eyes averted. I thought of asking the vampire if he was doing anything—if vampires can persuade, can they repel too?—but it was still daylight, if barely, so this didn't seem likely. Maybe my power-ripples were doing something. Maybe that was part of the adjustment they'd made at the edge of town. Maybe we were just lucky.

In the middle of all this I had a fierce implausible longing for my grandmother, who could have explained to me what I was doing—I was sure—and how I was doing it. As I started to slip over some kind of definitive last line, as I began to feel that the power-ripples were soon going to be all there was left of me, that my own personality was weakening, thinning, would blow away like the spidery gray stuff over my eyes, I suddenly, passionately, wanted to know what I was doing.

It wasn't the vampire the people were avoiding, though. It was me. I was the one reeling and mumbling and off my head and probably dangerous.

I was fading with the daylight. I had stretched myself too far.

I got us to the edge of the park at about the moment that twilight turned into darkness, and he picked me up again without so much as a break in his stride, and plunged under the trees, into the night that was his element. I could feel the power-ripples moving faintly through me even though I no longer needed them for a sun-parasol. I thought, mistily, maybe they're trying to keep me alive. Nice of them. He must be trying too. Funny sort of thing for a vampire to do. . . .

It was all darkness around us, darkness and trees, and the vampire speeding through it. Feebly I murmured, "I have no idea where we are any more."

"I do," he said. "I can smell your house."

Perhaps I fell asleep. That would explain the dreams: that I was flying, that I was dead, that I was a vampire, that I was standing by the lake with my grandmother, and I had just opened my closed hands, but instead of a flower or a feather or a ring, blood welled up and spilled over the edges of my hands, and welled up and welled up, as if my hands were a fountain. But a fountain of blood.

The vampire came to a halt. I blinked my eyes open and saw lights twinkling through a few trees, and made out the shape of my house. My house. We were on the far side of the garden. I could see the pale lavender of the lilacs by Yolande's sitting-room window. She was the sort of old lady who had a sitting room instead of a living room. And the lights on in it meant she was still awake, although usually she went to bed as early as a person who gets up at four A.M. to go make cinnamon rolls does. I wondered what time it was.

The vampire said, "You will need a key to open your door."

He could leave me here. I could ask him to let me down, and then he could go. I could knock on Yolande's door, and, once the fright of having a derelict on her doorstep had worn off, after she had recognized me, she would let me in with her spare key. She would be appalled and sympathetic. She would call the coffeehouse and the doctor and the police. She would run me a hot bath and help me into it, and cluck over my wounds. She would not ask me any questions; she would know I was too tired, and she would recognize the signs of shock. She would give me hot sweet tea and orange juice, and human warmth and company and understanding.

I couldn't face her.

Slowly I moved, to pull the knife-key out of my bra. The vampire knelt, holding me in his lap. I leaned against him, closed my hands round the small heavy bit of worked metal. I called on the power of daylight. It came from a lifetime away, but it came. I felt something snap, as if my stomach had parted company with my small intestine, or my liver from my spleen; but when I opened my hands again, there was the key to my front door.

The vampire picked me up again, gently. He walked round the garden. He went silently up the porch steps, which I could not have done. The steps all creaked and the porch itself creaked worse. He drifted, dark and silent as any shadow, to my door, and, still in his arms, I twisted the key in the lock, turned the handle, pushed the door a tiny way open, and whispered, "Yes."

He carried me upstairs and through the door at the top and into my front room, and laid me on the sofa. I didn't hear him stand up or move away, but I heard my refrigerator door open and close, and then he was kneeling beside me again. He slid an arm under my head and shoulders and raised me and stuffed pillows under me till I was half sitting, and said, "Open your mouth."

He dribbled a little of the milk into my mouth and made sure I could swallow it before he held the carton up steadily for me to drink. He cupped the back of my head with his other hand. What did he think he was, a nurse? I would have asked him but I was too tired. He got most of the carton of milk down me, eased my head back onto the pile of pillows and then started feeding me something in small scraps. After the first few, more of my senses came back from nowhere and I recognized one of my own muffins, left over at the end of that last day at the coffeehouse, several centuries ago. He was tearing off small bits and feeding them to me slowly, so I wouldn't choke. The muffin was still pretty good but three days old to a baker counts as over. I think he may have fed me a second one, still scrap by scrap. Then he held up the carton of milk again till I finished it. Then he pulled the pillows back out, except for one, and laid me down with my head on it.

I don't remember anything more.

I woke up I don't know how many hours later with the light streaming through the windows. It had finally reached the sofa where I was lying, and touched my face. I couldn't remember where I was—no I was at home—no, not my old childhood bedroom, this had been my apartment for nearly seven years—then why wasn't I in my own bed—why did I remember sleeping on a floor—no, that had been a dream—no, a *nightmare*—don't think about it—*don't think about it*—and at the same time I knew I had overslept and should have been down at the coffeehouse hours ago and Charlie would kill me—no he wouldn't—why hadn't one of them called to find out where I was?

I tried to sit up and nearly screamed. Every muscle in my body seemed to have seized up, and I didn't think there was a single nerve end that hadn't shouted *NO* when I moved. I ached all over, inside

and out. And furthermore I felt . . . I felt as if all my insides, the or-
gans, the organ systems, all that stuff you studied in biology class and
promptly forgot again, all those murky, semiknown bits and pieces,
no longer had the same *relationship* to each other that they had
before . . . before . . . silly sort of thing to feel, I must be delirious.
My mind would keep drifting back—*don't think about it*—but how
was I to make sense of where I was, at home, sleeping on the sofa, in
broad daylight? And so sore I couldn't move. If—all that—was a
nightmare, what *had* happened to me?

I tried to sit up again and eventually succeeded. There was a
blanket laid over me, and it fell off, and onto the floor.

I was wearing a filthy, stained, dark cranberry-red dress that clung
round me at the top and swirled out into yards and yards of hem at
my ankles. I was barefoot, and my feet were in shreds, scratched and
abraded and bruised and swollen. I had mud all over me (and now all
over the sofa and the floor as well) and a long, curved ugly slash
across my breast that had obviously bled and then clotted. Its edges
ground against each other and throbbed when I tried to move. My
lower lip was split and that side of my face felt puffy.

I started to shiver uncontrollably.

Painfully I picked up the blanket again, and wrapped it round
me, and made my way into the bathroom by feeling along the walls,
and turned the hot water on in the bath. The hot water was going to
hurt, but it was going to be worth it. I poured in about four times
as much bubble bath as I usually use, and breathed the sweet
lily-of-the-valley-scented steam. Even my lungs hurt, and my breathing seemed funny, there was something about the way I breathed
that was different from . . . While I waited for the bath to fill, I
groped my way into the kitchen. I ate an apple, because that was the
first thing I saw. There was an empty carton of milk on the counter
by the sink. I didn't think about this. I ate another apple. Then I ate a
pear. I moved into the light pouring through the kitchen window
and let it soak into me while I stood staring out at the garden. In the
welcoming, restorative sunlight, trying to keep my mind from
thinking anything at all, I felt the tiny, laborious stirring of a sense of
well-being: the convalescent's rejoicing at the first hint of a possible

return to health. I would have a bath, and then I would call the coffeehouse. I didn't have to tell anyone anything. I could be too traumatized. I could have forgotten everything. I *had* forgotten everything. I was forgetting everything right now. My feet and my face and the gash on my breast would stop anyone from pressing me too hard to remember something so obviously terrible. Yolande must be out; otherwise she would have heard the bathwater running, and have come upstairs to find out if I was all right. She would have known that I've been missing, that on a normal day I would have been at the coffeehouse hours ago, not up here running bathwater.

That I've been missing.

That I've been . . .

I didn't have to remember or think about anything. I could just stand here and let the sun heal me. I was relieved that Yolande wasn't here, asking questions, being appalled and sickened. Reminding me by her distress. I was relieved that no one would disturb me till I had finished forgetting.

The bath should be full by now. Now that the sunlight had begun to do its work I wanted to be clean. I might have to use every bar of soap I had, and bring the scouring pads in from the kitchen. I was going to burn this dress, wherever it came from. It was nothing I'd have ever chosen. I couldn't imagine why I was wearing it. When I was completely clean again, and wearing my own clothes, I would call the coffeehouse, tell them I was home again. Home and safe. Safe.

As I turned away from the window a square of white lying on the kitchen table caught my eye. It was my notepad, which usually lived beside the phone. On it was written:

Good-bye my Sunshine.
Constantine

PART TWO

It might not have been too bad, afterward, except for two things. The nightmares. And the fact that the cut on my breast wouldn't heal.

That's nonsense, of course. If I'd been able to face being honest, there was no way it *wasn't* going to be bad.

I suppose I didn't realize how rough I was that first morning. After I had one bath I had another. (Bless landladies with absurdly huge water heaters.) I washed my hair three times during that first bath and twice during the second. Hot water and soap and shampoo hurt like blazes, but it was a wonderful, human, normal, this-world sort of hurt. Getting dressed wasn't too difficult because my wardrobe specializes in soft, well-worn, and comfortable, but finding shoes and socks that didn't feel like they were scarifying my poor feet with steel wool was hard. Then I drank a pot of very strong tea and on the caffeine buzz I almost half convinced myself that I felt almost half normal and if I felt half normal I must look half normal.

Wrong.

At the last minute I didn't burn the dress. I put it in the sink with some handwash stuff and then hung it in a corner with a bowl under it to drip dry. It leaked thin bloody-looking water and this made me so queasy I almost screwed it up to be burned anyway. But I still didn't.

I did burn the underwear I'd worn. It was like I had to burn something. I took it out—nearly on tiptoe, clinging to the shadows, as if I was doing something illicit I might be caught at—and stuffed it into the ashes and wood chips on Yolande's garden bonfire heap. My hands shook when I struck the match, but that might have been the caffeine. It burned surprisingly well for a few scraps of cloth, as if my eagerness to see something go up in smoke was itself inflammatory.

I stuck that note in a drawer so I didn't have to see or think about it. Or about who had written it.

The house key that had been a jackknife lay on top of a pile of books next to the sofa. It had been one of the first things I'd seen when I'd managed to lever myself upright. I had done all of this other stuff—wash, rewash, inject caffeine, set fire to things—while not deciding what to do about it. It wasn't that an extra house key was an enormous problem. But it was a house key that had been a pocketknife. Was supposed to be a pocketknife. And I *missed* my knife. I wanted it back. And there was only one way to get it back, which would remind me of all that stuff I was working on forgetting. I had returned to the world where I made cinnamon rolls and was my mother's, not my father's, daughter, and I wanted to stay there.

I had opened all the windows, and the door to the balcony; I wanted as much fresh air as I could get. I wanted no faintest remaining scent here of anything that might have come back with me last night. The blanket that had covered me was soaking in the tub. I had brushed the sofa within an inch of its life, with a whisk broom that would take the hide off an armadillo. The cushion I had had my head on had spot remover troweled over it and was waiting to dry.

I stood on the balcony, closed my eyes, and let the sun and the soft breeze move over me. Through me. I heard—felt—the leaves of my tree stir and rustle. My grandmother had taught me that if you handle magic, you have to clean up after yourself. Just like washing (or burning) your clothes or troweling spot remover on a sofa cushion.

I went back indoors to pick up the house key that shouldn't be left a house key. I knelt on the floor inside the balcony door, in the sunlight, near enough the open door to smell the breeze from the garden.

It was so easy this time. I felt the change, felt the key slip from keyness to knifeness. It was like kneading dough, feeling the thing become what you want it to be under your hands, feeling it responding to you, feeling it transform itself as a result of your effort. Your power. Your knowledge.

I didn't like it being easy.

But I liked having my knife back. It lay in my hand, looking like it always had. "Welcome back, friend," I murmured, and refused to feel silly for talking to a jackknife. Maybe I was talking to myself too.

Then I put it in my pocket and went to look for incense. I never use incense in my life as a coffeehouse baker—I much prefer the smell of fresh bread—but it was one of those things that people who need to give you something but haven't a clue who you are give you. My aunt Edna, my mother's other sister, every year at one solstice or another, gives me a packet of the current hot fashion in incense. So there was probably some lurking in the back of a cupboard somewhere. There was. I lit a wand of World Harmonics Jasmine and put it in a glass and said the words my grandmother had taught me. I didn't have to remember them, they were right there, like my tree.

Then I called the coffeehouse to tell them I was back, and all hell broke loose. Especially after Mom belted out to my apartment when I explained I didn't have a car any more, to pick me up, and got her first look at me.

I won't go into a lot about that. It was not one of our finest mother-daughter moments.

I did go to the doctor because everybody said I had to. The doctor said there wasn't much wrong with me but minor dehydration and exhaustion, gave me a tetanus shot, and some cream to put on both my feet and my breast. He asked me how I'd got the cut on my breast because as he put it, in that portentously unruffled and infuriating way of doctors, "It looks a bit nasty." But I hadn't decided how much I was going to tell anyone, and having had everyone who had seen me so far freaking out (except the doctor, who was doing portentously unruffled like a kick to the head) wasn't helping. So I said I didn't remember. He said "mm hmm" and put some stitches in so it would heal neatly, muttered something about post-traumatic shock syndrome, offered me a reference to someone who could talk to me about remembering and not remembering, and sent me away. Mel had brought me. He borrowed Charlie's car so I didn't have to ride pillion on a motorcycle. (I hadn't known Mel could drive a car. He drove his motorcycles in all weather, including heavy snow and thunderstorms.) And he brought me back. To the coffeehouse. The thought of going back to my apartment was only fleetingly tempting. I wanted to return to my *life*, and my life, for better or worse, was in the coffeehouse bakery. Also, I wanted to get the freaking out over with so that I didn't have to keep coming back to it, and I knew Mom wasn't through yet. Charlie had nearly had to tie her up to let Mel take me to the doctor. Mom is a bit prone to overreacting. But Mel, when he first saw me, turned haggard, and his eyes seemed to go about a million miles deep, and I suddenly felt I knew what he was going to look like when he was ninety. And he didn't say anything at all, which was probably worse than the noise everyone else was making.

Mom tried to insist that I stay at the house—move back in with her and Charlie and my brothers. I said that I would do nothing of the kind. I meant it, but I was a little hindered by the fact that I no longer had a car. (They never did find my car. I had liked that car.) That afternoon, after talking to the doctor and about forty-seven kinds of cop, Mom and I had a big shouting match that I didn't have the strength for, and I burst into tears and said that I would *walk* home if I had to and then Mom started weeping too and it was all pretty ghastly. Charlie at this point reminded Mom in a reasonable facsimile of his normal voice (he kept starting to pat my shoulder and then stopping because I'd told him, truthfully, that I was sore all over) that there was no longer a bedroom for me: the spare bedroom and den had disappeared when Charlie knocked all the downstairs walls out, and Kenny had moved out of the boys' bedroom into my old bedroom upstairs. This only made Mom cry harder.

Then Mel, who had been left more or less singlehanded to run the coffeehouse while all the drama went on in the office, began collaring the staff who had crammed into the office door to watch and be a kind of Greek chorus of horror, and one by one heaving them physically toward what they ought to be doing, like minding the customers, before *they* all came back to see what was going on too, which, given Charlie's kind of customers, they would be quite capable of. When he'd forged his way through to me, he handed Charlie the spatula he was still holding in his other hand, like the relay runner handing on the torch at Thermopylae, and said, "Can you hold the kitchen a minute?" and hustled me off to the bakery. *My* bakery. Just standing in my own domain again, where I was Queen of the Cinnamon Roll, the Bran Muffin, the Orange-Date Tea Bread—the Caramel Cataclysm and the Rocky Road Avalanche—made me feel better. I had to cancel the immediate impulse to put on a clean apron and check my flour supply. It was far too *clean* in here for a Thursday. . . .

"Nobody's been in here while you've been gone. We gave Paulie the time off."

Paulie was my new apprentice. I had stopped crying for the moment but this made my aching eyes fill up again. "Oh . . ."

"Hey, we didn't know what to do. No carthaginian idea." Mel sounded grim but studiedly calm. For the first time I had some glimpse of what it must have been like for everybody here when I disappeared. I wasn't the disappearing kind. They would have feared the worst. It was the right response. And given what could have happened, I probably looked a lot worse than I was, so everybody was taking one look at me and fitting this vision against what their dreams had been churning out the last two days.

"Sweetheart. . . ."

I stiffened.

"Hey. Sheer. This is me, okay? I saw you not taking the name the doctor wanted to give you about someone to talk to. You don't have to talk to me unless you want to. Or anyone else, including Charlie and your mom. But if you tell me what you do want, I'll help you make it happen. If you'll let me."

Thanks to all the gods and angels for Mel. I couldn't explain that while yes, I'd always been a bit solitary, a bit disinclined to talk about what mattered to me, about what I was thinking about, it was *crucial* that I be able to go home, to *my* home, my private space, now. Alone. Where I didn't have to lie.

I hadn't forgotten nearly as much as I was pretending I had.

Mind you, I'd forgotten a lot. Post-traumatic whatsit, like the doctor said. The cops mentioned post-traumatic whatsit too. I had to check in with the cops because Mom and Charlie had, of course, reported me missing. I said that I'd driven out to the lake Monday night and didn't remember anything after that. No, I didn't remember where I'd been. No, I didn't remember how I'd got home two days later. No, I didn't remember why I was so beat up. Mel went with me for that too, even though he was pretty allergic to cops. (Charlie, trying to make a joke, said that he hadn't done so much cooking for years, and did I want Mel to take me anywhere else? Florida? The Catskills?) *And* the cop shrink they made me talk to had to go into it again. The gist is that you only remember what you can bear to remember. If you're lucky, as you get stronger, you can bear to remember a little more, and eventually you get round to remembering all of it and by remembering it then it can't mess up your life. That's the theory. Fat lot they know.

I didn't say "vampires" to anyone, and I sure remembered that much. If I had said it, SOF wouldn't have just talked to me, they'd've *kept* me. People don't escape from vampires. I wasn't going to think about how I'd escaped from vampires—let alone tell SOF about it—so let's just pretend I hadn't escaped from vampires. *Post*-traumatic shock, phooey. Seemed to me the trauma was trotting right along with me, like a dog on a leash with its owner. I was the dog.

I had to talk to SOF, because anything mysterious might be about the Others, and SOF were the Other police. But I told them I didn't remember anything too. By the time I talked to SOF I was getting good at saying I didn't remember. I could look 'em in the eye and say it like I meant it. They were cleverer about questioning me. They asked me stuff like what the lake had looked like that night, where exactly I'd sat on the porch of the cabin. They weren't trying to trick me; they were trying to help me remember, possibly to our mutual benefit, trying to help me find a way in to remembering. I pretended there was no door, or if there was one, it had six locks and four bolts and a steel bar *and* it had been bricked over years ago.

It was easier, saying I didn't remember. I walled it all out, including everybody's insistent, well-meaning concern. And it turned out to be easy—a little too easy—to burst into tears if anyone tried to go on asking me questions. Some people are mean drunks: I'm a mean weeper.

The first days started passing and became the first week. The bruises were fading and the scratches skinned over, and I began to look less like hell on earth. On the second Monday movies night at the Seddons' after my return, people began to make eye contact with me again without looking like it was costing them.

And I was making cinnamon rolls and bread and all like a normal crazed coffeehouse baker again, thus deflecting poor Paulie's imminent nervous breakdown. He was going to be good, but he was still new and slow from lack of experience, eager to gain that experience, he'd been several weeks going through the wringer, or the five-speed industrial strength mixer, with me, and then I disappeared and everybody was barking at him because his presence reminded them that I wasn't there, and sending him home. I wanted to cheer him up, so I let him in on the secret of Bitter Chocolate Death and he made it, beautifully, first time. This bucked him up so much he started humming while he worked. Gah. It was bad enough having someone in the bakery with me some of the time, so I could teach him what to do and keep an eye on him while he did it: humming was pushing it. Was it absolutely necessary to have a cheerful apprentice?

Charlie found someone who could loan me a car till I could replace the one they never found, and then found another one when the first one had to go back. The insurance took forever to cough up but it did at last. Their agent wanted to complain about my not remembering exactly what had happened, but he was promptly inundated by people from Charlie's, staff and regulars, offering to be character references, the doctor I'd seen and the cop shrink I'd seen said I was genuine, *and* then Mom started writing letters. The company might have held out against the rest, but no one resists Mom for long when she starts one of her letter-writing campaigns.

During borrowed-car gaps Mel gave me a lift on his motorcycle of the week (favors don't get much more serious than giving someone a ride at four A.M.), and then I started using Kenny's bicycle. Kenny was at an age when bicycles are deeply uncool and he didn't miss it. Downtown where the coffeehouse is is a drag on a bike, cars and buses first run you off the road and then leave you asphyxiating in their wake, but it's nice out near Yolande's and bicycling helped make me tired enough to sleep through the nights. Although it meant getting up at three-thirty to get in in time to make cinnamon rolls. Which is ridiculous. Also, Mom was having kittens about my riding a bike after dark (or before sunup), and she was perhaps not entirely wrong about this, even if she didn't know why, and even though there was no record of anyone ever being snatched off a bike in New Arcadia. There was no record of suckers at the lake either. So I did buy another car. The Wreck. It ran. I bought it from a friend of Mel's who liked tinkering with cars the way Mel liked tinkering with motorcycles, and the friend guaranteed it would *run*, just so long as I didn't want anything fancy like a third gear that was there all the time, or a top speed of over forty. It suited me fine. I didn't feel like getting attached to another car, and the sporadic absence of third gear was an interesting diversion.

The doctor took the stitches out of my breast. My feet healed. Life started to look superficially normal again. I took a deep breath and asked Paulie how he'd like to get up at four in the morning once a week to make cinnamon rolls. He was delighted. Another head case joins the inner cadre at Charlie's. He chose Thursday. I now had two mornings a week I didn't have to get up before sunrise. Theoretically. I didn't tell him what if he was paying attention he already knew, that the coffeehouse schedule was a thing that happened on paper and never quite worked out that way. But letting him think he got to choose should be good for morale. His morale. And even an unpredictable series of fours in the morning I didn't have to get up at was going to be good for *my* morale.

Aimil and I started going to junk and old-books fairs again. And when I went hiking with Mel we didn't go out to the lake. Not being able to decide what to tell anyone about anything had become the habit of not telling anybody anything. The funny thing was that the nearest I came to telling anyone was Yolande. There was something about the way she put me in a chair and made pots of tea and sat with me and talked about the weather or the latest civic scandal or some book we had both read, and not only didn't ask me anything but didn't appear to be suppressing the desire to ask me anything either.

The second nearest I came was one night with Mel, when I woke up out of one of the nightmares, and was out of bed and across the room before I had registered that the body I had been in bed with—had had my head on the chest of—had a heartbeat. Mel didn't say anything stupid. He sat up slowly, and turned the light on slowly, and made me a cup of tea slowly. By that time I was no longer twitching away from every shadow but I was too pumped with sick adrenaline to sleep. Mel took me downstairs and put a paintbrush in my hand. Every now and then he got talked into doing a custom job on one of the bikes he'd rescued. I had laid down primer and first coats for him a few times, and buffed finishes, but that's all. That night he had me filling in the outline of tiny green oak leaves. When I had to stop and get ready to report for cinnamon roll duty I felt almost normal again. No, not normal. Something else. I felt as if I'd accidentally re-entered my grandmother's world, where I didn't want to go. But if that was where I had been, it had done me good. I wondered who the bike was for, why they wanted an oak tree. Mel would never do the standard screaming-demon thunderbolt-superhero sort of thing, all jaw and biceps and skeggy-looking flames, and one of the few little dumb things that would ruffle that calm of his was the sight of a bike decorated with a flying sorcerer, but a tree was a . . . well, a funny symbol for something with wheels that was built to go lickety-split. Or look at it another way. The main symbolism around trees is about their incorruptibility, right? Their immunity to all dark magic. This is not something you expect your average biker to be deeply interested in.

I felt a little breeze—Mel had opened a window—heard leaves rustle. It hadn't occurred to me that my secret tree might be, say, an oak, or an ash, a beech, some particular kind of tree that related to a tree I might find in an ordinary landscape. I didn't want my grandmother's world to have anything to do with this one. I didn't want what had happened to me at the lake to have anything to do with this world, this ordinary landscape. I laid my paintbrush down and went and stood with Mel by the open window.

AFTER THE FIRST week or two of armed and sizzling silence after the argument, and all messages passed through pacifist intermediaries, Mom had started giving me charms. She'd turn up at the coffeehouse at about eight in the morning with another charm done up in the standard charm-seller's twist of brown paper. I didn't want them, but I took them, and I didn't argue with her. I didn't say anything at all except (sometimes) thank you. Mom and I hadn't gone in for light conversation in years, since it never stayed light, between us. I did things with the charms like wrap them around the telephone at home, to soften any bad news it might be bringing me, or drape them round my combox screen, ditto. This kind of abuse wears charms out fast. I'm not a big fan of charms—barring the basic wards, which I admit only a fool would dispense with, fetishes, refuges, whammies, talismans, amulets, festoons, or any of the rest, I can do without 'em. They take up too much psychic space, and the sooner these new ones crashed and burned the sooner they'd stop bugging me. But Mom was trying to behave herself, and the charms seemed to relieve her feelings. Once I had a car again I started stuffing them in the glove compartment. They didn't like it, but charms aren't built to quarrel with you.

The mark on my breast, which appeared to have closed over, cracked open again, and oozed. It was nearing high summer by then and I, who generally wore as little as decency allowed because it got so hot in the bakery, was suddenly wearing stranglingly high-necked T-shirts. You can't ooze in a public bakery. I went back to the doctor and he said "hmm" and had I remembered yet how I'd gotten the cut in the first place. I said I hadn't. He gave me a different cream for it and sent me home again. It seemed to heal for a while and then cracked open again. I grew clever about taping gauze over it and ripping the armholes out of my high-necked shirts and wearing lurid multicolored bras—fortunately there was a vogue on for lurid multicolored bras—so it looked like I was merely making a somewhat unfortunate fashion statement. Mel knew better, of course, and if it hadn't been for him I would have stopped going to the doctor, but Mel was a stubborn bastard when he wanted to be and he wanted to be about this, drat him. So I had to go back again. The doctor was starting to worry by now, and wanted to send me to a specialist. A specialist in *what*, I wanted to say, but I didn't dare. I was afraid I'd give something away, that my guilty conscience would start oozing through the cracks somehow, like blood and lymph kept oozing through the crack in my skin. I refused to see a specialist.

Some cop or other came by the coffeehouse at least once a week "to see how I was doing." Any of our marginally half-alert regulars knew the Cinnamon Roll Queen and chief baker had been absent a few days under mysterious circumstances and that whatever had happened to her was still casting a pall over the entire staff at Charlie's. That was everybody. And our SOF regulars are better than half alert or they wouldn't be working for SOF. So I had cops coming in and our SOFs watching the cops and the cops watching our SOFs. It should have been funny. It wasn't. I think Pat and Jesse actually suspected the truth, although I don't see how they could have. Maybe they thought it was ghouls or something, although ghouls don't generally have the foresight to, like, *store* a future meal. But something had happened and the law enforcement guys wanted to get out there and enforce something. They weren't fussy. If it was people, the cops were happy to do it. If it wasn't people, SOF was happy to do it. But I was supposed to choose my dancing partner and I wouldn't, and this was making the troops restless.

I did notice the difference between the people who were really bothered for me, or for the sake of the society they were paid a salary to keep safe, and the people who wanted to know more because it was like live TV or those cheesy mags with headlines like I ATE MY ALIEN BABY. Fried, with a side salad and a beer.

The most serious drawback to the telling-nothing approach is that it made that much more of a mystery of what had happened, and the nature of gossip abhors a vacuum of the unexplained. This meant that soon everybody "knew" that whatever had happened did indeed involve the Others, because that made a better story. I think they would have liked to assume that it involved the Darkest Others, because that made the best story of all, except that, of course, I was still *here*, and nobody escaped from vampires.

Nobody escaped from vampires.

I didn't know if the everybody who knew this included SOF or not, but I could hardly ask.

MEANWHILE THERE WERE the nightmares. There continued, relentlessly, to be the nightmares. They weren't getting any better or easier or rarer. There's not that much to tell about them because nightmares are nightmares on account of the way they feel, not necessarily by the mayhem and the body count. These felt bad. Of course they always had vampires in them. Sometimes I was being stared at by dozens of eyes, eyes that I mustn't look into, except that wherever I looked there were more eyes, and I couldn't shut my own. Sometimes there was just the knowledge that I was in a horrible place, that I was being contaminated by the horrible place, that even if I seemed to get out of it I would take it with me. The nightmares also always had blood in them, one way or another. Once I thought I had woken up, and my bed was floating in blood. Once I was wearing the cranberry-red dress and it was *made* of blood. But the worst ones were when I was a vampire myself. I had blood in my mouth and my heart didn't beat and I had strange awful thoughts about stuff I'd never thought about, that in the dream I would think

I *couldn't* think about because I was human, and then I'd remember I wasn't human, I was a vampire. As a vampire I knew the world differently.

I told myself that those two days at the lake were just something that had happened. That's all. The dreams were like the wound on my breast: my mind was wounded too. The bruises and scratches were the superficial stuff: of course they healed quickly. And everybody dreams about vampires; we grow up dreaming about them. They're the first and worst monster that lives under everybody's bed. You do get mad Weres or a demon that's tired of passing for human and not being able to do the less attractive demon things, but mostly it's vampires.

I never dreamed about . . . The funny not ha-ha thing was how hard I was trying to forget about him too. He'd saved my life, sure, but he'd destroyed my world view in the process. The only good vampire was a staked and burned vampire, right? So what if he'd shown a little enlightened self-interest about me—as well as having a sense of honor straight out of some nineteenth-century melodrama with dueling pistols and guys who said things like "begone varlet," which was how I'd lived long enough to present him with an opportunity to display enlightened self-interest. He was still a vampire. And everybody he'd . . . my brain wouldn't go there . . . was still dead. To put it another way: the loathly lady was still a loathly lady, she hadn't been cured by whatever, and there was no reason to suppose she wasn't going to go on eating huntsmen and their horses and hounds, and probably the occasional knight who didn't give her the right answers as well.

I didn't think there was a word for a human so sicko as to rescue a vampire, so he could go on being a vampire, because no one had ever done it. Before.

When I woke up out of one of these nightmares I didn't dare go back to sleep again. And they kept coming. So after a few weeks I segued from being flipped out and exhausted by what had happened to being flipped out and exhausted from being flipped out and exhausted.

During this first time in my life I didn't want to read lots of news reports about Other activity, there seemed to be more of them around.

Some of it was okay. There was another long heated debate—as a result of some statistical review stating that the numbers of those afflicted were rising—about whether incubi or succubi were living or undead, which is an old argument but no one has ever settled it. The obstacle to scientific study is that the moment the psychic connection is cut your object of investigation disintegrates, and by seizing one of the things for scientific study you are ipso facto severing the link. At least until the global council decides it's okay to keep a human being as a thing-thrall, which is at present even for purposes of pure research *highly* illegal, although the official language talks about corporeal and noncorporeal subjugation. The reason it's such a hot topic is that while incubi and succubi are a relatively small problem, some people think that finding out how they work would give us a handle on vampires, which is absolutely number one on everyone's list about Others, and the medical guys can cure someone who has been a thing-thrall, which isn't an option with vampire dinners. Well, *usually* they can cure someone who has been a thing-thrall, if they haven't been one for too long.

There was a project drawn up not too long ago with a list of volunteers to be thing-thralls but that never got off the ground, maybe partly because the 'ubis like choosing their own prey and bait on a string doesn't interest them, but mainly because there was this huge public outcry against it. Mind you, you have to wonder about the volunteers. 'Ubis may be a bigger problem than anybody knows because thing-thralls are usually having a *very good time* and it's their loving friends and families (sometimes their pissed-off colleagues) that start to wonder why they're sleeping twelve or fourteen hours a day and spending the rest of the time looking like they just had amazingly terrific sex. Nobody knows whether thing-thralls really are having sex with their things either, or whether they only think they are. But even the best sex your nerve endings can be made to imagine they're having has to be balanced against the fact that your IQ tends to drop about one point for every month you're a thing-thrall. The cleverer 'ubis cut and run before the brain drain gets obvious, and a lot of people aren't using their brains to begin with and don't miss them. But sometimes it's too late for the thrall to have any future more intellectually demanding than night shift shelf restocker. There is a bagger I know at our local Mega Food who had been New Arcadia's top criminal defense lawyer before an 'ubi got him. I used to read the reports of his courtroom antics and thought being a thing-thrall had improved his personality beyond recognition, but it had knocked hell out of his career prospects.

There was a series of articles about how many different kinds of Weres there are, another favorite topic. Wolves are the famous one, of course, but they're actually comparatively rare. There are probably more were-chickens than there are were-wolves, which if you're asking me explains why comparatively few Weres go rogue as against, say, how many demons. And possibly why the black market in anti-Change drugs is so slick, although the idea of black marketeers with either a sense of humor or of compassion is maybe stretching it a little. More likely the were-chickens will pay *anything* for the drugs, and do.

But there are were-pumas, for example, and were-bears. Were-coyotes are enough of a scourge that the SOFs go after them and do a horrible sort of mop-up about once a year. Were-raccoons are nasty little beggars and were-skunks are, well, beyond a nightmare. Get a were-skunk mad at you and your life isn't worth living. There's a special flying SOF unit for were-skunks. Every city over about a hundred thousand has a SOF were-rat unit, speaking of horrible mop-ups. New Arcadia has one. But according to Pat and Jesse you can stay one jump ahead (so to speak) of all the Weres, even the rats, as long as you don't get careless. Nobody ever stays a jump ahead of vampires.

Maybe because there was all this other stuff about the Others, and because, of course, I wanted not to be noticing, I ignored for a while that there were more local stories about vampires. Sucker sightings, sucker activity, which is to say fresh desiccated corpses, aka dry guys. As I say, New Arcadia is pretty clean, but nowhere is really clean of vampires. And so I didn't notice right away—who wants to notice bad stuff happening next door? And even if it was happening, it didn't mean it had anything to do with my little adventure. I could ignore it if I wanted to.

... *That we are both gone will mean that something truly extraordinary has happened. And it almost certainly has something to do with you—as it does, does it not?—and that therefore something important about you was overlooked. And Bo will like that even less than he would have liked the straightforward escape of an ordinary human prisoner ...*

The coffeehouse is in the old downtown area, called Old Town now. It had been a pretty grotty place when Charlie's first opened, and he catered to grotty people, figuring that everybody has to eat. Since he apparently didn't do anything—including, I swear, sleep—in the beginning but run the coffeehouse, he could do everything himself, including cook from scratch. He didn't even have a regular waitress the first couple of years; the kitchen, such as it was, was lined out along the fourth wall. This kept his overheads low, and I've already said he's a good cook. The cleaner and more lucid of his grotty clientele began to bring their less grotty friends there because of the food. When Mom and I moved in two blocks away the gentrification had only just begun—begun enough that Mom wasn't totally stupid to move in—but there were still drunks and hype heads on more corners than not, and Ingleby Street was still all old-books shops, the kind where walking in the door puts you at immediate risk of being crushed to death by a toppling pile of crumbly yellow magazines no one has looked at in fifty years. (This nearly happened to me when I was twelve, and the owner was so relieved I wasn't going to tell my mom on him—my mom even then had a local rep as someone you didn't mess with—that he gave me a great deal on them instead. This motley assortment included an almost unbroken run of *Vampire Tales and Other Eerie Matters* from the sixties, which among other Other things included the first serial publication of the early, less controversial volumes of *Blood Lore*. I was already Other-fascinated, but this may have confirmed the disease.)

When I was still in high school the city authorities got really ex-
cited because New Arcadia was going to be on the post-Wars map.
This was partly because we'd had—comparatively—quiet Wars, so
most of the city was still standing and most of its occupants were
still sane, and partly because our Other Museum by the mere fact
that it was still there had become nationally and perhaps globally
important. I had never liked it myself; the exhibits for the public
were real lowest-common-denominator stuff, and you had to have
six PhDs, no dress sense, and a face like a prune to get into the stacks
or any of their serious holdings, which included stuff you couldn't
get on the globenet. You could say my nose was out of joint. I was
going to like it even less if it was going to swamp us with the kind of
loony-tune academic that specialized in Others, but the city council
thought it was going to be totally thor.

One of their bright ideas about raising Old Town's attractiveness
level, since we were inconveniently close to the museum, was to dig
up all the paving and put down the cobblestones that the city authorities had dug up seventy years ago to put down paving, and replace the old (and, by the way, brighter) street lamps with phony gas
lamps with electric bulbs in them. Then they stuck a raised flower
bed in the middle of what had been the road, and made it a pedestrian precinct. The old-books stores left and the antique shops and
craft boutiques moved in, and for a while there Charlie and Mom
were thinking desolately about trying to relocate the coffeehouse
because we didn't want to learn to make Jackson Pollack squiggles
out of raspberry coulis, thank you very much. And if the taxes went
up as predicted they would have to sell the house even if they kept
the coffeehouse, which they probably wouldn't do either because
they wouldn't be able to bear putting up the prices enough for the
sort of hash and chili and chicken pot pie and succotash pudding and
big fat sandwiches on slabs of our own bread menu that we do so
well—this was before my bakery was built and so before we were
also known for toxic sugar-shock specials—to keep us in the black.
Our regulars wouldn't be able to afford it, even if the new upscale
crowd wanted to eat retro diner food, or we wanted to serve it to
them. Meanwhile the pedestrian precinct seemed to be pretty well

shutting down our trucker traffic, and Charlie's has had truckers from its first day. There used to be a joke that a New Arcadia route trucker wasn't the real thing till he could get his rig within two blocks of Charlie's.

But it turned out there were more of the old grotty people still clinging on than anyone realized—well, we realized it, because most of them ate at the coffeehouse (including the better class of derelicts who knew to come to the side door and ask for leftovers), but we thought the Rolex shiny-briefcase thugs would drive them out. Only it was the Rolex shiny-briefcase thugs that eventually left. So the old grotty people are still here, and the coffeehouse is still here, and Mom and Charlie still live around the corner, and most of the antique shops have subsided or are subsiding more or less gently into junk shops again, and some of them are beginning to have piles of old books in the corners, and most of our truckers still come in the back way, although they can't get within two blocks any more. And when the city in disgust told us to mind our own flower bed because they weren't going to do it any more, Mrs. Bialosky, who is one of our most stalwart and ubiquitous locals, organized working parties, and nearly every year since then our flower bed wins something in the New Arcadia neighborhood gardening festival, and I like to think I can hear the sound of city authority teeth grinding. Mrs. Bialosky owns a narrow little house on the corner of Ingleby and North where she can keep an eye on almost everything that happens, and the two-seater corner booth just to the right of the front door of Charlie's also belongs to her in all but real estate contract, and woe betide anyone who sits there without her permission. Mrs. B, by the way, is suspected of being a Were, but there is no consensus on a were-*what*. Guesses range from parakeet to Gila monster. (Yes, there are were-Gilas, but not usually this far north.)

For the most part our neighborhood is a good thing. Who wants to be dazzled by Rolexes and aluminum briefcases every time you want to have a quiet cup of tea sitting on the wall around the award-winning flower bed? I'll take the odd wandering vagrant any day. But it means that if you've got vampires moving in from the outside they're going to move into our neighborhood before they move into a neighborhood like the one the city authorities had planned for us. Suckers don't like their food in a bad state of preservation any more than humans do, but our population is predominantly sound and healthy, just not very well-off or important. Furthermore, when the city went into its snit about our bad attitude, they had finished tearing out all the old streetlights but hadn't finished putting in new ones, and since then they keep claiming they can't afford to finish the job. Some of our shadowy corners are really *very* shadowy.

And then one of the dry guys turned up on Lincoln Street, less than three blocks from Charlie's.

You might think the neighborhood would shut down, everyone staying indoors with the doors locked, iron dead-bolts stamped with ward signs and shutters hung with charms, but far from it. Charlie's was hopping the next evening, and since Charlie himself would almost rather die than turn away a customer—not because he always has his eye on his profit margin (Mom would say he *never* has his eye on his profit margin), but because a hungry and thirsty person must always be treated kindly—we had people leaning against the walls and outside against the front window. Maybe they were crowded a little closer than usual under the awning, where the coffeehouse lights were bright. Our dopey fake gas lamps dotted around the square looked even more pathetic than usual, but you're pretty safe if there's enough of you. Even a serious vampire gang won't tackle a big group of humans without an extremely good reason. But it was just as well no fire inspector came out for a stroll that night and checked the numbers against our license. Although the local fire inspector was an old friend of Charlie's, and would have stopped for a glass of champagne and a chat.

Things got really exciting when the TV van showed up. I was in the bakery, feverishly turning out whatever-took-the-least-time to feed the extra people, but I heard the commotion and Mary put her head in long enough to tell me what was going on. "I'm not here," I said. "If it comes up." She nodded and disappeared.

But too many other people knew I was there. I'd been interviewed—or rather they'd tried to interview me—right after it happened. SOF is supposed to "cooperate" with the media, but I know Pat and Jesse are in a more or less continual state of pissed-offness because someone is forever leaking more stuff from their office than they feel anyone but them needs to know, but their boss, or rather their sub-boss, widely known as the goddess of pain, refuses to try to shut it down, so they are stuck. In this case it meant that it had got leaked that SOF was very interested in whatever had happened to me, even if I hadn't given them any reason to be interested, and even though apparently nothing else had happened since (if I'd developed a rider, like an incubus, or a hitch, from a demon having me on a tether, there are signs, if you're looking). So now Mr. TV Roving In Your Face Reporter, exploring neighborhood response to a sucker in our midst, wanted to interview me, and at least eight people had told him I was on the premises. Mom, for good or bad, had gone home; she hates packed-out nights and in theory we didn't need her. She would have given Mr. TV Pain in the Butt Interviewer something to think about. It mightn't have been such great publicity for Charlie's but we don't really need to care what local TV thinks of us.

Charlie is great at blandishing. Few people can resist him when he's in Full Blandish. But he's nowhere near as good at getting rid of assholes as Mel is, and it was Mel's night off. Charlie came back after a while and asked if I could bear to come out and be stared at. "You can say no a few times and come back here; I'll keep 'em out after that. But if you'd be uncooperative in person first it would be easier."

Charlie knew I hated the whole business, which I did, but that wasn't the real problem. The ever-ready-for-fresh-disasters media guys had walloped my bruised and messed-up face onto TV seven weeks ago, though I'd refused to talk to them. I don't suppose I could have stopped them even if it had occurred to me to try. I'd thought about it later. I hadn't wanted to, but I did. Did vampires watch local news on TV? Seven weeks ago they might still have been prying up floorboards for where I might be hiding.

Most of what goes on TV, even on local TV, gets archived on the globenet within a few weeks. And vampires use the globenet all right. Some people believe vampire tech is better than human.

I went out front like Charlie asked. Mr. TV was there with his camera slave, half Quasimodo and half Borg. Mr. TV had amazing teeth, even for a TV presenter. "I don't have anything to say," I said.

"Just come outside a minute, where we can get a clearer shot," said Mr. Teeth. I wondered if vampires ever got their teeth capped. I went off on a teeny fantasy about specialist fang caps. Probably not.

"You don't have anything to get a clearer shot of," I said.

"Oh now you want to leave that up to us," said Mr. Teeth, grinning even wider. He put his hand on my arm.

"Take your *hand* off my *arm*," I said. I had meant to sound huffy but it came out sounding like a person about to fly into the ozone and loop the loop. Damn.

Mr. Teeth dropped my arm but his eyes (and his incisors) glinted with increased interest. *Damn.* He made a gesture to the slave, who raised his camera and pointed it at Mr. Teeth. I heard him start in with the TV introduction voice but there was a ringing in my ears. The scab on my breast started itching fiercely. I kept my hands clenched at my sides; if I scratched it it would start to bleed, and if it started to bleed it would leak through, and I didn't want the Contusion That Wouldn't Go Away to be on the eleven o'clock news too. Seven weeks ago I'd been home from the doctor for the first time and bristling with stitches (for the first time), which had been part of the shock effect of my appearance, since they showed. Back then while I hadn't exactly been aiming for the Frankenstein look it hadn't occurred to me I had anything to hide, and I didn't want the little stubbly ends catching on my clothing.

I had been avoiding thinking about any implications in a sucker victim found three blocks from the coffeehouse, as I had been avoiding noticing there was more local sucker activity at all. If I'd been avoiding it less hard, it might have occurred to me that some kind of news gang would turn up to pry a few ravaged expressions and maybe if they were lucky some sign of an incipient crack-up out of some of the natives. (Possibly not realizing that Old Town always had natives on the brink of a crack-up.) The police hadn't identified the body yet—they called it "the victim"—and nobody at the coffeehouse was missing anyone.

Vampire senses are different from human in a number of ways. The one that is relevant in this case is that landscape which is all one sort of thing is . . . more penetrable . . . to the extent of its homogeneity. . . .

I had no idea what the homogeneity of TV broadcasting might be from a vampire perspective. I didn't want to know.

The camera swung to point at me.

I raised a hand against it. "No," I said.

"But—" Mr. Teeth said. He was trying to decide whether more smiling was called for or if he should try a frown. I put up my other hand, blanking out most of the lens. Quasi-Borg said, "Okay, okay, I get the idea," and let the thing sag. If it was still taping it was getting a good shot of a dirty apron, purple jeans, and red sneakers.

Mr. Teeth, the mike still glued under his chin, said, "Miss Seddon, we only want a few words with you. You must understand that the assaults on any human by the Others are always of first importance to every other human, and it is the duty of a responsible media that we report anything of that sort as quickly and thoroughly as possible. Miss Seddon, a man *died* here."

"I know," I said. "Fine. Go report it."

Mr. Teeth looked at me a moment. I could see him deciding on the hard-man approach. "Miss Seddon, it is very plain to many of us that whether you wish to discuss your experiences or not, you too have been a victim of an Other attack, and the fact that a mere few weeks later a *vampire* victim should turn up near your place of employment cannot be considered insignificant."

"Two months," I said. "Not a few weeks."

"Miss Seddon," he said, "do you still deny that you were set on by Others?"

"I don't say anything one way or another," I said. "I don't remember."

"Miss Seddon—"

"She's told you she has nothing to say to you," said Charlie. "I think that's enough." He was so rarely hostile I almost didn't recognize him. In the back of my mind, a thought was forming: if he can get rid of a tanked up six-and-a-half-foot construction worker with a few friendly words, which he can, and if he just failed a few minutes ago to get rid of a tanked-up-on-his-own-importance TV asshole be-cause he had been unable to get confrontational about it, what does it mean that he's suddenly feeling so antagonistic toward Mr. Re-sponsible Media Reporter now? I didn't like the answer to that ques-tion. It meant that he thought Mr. Responsible Media—and our suddenly overwatchful Pat and Jesse and their friends—were right about what had happened to me. How could they *tell*? I hadn't said anything. And nobody gets away from . . . they *couldn't* think it was vampires.

Mr. Responsible Media was looking rebellious, but this was my country. I was Cinnamon Roll Queen and most of those assembled were my devoted subjects. "Hey, leave her alone, man," said Steve, idly rolling up to stand next to the counter stool he'd been sitting on. Steve isn't major league tall, but he is major league in the looming unspoken threat department. Things had gone kind of quiet in the last few minutes while everyone watched me refuse to be inter-viewed, and now they went quieter yet. One or two other people—that is to say, guys—stood up, just as idly as Steve had. I was suddenly glad it was Mel's night off after all; under the good-old-boy exterior he had a temper on him, and he'd been feeling kind of protective of me lately. Over Mr. Responsible Media's shoulder I met Jesse's gaze. He and Pat and John were sitting squashed together at a two-person table. I could see by their stillness that they *weren't* standing up . . . and I didn't have to think too hard to figure out that this was be-cause they knew Mr. Responsible Media would recognize them as SOFs and they were giving me a break. Because they knew I needed a break. Oh skegging *damn*.

"All right, all right," muttered Mr. Responsible, and he waved at his camera slave, and they left the coffeehouse reluctantly.

"Thanks," I said to everyone generally. I patted Steve's hamlike shoulder on my way back to the bakery (and sent him three cran-berry and sprouted wheat muffins via Mary, which were his favor-ite) and didn't come out again till closing, although Mary came in a few times to tell me what was going on. She had her break in the bakery too so she could tell me in detail about the interview Mr. Responsible had had with Mrs. Bialosky, who knew how to play an audience. She'd learned a lot in the years of running our flower bed, and she'd never been somebody any sane person would want to jerk around. Mary had me laughing by the time she had to go back to work.

Jesse came in right after Mary left. It was like he'd been listening at the door. He stood there looking at me. I went on hurling large spoonfuls of batter into millions of muffin cups. Muffin cups in my bakery were real sorcerer's apprentice material, like the dough for the cinnamon rolls every morning could have stood in for The Blob. "There isn't room to hang around back here," I said. There wasn't, although people often did. It was illegal to have customers back here, but the local food inspectors were all Charlie's friends, just like our local fire inspector was. We'd had the head inspector's daughter's fifteenth birthday party here about six months ago: the story was that the coffeehouse was the compromise reached between the party her parents wanted her to have and the party *she* wanted to have. I made six chocolate chip layer cakes for the event (and chocolate butter alphabet cookies to spell out HAPPY BIRTHDAY CATHY over the frosting, because I don't do fancy decorating, life is too short), and they were all gone that evening. Some of her friends were still coming back. I was going to need a second apprentice if Charlie's became a haunt of teenage boys.

"Mary was in here for fifteen minutes."

"You tell time real well," I said. "Is that an important skill in SOF? Mary will fit on the stool. You won't." I kept a stool wedged in the one semifree corner that wasn't next to the ovens, for staff on break, or anyone else I felt like letting into my territory. No SOF was on that list tonight, and I wasn't in a good mood.

Jesse went and sat on the stool. He did fit. SOF made you keep in shape to keep your job. No lard butts there. The SOFs weren't that much easier to keep topped up than teenage boys. All that fitness makes you eat. Pat in particular could put it away. When he sat on that stool I had to keep a sharp eye on him. He could make whole loaves of bread disappear in moments.

I opened the oven doors and dragon breath roared into the room. I shoved in muffin tins. I closed the doors and set the timer. I dumped the bowls in the sink and turned on the water. The coffeehouse doesn't have the most efficient layout in the world, and the dishwasher is in the main kitchen. When I had time, I washed up my own stuff.

I made as much noise as possible.

"Rae," said Jesse at last.

"Yeah," I said.

"We're on the same side."

I didn't say anything. Are we? Am I sure I'm on the right side any more? It was a very pretty conundrum. People don't escape from vampires. Since I'm alive . . . It wasn't really consorting with the enemy. It was just something that happened. Yeah, and it just *happened* that I could keep the sun off a vampire.

It wasn't him I needed to forget. It was *me*. It was what *I* had done.

Why would a vampire stick around to feed a human milk and muffins—and make sure she didn't choke on them? Honor among thieves? I'd said that. To him. Why the hell had I *wanted* to save him? He'd almost had me for dinner. He'd thought about it.

Why had my tree said *yessssss*? *What the hell was I?*

Maybe the fact that the vampire slash on my breast hurt all the time and wouldn't heal was a good sign. Maybe it meant I was still human.

Eventually Jesse got down from the stool and went away.

The nightmares that night were particularly bad, and apparently I'd been clawing myself in my sleep, because when the alarm went off at three-forty-five and I groaned and rolled over and turned the light on, not only had the scab split open again but my pillow had big ugly streaks and blotches of blood all over it.

The alarm was still going off a quarter hour earlier than it used to because it took me a quarter hour longer to get moving in the morning than it used to. I was still tired all the time. Okay, it was just the nightmares stopping me sleeping properly. Plus worrying about stuff like my face in the globenet archive and what all my friends thought. I wasn't losing enough blood from the vampire slash to make me tired that way. And it didn't hurt all that much. It was just a nagging nuisance.

I drove to the coffeehouse and made cinnamon rolls and rye bread—it was rye bread day—and then I made banana honey nut bread and fig bars and Hell's Angelfood and Killer Zebras and a lot of muffins, and by late morning I was done. I had the rest of the day off till six.

There was one thing that helped the tiredness a little, and stopped my breast prickling and itching as well. Sunlight. It was a glorious, blue, sunny day and I went home and lay in it. For nearly seven hours. I should have burned to a crisp, but I never sunburn. It goes *in* somewhere. I've always been like this. But since those two nights on the lake I'd been spending more time than usual when the sun was out, lying in it. And I seemed to be doing more and more of it. I'd missed an old-books fair with Aimil and Zora, and the last time Mel'd suggested we go hiking I'd opted to lie in the sun in his back yard while he took another motorcycle apart. This was fine with him but it wasn't at all like me. I wasn't even reading as much as usual; it was as if I had to concentrate on soaking in as much sunshine as I could, and didn't dare distract myself from that crucial activity.

Okay, I had a lot of catching up to do. The part of me that was my grandmother's granddaughter had been having a free ride the last fifteen years, and out of nowhere I'd tapped her flat. Whether for good cause or bad. Recharging was in order.

But it wasn't just that. It was like I was under attack. And it didn't feel like it was only from my own negative thinking.

THERE WERE MORE people than usual at the coffeehouse that evening too, but not as many as the night before, and there were no TV vans and nothing to make me jumpy, except maybe that six of our little SOF gang were there. *Six?* Didn't these people have *lives?*

No, they didn't have lives. SOFs weren't expected to have lives. You were a SOF, you stayed very fit and you didn't have a life. A bit like running a family coffeehouse really. Maybe that was why they felt we should be kindred spirits. And our SOFs had dinner at the coffeehouse more nights than they didn't, and a lot of the staff from our county SOF headquarters, which was only about a half a mile away north of Old Town, came by some time in the mornings for coffee and a cinnamon roll. Relax, Sunshine.

I tried to relax. They released the name of the poor bod that had got sucked: nobody any of us knew. He lived in our city, but not around here. Nothing else happened. No more dry guys, at least none left for us to find. By three days later when things appeared to be back to normal I managed to say, "Hey, how's it going," in an ordinary voice when I found Jesse and Theo sitting at the table next to the door when I walked in for the evening dessert shift. Paulie had been in the bakery all afternoon, and he was eager to leave. I was still letting him have most any evening he wanted off, letting him put his hours in during the days; I was chiefly interested in that second morning a week I didn't have to get up at three-forty-five. I was used to not having a life, and I wanted to hold on to Paulie. He was the first apprentice I'd hired who both had a brain and liked playing with food. Also he was the first guy who didn't seem to think his manhood was under threat by having to learn stuff and take orders from someone of my age and gender. He still had to live through his first August in the bakery with the ovens on, but I was hopeful.

We emptied out a little earlier than sometimes, especially surprising on a three-day-weekend Sunday. We'd be open tomorrow while most of the rest of the working world was celebrating the birth of Jasmin Aziz, the famous code-breaker of the Voodoo Wars and why we still have Michigan, Chippewa, and most of Ontario instead of the biggest smoking hole on the planet. But she had been nicknamed Mother Durga, "She Who Is Difficult to Approach," long before she was a hero, and the name stuck. Ha. Even if Charlie's didn't stay open automatically for three-day weekend Mondays, we'd've had to stay open for that one.

I'd pulled the last trays out of the ovens a while back, racked or frozen what wasn't going to get eaten that night, started roll and bread dough for tomorrow morning, and had come out front to sit at the counter and gossip for the last few minutes with Liz and Kyoko, who were on late that night, and Emmy, who had recently been promoted to assistant cook and wasn't sure she could take the pace. (I was slightly insulted by this, since I'd been using her in the bakery between apprentices, and felt that I must be at least as merciless and temperamental a taskmaster as anything the main kitchen crew could do.) Theo showed occasional signs of wanting to get fond of Kyoko, but she knew about SOFs, and she wasn't having any. Charlie was there, prowling; he didn't know how to sit down. Mel was closing down in the kitchen, which included preventing Kenny from sloping off early. A quiet night gave you time to catch up.

It was warm, and the front doors were open. There were still a few people sitting at one of the outside tables; another couple had drifted off with their cups of coffee to sit on the flower bed wall and smooch. One of the last closing-up rituals was to have a sweep through the square for coffee cups, champagne glasses, and dessert plates. If you paid your bill beforehand, we didn't stop you taking your sweetheart and your sweet thing on a plate to a quieter spot. (Your bad luck if you chose a spot already occupied by a wino or a hype head, but hey.) This was probably illegal too, by civil regulation 6703.4, subheading Behavior of Clientele at Eating Establishments and Potential Broadcasting of Crumbs to Deleterious Effect, viz., the Vermin Population, but no one had stopped us yet.

It was so quiet. Peaceful. Even the SOFs looked pretty relaxed, for SOFs.

And I heard a familiar goblin giggle.

Did I hear it? I don't know. I'll never know. But I *knew* it, one way or another, however it got to me. And I had picked up a table knife and bolted out the door long before any poor following-on function like rational thought had a chance to kick into gear.

No human has ever destroyed a vampire by thundering down on it brandishing a table knife. In the first place, vampires are fantastically faster than humans. You can't *race* up to a vampire to do anything, because it's done it several times already, waiting for you. And you can bet it's not going to stand there waiting to be staked.

In the second place, a table knife is a real bad choice. You can do it with wrought iron, although no one in their right mind is going to haul a wrought iron stake around with them when wood works better and weighs a lot less. But stainless steel, forget it: it slithers off, like a swizzle stick on an ice cube. You have as much chance of punching a hole in a vampire with stainless steel as you have racing up to it and getting it to hold still while you try.

Wood will break through that little layer of whatever-it-is, the electricity of the undead, and let your stake penetrate. You still have to ram it in hard, and you have to know where it's going, and it has to reach and enter the heart, or you've just died as the vampire rips your head off. A sucker repelling a staking doesn't bother to be cool about it. (Note that while a vampire may have to ask permission to suck your blood, it can kill you any time it likes. It just won't get a square meal out of the experience.) Macho SOFs will go straight in through the breastbone, but the more sophisticated approach—as well as the more likely to be successful—is up underneath it. The notch at the bottom of the breastbone is a useful road marker—so I'm told. It's still not at all easy to do. There are lots of dead people who have tried. There have been a lot of studies done about the best wood for stakes too. Turns out it's apple wood—and not any old apple, but a tree that is home to mistletoe. Retired or invalided-out SOFs (this latter category a small number: SOFs tend to live or die with nothing in between) often end up tending SOF orchards, and making sure the mistletoe is happy. Mistletoe is cranky stuff, and nobody knows why it sometimes grows and sometimes doesn't. Makes you wonder what the druids knew—or Johnny Appleseed. Of course the druids are a fairy tale and Johnny Appleseed never existed. They say. But then, they also say that no human has ever destroyed a vampire by charging at one flashing a table knife.

Maybe no human ever *had*.

I did have one advantage. He wasn't expecting *me*.

I had time to see the look on his face. I probably didn't figure out what I'd seen till later, but this was what it was: he was looking for me—for *me*—but he wasn't expecting to find me. He was working under his master's orders, all right, but privately he thought his master had a wild hair up his ass, and he wasn't going to find me, because I was dead. He didn't know how I was dead, or where I had

disappeared to, but I *had* to be dead. Therefore I was. I understood
this point of view completely.

Maybe it was just the surprise of seeing someone thinking they
could do anything with a table knife.

He paused. The girl he'd been pulling under stood swaying and
stupid while he turned to me. We stared into each other's eyes for
the last time fragment, my last few running steps, before I thudded
into him . . .

. . . and slammed the table knife up under his breastbone, and
into his heart. I remember the hot evil smell of his last breath on my
face. . . .

I'd never heard or read anywhere that vampires explode when
staked. Maybe it's only when you use a table knife. Vampires aren't
made of flesh and blood quite the way we are . . . but near kali goddam enough. It was . . . horrible. The contact, when I drove against
him, not just arm's length with the knife—The sense of the knife going in—maybe I didn't think I was going to be able to do it either;
maybe that was the plan—The *texture* of the knife sliding into—The
way it seemed to *know* where to go, with my hand on it—

The smell—

The surprise on his face, just before my knife reached his heart
and it stopped—being a face—

The *sound*—

The pressure of the—blast—which made me stagger, which smeared and stained me with—

From the taste in my mouth a few minutes later, I assume I threw
up. Maybe I passed out as well, although I was still on my feet when
I began to hear someone shouting, "Rae! Rae! It's over! You're okay!"
and also began to realize there were arms around me and they were
trying to stop me thrashing around. There was a lot of other noise;
someone screaming; other people shouting; and, coming closer, a
siren. The siren should have been reassuring: the sound of approaching authority. Authority would take over and I could relax. Relax,
Sunshine.

It wasn't reassuring. But it did have the effect of sobering me up.

I stopped flailing. The arms loosened—not very much—and let me stand on my own feet. It was Jesse, holding on to me.

There was already a crowd. I suppose the screaming brought them. We're the kind of neighborhood that responds to screams. Jesse and I were in a little alleyway—one alley over from where the corpse husk, the dry guy, had been found a week ago—and from somewhere someone had found a couple of halogen floodlights. This meant you could see. . . .

I started retching, and Jesse turned me round and started hauling me toward—what turned out to be a car, driven by Theo. It's a good trick, getting anything with four wheels, including a kid's little red wagon, this far into Old Town. Maybe that's part of SOF training too. The crowd was still gathering. Maybe they didn't understand what they were seeing—the dark, dribbling blotches on the ground, stickily trailing down the enclosing walls—the charnel house smell might have been a dead rat or a backed-up drain; Old Town can be like that—but the scene the floodlights illuminated. . . . I managed to look away before I heaved again, not, I think, that there was anything left to come up.

Jesse bundled me into the back seat and was now . . . wiping me down with a towel. I had . . . horrible stuff all over me. Did SOF vehicles automatically carry large absorbent towels for . . . cleanup? This one had hung outdoors on a line. I tried to think about the smell of the towel—laundry soap, fresh air, *sunlight*. I was crying. Less messy than throwing up anyway. Easier to clean up after. I cried harder. I'd cried more in the last two months than I had done in my entire previous life.

I croaked something. I didn't understand what I said either, and Jesse said, "Don't talk now. We're going to get you some clean clothes and a cup of cof—tea." He knew me well enough to know I didn't drink coffee. That should have been reassuring too, that I was with friends—but I wasn't with friends. I was with SOF. Who had seen me explode a sucker with a table knife. I wondered if they were getting me away so fast, before anyone from the coffeehouse had a chance to intervene. Mel. Charlie. Where were they taking

me anyway? And why? I could make a guess and it didn't make me
feel any better.

Jesse's dark face was invisible in the darkness of the back seat. I
was almost desperate enough to ask to turn the dome light on, just
so I could see his face. That he had a face. A human face.

I croaked again. "Will she be all right?"

"Who?" said Jesse.

"The girl. The . . . girl who was screaming. The girl who was . . .
under the dark."

Jesse said, "She'll be okay."

I was silent a minute. We were out of Old Town. I couldn't figure
what we were doing at first; I was used to the front door of the SOF
county building—not that I made a habit of going there—of course
there would be a back way. Where they parked their cars. Also perhaps where they brought people in they didn't want to be seen. How
soon before the TV van showed up in the alleyway and started pan-
ning over those blotchy walls, those gruesomely amorphous lumps
on the pavement?

"You don't know, do you? You don't know if she'll be all right."

Jesse sighed and sat back, leaving the towel in my lap. It didn't
smell like sunlight any more: it smelled like disintegrated vampire.
The car smelled like disintegrated vampire. Jesse, because he'd been
holding on to me, had disintegrated vampire all over him too. In the
flickering light as we went from one streetlight's aura to the next he
looked rather too much like a pied demon. Pied demons are not
among the nice ones. "No. I don't know. We don't snatch people out
from under the dark at the last minute like that very often. But I'm
pretty sure she'll be all right. I can tell you why, but you could tell us
something too. Something for something."

I grunted. I had been rolling my window down for some fresh
air, and had discovered that it would only roll down halfway, and
that the doorlock button was engaged, but not by me. No escapees
from the back seat of a SOF car.

He almost laughed. "It's not what you think. Hell, Sunshine,
what do we have to do to—"

The car stopped. We were in a parking lot tucked in among a lot of big civic-looking buildings. It was nothing like empty, as you might expect it should be at this time of night, although all the cars were parked at one end of the lot, near one particular building. I didn't recognize SOF HQ from the back, but I could guess that was what it was. Most municipal departments don't run a big night shift, and the ordinary cop station was across town.

The doorlocks popped open. We got out of the car, first Theo and then Jesse again holding my arm, as if I either needed support or might run away. They took me up some stairs and down a long ugly windowless hallway with doors opening off on either side. Eventually Jesse tapped on a cracked-open door with a light behind it. "Annie," said Jesse, "can you give us a hand?"

Annie wasn't reassuring either, but she was nice about trying to pretend that she didn't think there was something extremely fishy about why I was there and in what condition and at this time of night. After all, she was right: there was something extremely fishy about it. She took me to the women's shower room and gave me fresh towels, soap, and this shapeless khaki jersey fuzzy-on-the-inside one-piece thing to put on that was like little kids' pajamas only without the feet.

I walked into the shower with all my clothes on. It was harder getting them off wet, but I didn't want to wait even long enough to get undressed before I made contact with hot water. Then I knelt on the shower floor and scrubbed them—and my sneakers—and left them in a heap I had to keep stepping over while I washed myself. But I wanted *all* the blood and . . . muck . . . *drummed* out of them. I wasn't as long about it as I had been the morning after coming back from the lake, but I scrubbed myself till I hurt all over and came out feeling boiled because I'd had the hot water turned up as high as it would go. I was sweating as I tried to dry off: partly because of the hot water. The cut on my breast had opened again, of course. I put some toilet paper on it, like I'd cut myself shaving, hoping it would scab over enough not to leave bloodstains that might need explaining on the pajamas.

I belatedly rescued the contents of my pockets when I hung my sodden clothes over the midsummer-cold radiator. My knife didn't mind a wetting so long as I dried it off again right away but my leather key ring would probably never forgive me, and the charm loop on it was definitely a goner. It was one of Mom's charms and it was one of the sort that keep going *bzzzt* at you so you know they're paying attention and I hadn't meant to drown it but I wouldn't be sorry to have it stop pestering me.

I paused a moment when I was dry and dressed to gather together what faculties I had left. I was so tired.

Annie was lurking outside to take me to wherever. She offered me some shuffly fuzzy-on-the-inside slippers too, also khaki, but enough is enough with the regression to childhood, and I stayed barefoot. Besides, I hate khaki.

I figured it was Jesse's office, since he was the one sitting behind the desk, while Theo was tipped back in a straight chair to one side, his feet against the edge, the toes of his shoes curling up the messy pile of papers on that corner and leaving black marks on the bottoms of the pages. Tsk tsk. Jesse's jacket had disappeared and he was wearing a clean shirt that didn't fit. There was a coffee machine in the corner going *glub glub*.

Nobody said anything right away. If this was supposed to make me start talking to fill up the silence it didn't work. There wasn't anything I could say that wouldn't get me into more trouble than I was in now. Okay, here's another thing: magic handlers have to be certified and licensed. I had lied about what had happened by the lake for a lot of reasons, and needing to register myself as a magic handler was the least of them and barely worth mentioning from my point of view, but by not doing it I'd still committed the sort of crime that even the ordinary police don't like and SOF really hates. Tonight I'd totally, inexorably, undeniably, blown it. Even a magic handler shouldn't have been able to skeg a sucker with a table knife.

I wasn't going to be able to fudge that one either. The table knife in question was lying on the one clear space on Jesse's desk. I assumed it was the same knife. It was the coffeehouse pattern and while it had been wiped roughly off, the smear of remaining blood-stains was convincing.

I had no idea when I'd dropped it. But the fact that it was here meant that they knew what had happened. No escape.

And then Pat came in carrying a pot of tea and a paper bag with the Prime Time logo. I wanted to laugh. They were sure *trying*. The Cinnamon Roll Queen wasn't going to be bought off by a fast-food hamburger—supposing I ate hamburgers, which I didn't, and after tonight, even if I had, I'd've given them up—but Prime Time was a twenty-four-hour gourmet deli. Downtown, of course. Far too up-scale to open a branch in Old Town. Not that they'd survive on Char-lie's turf anyway.

I stopped wanting to laugh when I noticed that Pat looked like a man who had been got out of bed for an emergency.

It was even good tea.

Jesse said, "Can you tell us what you're afraid of? Why you won't talk to us."

I said cautiously, "Well, I'm not licensed. . . ."

There was a general sigh, and the tension level went down about forty degrees. Pat said, "Yeah, we thought that was probably it."

There was a little silence and then the three of them exchanged long meaningful looks. I had tentatively started to relax and this stopped me, like sitting down in an armchair and discovering there's a bed of nails instead of a cushion under the flowered chintz. Uh-oh.

Pat sighed again, this one a very long sigh, like a man about to step off a cliff. Then he shut his eyes, took a deep breath, and held it. And held it. And held it. After about a minute he began to turn, well, blue, but I don't mean human-holding-his-breath blue, I mean *blue*. Still holding his breath, he opened his eyes and looked at me: his eyes were blue too, although several degrees darker than his skin, and I mean *all* of his eyes: the whites as well. Although speaking of all of his eyes, as I watched, a third eye slowly blinked itself open from between his eyebrows. He was still holding his breath. His ears were becoming pointed. He held up one hand and spread the fin-gers. There were six of them. The knuckles were all very knobbly, and the hand itself was very large. Pat was normally no more than medium-sized.

Theo gently lowered the front legs of his chair to the floor, drifted over to the office door, and locked it. He returned to his chair, put his feet against the edge of the desk, and rocked back on two legs again.

Pat started breathing. "If I let it go any farther I'll start popping my buttons. Pardon me." He unfastened his belt buckle and the button on his waistband.

"You're a *demon*," I said.

"Only a quarter," said Pat, "but it runs pretty strong in me." His voice sounded funny, deeper and more hoarse. "My full brother couldn't turn if he held his breath till he had a heart attack. Nice for him. Sorry about the locked door, but it takes a good half hour for the effects to wear off again."

It's only really *illegal* to be a vampire, but people who too regularly call in sick the day after the moon is full somehow never get promoted beyond entry-level positions, and a demon that can't pass is an automatic outcast. And miscegenation is definitely a crime. Since the laws about this are impractical to enforce, what happens is that if you have a baby you know can't pass, you arrange to look as careworn and despondent as possible (which will be easy in the circumstances) and go wail at the Registry Office that no one had told you that great-granddad—or great-grandmother—had been or done or had, whatever, great-grand-something being safely dead, of course, and unavailable for prosecution. So the kid gets registered, and grows up to find out it can't get a job in any industry considered "sensitive," and if any of its immediate family had been on the fast track, they're probably now off it. For life. Even if nobody else shows any signs of being anything but pure human.

It's probably worse, the partbloods that are fine till they hit adolescence, and suddenly find out that the Other blood, which they may not have known about, is alive and kicking and going to ruin their lives. Every now and then it happens to a grown-up. There was a famous case a few years ago about a thirty-eight-year-old bank manager who suddenly grew horns. They fired him. He'd had an exemplary career till that moment. He appealed. The case got a huge amount of publicity.

They still fired him.

As "sensitive" industries go, SOF was at the top. No way any demon partblood was going to get hired by the SOFs.

Even someone like Mary might be turned down if she applied for basic SOF training, if anyone was so poor-spirited as to report to her recruitment team that the coffee she poured was always hot. Mary wasn't registered. If the government insisted on registering everyone who could sew a seam that never unraveled or pour coffee that stayed hot or patch a bicycle tire that didn't pop somewhere else a hundred feet down the road, they'd have to register sixty percent or something of the population, and fond as the government was of paper trails and tax levies, apparently this boggled even their tiny minds. But SOF cared down to this level. The deep widow's peaks you sometimes get with a little peri blood and which are so fashionable that models and actors are forever having cosmetic surgery to implant them, if one of these people had a sudden desire for a midlife career change to SOF they'd have to go in with their surgeon's certificate taped to their forehead, or they'd be turned away at the door. SOF didn't fool around.

Pat blinked his blue eyes at me and smiled. He had a nice smile as a demon. His teeth were blue too.

"SOF is rotten with partbloods," said Jesse. "I'm one. Theo's another. So is John. So are Kate and Millicent and Mike. We somehow seem to find each other to partner with. Safer, of course. 'Hey, doesn't that blue guy look a lot like Pat? Where *is* Pat, anyway?' 'Look like *Pat*? You must be joking. He's at home with a head cold anyway.' But Pat's the most spectacular of us, which is why we called him in tonight."

I had maybe about managed to keep my jaw from dropping round my ankles while Pat turned blue—it had taken several minutes, I could go with the flow—but this was absolutely one too many. This was on a par with, say, finding out the president of the global council was a sucker, the moon was made of green cheese, and the sun only rose in the morning because of this complicated system of levers and dials overseen by an encampment of the master race from Antares settled on Mars. . . . "What the hell d'you mean SOF is rotten with partbloods? What about the goddam blood test when they take you?"

All three of them smiled. Slowly. For a moment I was *the only human in the room*, and they were all bigger and tougher than I was. I went very still. Not, I'm sorry to say, the stillness of serenity and compassion. Much more like a rabbit in headlights.

The moment passed.

"It must have been a bastard in the beginning," said Jesse.

"When the only drug that worked made you piss green for a week," said Pat.

"Or indigo or violet," said Theo.

"Yeah," said Pat. "Depending on what kind of partblood you were."

"But the lab is pretty well infiltrated by now," said Jesse. "Once you get that far you're usually home already."

There was another pause. Maybe I was supposed to ask what "you're home already" meant, but I didn't want to know any more. I hadn't been so mind-blasted since I woke up next to a bonfire surrounded by vampires. As the silence lengthened I realized that the tension level was rising again, and there were more meaningful looks flashing back and forth. I tried to rouse myself. But I was so tired.

At last Pat spoke. "Okay," he said. "Where we were. Um. We've been thinking for a while that something like . . . turning blue must have happened to you out at the lake. Or—wherever. But we haven't had a good excuse to, well, ask you about it closely. Somewhere we could lock the door when I held my breath."

"Till tonight we haven't been totally sure that's what we were looking at anyway," said Jesse. "Arguably we still aren't."

They looked at me hopefully.

I thought about what I could say. They'd just handed me all their careers on a platter. All I had to do was walk out of here and tell someone—say, Mr. Responsible Media—that Pat turned blue, three-eyed, and twelve-fingered if he held his breath, and that several of his closest colleagues including his partner knew about it, and they'd tie Pat to a chair, put a plastic bag over his head, and await developments. They'd have to. Even if the twenty-four-star bigwig supreme commander honcho of SOF was a fullblood demon him- or herself and knew the name of every partblood in the service, the public furor would make them do it. Being an unlicensed magic handler was a mouse turd in comparison.

My brain slowly ground out the next necessary connection to be made. Oh . . .

"You know about my dad?" I said.

They all snorted. Pat sounded like the horn on something like a semi or a furniture van. *Ooooongk.* "Does the sun rise in the morning?" said Jesse.

With or without the help of the guys from Antares? "Then probably you know that my mom raised me to be, er, not my father's daughter."

"Yeah," said Pat. "Made us real interested, if you want to know."

I stared at him. "You had better not be telling me you have been hanging around the coffeehouse *for fifteen years* on the off chance that you could catch me—turning blue."

It wouldn't be turning blue, of course. Unlike demon blood, magic handling was welcomed by both government and corporate bureaucracy in its employees—sort of. What they wanted was nice cooperative *biddable* magic handling. Somewhere *between* a third cousin who could do card tricks and a sorcerer. The problem is that as the magic handling rises on the prepotency scale, the magic handler sinks off the other end of the biddableness scale. But there probably had been biddable Blaises. And no one had ever proved my dad was a sorcerer. I didn't think.

"We hang out at the coffeehouse because we're all addicted to your cinnamon rolls, Sunshine, and your lethal dessert specials, especially the ones with no redeeming social value," said Pat. "You didn't see us half so often before Charlie built the bakery. But your dad didn't hurt as an excuse on our expense accounts."

Another pause. I didn't say anything.

"And your mom seemed kind of . . . well, *extreme* about it, you know?"

And another pause. I seemed to be missing something they wanted me to catch on to. But I was so *tired*.

"And the coffeehouse is a good place to keep an eye on a lot of people. Gat Donnor." Poor old Gat. He was one of our hype heads. Sometimes when he got the mixture wrong—or right—he turned into a skinny orange eight-foot lizard (including tail) that would tell you your fortune, if you asked. The locals were used to him but tourists had been known to go off in the screaming ab-dabs if they came across him. SOF was interested because a slightly-above-the-odds number of the fortunes he told were accurate.

I brought myself back to the present. Sitting in a SOF office with a blue demon SOF and a few friends.

"I suppose you know your Mrs. Bialosky is a Were?"

I did laugh then. "Everyone believes she is, but no one knows were-*what*. No—don't tell me. It would spoil it. Besides—Mrs. Bialosky is one of the good guys. I don't care what her blood has in it." It is a violation of your personal rights to have blood taken by your doctor examined for anything but the disease or condition you signed a release form about before the lab tech got near you with the needle, but accidents happen. One of the other ways you could guess a Were or a demon is by their paranoia about doctors. Fortunately the lab coats perfected artificial human blood fifty years ago—or nearly perfected it: you need about one in ten of the real thing—so donating blood isn't so big a deal any more, and the nasty-minded don't necessarily get any ideas looking at blood donor lists about who isn't on them. Human magic handling doesn't pass through transfusions; demon blood won't make you a demon, and weak part-demon might not show at all, but strong part- or full-demon makes a fullblood human very sick, even if the blood type is right. And being a Were transfuses beautifully, every time.

"I couldn't have said it better myself," said Jesse. "So, you grew up being your mom's daughter, with no higher ambitions than the best cinnamon rolls in the country. Did you know about your dad?"

I hesitated, but not very long. "More or less. I knew he was a magic handler, and I knew he was a member of one of the important magic-handling families. Or I found that out once I was in school and some of the magic-handler kids mentioned the Blaises. I was using my mom's maiden name by the time I went to school, before she married Charlie. I knew that my dad being a magic handler was something to do with why my mom left him, and . . . at the time that was enough for me." I thought about the "business associates" my mom hadn't liked. That was what she'd always called them. "Business associates." It sounded a lot like "pond slime." Or "sorcerer." As I got a little older I realized that people like my mother mean "pond slime" when they say "sorcerer." Lunatic toxic kali pond slime.

"I *felt* like my mother's daughter, you know? And after we cleared off I never saw my dad again." I'd never said this to anyone before: "My mom was so determined to have nothing whatever to do with my dad's family that I wanted to be as much like her as possible, didn't I? She was all I had left."

They all nodded.

"So you didn't know anything about what your own heritage might be?"

"I did know something. My gran—my dad's mother—showed up again a year after we geared off. I used to visit her—at our old cabin at the lake. She'd meet me there. My mom wasn't happy about it, but she let me go. My gran told me some—taught me some."

"Taught you," Jesse said sharply.

"Yeah. Stuff changing mostly. Little stuff. Enough to know that I had something, but not so much that I—had to use it, you know?"

They nodded again. Magic handling, like Other blood, often makes its presence known, whether *you* want to know or not. But if it wasn't too strong, it would also leave you alone, if you left it alone. Probably.

"Then my gran disappeared. When I was about ten. Just before the Wars. And just when Charlie married my mom. Charlie didn't seem to mind having me around. He adopted me, let me get underfoot at the coffeehouse. And yeah. I *was* drawn to cooking. I've been cooking, or trying to cook, since I was like *four*. Pretty sad, huh?

A Blaise with frosting on the end of her nose. And once I got to Charlie's I thought that was the end of the story."

"And then two months ago," said Jesse. Why did I feel there was something else going on with these guys? Like we were having two conversations, one of them silent. It seemed to me that this out-loud one was enough.

I sighed. "All I did was drive out to the lake on my night off. I had a headache, I wanted some peace and quiet, you don't get that anywhere around my family, including away from the coffeehouse. I'd just had my car tuned, it was a nice night. There hasn't been any trouble at the lake that I know of since the Wars were over, so long as you stay away from the bad spots. I drove out to our old cabin, sat on the porch, looked at the water. . . ."

That was as much of the story as I had told before. I still wasn't expecting my heart rate to speed up, my stomach to hop back and forth like water on a hot griddle, and tears to start pricking the backs of my eyes at the prospect of telling even a little bit more. I looked down at my shapeless jersey kids'-pajama lap, and then glanced at the table knife on Jesse's desk. The world started to turn faster and at a funny angle.

Jesse reached into a bottom drawer and brought out a bottle of . . . oh, hey, single-malt scotch. Some SOFs did know how to live. Theo had turned the Prime Time bag upside down. There was an assortment of greasy-paper-wrapped bundles and they smelled . . . like food. Real human food. "Have a sandwich," said Theo. "Have some chips. Have—hey, Pat, you're living dangerously. Have a Prime Time brownie."

"No thanks," I said automatically. "Too much flour, too much raising agent, and the chocolate they use is only so-so."

"Your color's improving," said Jesse. "Tell us more about Prime Time's sins. I'm sure their bread isn't as good as yours either." It isn't. "Have some scotch." I held out my (empty) tea mug.

I had half a Swiss cheese and watercress sandwich (on mediocre anadama) to give my stomach something else to think about. *The dark stains on the walls in the alley. The gobbets among the cobblestones . . .* Stop that. Okay, I should maybe think about what Pat and Jesse and

Theo were trying to give me space to say. To be afraid of? Something that had to do with, however good their cover, how they must be afraid of being found out as partbloods?

. . . No.

It hadn't occurred to me before. *I didn't think there was a word for a human so sicko as to rescue a vampire, because no* human *had ever done it. Before.*

Dear gods and angels, *no.*

It's not only paranoia and bureaucratic oppression that demands partbloods be registered. Human magic-handling genes and certain demon genes mix really, really badly. There are lots of minor charm-twisters who have a touch of both the human capacity for magic and the demonic, and there's a story that some of them can do stuff no one else can, although it tends to be more goofy than useful. But this is strictly trivial magic handling.

Not all demons can do magic; some of them just *are*, although the areness of demons can seem magical when it isn't. A swallow demon—to take a rare but spectacular example—can fly less because of its hollow bones, although it has those too, than because something funny goes on with some of its atoms, which behave in certain ways as if they exist in some other universe. One of these ways is that they have no gravity in this one. So a swallow demon, despite being the size of anything from a large wardrobe up to and including a small barn, flies. It isn't magic. Swallow demons don't do magic. It only looks like magic. But a lot of demons also handle magic, some of them as powerfully as powerful humans do. And a drop of their blood into a strong human magic-handling gene pool is a disaster.

Strong magic-handling genes and even a weak unmanifested-for-generations magic-operating demon gene in the same person gives you about a ninety percent chance of being criminally insane. It might be as high as ninety-five percent. There are asylums specially built to hold these people, who tend to be extremely hard to hold.

Important magic-handling families for obvious reasons therefore become kind of inbred. Although this isn't an ideal solution either, because over the generations you start getting more . . . *third cousins*

who can maybe write a ward sign that almost works . . . say. And usually
fewer children total. In one way this is a relief. Someone whose human magic-handling DNA isn't up to more than a ward sign that almost works is in little if any danger from a big thor demon-blooded
great-great-grandmother on the other side even if her magic genes
have played very neat hopscotch over the intervening generations and
come through nearly intact. (That's actually another tale. Yes, there are
stories, at least one or two of them impressively documented, about
strong doers in apparently on-the-skids magic-handling families
whose magic turns out to be demonic in origin. But all of those stories—
all the ones with happy endings anyway—are about families whose
magic handling has been moribund for *generations*. People with fathers
under even the suspicion of being sorcerers need not apply.) On the
other hand, important magic-handling families need to go on handling magic to remain important magic-handling families.

The Blaises' name still casts a long shadow. But even I knew they'd
hit their peak a while back, and that there weren't many of them—
us—around any more. There didn't seem to be any at all left since the
Wars. I hadn't thought about this. It might have been an issue if I had
wanted to be a magic handler, but I didn't. It's pretty amazing what
you can *not* think about. To the extent that I thought about it at all,
I missed my gran, but it was a lot *simpler* to be Charlie Seddon's
stepdaughter.

Outcrosses in a magic-handling family on the decline . . . like
me . . . are viewed with mixed feelings. We may be salvation. We
may be catastrophe. It depends on the bloodline on the other side.

Dubious outcrosses are often exiled or repudiated by the family.
It's easier if the alien parent is the mother too, because then they can
claim she was fooling around. Paternity tests applied to bad-magic
crosses are notoriously unreliable.

No. There was no whisper of demon blood in my mother's family.

Would I know? My mother's sisters were both several sandwiches
short of a picnic in terms of common sense. They were not the kind
of people who would be entrusted with dark family secrets. And I
didn't have to waste any time wondering if my mother would have

told me. "Overprotective" is my mom's middle name. She wouldn't have told me.

My mother's parents had been *dead* against the marriage. They hadn't spoken to her since she refused to give my dad up. She'd been very young, and in love, and I could guess that even in those days she didn't take direction well. Maybe they didn't tell her. Just booted her out: never darken our door again, etc. They'd never made any attempt to meet me, their first grandchild, either. Maybe my mother found out later, somehow, after I was born. Maybe it was my dad who'd found it out. . . .

I'd never seen my father again after my mother left him, nor any of the rest of his family. Only my gran. Who was maybe choosing to see me privately and alone not in deference to my mother's feelings but because her own family had ordered her to have nothing to do with me.

Maybe my gran had some other reason for believing I was okay. Or maybe she didn't know why my mom had left. Maybe she thought it was my dad's business associates. Magic-handling families can be pretty conceited about their talent, and pretty offended by common-ers feeling they have any rights to inconvenient opinions. Maybe my gran thought her family were just being arrogant.

If you were in the ninety percent, it showed up early. Usually. If you weren't born with a precocious ability to hoist yourself out of your crib and get into really *repulsive* mischief, the next likeliest time for you to begin running amok was in the preteen years, when magic-handling kids are apprenticed for their first serious magic-handling training. When my gran taught me to transmute.

The sane five or ten percent most often have personalities that are uninterested in magic. One of the recommendations, for some-one who finds out they're in the high-risk category, is *not* to do magic, even the most inconsequential. My mother would never have let me have all those meetings with my gran if there'd been any chance. . . .

She might have. My mother makes Attila the Hun look namby-pamby. If she wanted me not to be a bad-magic cross, then I *wouldn't* be, by sheer force of will if necessary. But she might still have wanted to know what she was up against.

I hadn't come home and started knifing old ladies or setting fire to stray dogs.

I was kind of a loner though. A little paranoid about being close to people. A little too interested in the Others.

My mother would have assumed that my gran had tried to teach me magic and that she hadn't been successful. So my mother would have assumed the Blaise magic genes were weak enough in me, or her own compromised heritage had missed me out.

Maybe my mother could be forgiven for being a little overcontrolling. Because she'd never be sure.

Bad-magic crosses don't invariably show up early. Some of our worst and most inventive serial murderers have turned out to be bad-magic crosses, when someone finally caught up with them. Sometimes it turns out something set them off. Like doing magic. Like finding out they could.

And I hadn't done any magic in fifteen years.

No.

I stopped chewing.

Pat and Jesse assumed I'd thought of all this before. They were assuming that's why I hadn't been able to talk to them. Had been afraid to talk to them. The licensing thing was piffle. They would know that I knew that too. If it was just a question of not being a certified magic handler, hey, I could get my serial number and my license. The bureaucrats would snuffle a little about my not having done it before, but I was a model cinnamon-roll-baker citizen; they'd at least half believe me that I'd never done any magic before, they probably wouldn't even fine me. Licensing was a red herring. Pat wouldn't have turned blue over a question of late magic-handling certification. So I had to be afraid of something else.

I *was* afraid of something else. They'd just guessed wrong about what it was and how I got there.

They were, in fact, offering me a huge gesture of faith. They were telling me that they believed I wasn't a bad cross.

They must really love my cinnamon rolls.

What they didn't know was that I'd rescued a vampire. Which might be read as the polite, subtle version of becoming an axe murderer.

"Have some more scotch," said Jesse.

And now, of course, they only thought I was dreading telling them about what had happened two months ago.

Okay. Let this dread be for the telling of the story. Nothing else.

The story of how I rescued a vampire.

Which I wasn't going to tell them.

I put my mug down because my hands were beginning to shake. I crossed my arms over my breast and began rocking back and forth in my chair. Pat dragged his chair over next to mine, gently pulled my hands down, held them in his. They were a pale blue now, and not so knobbly. I couldn't see if he still had the sixth fingers.

I said, speaking to Pat's pale blue hands, "I didn't hear them coming." I spoke in a high, peculiar voice I didn't recognize as my own. "But you don't, do you, when they're vampires."

There was a growl from Theo—not what you could call a human growl.

It was a creepy, chilling, menacing sound, even knowing that it was made on my behalf. Briefly, hysterically, I wanted to laugh. It occurred to me that maybe I *hadn't* been the one human in the room, a few minutes ago, when I'd felt like a rabbit in headlights.

Jesse let the silence stretch out a little, and then he said softly, "How did you get away?"

. . . *There was another muddle leaning up against the wall in front of us . . . someone sitting cross-legged, head bowed, forearms on knees. I didn't realize till it raised its head with a liquid, inhuman motion that it was another vampire. . . .*

I took a deep breath. "They had me shackled to the wall in—in what I guess was the ballroom in—in one of the really big old summer houses. At the lake. I—I was—some kind of prize, I think. They—they came in to look at me a couple of times. Left me food and water. The second day I—transmuted my jackknife into a shackle key."

"You transmuted *worked metal?*"

I took another deep breath. "Yes. No, I shouldn't have been able to. I'd never done anything close. I hadn't done anything at all in fifteen years—since the last time I saw my gran. It almost . . . it almost didn't occur to me to try." I shivered and closed my eyes. No: don't close your eyes. I opened my eyes. Pat squeezed my hands. "Hey. It's okay," he said. "You're here." I looked at him. He was almost human again.

I wondered what I was. Was I *almost* human?

"Yeah," he said. "What you're thinking."

I tried to look like I might be thinking what he thought I was thinking. Whatever that was.

"SOF is full of Others and partbloods because it's vampires that are *our* problem. Sure there are lousy stinking demons—"

And bad-magic crosses.

"—but there are lousy stinking humans too. We take care of the Others and the straight cops take care of the humans. If we got the suckers sorted the humans would calm down—sooner or later—let the rest of us live, you know? And then we'd be able to organize and *really* get rid of the 'ubis and the goblins and the ghouls and so on and we'd end up with a relatively safe world."

There was a story—I hoped it was no more than a myth—that the reason there still wasn't a reliable prenatal test for a bad-magic cross was the prejudice against partbloods.

Jesse said patiently, "You transmuted worked metal."

I nodded.

"Do you still have the knife?"

I dragged my mind back to the present. I'd decided earlier that the light in the office was good enough, so I nodded again.

"Can we see it?"

Pat let go of my hands, and I pulled the knife out of my fuzzy pocket and leaned forward to lay it on a pile of paper on Jesse's desk. It lay there, looking perfectly ordinary. Jesse picked it up and looked at it. He passed it to Theo, who looked at it too, and offered it to Pat. Pat shook his head. "Not when I'm coming down. It might crank me right back up again, and we can't keep the door locked all night."

"What would happen if someone knocked?" I said. "You're still a little blue around the edges."

"Closet," said Pat. "Nice big one. Why we chose Jesse's office."

"And we would be so surprised that the door was locked," said Jesse. "Must be something wrong with the bolt. We'll get it checked tomorrow. Miss Seddon is all right, isn't she?"

"Miss Seddon is fine," I lied. What was wrong with her was not their fault.

"Rae—" said Jesse, and hesitated.

I was holding myself here in the present, in this office, so I was pretty sure I knew what he wanted to ask.

"I don't know," I said. "I haven't been back to the lake since. There's a really big bad spot behind the house, maybe that's part of why they chose it, and when—when I got out of there I just—followed the edge of the lake south."

"If we take you out there—let's say tomorrow—will you try to find it?"

It had little to do with what I hadn't told them that made the silence last a long time before I answered. What I had told them was plenty for why I didn't want to go there again. "Yes," I said at last, heavily. "I'll try. There won't . . . be anything."

"I know," said Jesse. "But we still have to look. I'm sorry."

I nodded. I picked up my jackknife and put it back in my pocket. I looked at Jesse. Then I looked at the blood-smeared table knife lying on his desk, and he watched me looking. "That's the next thing, isn't it?" he said. "Okay—you have some kind of line on worked metal. Some pretty astonishing line, it must be. But that doesn't explain. . . ."

The phone rang. He picked it up. "Ah. Well, better send him up then." We all looked hard at Pat. He wasn't blue at all. Theo unlocked the door.

Mel came through it about ten seconds later, looking fit to murder battalions of SOFs with nothing more than a table knife. "What the dharmic *hell* do you red-eyed boys think you are up to, keeping a law-abiding member of the human public incommunicado for over an hour?"

I managed to keep a straight face. "Red-eyed boy" (or girl) is an accusation of Other blood: just the sort of thing a pissed-off civilian would say to a SOF. They all looked perfectly blank. "Sorry," said Jesse. "We didn't mean to keep her incommunicado. We were getting her out of a bad situation as fast as possible—brought her in the back way, of course. The media jokers can't get to her here. But we forgot to send word to the front desk that we weren't—er—holding her."

Sure you forgot, I thought. Mel, still quivering with fury, and equally aware Jesse was lying, turned to me. "I'm okay," I said. "I was a bit—hysterical. They let me have a shower," I added inconsequentially. I'd had a rough night, and it was getting harder and harder to remember what I'd told whom and why.

"A *shower?*" said Mel, taking in my fuzzy-bunny clothing—probably the first time he'd ever seen me in anything that didn't involve red or pink or orange or yellow or at least peacock blue or fluorescent purple—and I realized he didn't know what had happened. He wouldn't, would he? You don't destroy vampires by rushing up to them and sticking them with table knives. The only sure thing about the night's events was that there'd been some kind of fracas—some messy kind of fracas—and I'd disappeared with some SOFs. There were probably half a dozen incompatible versions of what had happened out there by now.

No wonder Mel was feeling a little wild.

"It's sort of a long story," I said. "May I leave now, please?" Before you start asking me about tonight, I thought.

"That's what I'm here for," said Mel, throwing another good glare around.

"See you tomorrow," said Jesse.

"What?" said Mel.

"I'll tell you on the way out," I said.

"Sleep well," said Pat.

"You too," I said.

They gave me my soggy clothes in a plastic Mega Food bag and I managed to jam my feet into the clammy, curled-up sneakers so

I could walk. Jesse offered to call a taxi, but I wanted some outdoor air. Even midtown civic center outdoor air.

We had to go back to the coffeehouse: the Wreck was there. Mel had walked over. Well, I don't know about *walked*. He had come over without vehicular assistance anyway. He was still putting out major anger vibes, even after a successful rescue of the damsel from the dragon-encircled tower. The dragon had been blue, and essentially friendly. The real problem was about the damsel. . . . I had never wanted someone to talk to so badly, never been so unable to say what I wanted to talk about.

And if I managed to tell him, what was he going to say? "I'll start ringing up residential homes for the lethally loony tomorrow, see where the nearest openings are"?

"Don't even try to tell me what happened till you've had some sleep," said Mel. "The goddam *nerve* of those guys. . . . I thought Pat and Jesse were okay."

"I think they are okay," I said, regretfully. In some ways it would have been easier if they weren't. "Jesse and Theo did get me out of there—um—and they couldn't help being, you know, professionally interested."

Mel snorted. "If you say so. Listen, the whole neighborhood is talking about it. Whatever it is. The official SOF report—what they've already fed to the media goons—is that you were an innocent bystander. None of us is going to say anything, but there were a lot of people in that alley by the time Jesse and Theo got you away, and it's unanimous that you were . . ."

There was a pause. I didn't say anything.

He added, "Charlie seemed to think Jesse *was* doing you a favor. That SOF could protect you better than we could."

Yeah. Further destruction of personal world view optional.

Mel sighed. "So we hung around the phone at the coffeehouse, waiting—Charlie and me. We sent everybody else home—including Kenny, sworn on pain of having his liver on tomorrow's menu not to tell your mother anything. The phone didn't ring. So then we rang SOF and got yanked around by some little sheepwit on the switchboard, and that's when I came over. . . ."

"I'm sorry," I said.

The coffeehouse was dark and the square silent and empty, al-though there was some kind of distantly audible fuss going on some-where it was easy enough to guess was a block or two over and down a recently defiled alley. We went round the side of the coffee-house and I could see a light on in the office. Charlie, drinking coffee and pacing. He had his arms wrapped around me so tight I couldn't breathe almost before I was inside. Charlie is such a *mild* little guy, most of the time.

"I'm okay," I said. Charlie gave a deep, shuddering sigh, and I remembered him backing me up with Mr. Responsible Media. I also remembered all the time he'd spent in years past, encouraging my mundane interest in learning to make a mayonnaise that didn't crack, how much garlic went into Charlie's famous hash, my early experiments with what turned out to be the ancestors of Bitter Chocolate Death et al. There was no magic about Charlie. Nor about most restaurants, come to that. Human customers tend to be a little twitchy about anything more magical than a waitress who could keep coffee hot. I wondered about my mother's motive in ap-plying for a job as a waitress all those years ago: I was already mak-ing peanut butter and chocolate chip cookies while we were still living with my dad (if there was a grown-up to turn the oven on for me), and if she was looking for nice safe outlets. . . . "Tonight. It's—it's connected with what happened—when I was gone those two days."

"I was afraid of that," said Charlie.

"Jesse wants me to try to find the place it all happened. Out at the lake. They're taking me out there tomorrow."

"Oh bloody *hell*," said Mel. "It's been two months. They don't have to go tomorrow."

I shrugged. "Might as well. I have the afternoon off."

"The lake," said Charlie thoughtfully.

I'd told everyone I'd driven out to the lake. I hadn't said that what happened afterward also happened at the lake. Till tonight my offi-cial memory had ended sitting on the porch of the old cabin.

"Yes. I was—er—held—at a house on the lake. They want me to try to find it."

Either Mel or Charlie could have said, when did you remember this? What else do you remember? Why did you tell SOF when you haven't told us? Neither of them did. Mel put his arm around me. "Oh, gods and frigging angels," he said.

"Be careful," said Charlie.

ONE OF THE (few) advantages to getting to work at four-thirty A.M. is that you can be pretty sure of finding a parking space. When I come in later I'm not always so lucky. I'd had to park the Wreck in a garage lot that evening, and it was locked at eleven. Mel took me home. When we got there and he turned the bike off the silence pressed against me. The sudden quiet is almost always loud when you've been on a motorcycle and got somewhere and stopped and turned it off, but this was different. Mel didn't say any more about the night's events. He didn't say any more about SOF taking me out to the lake the next day. I could see him *wanting* to . . . but as I've said before, one of the reasons Mel and I were still seeing each other after four years was because we could *not* talk about things sometimes. This included that we both knew when to shut up.

It was *blissful*, spending time with someone who would leave you alone. I loved him for it. And I was happy to repay in kind.

It had never occurred to me that leaving someone alone could harden into a habit that could become a barrier. It had never occurred to me before now.

I had to repress the desire that he not shut up this time. I had to repress the desire to ask him if I could talk to him.

But what could I have said?

We stood there in the darkness for a minute or two. He was rubbing another of his tattoos, the sand wheel, on the back of his left hand. Then he came with me to check that I still had Kenny's bicycle and the tires weren't flat. Then he kissed me and left. "See you tomorrow," is all he said.

I reached over my head to touch the wards strung along the edge of the porch roof on my way indoors. These were all Yolande's. Her wards were especially good and I'd often thought of asking her where she got them, but you didn't really ask Yolande questions. I had noticed that her niece, when she was visiting, didn't seem to ask questions either, beyond, "I'm taking the girls downtown, can I bring you anything?" And the answer would probably be "No, thank you, dear."

I wiggled my fingers down the edges of my pots of pansies on the porch steps, to check that the wards I'd buried there were still there, and that a *ping* against my fingers meant they were still working. I straightened the medallion over my downstairs door and lifted the "go away" mat in front of the one at the top of the stairs to check that the warding built into the lay of the planks of the floor hadn't been hacked out by creature or creatures unknown. I fluttered the charm paper that was wound round the railing of my balcony to make sure it was still live, blew on the frames of my windows for the faint ripple of response. I didn't like charms, but I wasn't naïve enough not to have good basic wards, and I'd been a little more meticulous about upkeep in the last two months.

Then I made myself a cup of chamomile tea to damp down the scotch and the cheese. I took off the bunny pajamas and put on one of my own nightgowns. The toilet paper had held; there wasn't any blood on the SOF thing. I put my still-wet clothes in a sinkful of more soap and water. Tomorrow I would put them through a washing machine. I might throw them out anyway, or burn them. (I still hadn't burned the cranberry-red dress. It lived at the back of my closet. I think I knew I wasn't going to burn it after the night I dreamed that it was made of blood, not cloth, and I'd pulled it out of the closet that night, in the dark, and stroked and stroked the dry, silky, shining fabric, which was nothing like blood. Nothing like blood.) My sneakers would live. I had dozens of T-shirts and jeans if I decided I wanted to burn something but I wasn't going to sacrifice a good pair of sneakers if I could help it.

I pushed open the French doors and went out and sat on my little balcony. It was a clear, quiet night with a bright quarter moon.

When Yolande had had mice in her kitchen I had set take-'em-alive traps and driven the results twenty miles away and released them in empty farmland. (Wards against wildlife are notoriously bad: hence the electric peanut-butter fence to keep the deer from eating Yolande's roses. And a house ward successful against mice and squirrels would be almost the money-spinner that a charm to let suckers walk around in daylight would be.) I couldn't kill anything larger than a housefly. I'd stopped putting spiders outdoors after I read somewhere that house spiders won't survive. When I dusted, I left occupied cobwebs alone. I hadn't drawn blood in anger since the seventh-grade playground wars.

I don't eat meat. I'm too squeamish. It all looks like dead animals to me. On the days I cover in the main kitchen, the only hot food is vegetarian.

Maybe my mother had successfully coerced and brainwashed her daughter into being a nice, human wimp.

But I'd blown it. I'd blown it when I'd turned my knife into a key, because it was the only way to stay alive. Because—maybe only because I didn't know any better—I wanted to stay alive. I looked down at my arms, at my hands cupping the tea mug, as if I would start growing scales or fur or warts—or turning blue—immediately. Most demon blood doesn't make you big or strong or blue though, whether it comes with magic ability or not. A lot of it makes you weaker or stupider. Or crazier.

I'd been doing okay as my mother's daughter. My life wasn't perfect, but whose was?

Yes, I'd always despised myself for being a coward. A wuss. So? There are worse things.

And then I had to drive out to the lake one night.

They'd started it. And I may be a wuss, but I've never liked bullies. Maybe, if it was all about to go horribly wrong, I could at least go out with a bang.

How cute and sweet and winsome and philosophically high-minded, that I didn't like bullies, that I wanted to go out with a bang. I was still a coward, I had a master vampire and his gang on my tail, I was all alone, and I was *way* out of my league.

"Oh, Constantine," I whispered into the darkness. "What do I do now?"

I slept the moment my head touched the pillow, in spite of everything that had happened. It was very late for me though, and I'd had two generous shots of scotch. The alarm went off about three hours later. I woke strangely easily and peacefully. I can get by on six and a half hours, just, and only if I'm feeling lively generally, which I hadn't been lately. Three hours' sleep doesn't cut it under any conditions. But I sat up and stretched and didn't feel too bad. And I had the oddest sensation . . . as if someone had been in my bedroom with me. Given the events of the night before, this should have been panic stations, but it wasn't. It was a reassuring feeling, as if someone had been guarding me in my sleep.

Get a grip, Sunshine.

I had to get moving quickly however I was feeling, because it took so much longer to bicycle than to drive into town. But as it turned out, it didn't. When I went round to the shed to fetch Kenny's bike there was a car parked at the edge of the road, engine off, but SOF spotlight on, illuminating the SOF insignia on the door, and the face of the man leaning against the hood. Pat. " 'Morning," he said.

"We are *not* going to the lake at this hour," I said, half scandalized and half disbelieving. "I am going to make cinnamon rolls and oatmeal bread and brownies and Butter Bombs, and you can call out the cavalry at about ten."

"Sheer. I know you're going in to make cinnamon rolls. You want to be setting some aside to bring with you later on. The only good Monday is a holiday Monday when Charlie's is open. But we figured that Mel would bring you home last night which would leave you with only two unmotorized wheels this morning. And we don't want you tired this afternoon."

Tired but alive would do, I thought. Dawn isn't for another hour and a half, and if I'm the first person to stake a sucker with a table knife I could be the first person to get plucked off a bicycle. . . . I had been thinking about this as I walked downstairs in the dark. Living alone has its advantages in terms of warding: your wards don't get confused, nor do they blunt as fast as they will if there are several of you. A big family with a lot of friends will go through wards like the Seddons through popcorn on Monday nights. And unless you are so fabulously wealthy that you can spend millions on made-to-order wards, there are always going to be some holes in the barrier. Someone living alone who isn't constantly having different people over can probably build up a pretty good, solid, home ward system. That's *probably*.

But wards are unstable at best, and they tend to blow up or fall over or go rogue or get their attributes crossed and morph into something else, almost certainly something you don't want, pretty easily, and generally speaking the more powerful they are the more likely they are to go nuts. And wards are the *sober* end of the charm family. Most of the rest of them are a lot worse. One of the most dependable ways to make a ward kali on you is to expect it to travel. All charms, including wards, that you wear next to your skin, are different—hence the perennial, if problematic, popularity of tattoos—but wards you hang at a distance have to stay put.

Consequently the eternally vexed question of warding your means of transportation. And while it's true that the chauffeur-driven limos of the global council are almost more ward than limo, it's also true that no council member travels anywhere without a human bodyguard stiff with technology, including to the corner store for a newspaper. If there are any global council members that live in neighborhoods with corner stores, which there probably aren't.

The irony is that the best transport ward for us ordinary schlemiels remains the confusing fact of motion itself. (There's a crucial maintenance speed of a little under ten mph. This is a *brisk* pedal on your bicycle and sensible joggers, if this isn't a contradiction in terms, get their exercise during the day. In the horse era a harness or riding horse that couldn't maintain a nine-mph clip for a useful distance was shot. This made horses short-lived and expensive and most people stayed at home after dark: but at least travel was possible.) The protection of movement is nothing like perfect, which is why they keep trying to create transport wards, but it exists—and thank the gods and angels for it, since without it I don't think there would be many sane humans left. There's only so much constant relentless constrictive dread you can live with. Anyway I knew to be grateful for it, but it had never made much sense, at least not till a vampire had told me *it is not the distance that is crucial, but the uniformity* and given me an inkling.

But what kind of homogeneity is it, about sucker senses? Had the goblin giggler's last sight of the human who offed him been *transmitted* anywhere?

I'd felt relatively safe inside my apartment. I had good wards, and you can kind of feel the presence of the screen they put up, that it's there, and there aren't any big drafts coming through it. And you feel it when you come out from behind it too.

But I'd never been able to bear a charm against my skin. They make me a total space cadet. I'd agreed to the key ring loop to make Mom feel good, and that was pushing it. Poor thing. It had probably been grateful to be drowned in the shower, last night, if it had survived the little incident shortly before.

I said to Pat unkindly, "You might have thought of that last night."

He grinned, and opened the passenger door. I got in. "Why did you draw the short straw?"

"'Cause I'm best at going without sleep. My demon blood has its uses."

There were at least two classes of demons who didn't sleep at all. My favorite is the Hildy demon, who gets all the sleep it needs during the blinking of its eyes. You'd think this would seriously interrupt any train of thought that takes longer to pursue than the time between one eye blink and another, but not to a Hildy. (They're called Hildies after Brunhilde, who slept for a very long time surrounded by fire. Hildies also breathe fire when they're peeved, although they're even-tempered as demons go.) Hildies aren't blue though.

I certainly couldn't get all the sleep I needed by blinking my eyes.

I stayed in the bakery all morning. Charlie and Mel kept everyone who didn't belong behind the counter on the far side, Mom answered more phone calls than usual and said "she has nothing to say" a lot. With the bakery door open I could sometimes hear conversations in the office. Mom is good at hanging up on people. It's one of her great assets as a small-business manager. (She and Consuela had lately been working up a good cop/bad cop routine that was a joy to eavesdrop on.) I had no idea what Charlie had told her about the events of the night before. I didn't want to know. But he must have told her something. Miraculously, she left me alone, although a particularly lurid new charm was waiting for me on my apron hook that morning. I left it there, glowering to itself. I like orange, but not in overdecorated feather whammies.

It wasn't as bad as it might have been by a long shot. I felt some grudging admiration for SOF.

Nobody tried to follow me when I left the coffeehouse at ten, or at least nobody but some of the overweight so-called wildlife that hangs around the pedestrian precinct and tries to cadge handouts from the weak-willed. They know a white bakery bag when they see one, and I was carrying a dozen cinnamon rolls. I swear some of our sparrows are too fat to fly, but the feral cats are too fat to catch them. And the squirrels should have had teeny-weeny skateboards to keep their bellies off the ground. One of the recent rumors about Mrs. Bialosky's neighborhood activities was that she ran a commando unit that protected us from some of Old Town's larger, more threatening wildlife, the rats and foxes and mutant deer that never shed their short but pointy horns. If Charlie's had had to keep *all* of that lot too fat to intimidate anybody we'd have gone out of business.

It was just Jesse and Pat today. They put me in the front seat—of an unmarked car—with Pat alone in the back. Jesse ate four cinnamon rolls and Pat ate five. I didn't think this was humanly possible—but then maybe it wasn't. I ate one. I'd had breakfast already. Twice. Ten o'clock is a long time from four in the morning.

We drove first to the old cabin. I was still clinging to that mysterious sense of someone keeping a protective eye on me, but I was beginning to feel a little rocky nonetheless. Maybe I should have brought the feather whammy instead of hiding it under my apron when I left. As the weed-pocked gravel of what had once been a driveway crunched under my feet, I put my hand in my pocket and closed it round my little knife. I had been not remembering what had happened two months ago so emphatically that the edges of my real memory had become a little indistinct. Standing on the ground where it had begun brought it horribly back. I looked at the porch, where I hadn't heard them coming from. I looked at the place where my car had no longer been, two days later.

I went down to the marshy reach near the shore, where the stream had run fifteen years ago. It didn't look like anybody had been there playing in the mud recently. I went back to the cabin.

"Yeah," Pat was saying.

"But it's been a long time, and they haven't been back," said Jesse.

They were just standing there, no gizmos in sight, no headsets, no wires, no portable com screens with flashing lights making beeping noises. I guessed it wasn't technology that was helping them draw their conclusions.

What a good thing Pat hadn't walked on my porch this morning, and up my stairs and knocked on my door and, maybe, walked into the front room where the same, if savagely stain-removed, sofa still stood, and the little square of carpet beside it, and maybe even the handle of the fridge door, the same handle that had been there ready to expose a carton of milk behind it if someone pulled on it, two months ago.

What a good thing that good manners dictate that you don't idly cross people's probable outer ward circle and knock on their doors unless invited.

Carthaginian hell.

We got back in the car and drove on the way we'd been going, north.

There was a bad spot almost at once. I picked it up first, or anyway I was the one who said, "Hey. I don't know about you, but I don't want to go any farther this way."

"Roll up your windows," said Jesse. He hit a couple of buttons on the very peculiar dashboard I was only now noticing and suddenly there was something like heavy body armor enclosing me, oppressive as chain mail and breastplate and a full-face helm, plume and lady's silk favor optional. I could almost smell the metal polish. "Ugh," I said.

"Don't knock it, it works," said Jesse. Our voices echoed peculiarly. We drove very slowly for about a minute and then a red light on the dashboard blinked and there was a manic chirping like a parakeet on speed. "Right. We're clear." He hit the same buttons. The invisible armor went away.

"Spartan, isn't it?" said Pat.

"No," I said.

We drove through two more bad spots like that and I hated the body armor program worse each time. It made me feel trapped. It made me feel as if when I woke up again I'd be sitting at the edge of a bonfire with a lot of vampires on the other side.

It was a long drive. Thirty miles or so. I remembered.

Then we reached a really bad spot. Jesse hit his buttons again but this time it really *was* like being trapped—held down while Things slid through the intangible gaps between the incorporeal links, reached out long taloned fingers and grabbed me. . . .

Big. Huge space. Indoors; ceiling up there somewhere. Old factory. Scaffolding where the workers had once tended the machines. No windows. Enormous square ventilator shafts, vast parasitic humps of silent machinery, contortions of piping like the Worm Ouroboros in its death throes. . . .

And eyes. Eyes. Staring. Their gaze like flung acid. No color. What color is evil? . . .

When I came to, I was screaming. I stopped. Even the guys looked shaken. I could see the scuff marks in the road ahead of us, where Jesse had slammed us into reverse. Good thing the driver hadn't gone under. I put my hands over my mouth. "Sorry," I said.

"Nah," said Pat. "If you hadn't been screaming, I'd've had to do it."

"What now?" said Jesse. They both looked at me.

"Maybe this is the really big bad spot behind the house," I said.

"I told you there was one. We're pretty well north of the lake now, aren't we? Seems like we've come far enough, but I keep losing the lake behind the trees."

"Yeah," said Jesse. "The road's well back here, because this is where the big estates are. Were."

"Okay," I said. "So we walk." I opened the car door and clambered stiffly out. This was harder than it would have been if I hadn't been squashed by SOF technology four times, especially the last time when it didn't work. I patted my stomach as if checking to make sure I was still there. I seemed to be. The cut on my breast was itching like crazy: the sort of variable itch that reinforces its performance by regular nerve-fraying jabs of pain.

My jackknife seemed to be trying to burn a hole through its cotton pocket to my leg. I wrapped my hand around it. The heat was presumably illusory, which perhaps explained why the sense of being *fried* felt so comforting. I set off through the trees without looking behind me. They'd follow, and I had to get myself moving before I thought much about it or I wouldn't do it at all.

I didn't bother trying to figure out where the bad spot ended. I went down to the shore of the lake and turned right. Walking on the shore, while awkward, all shingle and teetery stones and water-tossed rubbish, wasn't so bad as walking through the trees. I was in sunlight out here, and the memories were under the trees. I hadn't walked on the shore before.

It was the right bad spot. I came to the house much too soon. I could half-convince myself I was enjoying walking by the lake. I like walking by water in the sunshine. I'd often enjoyed walking by this lake. Before. I stopped, feeling suddenly sick, and waited for the other two to catch up with me. "I'm not sure I can do this," I said, and my voice had started to go funny again, as it had last night, when I told them you don't hear vampires coming.

"It's daylight, and we're with you," said Jesse, not unsympathetically.

I said abruptly, "What if we get back to the car and it won't start? We'd never get out of these woods before dark."

"It'll start," said Pat. "You're okay. Hold on. We're going to walk up the hill toward the house real slow. You just keep breathing. I'm walking up on your left and Jesse is walking up on your right. We'll go as slow as you want. Hey, Jesse, how's your nephew doing with that puppy he talked your folks into buying him?"

It was well done. Puppy stories got me to the stairs. By that time Pat had me by the elbow because I was gasping like a puffer demon, except they always breathe like that, but having a hand on my elbow was too much like having been frog-marched up those stairs the last time I'd been here. "No," I said. "Thanks, but let me go. Last time, you know, I had help."

The porch steps creaked under my weight. Like last time. Unlike last time, the steps also creaked under the weight of my companions.

Almost dreamily I went through the still-ajar front door and left across the huge hall toward the ballroom. It was daylight, now, so I could look up, and see where the curl of grand staircase became an upstairs corridor lined by what had once been an equally grand balustrade, but some of the posts were cracked or missing. There were still glints of gold paint in the hollows of the carving. In the dark I hadn't known the railings were anything but smooth. I wouldn't have cared.

The ballroom was smaller than I remembered. It was still a big room, much bigger than anything but a ballroom, but in my memory it had become about the size of a small country, and in fact it was only a room. As ballrooms go it probably wasn't even a big one. The chandelier, very shabby in daylight, still had candle stubs in it, and there was a lot of dripped wax on the floor underneath. There was my corner, and the windows on either wall that had bounded my world for two long nights and a day in between . . .

I shuddered.

"Steady, Sunshine," said Pat.

I had been worrying about the shackles in the walls. I was going to have to revert to not remembering, when Pat and Jesse asked me about the second shackle, the one with the ward signs on it.

There were no shackles. Just holes in the walls. I almost laughed. Thanks, Bo, I said silently. You've done me a favor.

Pat and Jesse were examining the holes, Pat still half keeping an eye on me. The holes looked like they'd been torn—as if the shackles had been ripped out of the walls by someone in a rage. By some vampire: no human could've done it. But I guessed the rage part was accurate. A frustrated—possibly frightened—rage, or on orders? On orders, I thought. I doubted Bo's gang did anything that Bo hadn't told them to do first. But however it had happened, I didn't have to explain a shackle with ward signs on it.

They did, of course, want to know about the second set of holes.

"This is where I was," I said, pointing to the holes nearer the corner.

"And this?" said Jesse, kneeling in front of the other holes.

"I don't remember," I said automatically.

There was a silence. "Can we have an agreement, maybe," said Pat. "That you stop saying 'I don't remember' and do us the kindness of telling the truth, which is that you're not going to say what you remember."

There was a longer silence. Pat was looking at me. I met his eyes. He had held his breath till he turned blue last night. He'd already made up his mind to trust me, even knowing that I was lying about what had happened. That made me feel pretty bad until it occurred to me that there was another angle on last night's demonstration: not only that Pat and Jesse and Theo were willing to trust me, but that they understood sometimes you had to lie.

"Okay," I said.

"So," said Jesse. "This second set of holes."

I took a deep breath. "I'm not going to tell you."

"Okay," said Jesse. "I think these holes are from another shackle. If it had been empty while you were here, Rae, you wouldn't mind telling us that. So, there must have been another prisoner, and it's this other prisoner you aren't going to tell us about."

I didn't say anything.

"Interesting," said Jesse.

Pat stared out one of the windows, frowning. "Shackles in a ballroom aren't standard equipment, so the suckers will have put them in special. The thing is, the space cleared around this house has been done recently too. You have to assume they did that as well. Why?"

I could keep silent on this one a little more easily. It seemed pretty weird if you didn't know. And this one they couldn't guess. I hoped.

They went off to look at the rest of the house. I stayed in the ballroom. I sat on the windowsill nearest my shackle, the one on the long wall—the window I'd peed out of. The window I'd knelt in front of when I'd changed my knife to a key. The lake looked a lot like it had the day I'd been here: another blue, clear day. It was hotter today though, summer rather than spring. I leaned back against the side of the window and thought about cinnamon rolls and muffins and brownies and the cherry tarts I'd started experimenting with since Charlie had ordered an electric cherry pitter out of a catalog and gave it to me hopefully. Charlie's idea of post-traumatic shock therapy: a new kitchen gadget. I thought about the pleasure of sitting in bright sunlight. With two humans in easy call. I might have opened my collar and let the sun shine there, but I had the gash taped up and I wasn't going to risk Pat or Jesse seeing it.

I thought about the fact that Mel, easygoing, laid-back, mind-your-own-business Mel, kept nagging me to look for a doctor who *could* do something about it, and found my refusal inexplicable and dumb.

Jesse and Pat came back into the ballroom and hunkered down on the floor in front of me in my window. There was a silence. I didn't like this. I wanted to leave. I wanted to get away from the lake, from what had happened here, from being reminded of what had happened here. I'd done what they'd asked, I'd found them the house. I didn't want to talk about this stuff any more. I wanted to go back to the car and make sure it was going to start, and get us out of here before sundown. I wanted to sit in the sun somewhere other than beside the lake.

"So, last night," said Jesse. "What happened?"

"I don't—" I said. Pat looked at me and I smiled faintly. "I wasn't going to say I don't remember. I was going to say I don't know. It was—it was like instinctive, except who has that kind of instinct? If it was an instinct, it was a really *stupid* instinct."

"Except that it worked," Pat said dryly. "So, you didn't think, ah ha, there's a sucker a couple of streets over, I think I'll go stake the bastard? Never mind that I don't know how I know it's there or that I'm going to stake it with a goddam *table knife?*"

"No," I said. "I didn't think at all. I didn't think from the time I—I stood up from where I was sitting at the counter to when—when Jesse had hold of me and was yelling that it was all over."

"So why did you stand up—and pick up a table knife—and take off at a speed that wouldn't have shamed an Olympic sprinter?"

"Um," I said. "Well, I heard him. Um. And I didn't like having him . . . on *my* ground. I was, um, angry. I guess."

"Heard him. Heard him what? Nobody else heard anything."

"Heard him, um, giggle."

Silence.

"Was this by any chance a sucker from two months ago?" Pat said gently. "From what happened here?"

"Yes."

"Can you tell us any more?"

He's the one that made this mark on me, I thought. This slice in my flesh that won't close. You could say I had a score to settle. That doesn't explain why I managed to settle it though. "He was—he was the other one that had hold of me, coming here. I don't know how many of them there were altogether—a dozen maybe." I thought of the second evening, the twelve of them fanning out around me and the prisoner of the other shackle, coming closer. Slowly coming closer. How I'd been pressing myself against the wall so hard my spine hurt. "Most of them didn't say anything. The one I think was the Breather—he seemed to be giving the orders. I thought of him as—as the lieutenant of the raiding party. He talked. And he held one of my arms, bringing me here. This—the one from last night, he held my other arm. He talked. He was the one with the . . . sense of humor." *Her feet are already bleeding. If you like feet.*

"The lieutenant of the raiding party," said Jesse thoughtfully. "That sounds like there was a colonel back at headquarters."

"You'd expect that, a setup as elaborate as this one," said Pat. "This is a gang run by a master vampire."

They both looked at me. "Do you know anything about the master?" said Jesse.

I could have said, I'm not going to tell you. I said, "No."

There was another silence. I tried not to squirm. This should be when the SOFs revert to type and start yelling at me for withholding important information and so on.

"We have a problem, you see, Sunshine," said Pat at last. "Okay, we know you're not telling us everything. But . . . well, I probably shouldn't be telling *you* this, but that happens oftener than you might think, people not telling SOF everything. Hell, SOF not telling SOF everything. I mean aside from the nomad blood of guys like Jesse and me. We could probably live with that if that was all it was. We wouldn't like it, maybe, but we've had a lot of practice not being told everything, and if you get too pissed off at people then they *really* won't talk to you.

"But you've done something pretty well unprecedented. Twice. You got away from a bunch of vampires—alone, and out in the middle of nowhere. It happens occasionally that a sucker gang gets a little carried away, teasing some kid from a human gang that has been jiving in the wrong place, hoping to see vampires. The kid gets a little cut up, but we take him to the hospital and they stitch him up and give him his shots, and he goes home good as new if a little more prone to nightmares than he used to be. It doesn't happen that a young woman alone in a wilderness gets away from a sucker gang so determined to keep her they have her chained to the wall. So far as I know it hasn't ever happened before."

I wished he would stop saying "alone." He hadn't forgotten the second set of holes in the wall any more than I had. Thank the gods at least the telltale shackle itself was gone.

"And that's only the first thing. The second thing is that you sauntered up to a sucker last night that in the first place you had no way of knowing was there, in the second place he stood there while you staked him without any warning or any backup, and in the third place staked him with a stainless steel table knife. People have staked suckers without backup, but they've never done it by running up to one in full sight and they sure as suckers hate daylight don't do it with a goddam table knife. I pulled the research on it that proves it can't be done, last night. Stainless steel is a no-hoper even if you've had the best wardcrafters and charm cutters in the business do their number on it first.

"I told you I don't need much sleep. I spent the rest of last night going through the files for *anything* about sucker escapees and unusual stakings. There isn't much. And nothing at all like you, Sunshine.

"We ought to put all this in our report, and pass it on up the line, and then you'd get a horde of SOF experts down on you like nothing you've ever imagined, and, speaking of shackles, you'd probably spend the rest of your life chained to the goddess of pain's desk. She'd *love* you.

"But we don't want to. Because we *need* you. We need you in the field. Dear frigging gods and angels, do we ever need you in the field. We need anything we can get because, frankly, we're losing. You didn't know that, did you? At the moment we still got the news nailed shut. But it isn't going to stay nailed shut. Another hundred years, tops, and the suckers are going to be running our show. The Wars were just a distraction. We think we won. Well, maybe we did, but we skegged our future doing it. It blows, but it's the way it is. So little grubby guys like me and Jesse feel we need you in the field a hell of a lot more than we need you disappeared into some study program while they try to figure out how you've done what you've done and how they could make a lot of other people do it too. Which they wouldn't be able to because it's gonna turn out not to work that way. And we guess you don't want to be disappeared either?"

I shook my head on a suddenly stiff neck.

"Yeah. So, anyway, if you can off suckers with common household utensils, we want you out there doing it. We'll even lie to the goddess of pain about you to keep you to ourselves, and babe, that takes balls."

Would they still want me out there doing what I could do if they knew what else I could do? If they knew the truth about the second shackle?

Were the vampires really going to win within the next hundred years?

WHEN WE GOT back to the car it started the first time. There wasn't much conversation. We were most of the way back to town when Pat said, "Hey, Sunshine, talk to us. What are you thinking?"

"I'm trying not to think. I'm—" I stopped. I didn't know if I could say it aloud, even to make my point. "I'm trying not to think about those stains on the walls in the alley, last night."

There was a pause. "I'm sorry," said Jesse. "We do have some idea what we're asking you. Don't let Pat's pleasure in his own rhetoric get to you."

"Hey," said Pat.

"I haven't been your age in a long time," Jesse went on, "and I grew up wanting to join SOF. I knew it was going to be bad, what I was going to be doing, if I stayed a field agent, which I wanted to be. And it is bad, a lot of it, a lot of the time. You get used to it because you have to. And SOF doesn't throw you in like you've been thrown in. Last night was rough even for a grizzled old vet like me.

"Rae, we aren't asking you to make a decision to save the world tomorrow. But please think about what Pat said. Think about the fact that we really, really need you. And think, for what it's worth, that we'll back you up to the last gasp, if you want us there. If last-gasp stuff turns out to be necessary."

"And just by the way, kiddo," said Pat in his mildest voice, "I'm not accusing you of anything, okay? But it must be fifty miles from here back to where you live with that weird siddhartha type. I ain't saying it's not possible, Sunshine, but that's a hell of a hike for anyone, let alone someone who's spent two days chained to a wall expecting to die. I'm thinking your last gasp is pretty worth having."

I stared out the window, thinking about the second shackle.

I GOT THROUGH dessert shift that night on autopilot. Nobody asked me how my afternoon had gone and I didn't volunteer anything.

The atmosphere of Repressed Anxiety was thick enough to cut chunks out of and fry, however. I wondered what you'd have on the side with a plate of Deep Fried Anxiety. Pickles? Cole slaw? Potato-strychnine mash? Things were so fraught that Kenny came into the bakery long enough to say "Hey big sis" and give me a hug. He hadn't called me Big Sis since the time he was eight and I was eighteen and I'd caught him spying on my then-boyfriend Raoul and me and he went around the house yelling Big Sissy Kissy Kissy and I sent Raoul home and went into my brothers' room and destroyed the backup discs to every one of their combox games that I could find. Which was a lot. You might think this was overreacting (Mom, Charlie, and Billy did), but I was lucky he'd only caught us kissing, and I wanted to be sure I'd been discouraging enough about this sort of fraternal behavior. Anyway neither Kenny nor Billy spoke to me at all for about six months, by which time I'd graduated, the Big Sis era was over, and shortly after that I'd moved into my own apartment.

Mary took her break in the bakery again, and told me the latest Mr. Cagney story, but her heart wasn't in it.

"I'm okay," I said. "Really."

"I know you are," she said, but she hugged me anyway, and got streaks of flour and cinnamon all down her front.

I was due to stay till closing but they packed me off an hour early. I didn't argue. I fetched the Wreck and drove home slowly. I was so tired—bone tired, marrow tired, what comes after that? Life tired? That's the kind of tired I was. It wasn't just lack of sleep tired, though I did have a few fuzzy cobwebs at the corners of my vision.

I could hear some of Mom's charms moving around in the glove compartment. Once a charm has been given someone's name, if that someone doesn't snap it and let it go live, it may pop itself, and try to come after you. When I opened the glove compartment to put a new one in now, half a dozen of the old ones tried to climb up my arm. They were probably all totally cracked from driving around in a car though.

It had been dark for two hours. The moon was rising. I thought about trying to talk Charlie into keeping the coffeehouse open twenty-four hours, drive those inferior Prime Time brownies right out of town. Then I could never leave the coffeehouse again, for the rest of my life. Pat and Jesse would be disappointed, of course, and we'd have to gear hard after the insomniac market, to keep the customer flow up, all night long, since you can't ward a restaurant. But these were mere practical problems. The thing that really bothered me was that I'd have to tell everyone why.

That there was a vampire—a master vampire, and his gang— after me. Specifically the ones I'd got away from two months ago, and it turns out suckers are poor losers. And persistent bastards.

That maybe I was the first bad-magic wuss in history. The lab-coat brigade would probably want to do exhaustive research on my mother's child-rearing techniques as well as on my blood chemistry. Academic prunes would write papers. If they knew.

If I lost it and they found out.

There was a light on in Yolande's part of the house, spilling across the porch and toward the drive. I still went up my own stairs in the dark; there was a hall light, but electric light in that narrow windowless way made me feel claustrophobic. When I got upstairs, and bolted the door behind me, I still didn't turn the light on. I had another cup of chamomile tea on the dark balcony. Moonlight was beginning to glimmer through the trees at the edge of the garden. And I turned off thinking. I sat there, listening to the almost-silence. There were tiny rustling noises, the hoot of an owl, the soft stirring of the wind through leaves. External leaves. Internal leaves.

A tree? It shouldn't be a tree. My immaterial mentor should be one of those things in one of my brothers' combox games that you zapped on sight, all teeth and turpitude.

And nothing at all like you, Sunshine . . . we need *you.*

I was so tired. At least tonight I had the option to go to bed early. I put my cup in the sink, put my nightgown on. Like last night, I was out as soon as I lay down.

BUT I WOKE again only a few hours later, knowing he was there. I lay curled up, facing the wall; the window, and the rest of the room, were behind me. I didn't hear him, of course. But I knew he was there.

I turned over. There was a bright rectangle of moonlight on the floor, and a dark shape sitting motionless in the chair beyond it. He raised his head a little, in acknowledgment, I think, of my waking. He'd been watching me.

I thought about being in the same room with a vampire. I thought about the fact that he'd come in, however he'd come in, through some charmed and warded door (or window). I thought about the fact that I had, of course, invited him in, when he had brought me home, two months ago. I hadn't thought about inviting him in, but I'd been beyond that kind of thinking then anyway, and he'd been doing me the small service of saving my life at the time. I shouldn't now object to the idea that once I'd invited him over my threshold the welcome was, apparently, permanent.

You can kind of feel the barrier your wards are making for you, feel if there are any big drafts flowing through any big holes. There weren't any drafts. None of my wards were reacting to his presence.

I assumed the invitation was particular to him. That I hadn't thrown the way open for vampires in general. Not a nice thought.

Maybe I'd invited him over my threshold a second time when I stood on the edge of the darkness two nights ago and said, *What do I do now?*

There were things I'd forgotten. I'd forgotten the *wrongness*. What was new was the fact that, despite my heart doing its fight-or-flight, help-we're-prey-and-HEY-STUPID-THAT'S-A-VAMPIRE number, I was glad to see him. Ridiculous but true. Scary but true.

The one person—creature—whatever of my acquaintance who wouldn't be in any danger if I snapped. Even a criminally deranged almost-human berserker is no match for a vampire.

The one whatever of my acquaintance who probably would still make me look virtuous and morally upstanding if I did snap.

I didn't find this very comforting.

"You came," I said.

"I was here last night," he said. "But you slept deeply, and I did not wish to disturb you."

I'd also forgotten how uncanny his voice was. Sinister. Not human.

"That was nice of you," I said, listening to myself and thinking *you pathetic numbskull.* "I had three hours of sleep last night and it—it's been a long couple of days."

"Yes," he said.

Silence fell. Some things hadn't changed.

"Bo is looking for me," I said at last.

"Yes," he said.

"I'm sorry," I said humbly, "I don't know what to do. I . . . I . . . All I did was drive out to the lake, that night, and everything else . . . I'm sorry," I said again, a little wildly, and only too aware of the irony: "I don't want to *die*, you know?"

"Yes," he said again.

This time I heard the pause as one of those "you're not going to like this" pauses.

"Bo is looking for me too," he said. "When he finds me, he will be careful to destroy me. Last time was theatrics. This time he will take no chances."

Well, that was the most cheering news I'd heard all week. Even better than ghastly revelations about the possible truth of my genetic composition. No one really understands genetics any more than anyone really understands world economics, and what I'd been guessing might not be true. I could just *worry* about it for the rest of my life. If I was going to *have* a rest of my life. As guaranteed bad news, vampires are a much surer bet. Great. Spartan. Let's have a party. "Oh," I said carefully.

I looked into what was probably a short, bleak future, and realized that one of the reasons I'd been glad to see that dark shape in the chair was that with him here, for the first time since I'd come home after those nights at the lake I'd felt maybe . . . not totally clueless and overwhelmed. Yes, he'd been the one shackled to the ballroom wall with me, but they'd been *afraid* of him. Twelve against one, and him chained to the wall, and they were afraid. The fact that they'd caught him could have been some kind of trick. It happened. Presumably among vampires too.

And now he was saying that he was out of his depth too. That it *was* hopeless. I wanted some nice human equivocation and denial. No, no, it'll be all right! The table knife was an ugly accident! And by the way you're not going to morph into an axe murderer!

Rescuing the odd vampire from destruction had already fulfilled my bad-gene quota of antisocial behavior. Please.

"Why does he hate you so much?" I said.

The silence went on for a while, but I could wait. What else was there to do? Walk outside and shout, "Here I am"? I might be due for a short, squalid future, but as a basic principle I was going to hold on to what there was of it.

He hadn't refused to answer yet.

"It's a long story," he said at last. "We are nearly the same age. There are different ways of being what we are. Mine is one way. His is another. Mine, it turns out, has certain advantages. If others perhaps thought the implications through, some things might be different. Bo does not wish anyone to think those implications through. Destroying me is a way to erase the evidence. Plus that he does not care for me to have advantages no longer available to him."

This was interesting, and under other circumstances would have made me curious. Constantine couldn't be very old—by vampire standards—only young vampires can go out in strong moonlight, like tonight. Middle-aged ones can go out when the moon is young or old enough. Later middle-aged ones can only go outdoors when there is no moon. Really old ones can't be outdoors under the open sky at all, with any possibility of the dimmest reflected sunlight touching them. That was one of the reasons older ones began running gangs.

If they survived to be old they'd also developed other powers.

"He has another urgent reason, now. If he does not destroy me, he will lose control of his gang. Bo likes ruling. It is also necessary to him that he rule—to do with those advantages I possess and he does not. And while as the leader of his gang he is much more powerful than I am, alone, I am the stronger."

"And you don't run a gang," I said.

"No."

I thought of saying, So, what now, do we hold hands and jump? How long a fall can a vampire walk away from? How high do we have to climb first? A mere almost-human pretty reliably goes splat after about four stories, I think. I was beginning to feel sorry that he'd come. No. I'd rather jump out a window and get it over with fast than fall into Bo's clutches again. I was merely resisting the idea that jumping was my best choice.

"I have thought of it a good deal, these last weeks," he was saying, "for I knew what happened at the lake would not be the end. Not with Bo. I also know that singly you and I have no chance."

I do wish you'd stop saying that, I thought.

"But together," he continued, "we may have a chance. It is not a good chance, but it is a chance. I do not like it. You cannot like it. I do not understand what it is that you do, and have done. I am not sure we will be able to work together, even if we attempt it. Even if we are each other's only chance." He was sitting in the darkness beyond the moonlight, and I could not see his face. I could—a little—see movement as he spoke; vampires also speak by moving their mouths. But this conversation was a little too like talking to a figment of your own imagination. Your darkest, spookiest, most bottom-of-your-unconscious-where-the-monsters-lurk imagination. Even the shadow in the chair was half-imaginary.

No it wasn't. There's really no mistaking the presence of a vampire in the room.

"Will you help me?" he said. It is very peculiar being asked a life-or-death question in a tone of voice that has no *tone* in it. Emotionally speaking the response feels like it ought to be something like passing the salt or closing the door.

"Oh," I said intelligently. "Ah—er. Well. Yes. Certainly. Since you put it so persuasively."

There was a pause, and then there was a brief noise that, mercifully also briefly, unhinged my spine. He had laughed.

"Forgive my persuasiveness," he said. "I would spare you if I could. I do not wish this any more than you do."

"No," I said thoughtfully. "I don't suppose you do." If I'd been honest I suppose what I'd really wanted him to do was say, "Oh don't worry about it. This is vampire business and I'll take care of it." Dream on. "So," I said. I didn't want to know, but I guessed I should make an effort. "What do we do now?"

"We start," he said, and paused. I recognized this as the middle of an unfinished sentence, and not one of his cryptic pronouncements, and waited. Then there was a funny breathing noise that I translated provisionally as a sigh. Vampires don't breathe right, why should they sigh right? But maybe it means vampires can feel frustration. Noted. "We start by my trying to discover what assistance I can give you."

Somehow this didn't sound like the usual movie-adventure sort of "I'll keep you covered while you reload" assistance. "What do you mean?"

"We must face Bo at night. Your abilities would not get us past the guards that protect his days."

I didn't even consider asking what those guards might be.

"Humans are at great disadvantage at night. I think I may be able to grant you certain dispensations."

Dispensations. I liked that. Vampire as fairy godmother. Or godfather. Pity he couldn't dispense me from getting killed. "You mean like being able to see in the dark or something."

"Yes. I mean exactly that."

"Oh." If I could see in the dark I would never again have to trip over the threshold of the bathroom door on the way to have a pee at midnight. If I lived long enough to need to.

"I will have to touch you," he said.

Okay, I told myself. He's not going to forget himself and eat me because he comes a few feet closer. I thought of the second night in the ballroom: *Sit a little distance from the corner—yes, nearer me. Remember that three feet more or less makes no difference to me: you might as well.*

And he'd carried me something like forty-five miles. And only about the first forty-two of them had been in daylight.

And somehow pointing out that I now was in bed and wearing nothing but a nightgown and would like to get up and put some clothes on first, please, was worse than not mentioning my inappropriate-for-receiving-visitors state of undress. So I didn't mention it.

"Okay," I said.

That fluid, inhuman motion again as he stood up and stepped toward me. I'd forgotten that too—forgotten how strange it is. How ominous. Too fluid for anything human. For anything alive.

He sat down near me on the bed. The bed dipped, as if from ordinary human weight. I pulled my feet up and turned toward him, but I did it carelessly, more conscious of him than of anything else—which is to say, more carelessly than I had learned to move over the last two months, carelessly so that the gash on my breast didn't just seep a little, but cracked open along its full length, as if it were being cut into me for the first time. I couldn't help it: it hurt: I gave a little gasp.

And he *hissed*. It was a terrifying noise, and I had slammed myself back into the pillows and headboard before I had a chance to think anything at all, to think that I couldn't get away from him even if I wanted to, to think that he had declared us allies. To think that there might be any other reason for a sound like that one but that he was a vampire and I was alive and streaming with fresh blood.

"Stop," he said in what passed for his normal voice. "I offer you no harm. Tell me about the blood on your breast."

He didn't linger on the word "blood." I muttered, "It won't heal. It's been like this for two months."

He wasn't as good at waiting as I was. "Go on," he said immediately.

I'd stopped shrugging in the last two months too: you can't shrug without pulling at the skin below your collarbones. "I don't know. It doesn't heal. It seems to close over and then splits again. The doctor put stitches in it a couple of times, gave me stuff to put on it. Nothing works. It just splits open again. It's a nuisance but I have been kind of learning to live with it. Like I had a choice. This is—er—worse than usual. Sorry. It's only a shallow gash. You may—er—remember."

"I remember," he said. "Show me."

I managed not to say, *What?* It took me a minute to gather my dignity as well as my courage, and my hands were shaking a little when I raised them to unbutton the top two buttons of my night-gown, and peel the edges back so he could see the bony space below my collarbones and above the swell of my bosom, where the blood now ran down in a thin ragged curtain from the wicked curved mouth of the long ugly slash. I barely flinched when he reached out a hand and touched the blood with his finger and . . . tasted it. Then I closed my eyes.

"I offer you no harm," he said again, gently. "Sunshine. Open your eyes."

I opened them.

"The wound is poisoned," he said. "It weakens you. It is very dangerous."

"It was for you," I said, dreamily. I felt like one of those oracle priestesses out of some old myth: seized by some spirit not her own, a spirit that then speaks from her mouth. "They wanted to poison you."

"Yes," he said.

I thought, I have been so tired, these last two months. I have got used to that too. I have told myself it is just part of—having had what happened, happen. You do not get over something like that quickly. I had told myself that was all it was. I had almost believed it. I *had* believed it. The cut didn't heal because it didn't heal.

Poisoned. Weakening me. Killing me is what he meant. Note that vampires can also be tactful.

All those hours in the sunlight, baking the thing, the hostile presence on my body. I'd known it was hostile, although I hadn't admitted it. I hadn't taken the next step of thinking "poisoned." Sunlight was my element; and so I turned to sunlight. And sunlight was the only thing that did any good, and it didn't do enough. Because the wound was poisoned. That was out of some story where there would be an oracle priestess somewhere: the poisoned wound that did not heal. I'd already been wondering how I was going to get through the winter, when I couldn't lie outdoors and bake some hours every week. Been learning not to think about wondering how I was going to get through the winter.

He was silent, waiting for me to finish thinking. I looked at him: glint of green eyes in the moonlight. Don't look in their eyes, I thought. Tiredly.

This would have been a nasty shock to him too, of course. Finding out his ally is a goner.

I was too tired to look at him. I was too tired for almost anything. Sometimes it is better not to know. Sometimes when you do know you just fold up.

"Sunshine. I know a little about poisons. This is not something your human doctors can distill an antidote for."

This was even better than his repeating that neither of us had any chance against Bo. By dying I was going to ruin his chances too. It's funny: I was actually sorry about this. Maybe I was a little delirious. Maybe too much had been happening lately. Maybe I was just very, very short of sleep.

"There is something that can be done. Can be tried." Pause. "It is not easy."

Oh, big surprise. Something wasn't going to be easy. I tried to rouse myself, to react. I failed.

"But can you trust me?"

More happy news. Not just *something* to be done, but a *vampire* something. Which doubtless meant it would have more blood in it. I don't *like* blood. I mean, I like it fine, inside, circulating, carrying oxygen and calories to all your stay-at-home cells, but slimy seeping pink *hamburger* gives me the whim-whams.

Can you trust me, he said. Not *will* you. *Can* you. Good question. I thought about it. It will not be easy. Yes, okay, that was a given. I didn't have to think about that. Can I trust him?

What have I got to lose?

What if his something is something I can't bear? There are all sorts of things I can't bear. I'm not brave to begin with, I'm very, very tired, I'm spongy with post-traumatic what have you, and I very nearly can't bear what I did last night with a table knife. And I may be a homicidal maniac.

"Yes," I said. "Yes. I think so."

He didn't exhale a long breath, as a human might have done, but he went motionless instead. It was a different kind of motionlessness than not moving. Having said yes I felt better. Less tired. Evidently still delirious, however, because I bent toward him, touched the back of his hand. "Okay?" I said.

A little silence.

"Okay," he said. I had the sudden irreverent notion that he'd never said "okay" before. Spend time with humans and have all kinds of unusual experiences. Laughter. Slang.

"It will not be tomorrow night," he said. "Perhaps the night after."

"Okay," I said. "See you."

"Sleep well," he said.

"Oh, sure, absolutely," I said, trying for irony, but he was already gone.

I left the window full open. I wanted as much of the fresh night air in the room with me as possible. There was a tiny chiming from one of the window charms. It was a curiously serene and hopeful noise.

I MUST HAVE looked pretty rough that morning too. It occurred to me that everybody at the coffeehouse was treating me like an invalid while trying to pretend they weren't treating me like an invalid. I wanted to tell them that they were right, I was an invalid, that mark on my breast that only Mel knew was still there was poisoned, and I was dying. I didn't say any of this. I said I was still short of sleep.

Paulie turned up an hour before time that morning saying he didn't have anything better to do, but I was pretty sure Mom had called him and asked if he could come in early. I think Mom had figured out that the charms she was giving me were going somewhere like into the Wreck's glove compartment, so she had begun stashing them around the bakery where maybe I wouldn't find them but they could still do me some good. Since my unwelcome speculations about dark family secrets the other night in Jesse's office I had begun to wonder what all Mom's charms were for, exactly. She's always been something of a charm freak; I'd put it down to eight years in my dad's world. I found two new ones that morning: a little curled-up animal of some sort with its paws over its eyes and a red bead where its navel should have been, and a shiny white disc that rainbows ran across if you held it up against the light. I left them where I found them. Maybe I should let them try to defend against whatever they could. I had some fellow-feeling for the small curled-up creature with its hands over its face, even if the red alien parasite was lower down on it than it was on me. Charms are often noisy, which is another reason I don't like them much, but you aren't going to hear extraneous buzzing and burbling above the general din at Charlie's. Especially on shifts when I had to spend some time in the company of a genially humming apprentice.

Mel was working that afternoon but Aimil had the day off from the library. She wandered back into the bakery with a cup of coffee toward the end of my stint, said she'd just found out about an old-books-and-junk sale in Redtree, which was one of the little towns between us and the next big city to the south, she was going to go, and did I want to come along? I should probably have gone home and taken a nap, but I didn't want to. So I said yes. A nice little outing for the doomed. Furthermore Aimil talked about library politics the whole way there and didn't once mention nocturnal neighborhood excitements. So by the time we arrived at the village square in Redtree I was in the mood.

Ordinarily I love this kind of thing without any effort. Someone who does coffeehouse baking for a living doesn't have huge amounts of disposable income, but the point about books-and-junk sales is that you never know what you may find for hilariously cheap. There are fewer people since the Wars than there had been before, and less money (don't ask me how this works: you'd think if there were fewer people there would be more money to go around), so there is a lot less motive for dealers to discover specialist markets for old, beat-up, weird, or obscure-looking and possibly Other-related stuff. Plus a lot of people don't want to think about old, beat-up, weird, obscure-looking, and possibly Other-related stuff because it reminds them of the Wars, or what life had been like before the Wars, i.e., better. The result is that a lot of very interesting nonjunk gets heaved into the nearest box for the next garage sale.

Furthermore, almost nobody wants to read the gormless old fiction about the Others which is my fave. I picked up a copy of *Sordid Enchantments* on the title alone, and the fourth, and most icky and rare, volume of the *Dark Blood* series, which I was no longer sure I wanted to read—the heroine has a choice to die horribly or become a vampire horribly, and she chooses to die. If I'd realized how *gross* it was going to get after the first volume I wouldn't have bothered—but I'm a completist, I had the first three, and hey.

I was feeling pretty good. In spite of last night. Or in an even funnier way, because of it. It was like I had two days out of time. Everything was on hold until . . . either the vampire-something worked, or it didn't. Jesse and Theo had been at a table under the awning when Aimil and I left Charlie's, and I'd nodded and kept going. I hoped nothing had come up they wanted to talk to me about. Nothing was allowed to come up for the next two days. I was on vacation in my own mind, cinnamon rolls at four A.M. or not.

It must have been Paulie's influence, but I was positively humming a tune—an old folk song about keeping a vampire talking till sunrise: not one of your brighter vampires—while I burrowed through a big sagging cardboard box of junk. Chipped china teacups. Dented tin trays. Small splintery wooden boxes with lids that no longer closed. A bottle opener shaped like a dragon with an extremely undershot lower jaw and pink glass eyes. *Pink.* The Dragon Anti-Defamation Society should hear about this.

At the bottom, when I touched it, it fizzled right through me, like I'd put my arm in a cappuccino machine. I knew it had to be some kind of ward—nonwarding charms are kind of *stickier*—but a live ward shouldn't be in the bottom of a box of cheap junk at a garage sale. Maybe it had fallen out of one of the splintery boxes. I hesitated, then picked it up to get a better look. Gingerly. It had now got my attention, so presumably it wouldn't feel the need to scramble my arm like an egg again.

I didn't recognize the style or the design. It was an oval, not quite the length of the palm of my hand, with a slightly raised edge, the whole of it thick and heavy, like an old coin, before the mints got mean and started stamping out pennies that sometimes bent if you dropped them edgewise on a hard floor. It was silver, I thought, or plate; it was so tarnished I couldn't make out clearly what was on it, except that something was. Three somethings: one each on top, middle, and bottom, rather like an old Egyptian glyph. The only thing I could say for sure was that they weren't any of the standard Other-preventive sigils I knew of, nor the all-purpose circle-star-and-cross one.

The most interesting thing was that it was live. Very live. Wards aren't necessarily as master-specific as most charms, and if they aren't actively in use they can molder quietly for a long time and still be capable of being wakened and doing some warding; but even one that's been tuned to you specifically shouldn't leap avidly out at you and wag its tail like a dog wanting to go for a walk.

I could have put it back. I could have taken it to someone in charge and said "You've made a mistake. This one still works." But I didn't. It seemed to like lying there in my hand. Don't be ridiculous, I thought. It's not responding to me personally.

As a soldier in the dented-tin-tray army they shouldn't be expecting real money for it, but that could only be because they hadn't noticed it was live. It was still worth a try. I took the two books and the tarnished ward to the suspicious-looking character at the card table with the rusty money box, who snatched them out of my hands as if he knew I was trying something on. But he was so preoccupied with whether or not he should sell me *Altar of Darkness* (in which it takes the heroine four hundred pages to die), which was certainly worth more than the seventeen blinks for two, which is what the sign on the drooping book table said, that he barely registered my little glyph. I'd done piously outraged innocence when he started haranguing me about *Altar* and a few of his other customers scowled at him and muttered about fairness. I won that round. So when he looked at the glyph and said "fifty blinks" I sniffed so he would know that I knew he was a brigand and a bandit, and let it pass. He knew more about

books. Even a dead ward made out of silver plate was worth more. A
blink is a dollar, and has been since after the Wars, when our economy went to pieces, and the average paycheck disappeared in the
blink of an eye.

What was more interesting was that he'd touched the glyph and
hadn't said "Wow! That was like putting my hand in a cappuccino
machine!"

Aimil had been watching my performance with a straight face.
"Well done," she said, when we got back to the car. "*Dark Blood Four*
as two for seventeen blinks! Zora will be mad with jealousy. Now
what is that little thing?" I was balancing my glyph on the top of the
books, and I watched as she picked it up. That Mr. Rusty Money Box
hadn't registered anything was one thing; if Aimil didn't register either it was something else.

She didn't say anything about a feeling like having her funny
bone hit with a hammer. "Hmm. It's quite—appealing, isn't it? Even
all blackened like this."

"Appealing"? Maybe it had decided that making people's hair
stand on end wasn't such a good way of making friends and influenc-
ing people. "Can you figure out any of what's on it?"

She frowned, turning it this way and that in the light. "No clue.
Maybe after you get it polished."

Dessert shift that night was notable only for the number of people
who wanted cherry tarts. They were catching on. Rats. I didn't really like little electrical gadgets—most of the other so-called home
bakeries in town used kneading *machines*, for example, which I thought
beneath contempt—but there was no way I was going to be making
cherry tarts without one. I'd already said I would only make individual tarts and customers had to order them with the main course
to give me enough lead time. And they were *still* catching on. I didn't
want cherry tarts to turn into another Death of Marat. When I was
first installed in my new bakery and messing around with the heady
implications of Charlie's having built it for *me*, I'd been having fun

with puddings that look like one thing and you stick a fork in them and they become something else. A Gothic sensibility in the bakery is not necessarily a good thing. I'd made this light fluffy-looking number in a white oval dish with high sides and presented the first one with a flourish to a group of regulars who had volunteered to be experimented on. Aimil was the one with the knife, and she stuck it in and the raspberry-and-black-currant filling had exploded down the side and over the edge of the dish onto the counter. It was, I admit, a trifle dramatic. "Gods, Sunshine, what is this, the Death of Marat?" she said. Aimil reads too much. Everybody at Charlie's that night wanted a taste, and the Death of Marat, the first of Sunshine's soon-to-be-notorious, implausibly named epic creations, was born, although I think most of our clientele thought Marat was some kind of master vampire. (Aimil is good at names. She's responsible for Tweedle Dumplings and Glutton's Grail and Buttermost Limit too.) The problem is that for months after I was getting constant requests for the damn thing, and light, fluffy puddings with heavy fillings are a brute to make. Our long-time regulars still ask for it occasionally, but I'm older and meaner now and say "no" better. I will make it if I like you enough. Maybe.

Well, the cherry season doesn't last long around here; I'd be back to apple pie before Billy'd had time to miss doing the peeling. (Unless I found some other source of cheap child labor I might have to get an electric *peeler* in another year.) It was true that Charlie's did almost everything from scratch and that anything that one of us wasn't good at didn't get done at all, but it was also true that our loyal customers were compelled to be biddable. If I decided I didn't feel like doing cherry tarts outside of fresh cherry season they could like it or eat at Fast Burgers 'R' Us.

When I got home I fished last night's sheets and nightgown out of the tub where they'd been soaking the bloodstains out (just like the Death of Marat without Marat), hauled them downstairs, and stuffed them in the washing machine. If Yolande had noticed the amount of laundry I'd been doing in the last two months she never said anything.

I put *Altar* and *Sordid Enchantments* on one of the hip-high piles of books to read next in the corner of the living room, and got out the silver polish. Not standard equipment in my household: I'd bought some before I came home. The glyph came up beautifully. Except I still couldn't make out the figures.

It was weirdly heavy for plate. And doesn't plate tend to look platy when you've shined it up? Maybe I only knew cheap plate. Even so.

The symbol at the top was round, with snaky and spiky lines woven through it. The symbol at the bottom was narrow at the base and fat at the top. The one in the middle . . . might conceivably have four legs, which would presumably make it some kind of animal. Right. Two squiggles and an unknown animal.

The top squiggle *could* be a symbol for the sun. The bottom squiggle *could* be a symbol for a tree.

And if it was solid silver—even if the round squiggle wasn't the sun and the fat-on-the-top squiggle wasn't a tree—it was still a shoo-in as an anti-Other ward. None of the Others liked silver.

Whatever it was, looking at it made my spirits lift. For someone under two death threats—plus, I suppose, the incompatible threats of Pat and Jesse's idea of what my future should include, supposing I had a future, because, if I did, I would spend it incarcerated in a small padded room—this was good enough. I put it in the drawer in the little table next to my bed. I slept that night, you should forgive the term, the sleep of the dead.

So WHEN THE alarm went off I was almost ready to get up. The prospect of the night to come started to creep up on me almost immediately, but there were distractions: Mr. Cagney complained that his roll didn't have enough cinnamon filling at seven A.M., Paulie called at seven-fifteen with a head cold, and Kenny dropped a tray of dirty plates at seven-thirty. He'd been doing better since Mel'd had his word, but he'd decided he'd rather do the early hours than the late ones, and this was only going to work if he got home sooner to do his homework sooner to get to bed sooner. Not my problem. Except in terms of Liz spending time helping to clean the floor instead of unloading cookie trays and muffin tins for me.

Pat came in about midmorning and penetrated my floury lair. "Thought you'd like to know—the girl from the other night. She's come round. She doesn't remember a thing from the time the sucker spoke to her to waking up in the hospital the next morning. She doesn't remember the guy *was* a sucker. And she's fine. A little spooked, but fine." Translation: the only on-the-spot witness doesn't remember what she saw, or at least isn't saying anything. And Jesse and Theo, who were claiming the strike for SOF (you don't *kill* vampires, of course, although most of us civvies use the term; in SOF-speak you *strike* them), were there only seconds after me and before anyone else. Except maybe Mrs. Bialosky.

But it was one of those days when the coffeehouse schedule breaks down, and Charlie and Mel and Mom and I held the pieces together with our teeth. We always have at least one of these days during a seven-day (or thirteen-day, depending on how you're counting) week. Not to mention the prospect of getting up at three-forty-five on Thursday. During a thirteen-day week. My sense of occult oppression tightened anyway, but it had its work cut out for it. I had forty-five minutes off from ten-forty-five to eleven-thirty, between the usual morning baking and the beginning of the lunch rush, and almost an hour off at three-thirty, while a skeleton staff got us through the late-afternoon muffin and scone crowd, before the more gradual dinner swell began—plus two or three tea with elective aspirin breaks. I went home at nine. Anyone who wanted dessert after that could have ginger pound cake or Indian pudding or Chocoholia. It wasn't a night for individual fruit tarts.

Fortunately I was tired enough to sleep. Before I'd found out I was going to be working all day I had thought I wouldn't sleep at all; by the time I got home I knew I'd sleep, but assumed I'd get a couple of hours and be awake by midnight, waiting for something to happen.

I'd spent some time considering what I should, you know, wear. This vampire in the bedroom thing was a trifle more intensively

perturbing than this vampire around at all thing. Even if the discon-
certingness was only happening in my mind. There was a corollary
to the story about male suckers being able to keep it up indefinitely:
that you had to, er, invite them over that threshold first too. But if
they could seduce you into *dying* just by looking at you, then they
could probably perform other seductions as well. Okay, this particular vampire had declined to seduce me to death when he could have.
This was a good omen as far as it went.

I reminded myself that the sound of his laughter made me want
to throw up, and that in sunlight he looked . . . well, dead. Let's get
real here. I couldn't possibly be *interested* in . . .

I involuntarily remembered that sense of *vampire in the room*. It
wasn't like the pheromone haze when your eyes lock with someone
else's across a room, crowded or otherwise, and *wham*. It really was
not at all like that. But it was more like that than anything else I could
think of. It probably had something to do with the peak-experience
business: with a vampire in the room you are sitting there expecting
to die. Sex and death, right? Peak experiences. And since I didn't go in
for any of the standard neck-risking pastimes I didn't have a lot of
practical knowledge of the hormone rush you get when you may be
about to snuff it. Perhaps someone who loved free-fall parachuting or
shark wrestling would find vampires in the room less troubling.

Never mind. Let's leave it that vampires infesting your private
spaces are daunting, and one of the ways to stiffen—er—boost morale is to wear carefully-selected-for-the-occasion morale-boosting
clothing.

I went to bed wearing my oldest, most faded flannel shirt, the bra
that had looked all right in the catalog but was obviously an escapee
from a downmarket nursing home when it arrived, white cotton pan-
ties that had had pansies on them about seven hundred washings ago
and were now a kind of mottled gray, and the jeans I usually wore for
housecleaning or raking Yolande's garden because they were too
shabby for work even if I never came out of the bakery. Food inspector arrest-on-sight jeans. Oh, and fuzzy green plaid socks. It was a
cool night for summer. Relatively. I lay down on top of the bedspread.

And slept through till the alarm at three-forty-five. He hadn't come.

THAT WAS NOT one of my better days at work. I snarled at everyone who spoke to me, and snarled worse when no one snarled back. Mel, who would have, wasn't there. Mom, fortunately, didn't have time to get into a furious argument with me, so we shot a few salvos over each other's bows, and retired to our separate harbors.

We did try to stay out of each other's way but it wasn't like Mom to avoid a good blazing row with her daughter when one was *offered*. What had she been guessing while I'd been doing my guessing? There was quite a lot in the literature of bad crosses about petty, last-straw exasperations that tipped the balance. I'd been checking globenet archives when I could have been reading *Sordid Enchantments*.

"I'm not a goddam invalid!" I howled at Charlie. "I don't need to be treated with gloves and—and bedpans! Will you please tell me I'm being a miserable bitch and you'd like to upend a garbage bin over my head!"

There was a pause. "Well, the idea had crossed my mind," said Charlie.

I stood there, buttery fists clenched, breathing hard. "Thank you," I said.

"Anything you want to talk about?" Charlie said in his best off-hand manner.

I thought about it. Charlie ambled over and closed the bakery door. Doors don't get closed much at the coffeehouse, so when one is, you'd better not open it for anything less than a coachload of tourists who didn't book ahead, have forty-five minutes for lunch before they meet their guide at the Other Museum, which is a fifteen-minute coach ride away (it's only seven minutes on foot, but try to convince a coach-load of tourists of that), they all want burgers and fries and won't look at the menu, we're not heavily into burgers so our grill is kind of small, and we don't do fries at all, except on special, when they're not what burger eaters would call fries anyway.

This really happened once, and by the time Mom got through with that tour company the president was on his knees, offering her conciliatory free luxury cruises for two in the Caribbean, or at least all future meal bookings of his tour groups when they came to New Arcadia, made *well* in advance. She accepted the latter, and the Earth Trek Touring Company (the president's name is Benjamin Sisko, but I bet that wasn't the one he was born with, and you should *see* the logo on their coaches) was now one of our best customers. We could almost retire on what they brought us in August. And we taught his regular tour leaders how to find the Other Museum on foot. This made the coach drivers love us too.

This is not what the city council had in mind when they were drooling over the prospect of seeing New Arcadia on the new post-Wars map, but the Other Museum is why coachloads of the kind of tourists who sign up with a company called Earth Trek now come to New Arcadia. The public exhibits are still lowest common denominator, but there are more of them than there used to be, and the Ghoul Attack simulation is supposed to be especially good: yuck-*o*, I say. We do also have a few more prune-faced academics on teeny stipends renting rooms in Old Town, but it's nowhere as bad as I'd feared. The proles win again. Ha.

Charlie ambled back from closing the door and sat on the stool in the corner. It wasn't so hot a day that we were going to die of being in the bakery with the ovens on and the door closed for at least ten minutes.

"Because of the other night," I said, "the SOF guys want me to be a kind of—unofficial SOF guy."

Charlie said carefully, "I didn't think a table knife was . . . usual."

I sighed. "What did you think, when you followed me out there that night? Just that I'd lost my mind?"

Charlie considered this before he answered. "I thought something had snapped, yes. I didn't think it was your mind. . . . But I didn't have much time to think. By the time I got there it was all over. And I guess I realized then that I'd, we'd, had the wrong end of the . . . table knife all along."

"Since I disappeared for a couple of days."

"Yeah. It had to be the Others, one way or another. Sorry. It just . . . the way you were . . . you didn't want to talk to any cops, but you *really* didn't want to talk to SOF."

I hadn't thought it was that noticeable.

"You were okay with the rest of us at Charlie's, us humans, not just *us*, strangers too. Nervy—like something really bad had happened, which we already knew—but okay. Anyone, you know, pretty human."

Except TV reporters. If they were human.

"It wasn't Weres, because you were here on full-moon nights like usual, after. And they don't usually go around biting people except *at* the full moon."

And however fidgety and whimsical I'd felt, I wouldn't have driven out to the lake alone on a full-moon night. There *are* some Weres out there. Just like there are a few Weres in Old Town. More than few. It doesn't hurt to be nice to them; they'll remember that you were, the other twenty-nine days of the month. Unlike suckers, who tend to prefer the urban scene, the Weres you really want to avoid mostly hang out in the wilderness.

"And—sorry—since you didn't have any visible pieces missing it couldn't be zombies or ghouls."

I was the Other expert at Charlie's. Most of the staff didn't want to know, like most of the human population didn't want to know, and our SOFs were just customers who wore too much khaki. Mel said stories about the Others made his tattoos restless.

"Sadie and I thought it must be some kind of demon. Sadie . . . well, Sadie talked to a couple of those specialist shrinks you wouldn't talk to, and they said this stuff can be as traumatic as it gets, and to leave you alone about it if you didn't want to talk."

I wished that was the only reason for the charms and the uncharacteristic reserve. Maybe it was. Or maybe I could *make* it be all. I was my mother's daughter, after all. Maybe I had hidden depths of Attila the Hun-ness. I said cautiously, "Did she tell them about my dad?"

Charlie shook his head. "I'd nearly forgotten about your dad myself, till the other night. It had never seriously occurred to me that what happened to you had anything to do with vampires. Uh—people don't get away from vampires. Any more than people get rid of vampires with table knives."

Even Charlie knew that much. "Yeah. That's what the SOFs say too."

Charlie was silent a minute. I was thinking, if Charlie had forgotten about my dad then he must not be a part of the Bad Cross Watch. My mother had never told him about Great-Great-Aunt Margaret, who had a limp because her left foot was short, horny, and cloven. Or whoever Great-Aunt Margaret had been and whatever demon mark they'd had. I mean Mom was keeping her fears to herself. I told you she was brave: she'd let her parents cut her off to marry my dad, she'd taken on the Blaises singlehanded when she left him. Any sensible woman who was not Attila the Hun in a previous existence would have been more than justified in leaving me behind for my dad's family to cope with. And they would have: if I had gone bad they might have denied I was theirs, but they'd have *coped*. And if I *had* gone bad, they'd've *wanted* to be there, performing damage control, for their sake if not mine. So she'd been doubly brave, or foolhardy. And there may not have been very many Blaises left before the Wars but they were *formidable*.

Some demons are *very* tough. Tougher than any human. Although the tough ones also tend to be the stupid ones.

Charlie said: "What do you want to do?"

"Go on making cinnamon rolls," I said instantly.

Charlie smiled faintly. "That's what I want to hear, of course—"

"*Is* it?" I said. "Do you want someone so—so obviously—not just some kind of freak magic handler but someone who—someone who—I mean with *vampires*—do you want someone like this—like me—making your cinnamon rolls?"

"Yes," said Charlie. "Yes. You make the best cinnamon rolls, probably in the history of the world. Never mind all the rest of it. We pay taxes for SOF to take care of the Others. We need *you* here. If you want to be here. I don't care who your dad is. Or what else you can do with a table knife."

I looked at him. He'd have every right to fire my ass—humans don't like weird magic handlers on the cooking staff of their restaurants. But I was a member of this family, this clan, a member of the bizarre community that was Charlie's. A key member even. I *owed* it to these people not to go mad. With or without an axe.

And to stay alive.

Charlie's Coffeehouse: Old Town's peculiar little beacon in the encroaching darkness.

An interesting perspective on current events.

"That's all right then," I said.

"Good." Charlie opened the door again and ambled out.

I WENT TO bed wearing jeans and a flannel shirt again that night. I woke at midnight and stumbled into the bathroom for a pee, tripping over the sill on the way. I went back to bed and fell asleep again immediately. The alarm went off at three-forty-five.

He hadn't come.

THE SENSE OF outrage of the day before—the absurd sense of having been stood up like a teenager on her way to the prom—was gone, as if it were a candle flame that had been blown out. I was worried.

The fact that the wound on my breast, for the past four days, since he'd told me it was poisoned, was burning like the 'fo had set a match to my skin, was almost by the way. It was as if now that I had the diagnosis I didn't care what the diagnosis was: knowing was enough. For a few days. It was seeping so badly I not only had to keep it bandaged, I had to change the gauze pad at least once a day. I didn't care. I did it and didn't think about it. The heavy, permanent sense of tiredness made this easier than it might have been if I'd been sharp and alert. The only problem was finding places to put the adhesive tape that weren't already sore from having adhesive tape there too often already. I could have bought the surgical tape that doesn't take your skin off with it, but that would have been admitting there was a problem. I wasn't admitting anything. So the area around the slash looked peeled.

The thing that really wasn't all right was that he'd said he'd be back, and he wasn't.

Things are getting *bad* if I was worried about a vampire. Well: they were bad, and I was worried. I didn't see him as the stand-you-up kind. If you could apply human guidelines to a vampire, which you couldn't.

But if he'd said he'd be back, he'd be back. I was sure. And he wasn't.

I had the rest of the day off after I finished the morning baking. Paulie, still hoarse but no longer sneezing, came in and started on Lemon Lechery and marbled brown sugar cake, and I went home to comb every globenet account I could find on vampire activity. Because of my peculiar hobby I paid for a line into the cosworld better than most home users bothered with, so I didn't have to go to the library every time I wanted the hottest new reportage on the Others. If there was anything to find I should be able to find it. When some big vampire feud came to a head there was usually more than enough mayhem to alert even the dimmest of the news media. And maybe this was only a tiny, local feud, but our media aren't among the dimmest. I couldn't believe that, this time, knowing what he knew, he wouldn't sell himself dearly, if Bo had caught him again.

If, that is, he hadn't come back because he'd been prevented. If I hadn't been stood up like a teenager going to the prom with a known loser. One might almost say a deadbeat. Ha ha.

I couldn't find anything. After I looked through all the local stuff I started on the national, and then the international. The nearest report of anything like what I thought I might be looking for was happening in Macedonia. I didn't think it would happen in Macedonia.

I wanted to start looking up glyphs, to see if I could translate mine, but I couldn't make myself be interested enough. I cleaned the apartment instead. I rearranged the piles of books to be read immediately. *Altar of Darkness* went on the bottom, although I dusted it first. I mopped floors. I scrubbed sinks. I baking-soda'd the tea stains out of the teapot and my favorite mugs. I vacuumed. I folded laun-

dry. I even cleaned a few windows. I hate cleaning windows. I was
too tired to work this hard but I couldn't sit still. And it was overcast
outdoors: not a day that insisted I go out and lie in it.

By evening I was exhausted and slightly queasy.

I had an egg-and-Romaine sandwich on two slabs of my pumpernickel bread at six, and went to bed at seven. I gave up. I wore the
nightgown I'd been wearing four nights ago, and got between the
sheets. I had a little trouble going to sleep, but it was as if my thoughts
were spinning so fast—or maybe it was effect of the poison winning
at last—eventually I got dizzy and fell over into unconsciousness.

WHEN I WOKE up three hours later he was there. Darkness, sitting in
my bedroom chair. Darkness, I noticed, barefoot. I couldn't remember if he'd been barefoot the other night or not.

I sat up. I was too sleepy and too relieved not tell the truth. "I've
been worrying about you."

I'd figured out last time that vampires don't move when they're
startled, they go stiller. He did that different-kind-of-stillness thing.

"You know," I said. "Concern. Unease. Anxiety. You said you'd
come back two nights ago. You didn't. There's this little threat of annihilation going on too, you know? I thought maybe you'd got into
trouble."

"The preparations took longer than I anticipated," he said. "That
is all. Nothing to . . . worry you."

"Nothing to worry me," I said, warming to my theme. "Sure.
The annihilation threat includes me and I'm wearing a poisoned
wound that is slowly killing me. I wouldn't dream of worrying about
anything."

"Good," he said. "Worry is useless."

"*Oh*—" I began. "I—" I stopped. "Okay. You win. Worry is useless."

He stood up. I tried not to clutch the bedclothes into a knot. He
pulled his shirt off and dropped it on the floor.

Eeeeek.

He sat on the edge of my bed again. He had one leg folded under
him and the other foot still on the floor, sitting to face me cringing

into the headboard. I thought, okay, okay, he still has one foot on the floor. And he only took his *shirt* off.

"Do you still have the knife you transmuted?" he said. "That would be the best."

The best *what*. I knew this was going to have blood in it. I knew I wasn't going to like it. And that particular knife, of course . . . "Uh. Well, yes, I still have it." I didn't move.

"Show me," he said. A human might have said, what's your problem? So where is it? He just said, show me.

I opened the bedside table drawer. When my jeans went in the wash, the contents of my pockets went in there. The knife was there. It was lying next to the glyph as if they were getting to know each other.

The light was visible at once in the darkness. I picked the knife up and cradled it in my hand: a tiny, clement sun that happened to look like a pocketknife. In ordinary daylight or good strong electric light it still looked like a pocketknife. I held it out toward him.

"This has been—since that night?"

"Yes. It happened—do you remember, right at the end, I transmuted it again, into the key to my door?"

"Yes."

"I'm pretty sure that's when it happened. It had been something-in-the-dark-colored when I pulled it out. I don't . . . it was something to do with making the change at night, I think. I think I'm not supposed to be able to do stuff after dark. But I did do it. I felt something . . . crack. Snap. In me. And since then it's been like this. I shifted it back to a knife the next day—didn't notice till evening what had happened. I thought it would fade after a while, but it hasn't."

I think I'm not supposed to be able to do stuff after dark. I had done this somehow though. And I happened to have been being held in the lap of a vampire at the time. That had been another of the things I hadn't been thinking about, the last two months. Because if it was something to do with the vampire—this vampire—why had my knife become impregnated with *light*?

I hadn't told anyone, shown anyone. It was very odd, finally having someone to tell. I hadn't wanted to tell anyone at the coffee-house, any of the SOFs. When I spent the night with Mel, I was careful to keep my knife in its pocket. I was still trying to be Rae Seddon, coffeehouse baker, in that life. Even after I'd exposed my little secret that it had been vampires at the lake—that I was a magic handler and a transmuter—I still hadn't wanted to tell anyone about my knife. The only person, you should forgive the term, left to tell was him. The vampire. The vampire I had now agreed to ally myself with in the hopes of winning against a common enemy.

It was a relief, telling someone.

I wondered what else an unknown *something* breaking open in-side me might have let loose, besides a little radiant dye leak. I won-dered if the jackknife of a bad-magic cross would glow in the dark. Sure. And when I went nuts it would transmute into a chainsaw.

He looked at it, but made no attempt to touch it. "That helps to explain. One of the reasons it has taken this extra time for me to come to you is that it has puzzled me you are not weaker, having borne what you bear two months already. I have been seeking an explanation. It could be crucial to our effort tonight." He paused. When he went on, his voice had dropped half an octave or so, and it wasn't easy to hear to begin with because of the weird rough half-echo and the tonelessness. "What you show me is a judgment on my arrogance; it did not occur to me to ask you for information. I have much to learn about working with anyone, for all that I believed I had thought through what I said to you last time. I ask pardon."

I gaped at him. "Oh *please*. Like I'm not sitting here half expecting you to change your mind and eat me. Oh, sorry, I forgot, I'm poison-ous, I suppose I'm safe after all, I get to bite the big one without your help. I'm your little friend the deadly nightshade. But that's just it: humans and vampires *don't* ally. We're implacable enemies. Like co-bras and mongooses. Mongeese. Why should you have thought of asking me anything? If there is going to be pardoning between us, it should be for lunacy, and mutual."

At least he didn't laugh.

"Very well. We shall learn together."

"Speaking of learning," I said. "I take it you have learned what to do about this," and I gestured toward my breast. "Since you're here."

"I have learned what will work, if anything will."

"And what if it doesn't work?"

"Then both of us end our existence tonight," he said in that impassive we're-chained-to-the-wall-and-the-bad-guys-are-coming voice I remembered too well.

Oh gee. Don't pull your punches like that. I can take the truth, really I can. I said something like, "Unnngh."

"I believe it will work."

"I'm delighted to hear it."

"Your wound is worse."

"Oh well. No biggie." I was a trifle preoccupied with his little revelation about our joint even-more-immediate-than-Bo impending doom. He'd *said* he wasn't sure what he was doing. "It comes and goes."

"Will you remove the bandage?"

Or you will? I thought nervously. I unbuttoned the top two buttons of my nightgown again and peeled the gauze away. *Ouch.* Of course the cut began to bleed at once.

"Er—I don't suppose you want to tell me what you're going to do?"

Badly phrased question.

"No," he said.

"*Will* you please tell me what you are going to do."

"If you would take your knife, and open the blade."

My heart, having tried to accustom itself to *vampire in the room*, began to thump uncomfortably. The knife lay between us on the bed, where I had set it down. I looked at him a little oddly as I picked it up, and he, I suppose, well accustomed to blood-letting and thinking nothing of a little more or less of the same, misinterpreted my look.

"I would prefer not to touch your knife, it will burn me. And it is better if you cut me yourself."

EEEEK.

"*Cut you?*"

"Yes. As you are cut. Here." And he touched the place below his collarbones. A lot less bony on him, it occurred to me. I hadn't registered it before, but he was a lot more filled-out-looking generally than he had been when we first made acquaintance.

When he was half-starved and all. I hadn't seen him with his shirt off four nights ago. Well.

I could have sat there quite a while thinking ridiculous thoughts—anything was better than thinking about the prospective hacking and hewing: a two-and-a-half-inch blade is plenty big enough to do more damage than I wanted to be around for—but he said patiently, "Open the blade."

The knife seemed much heavier in my hand than usual, and the blade more reluctant to unfold. I snapped it open and the blade flared silver fire.

"You said it would *burn* you."

"And so it will. I would appreciate it if you made the cut quickly."

"I can't," I said, panicky. "I can't—cut you—at *all*."

"Very well," he said. "Please set the tip of it, here," and he touched a spot below his right collarbone.

I sat there, frozen and staring. I even raised my eyes and looked into his: green as grass, as my grandmother's ring, as my plaid socks from last night. He looked steadily back. I could feel my own blood—my poisoned blood—seeping slowly down my breast, staining my nightgown, dripping on the sheet.

He reached out, and gently closed his own hand around mine holding the knife. He drew hand and knife toward him, set the point where he had indicated. I *felt* the slight give of his flesh under the blade. His hold tightened, and he gave a tiny, quick twist and jerk, and the knifepoint parted the skin; I *felt* the moment up the blade into my hand when the skin first divided under the glowing stainless-steel blade, when it sank into him. There was a *sound*, as if I could hear that sundering of flesh, or perhaps of the undead electricity that guarded that flesh, a minute fizz or hiss; then he drew the sharp—the burning sharp—edge swiftly across his chest in a shallow arc—just like the wound on me. And pulled the knife away again. It was over in a moment.

The slash he had made was deeper, and the blood raged out.

I was—whimpering, or moaning: "Oh no, oh *no*,"—I dropped the knife and reached toward him as if I could close the awful gash with my hands. The blood was black in the moonlight, there was so much of it, too much of it—it was hot, *hot*, running over my hands. . . .

"Good," he said. He took my bloody hands and turned them back toward me, wiped them down the front of my poor once-white nightgown, firmly, against the contours of my body; pulled my hands toward him again, smeared them across his chest, and back to press them against me: repeated this till my nightgown *stuck* to me, sopping, saturated, as if I had been swimming, except the wetness was his blood.

I was weeping.

"Hush," he said. "Hush."

"I don't understand," I said, weeping. "I don't understand. This cannot be—healing."

"It can," he said. "It is. All is well. Lie back. Lie down," he said. "You will sleep soon now."

I lay down, bumping my head against the headboard. My tears ran down my temples and into my hair. The smell of blood was thick and heavy and nauseating. I saw him leaning, looming over me, felt him lie down upon me, gently, so gently, till our bleeding skins met with one thin sodden layer of cotton partially between: till the new wound in him pressed down against the old wound in me. His hair brushed my face as he bowed his head; his breath stirred my hair.

"Constantine," I cried, "are you *turning* me?"

"No," he said. "I would not. And this is not that."

"Then what—"

"Do not talk. Not now. Later. We can talk later."

"But—but—I am so frightened," I pleaded.

In the moonlight I could see his silhouette clearly. He raised his head away from me, arching his neck backward so our bodies remained touching. I saw him rip, quickly, neatly, his upper lip with his lower teeth, his lower lip and tongue with his upper. He bent his head to me again, and when he stopped my mouth with his, his blood ran across my tongue and down my throat.

IT WAS STILL dark when I woke. I had turned on my side—I always sleep curled up on one side or the other—but this time I was facing the room. My first thought was that I had had a terrible dream.

I was alone in the bed. I looked down, along my body. Gingerly I touched my white nightgown. It had been a dream. I had imagined it. I had imagined all of it. Although my nightgown felt curiously—*tacky*, as if I had worn it too long, although it had come fresh out of the dryer this morning. But it was white. The sheets were white too.

No bloodstains.

I had imagined it.

I knew he was sitting in the chair. After four nights he had returned after all. I couldn't bear to look at him—not yet—not while the dream was so heavy on me—so shamefully heavy. What a horrible thing to dream. Even about a vampire. At least he wouldn't know that I'd dreamed—at least he wouldn't know. I didn't have to tell him. I sat up, and as I sat up, I felt a small heavy something fall to a different position on top of the bedclothes.

My small shining knife. The blade still open.

No.

I looked at him. Although the chair was in shadow I saw him with strange clarity: the mushroomy-gray skin, the impassive face, the green eyes, black hair. I *knew* it was nighttime—I felt it on my own skin—why could I see as if it were daylight?

It occurred to me that he wasn't wearing his shirt.

No.

I had climbed out of bed and taken the two steps to the chair and laid my hands on his unmarked chest before I had a chance to think—before I had a chance to tell myself not to—laid my hands as I had laid them—an hour ago? A week? A century?—with the blood welling out, sluicing out, from the cut I had made with my knife. I touched his mouth, his untorn lips.

"Poor Sunshine," he said, under my fingers. "I told you it would not be easy. I did not think how difficult the manner of it would be for you."

"It—it happened, then?" I said. My knees suddenly wouldn't hold me, and I sank down beside his chair. I leaned my forehead against the arm of it. "What I remember . . . I thought it must be a bad dream. A . . . shameful dream."

"Shameful?" he said. He bent over me, took my shoulders so I had to sit up, away from the support of the chair. The top two buttons of my nightgown were still undone, and the edges fell open as I moved. He put one hand on my breast just below the collarbones, so that it covered the width of my old wound. He left his hand there for two of my breaths, took it away again, held it, palm up, as if he might be catching my tears; but I was dry-eyed.

"You are healed," he said. "There is no shame in healing."

I looked down, touched the place he had touched. The skin was clear and smooth: I could see it plainly. I could see plainly too, a thin pale scar, where the wound had been, but this was a real scar. The wound was gone, and would not reopen.

"The blood," I said. "All the blood."

"It was clean blood," he said. "It was for you."

I was remembering the real dream I had had after I slept—the blood dream. Daylight, sunshine, grass, trees, flowers, the warmth of life, gladness to be alive. . . .

Gladness to be alive. Gladness was the wrong word. It was much simpler than that, more direct. There was no translation of sensation into a *word* like gladness. It was the sensation itself. Smells, sounds, tastes, all perceptions so different from anything I knew in waking life, so unequivocal, uncluttered . . . uncontaminated. The wide world around me seemed vast and open and immediate in a way I did not recognize. But my sense of self was—there was no thought to it. There was a place where all those strange vivid sensations met, and there *I* was. A feeling, instinctive, responsive me—but no *me*.

On four legs. This life I dreamed—this life I borrowed—this life I knew so strangely from the inside—this life, I abruptly knew, that had been taken for me—it was no human life. I was remembering life as some creature—she, I knew her as she; I knew her as a grass-eater, a scenter of the breeze, and a listener with wide ears; I felt her long lithe muscles, rough brown fur, smelled the sweet gamy smell of her; I knew her as a runner and a leaper and a hider in dappled shadow. A deer.

I searched for the horror of her death, for the fear and the pain, the helpless awareness of coming final darkness. I remembered waking up, sick and dazed but with a kind of drugged tranquillity, after Bo's lieutenant had used the Breath on me. I looked for some equivalent in my doe's last minutes. I could not find it.

"The doe," I said.

"Yes. It would not have been right for you to remember the last day of a human woman."

There was a laugh that stuck in my throat. "No," I said soberly. "It would not have been right for me." I sagged forward again, but this time I was leaning against his leg, my cheek just above his knee. "How did she die?" I said dreamily, resting against the leg of the vampire who had cured my poisoned wound with the death of a doe.

"How?" he repeated. There was a long pause while I remembered the wild grass against my slender legs, the way my four hoofs dug into the ground as they took my weight as I ran, how much more fleetly and steadily I ran on four two-toed hoofs than I would ever run on two queerly inflexible platterlike feet and thick clumsy legs.

He said: "There are many myths about my kind. It is not true that we cannot feed unless we torment first. She died as any good hunter kills his prey: with one clean stroke."

"But . . ." I said, groping for the answer I wanted. Needed. "You told me—long ago. By the lake. You have to ask. You can take no . . . blood that is not offered. She has to have said 'yes.'"

After a little while he said: "Animals do not draw the distinction between life and death that humans do. If an animal is caught, by age, by illness, by some creature stronger than it, and cannot escape, it accepts death." A longer pause. "Also . . . my kind were all once human. There perhaps can be no truly clean death between one of your kind and one of mine."

I thought: If that is true, then it works both ways. The death of the giggler at my hands is no cleaner than the death he was offering that girl. I shivered. I felt Constantine's hand on the back of my neck.

"I told you last time that Bo and I chose different ways of being what we are. You magic handlers know you risk, with every sending, the recoil. Bo is burdened by many years of the recoil of the torment that provides the savor to his meals. The savor is real—yes, I too have tasted it—but it is not worth the price."

I was looking across the room, at a corner near the ceiling, where one of the occupied cobwebs hung. I could see the tiny dot that was the folded-up spider at the center.

I raised my head and turned round, knelt up, put my hands on his knees, stared into his face, into his eyes. I had looked full into his eyes briefly last night, while I held the knife, before he had taken from me the action I could not perform. I stared at him now, minute after minute, night flowing past us as morning had done by the lake, two months and a lifetime ago, when I told him I would take him with me, through the daylight, out of the trap we shared. "You used the blood of a doe, to spare me the death of a human. You said you would not—were not—turning me. Why are you not telling me not to look in your eyes?"

"I have not turned you," he replied. "In three hours, when the sun rises, you will find that sunshine is your element, as it always has been. I do not think you can be turned. You can be killed, as any human can be, as the poison Bo set in your flesh would at last have killed you, but I believe you cannot be turned.

"There is nothing I can do to you with my gaze, any more, whether I wish it or not. I was not able . . . to give you the doe's clean blood cleanly. I caught and carried her blood for you, for tonight's necessary rite, but I am not a clean vessel. Sunshine, we are on territory neither of us knows. We are bound now, you to me as I already was to you, for I have saved your life tonight as you saved my existence two months ago."

"I think the honors were about even, two months ago," I said, struggling. He picked my hands up off his knees, held them between his hands.

"That-which-binds did not judge so; the scales did not rest in balance. You will begin, now, I think, to read those lines of . . . power, governance, sorcery, as I can read them. By what has happened between us tonight. Onyx Blaise's daughter—the daughter who did what you did, that second morning by the lake—always held that capacity. Now you must learn to use it. That-which-binds reckons I have been bound to you by what happened two months ago. I could not come to you if you did not call me, but if you called I had to come. You are now bound to me as well. I did not do this deliberately; to save your life, it was the only choice I had, and I was *bound* to try.

"When I came to you four nights ago, I had no knowledge of the wound you still carried. I was thinking only of how I could convince you—to go into battle with me. That I should succeed did not seem likely, though you were calling to ask me for help. I came here that night thinking how I might give you—anything I could give you—to help you in that battle, if you agreed. It would have required some greater tie between us, but nothing like . . .

"I do not know what I have given you tonight." Another silence. He added, "I do not know what you have given me."

Another, longer silence.

"Well," I said, shakily, clinging to his hands holding mine, "I think I can see in the dark."

PART THREE

So, I would have said that not much could be worse—short of being dead or undead—than those first weeks after the night I went out to the lake and met some vampires up close and personal. I would have said that being paralyzed from the neck down or having an inoperable brain tumor would be worse. Not a lot else. Just shows how limited the human imagination can be.

The first weeks after Con healed the wound on my breast were worse.

It's funny, because I had thought, living through those first two months after the nights at the lake, that the great crisis *was* about What I Was or Who I'd Become or What Terrible Thing Was Wrong With Me (and About to Go Wronger) and Why All Was Changed As a Result. But I was still struggling against the idea that all *was* changed.

Sticking the giggler with the table knife should have shaken me out of this fantasy even if the sucker-sunshade trick hadn't, but I was too busy being grossed out by the sheer grisliness of the latter experience to have thought much about the philosophical implications. What the little chat with Jesse and Pat had revealed to me had done my head in worse, and the news that the suckers were on to conquer the world within the next century had been worse yet. I felt like a pancake in the hands of a maniac flipper. But when you're being caromed around your life like a squash ball you haven't got leeway to think about what happens *next*. When you're feeding the second coachload of tourists that day you aren't thinking about the birthday party for fifty next week. Maybe you should be, but you aren't. *Now* is more than enough.

Before the detox night with Con I still thought I could say *no* somehow, could still stick my head back in the sand. Hey, I wasn't going to be around in a hundred years—unless maybe I started handling a lot of magic, which I didn't *want* to, right? That was exactly what I *didn't* want to be doing; magic handling extending your life span was a myth anyway—so what did I care?

You can be a really nasty, selfish little jerk when you're scared enough. I was scared enough.

Of course I had had this apparently permanent leaking wound on my breast, I had had these nightmares, and I had been doing a pretty bad job after all of suppressing thinking about what it all *meant*, what had happened at the lake. But I was still obstinately trying to pretend I'd only had a piece of very, very bad luck, and the fact of my having survived it wasn't . . . irredeemable. My gran had shown me all that transmuting stuff fifteen years ago, and I'd never used it before. Maybe it would be another fifteen years before I used it again. Maybe thirty this time. And one vampire more or less? Who cares?

And the table knife venture was just that the giggler'd been the one who cut me, poisoned me. It was a one-off. There was an answer in there somewhere: it wasn't me, it wasn't my warped, screwed-up genetic heritage.

And if I'd delivered the world of one sucker, sort of accidentally having preserved it another one, then my final effect on the vampire population was nil, invisible, void. Which was exactly the profile I'd choose.

I told myself I had always been my father's daughter. I was facing what had been there all the time.

But I was also facing stuff that hadn't been there.

Being able to see in the dark sounds great. Never trip over the bathroom threshold on your way for a pee at midnight again, right? But it's not that simple. Human eyes *don't* see in the dark. They don't have the rods and cones for it or whatever. Therefore you are doing something that *isn't human*. It's not like you've awakened a latent talent, like someone who finds out they have a gift for playing jazz piano after a life previously devoted to Bach. That may be odd, but it's within human scope. Seeing in the dark isn't. And you know it. That doesn't mean I know how to explain it; but trust me, you can tell the difference between seeing because there's enough light and "seeing" because something weird and vampiry is going on in your brain that chooses to pretend to be happening in your eyes because that's the nearest equivalent. Like if some human had had a poisoned wound healed by some weird reciprocal swap with the phoenix, maybe they'd be able to fly afterward, *apparently* by flapping their arms.

(Mind you no one has seen the phoenix in over a thousand years, and it has never been inclined to do humans any good turns. Rather the opposite. Very like vampires, I suppose. Except a lot of people think the phoenix is a myth, and not many are stupid enough to think vampires are. I think the phoenix has at least a fifty-fifty chance of being true, because it's nasty. What this world doesn't have is the three-wishes, go-to-the-ball-and-meet-your-prince, happily-ever-after kind of magic. We have all the mangling and malevolent kinds. Who *invented* this system?)

I saw in the dark pretty well. I thought, do I want to see Bo coming?

Oh yeah, and seeing in the dark doesn't mean when the sun goes down. It also means all the shadows that fall in daylight. This would not be a big issue for a vampire, of course, but it troubled the hell out of me. Even an ordinary table knife throws a shadow—although I didn't really need any more reminders that table knives would never be ordinary to me again.

It throws your balance off, seeing through shadows. Your depth perception goes wrong, like trying to look through someone else's glasses. Everything has funny dark-light edges to it, and sometimes those edges have themselves threadlike red edges. You get your new looking-through-bad-spectacles distortion on everything, including your own hands, your own body, the faces and bodies of the people you love and trust. Oh, the one time this goes away is when you look in a mirror. Or it did with me. Just in case I needed reminding that I got it from a vampire. Thanks.

I hated it that I now "saw" more easily in the dark than I did in the light. In the dark it all made sense. I *hated* this.

I was so clumsy for the first ten days or so that Charlie did another of his drifting-into-the-bakery-and-closing-the-door numbers. Golly, twice in two weeks: I must be a worse pain in the butt than I realized. Damn. He wandered around the bakery for a minute like he was thinking about what to say. I knew better; he figures this stuff out beforehand. When I still lived with him and Mom I used to see him ambling around the house in that fake idle way, figuring out what he was going to say to someone, what they might say back. He thinks of it on the move and he says it on the move. He wandered a lot during the time the city council was trying to upgrade us. The media, who love a good story and truth is noncompulsory, presented Charlie's as the focus of the neighborhood campaign to stay the way we were: downmarket and crappy. This was not entirely false. That's when Charlie's kind of got on the New Arcadia map rather than merely the Old Town map, and one of the results was that Charlie could afford to build my bakery. (I have to say he used to wander a lot when Mom and I were at each other's throats the worst too. There was some overlap between these two eras. Kenny and Billy are probably scarred for life.)

But having him wandering around again in that way I recognized made me feel bad. I didn't live with him any more, but I had the impression he didn't wander as much as he had then: that he'd mostly figured out how to say the sort of things he needed to say as Charlie of Charlie's.

I suppose a magic-handling baker with an affinity for vampires is kind of an unusual problem for a coffeehouse. Maybe the bitchiness factor was trivial.

"You've been having a little trouble lately," he said, mildly and gently, addressing one of the ovens.

"That oven is working fine," I said, thinking, if you're going to *manage* me you can just *do* it.

He turned around. "Sorry. We . . . Charlie's has had its rough times, but . . . having SOFs interested in one of my staff is a new one."

I refrained from pointing out that our regular SOFs had always sort of jived with me. I had thought because I was the one who wanted to hear their stories, but as it turned out, I now knew, because they remembered my father, even if Charlie—and for that matter Mom and I—didn't. "Yeah," I said. "It blows. I've been thinking, okay, my dad has always been my dad, but that doesn't help. I could have gone on not knowing what it meant."

Charlie hesitated. "Well . . . I doubt it, Sunshine. If you just kept coffee hot, maybe. But someone who can . . ." His voice faded. "Have you talked to Sadie about it?"

I shook my head. Have I sawn myself in half with a blunt knife? No.

"You know what Sadie is like—no one better. You inherited her backbone, her doggedness."

The big difference between my mom and me—besides the fact that she is dead normal and I'm a magic-handling freak—is that she's the real thing. She may have a slight problem seeing other people's points of view, but she's *honest* about it. She's a brass-bound bitch because she believes she knows best. I'm a brass-bound bitch because I don't want anyone getting close enough to find out what a whiny little knot of naked nerve endings I really am. "And her nasty temper," I said.

Charlie smiled. "She knew your dad pretty well. Do you know she loved him? She really did. Still does, in her secret heart. Oh, she loves me, don't worry. And we're happy together—that's the point. She's happy running the admin side of Charlie's."

And ripping self-important assholes to shreds, I thought. But get under cover if there haven't been any self-important assholes around lately.

"She was often joyful—euphoric—with your dad, especially at the beginning. But his wasn't a world she could live in. Mine is.

"My guess is she got out of your dad's world when she did and took you with her *because* she knew what you were. I think she knew you were going to be someone pretty unusual. I think she was hoping that what she's given you—both by being your mom and by raising you in a place like Charlie's—is going to be enough. Enough ballast. When what your father gave you started coming out."

I'd already figured out that she hadn't included him in the Bad Cross Watch, so what I was in Charlie's version of events didn't include the possibility of a demon taint. On the whole I thought my version was more plausible than Charlie's. Possibly because it was more depressing.

I drifted in a very Charlie-like manner over to the stool and sat down. I looked at my hands, which had a funny red-outlined light-dark edge. I thought about bad gene crosses. I put my head in my hands and closed my eyes.

"What do you think, Sunshine?" said Charlie. "Is it going to be enough?"

"I don't know," I said. "Charlie, I don't know."

AUGUST WAS LESS death-defying than usual in terms of temperature (which among other things meant that I hadn't had to beg Paulie not to quit) if not in terms of numbers of Earth Trek coachloads, and possibly, because all the heat August hadn't used had to go somewhere, we went straight into Indian Summer September, do not pass Go, do not collect two thousand blinks. So I got out all my least decent little-bit-of-nothing tank tops and wore them. The scar was visible but the skin was flat and smooth, no puckering, and the white mark itself seemed weirdly *old* and sort of half-worn-away-looking the way old scars get sometimes.

I was still having trouble with the idea that what had happened that night counted as *healing*, but whatever it was, it had worked.

I started going home with Mel a lot. He was glad to have me around—glad to stop arguing about my going to another doctor. He didn't know about Con, of course, but he knew plenty—too much—about recent events. He would know that I needed reassuring without knowing I needed to feel . . . *human*.

This is really stupid, but I also discovered that I somehow believed that he was the one human at Charlie's who might be able to stop me in time if my bad genes suddenly kicked in and I picked up my electric cherry pitter and went for the nearest warm body. That he'd drown me efficiently in a vat of pasta sauce while everyone else was standing around with their mouths open wringing their hands and saying, who are we going to get to cover the bakery on such short notice?

This was at its worst during Monday movie evenings. The Seddon living room had never seemed so small, or so packed with flimsy, vulnerable human bodies. If Mel didn't feel like going I didn't go either.

As a romantic fantasy I don't think it's going to make it into the top ten—most women pining for the presence of their lovers aren't worrying about needing their homicidal tendencies foiled—but it did mean I felt a little safer with Mel around.

I probably didn't believe it at all. I just didn't want to give him up. He was warm and breathing and had a heartbeat.

Human. Yeah. I hadn't been willing to go see a specialist *human* doctor, as Mel had kept asking me to. No. I asked a *vampire* for help. And took it instantly when he offered it.

Mel must have wondered what happened to the wound on my breast. But he didn't say anything. He was very good at not saying things. It had only been since the Night of the Table Knife that I'd begun to wonder if his reticence was for my sake or his.

And if it was for his . . . No. I needed him to be steady, solid, secure. I needed it too badly to pursue that one. Too badly to wonder about the number of live tattoos he had. Even for a motorcycle thug.

Another of the things I'd never thought about was the way when we went home together it was always his home. He'd been inside my apartment a handful of times. If we had an afternoon together we went hiking or went back to his place. If we had an evening together and we decided to go out, we went where he wanted to go because there wasn't anywhere I wanted to go. I knew his friends. He didn't know mine. His house wards were set to know me. Mine weren't set to know him.

I didn't have friends. I had the coffeehouse. A few librarians—chiefly Aimil, who had been a Charlie's regular all her life—was as far afield as I went.

It is halfway true that if you are involved in a family coffeehouse you don't have a life. But only halfway. Mel had a life.

I've said before that Mel had been a bit of a hoodlum in his younger days, although nobody seemed to be quite sure how much, or maybe his War service had wiped earlier misdeeds off the record. He wasn't old now but he'd had time to go wrong and then change his mind. There must have been signs he wasn't going wrong right, though, even at the time. Some of his tattoos were for pretty strange things. Some of them I didn't know the purpose of because when I'd asked he'd said "Um" and gone silent.

Anybody who spent a lot of time on or about motorcycles would have a couple of the regulation anti-crushed-by-flying-metal-or-running-into-trees-at-high-speeds wards, either pricked into your skin or on a chain round your neck or a secret pocket in your belt or the soles of your biker boots. He had those. But he also had a seeing-things-clearly charm that I hadn't recognized when I saw it the first time: okay, a useful thing for someone on the wrong side of the law (or the wrong side of the battle zone) who needs to have his eyes peeled for trouble, but Mel's wasn't the conventional block-and-warn ward that most petty crooks used for the purpose.

(You could sometimes half-identify the variety of malfeasant you were dealing with by whether or not you could see that ward. Scammers, of course, kept it well hidden: wouldn't do to have it dangling on a bracelet or tattooed on your wrist when you popped your cuffs at someone you were trying to schmooze. A couple of Mel's old gang who had also changed their minds about being professional bad guys had it on the backs of their gonna-punch-you-in-the-nose hands, so the guy who was about to get punched would see it on the fist being held under his nose.)

Anyway. Mel still bought and sold motorcycles. He still drank beer with friends at the Nighthouse or the Jug. Wives and steady girlfriends (very occasionally boyfriends) were expected to show up if they wanted to. (Better yet, we were expected to *talk*. Of course the women who could talk about ignition mixtures and piston resistance were preferred, but you can't have everything.) He'd bought a house in what had been Chesterfield but was now called

Whiteout, the worst-Wars-hit section of New Arcadia, had it cleared and re-warded, and was slowly doing it over into something even my mother would recognize as habitable (although the motorcycle-refit garage on what had been the ground floor would probably have given her spasms). He loved cooking and Charlie's but he wasn't *owned* by them.

I felt like maybe I should be asking to borrow his survival text-book. Maybe the problem was that the first chapters in it were about running away from home at fourteen and lying about your age, and then being a biker bandit for a few years before deciding that the fact you always seemed to wind up frying the sausages over the fire for everybody was maybe a pointer toward a different way of life with better retirement options, which five years of the Wars had given him plenty of time to consider.

Mel would have understood why I drove out to the lake that night. He probably did understand without my telling him. I would have liked hearing him understand. But I didn't want to tell him. Because I couldn't—*couldn't*—tell him what happened after.

But you don't have to talk when you're making love, and bodies have their own language. Also you don't have to use your eyes so much. There are other things going on.

Meanwhile I was still reaching the wrong distance to pick up the edges of baking sheets and muffin tins or the handles of spoons, and fumbling them when I managed to grab them at all, and I walked into doors a little too often instead of through them. At least I knew the recipes I used all the time by heart and didn't have to bother peering at print midmix or identifying the lines on measuring jugs. Nor had I lost my sense of whether a batter or a dough was going together right or not, or what to do if it wasn't.

I could tell Jesse and Pat about seeing in the dark and let *them* tell me what to do about it. Or with it. As far as my strange new talents went it beat hell out of Unusual Usages of Table Knives. And maybe if I told them I could bear to tell the people at Charlie's.

Nobody had to know anything about *why* I could now see in the dark. Including the dark of the day.

One day when Pat and John came in for hot-out-of-the-oven

cinnamon rolls at about six-thirty-two, I tipped them onto a plate myself and took them out while Liz was still yawning over the coffeepot. "You have some free time soon maybe?" I said, trying to sound casual in my turn. They both shifted in their seats, trying not to point like hunting dogs. Not very many people, even at Charlie's, are at their best at that hour, but it doesn't pay to be careless. And Mrs. Bialosky was there, pretending to read a newspaper while waiting for one of her confederates to turn up to make a clandestine report. "For you, Sunshine, anything," said Pat.

"I'm off at two," I said.

"Come round the shop," said Pat. "There are two desks in the entry, okay? You go up to the right-hand one and say Pat's expecting you and they'll let you straight in."

I nodded.

THERE WAS A young woman at that desk with a nameplate and a sharp uniform and a sharp look like she should have had a rank to go on the nameplate, but what do I know? She hit two buzzers, one that opened the inner door and one that, presumably, warned Pat, because he came walking out to meet me before I'd gone very far down the faceless hallway Mel must have brought me out of the last night of the giggler's existence on this earth, but it was so characterless I was ready to believe I had crossed one of those distance-folding thresholds and was now on Mars. If so, Pat was there with me. Maybe we'd been on Mars that night too. "What if the wrong person showed up first and said you were expecting them?" I said.

"I told them middling tall, skinny, weird-looking hair because it will have just been let out of being tied up in a scarf for working in a restaurant and you never comb it, wearing a fierce look," said Pat. "I was pretty safe."

"Fierce?" I said. I also thought, *Skinny?*, but I have my pride. The part about my hair is true.

"Yeah. Fierce. Through here," and he opened a door and shepherded me through. This was, presumably, Pat's office. The chair behind the desk was empty, but had that pushed-back-someone-just-got-up look. Jesse was sitting on a chair to one side of the desk. "Someone I want you to meet," Pat said, nodding toward the other person in the room, who stood up out of her chair, and said in a rather stricken voice, "Hi."

Aimil.

I looked at her and she looked at me. With my funny vision the sockets of her deep eyes and the hollows of her cheeks had a glittering dark periphery. "Okay," I said, planning not to lose my temper unless it was absolutely necessary. "What are you doing here?"

"Tea?" said Pat blandly.

"Tell me what Aimil is doing here first," I said.

"Well, we're in putting-all-our-cards-on-the-table vogue now, aren't we?" said Pat, still bland. "Since the other night. So it's time you knew Aimil is one of us."

"One of *you*," I said. "SOF. And here I thought she was a librarian."

"Undercover SOF," Jesse said.

"Part time," added Pat.

"I *am* a librarian," said Aimil. "But I'm sometimes a—er—librarian for SOF too."

I thought about this. I'd known Aimil since I was seven and she was nine. She and her family had had Sunday breakfast at Charlie's most weeks for years, were already regulars when Mom started working there and then when I started hanging out there. She was one of the faces I recognized at my new school. I'd lost half a year being sick and then Mom crammed the crap out of me the second half of the year so I didn't lose a grade when I went back to school in the fall. (Yes, I mean *crammed*. Second grade is freaking hard work when you're seven or eight.) In hindsight that was the beginning of Charlie's being my entire life: I didn't have time to make friends the six months I was being crammed. The only kids I met were kids who came to Charlie's, not that I got to know many of them because I wasn't allowed to annoy the customers. But Aimil used to ask for me, so I was allowed to talk to her. She talked to me because she felt sorry for me: I was weedy and undersized and hangdog that half year, and always doing homework. I forget how it started—maybe she saw me sitting at the counter studying, which I was allowed to do when it wasn't too crowded.

We'd managed to stay friends outside of school although not inside so much; two years is the Grand Canyon when you're a kid. She'd gone off to library school my junior year and did an internship at the big downtown library the year after I started working full time at Charlie's and we used to get together to complain about how hard working for a living was. Two years later she got a job at the branch library near Charlie's. Sometimes she still had Sunday morning breakfast at Charlie's with her parents.

"*When* did you become SOF—undercover, part time, or hanging upside down on a trapeze?" I said. I did not sound friendly. I did not feel friendly.

"Twenty months ago," she said quickly.

I relaxed. Slightly. "Okay. So *why* did you?"

Aimil sighed. "It seemed like a good idea at the time." She glanced at Pat and Jesse. I glanced at Pat and Jesse too. If they looked any more bland and nonconfrontational they were going to dissolve into little puddles of glop.

Aimil looked back at me. "You're not going to like this," she said.

"I know," I said.

"SOF monitors globenet usage for who likes to read up a lot on the Others," said Aimil. "That's how they found me. They have a note of everybody who subscribes to the Darkline." Which included both her and me. In theory any heavy-duty line into the cosworld will let you look up anything you like on the globenet, and the parameters are drawn only by your subscription price and the weight of the line. But in practice it is a little more specific than that. The Darkline is what you are going to choose if what you are chiefly interested in is looking up all the latest the globenet could give you on the Others without going to a Darkshop or the library or some other public hook-in for it.

If I'd ever given a passing real-world thought to anything outside my bakery, I would have known SOF must do stuff like monitor the

Darkline. Which would mean they would know I used it. That, with my dad, was easily enough to interest them in me.

If I'd ever given a passing real-world thought to it, which I hadn't. I'd lived in my own swaddled-up little world. I who had been the star pupil in June Yanovsky's vampire lit class. But that was the point, really. The Others were still something that happened between the covers of books like *Vampire Tales and Other Eerie Matters*. SOF shop talk overheard at Charlie's was just live stories. Dry guys happened, but never to anybody I knew. Vampires were out there, but nowhere near me.

Until recently.

"We'd already found you, of course," Pat said to me, "because of your dad."

"Yes," I said. "You could stop reminding me. Nothing wrong with your dad, is there?" I said to Aimil.

Aimil laughed a little bitterly and bowed her head. As her bangs fell across her forehead they left flickering mahogany bars against her skin. I blinked. "Nothing that I know of. Or with my mom either. That's why it came as such a shock to them when I had two sets of adult teeth come in, one inside the other. Fortunately my mom has a cousin who's a dentist. A discreet dentist. And scared to death there might be something wrong with *his* blood. Also fortunately my second set wasn't the kind that keeps growing, although they were a funny shape. Once they were out they've stayed out. And my mom's cousin doesn't have anything to do with our branch of the family any more. But I'm not registered. Remember Azar?"

I was already remembering Azar.

He'd been the year between Aimil and me. My freshman year in high school, he was the only sophomore on the varsity football team. That was before his lower jaw began to drop and widen to hold the spectacular pair of tusks that started to grow at the same time. They took the tusks out, of course, but they couldn't do much reconstructive surgery on his face till his jaw stopped expanding. After the first surgery his family left town so that he could start school again somewhere they hadn't known him before. That was after he'd been registered. After our school had taken away all his sports awards because he was a partblood and must have had—ipso facto—an unfair advantage. Which is crap. And he'd been a nice guy. He wasn't stupid or a bully.

"It's an interesting situation," Pat interrupted, "because one of SOF's official purposes is to find unregistered partbloods, register them, and fine their asses good, if not arrest them and throw them in jail, which happens sometimes too. One of SOF's *unofficial* purposes is to find certain kinds of unregistered partbloods, protect them from getting found out, and persuade them to work for us. We really like librarians. They tend to have tidy minds."

"Librarian partbloods are probably flash easy to find," said Aimil. "We'll be the ones who belong to Otherwatch and Beware." These are the two biggest globenet trawlers for Other 'fo, exclusive to the Darkline. For a modest extra monthly fee you too can download eleventy jillion gigabytes every week and experience mental overkill paralysis, unless you are a trained member of SOF or a research librarian or a prune-faced academic and have a cyborg overdrive button for taking in 'fo. I didn't have the overdrive button. Besides, I'd always had a guilty preference for fiction. Since I seemed now to be *living* fiction, this proved to have been an entirely reasonable choice.

"I spend a few hours every week reading certain threads and—well—following my nose."

"We contacted her because the filters she'd set up herself on her subscription passwords seemed to bring her a peculiarly high level of source traffic by Others and partbloods, not just about them. So we had her in for a few chats and once she softened up a little. . . ."

"Did someone turn blue for you too?" I said.

Aimil smiled. "Yeah."

"—We found out that that nose of hers often told her when your actual Other had actual fingers on the keyboard, and that has sometimes been very interesting," said Jesse.

"Especially when she picks up a sucker," said Pat.

They all saw me freeze. "Hey, kiddo," said Pat. "That's kind of the point, you know? Nailing vampires. Remember?"

I nodded stiffly. The rift—or did I mean rifts—in my life were getting deeper and wider all the time. I only just stopped myself from reaching up to touch the thin white scar on my breast. If any of these people had noticed that I'd spent the entire sweltering summer wearing high-necked shirts they hadn't mentioned it, and they weren't mentioning that I had suddenly stopped wearing them for a mere autumn burst of pleasantly warm weather either.

"I—I just don't like talking about vampires," I said, after a moment. If one-fifth of the world's wealth—or possibly more—lay in vampire hands, of course there were a lot of them out there with not just basic com gear to handle their bloated bank balances but monster com networks that meant they had probably stopped noticing they weren't able to go outdoors in daylight. Plenty of human com techies never went out in daylight either. But com networks would include trog lines into the globenet. And some vampires who had them no doubt amused themselves chatting up humans.

I *knew* this. But those vampires were scary faceless bogeypeople that SOF existed to deal with. What was I doing here in a SOF office?

Partbloods sticking together, I suppose. What if I told them I *didn't* know I was one of the lucid ten percent? I shivered.

Did Bo have a line into the globenet? He was a master vampire. Of course he did.

Did Con?

I shivered again. Harder.

"Sunshine, I'm *sorry*," Aimil said. "I know it doesn't mean much, but sometimes when I'm tracking some—some *thing*, even that much contact, through however many miles of trog and ether, it starts to make me sick. I can't imagine what it must be like for you."

True.

"Now, about that tea," said Pat.

"You still haven't told me why you're here, like, today, now, this minute, in Pat's office," I said to Aimil.

She shook her head. "Serendipity, I guess. I showed up this afternoon to plug in my usual report and Pat brought me in here, said I was about to meet an old friend who was also a new recruit, and maybe I could reassure her that having anything to do with SOF doesn't automatically mean you're going to lose your interest in reading fiction and will wake up some morning soon with an overwhelming urge to wear khaki and start a firearm collection."

Pat, who was wearing navy blue trousers and a white shirt, said, "Hey."

"Navy blue and white are khaki too," said Aimil firmly. "But Rae, I didn't know it was you till you walked through the door."

"Then why are you saying you're sorry about what happened to me? What do you know about it?"

Aimil stared at me, visibly puzzled. "What happened—? Since the—the other night all of Old Town knows you were in some kind of trouble with suckers, those two days you went missing last spring—and a lot of us were already wondering. What else could it have been?"

Right. What else could it have been?

"It could have been a rogue demon," I said obstinately.

Aimil sighed. "Not very likely. A lot of partbloods can spot other partbloods, right? I haven't got Pat's gift for that. But a fullblood demon—if you'd been held by rogues, I'd've known it. Like cat hair on your shirt. So would whoever from SOF interviewed you have known it. SOF wouldn't have assigned someone to interview you who *wouldn't* have known it."

"And Jocasta's *good*," said Pat. "Even better than me."

"Good" wasn't the adjective I'd've chosen for my experience of that interview, but I let it pass.

"So would a lot of other people who come into Charlie's have known it," Aimil continued. "Haven't you noticed—well, like that Mrs. Bialosky hardly lets you out of her sight these days?"

"Mrs. Bialosky is a *Were*," I said.

"Yeah. And her sense of smell is *real* good," said Pat.

"She's another undercover SOF, I suppose," I said.

Pat laughed. "SOF couldn't hold her," he said.

She and Yolande should get together, I thought, but I didn't say it out loud. If SOF had no reason to look into my landlady I wasn't going to suggest it to them. If Pat thought she was a siddhartha, all the better.

And if they already had looked, I didn't want to know.

Jesse said gently, "You know there's such a thing as friends as well as colleagues and neighbors, don't you?"

I had my mouth open to say, "Sure, and you'd've been hanging around Charlie's watching me with at least four eyes a day if I'd just been some poor mug that got mixed up in something ickily Other, right?" And then I closed it again, because I realized that the answer was yes. They might not have been watching me so intensely, and they might not have been watching me in the hopes that whatever had happened might lead them to something they could use without reference to a continuing and uninterrupted supply of cinnamon rolls, but they would have been watching me. Because that was what SOF was for—in theory the first and most important thing it was for—to keep our citizens safe. And SOF for all its faults took that pretty seriously. I sighed. "So, how about that cup of tea? And then maybe you'll finally tell me why you wanted me to meet Aimil here."

Pat spun his combox around so the screen faced Aimil. She sat down and tapped herself in, and the screen cleared to the globenet symbol. I averted my eyes. Since I'd started seeing in the dark I couldn't look at any comscreen for long, TV, net, personal, GameDeluxe (not my territory, but Kenny had an amazing one), whatever. Brrrr. Vertigo wasn't in it, although migraine came close. At least I wasn't wasting subscription fees on Otherwatch and Beware by not having gone near my combox lately.

I could tell, however, watching out of my peripheral vision, that Aimil was calling up lists of mailsaves. She chose a list, hit a button, and mailtext blocks appeared. I felt an almost physical jolt, and reached out to steady myself on the back of her chair.

"Aah," said Pat, watching me.

"*What*," I said nastily. I don't like surprises. Especially this kind of surprise, and this was my second since I came through the front door of SOF HQ.

Aimil said, studying the screen, "I save anything that—well, that I guess comes from an Other, right? That feels funny. That's what these guys pay me for. There are a lot of us doing it—we don't know who each other are of course but I doubt we're all librarians—and when some nettag is making a lot of us jumpy, SOF tries to find out more about who's—or what's—behind it. Jesse asked me to separate off some tags that are on SOF's active list that I personally think feel like vampires rather than something else, and . . ."

"We wondered if any of them might mean something to you, you know, locationally," said Jesse.

Locationally? I thought irrelevantly. Is this the same English I speak?

"After what happened the other night," said Jesse. "The way you knew where it was even though it was too far away for you to, er, hear, in the usual way. Or see. What made you jump when Aimil opened her mailsave list?"

I shook my head. "Presumably I'm reacting to what you want me to be reacting to, yes," I said. "But whether it's going to be anything but a sensation like putting your finger in an electric socket I don't know."

"Try it," said Jesse.

Aimil stood up from the chair and I sat down, trying to examine myself for signs that my evil gene was waking up. This would be a logical moment for it, I felt, and probably quite a practical one too, from the perspective of lingering final moments of philanthropic sanity. Jesse and Pat would be trained in hand-to-hand, and even amok, and thor as hell with the muscles you get if you bash The Blob into trays of cinnamon rolls every morning, I should be a pushover for a couple of veteran SOF field agents.

The screen glowed at me balefully. I shut my eyes. Nothing was happening. My body went on breathing quietly, waiting for me to ask it to do something. "What do I do?"

"If you hit *next*," Aimil said, "you go to the next message."

I opened my eyes long enough to find the NEXT button. I could look at the keyboard. I glanced at the screen. The words there wriggled. I didn't like it but it didn't say "vampire" to me either. I hit NEXT.

More wriggly words. Ugh. Nothing else though. I hit NEXT.

And the next NEXT.

There was an odd building-up of internal pressure that I couldn't quite put down either to trying to look while not looking at a com-screen that was longing to give me a lightning-bolt-thunder-roll odin-bloody headache or to the knowledge that I was surrounded by SOFs avidly waiting for me to do something. Or that *I* was waiting to pop into Incredible Hulk mode and try to eat somebody. So I could guess that my shady rapport, affinity, Global Navigational Pin-point Precision Positioning Device (patent pending), or whatever, was acknowledging the presence of vampires somewhere out there behind the screen, but—so?

Next. Next. Next. I was sweating.

I realized what the pressure was. Expectation. I was getting close.

Close to *what*?

Next.

HERE.

I snapped my eyes closed and flung myself back in the chair, which rolled several feet away from the desk till it hit the corner of a table pushed against the wall. An unhandily stacked heap of paper spilled off onto the floor with a *swoosh*.

I got up, shakily, keeping my eyes averted from the screen. I could feel the beating of the HERE. I turned my head back and forth as if I was standing in a field looking for a landmark. No. Not there. I moved round a quarter turn, and waited to reorient the HERE. No. I moved another quarter turn . . . almost. An eighth turn back. No. An eighth turn forward, then another eighth. Yes. HERE.

I raised an arm. "That way. Now turn whatever it is off, because it's making me sick."

Aimil dived for it, and the screen went blank.

I sat down.

"Well, well, well," said Pat. The satisfaction in his voice made me suddenly very angry, but I felt too tired and sick to tell him so. I closed my eyes.

I opened them again a minute later. Steam from a cup of hot tea was caressing my face. I accepted the cup. Caffeine was my friend. I wasn't sure if I had any other friends in that room or not.

The Special Other Forces exist to control, defeat, neutralize, or exterminate all Other threat to humans. That was easy and straight-forward, and as a human it sounded—had sounded—pretty good to me, although at the same time I'd had a problem with the politics of anything Other defined as bad, which seemed to be the unofficial SOF motto. Now I was learning that in fact SOF was—apparently—full of partbloods, maybe fullbloods, and presumably Weres, and was clandestinely sympathetic to the registry dodgers.

It should have cheered me up. If I was a partblood myself, I was a partblood among partbloods. I should be eager to cooperate with my own little group of SOFs.

Who hated vampires. All vampires. By definition. Who hated and targeted vampires because they believed that vampires were not merely making everybody's lives more dangerous, but their own lives harder, their lives as good, socially well-adjusted and well-disposed part-demons or demons, as Weres who only needed a night off once a month. If it wasn't for vampires (so Pat's theory went) the humans would probably repeal the laws that automatically prevented anyone with Other blood from enjoying full human rights.

The theory was probably right.

Not to mention the less-than-a-hundred-years-before-we-all-go-under-the-dark thing.

It wasn't only that seeing in the dark creeped me out because it came from a vampire. It was that it made me permanently, relent-lessly, continuously conscious of being *connected* to . . . vampireness.

I do not know what I have given you tonight. I do not know what you have given me.

I was aware of it standing motionless outdoors at noon on a sunny day. Even the absence of shadow is a kind of shadow. You may not know that but I do. I did now. I wondered if this was anything like the dare-I-say *usual* realization of partbloodedness: knowing that you are—and are not—human, but angrily, frustratedly believ-ing that this didn't make you any less of a . . .

A what, exactly? A human? A person? An individual? A rational creature?

Remind me that you are a rational creature.

I wished I could ask somebody. But nobody was part vampire, it wasn't possible. Whatever I was, that wasn't it. Was it. Was it?

Drink your tea, Sunshine, and stop thinking. Thinking is not your strong suit.

There was something else that was bothering me about all this, but I couldn't get that far yet. I didn't have to. Where I was was far enough to feel nomad about.

"Feeling better?" said Pat.

"No," I said.

"Do you know what you were pointing at?"

"No," I said. I looked up, along the line I had indicated, and thought about which way the SOF building lay and where I thought I was in it. I'd probably been pointing west, something like west. That wasn't a big help; west was where all the deserted factories were, where the worst of the urban bad spots were. Nobody lived out that way now; as the population slowly began to recover from the Voodoo Wars, rather than trying to reclaim any of that area, new malls and office blocks and housing developments were going up in the south and east and—also avoiding the lake and its bad spots—curling around eventually (avoiding druggie nirvana) up to the north. The reason anybody was trying to salvage Chesterfield was because it was south. In twenty or thirty years we and the next town to the south, Piscataweh, would probably be one big city. Unless we all went under the dark early.

The western end of New Arcadia isn't entirely deserted; it has some rather murky small businesses scattered around and some clubs the police keep closing down that open again a day or a week later. Sometimes they reopen briefly somewhere else, sometimes they don't bother to pretend to move. It is the western end of town where gangs of mostly human, mostly teenage boys go to play chicken and look for vampires. It is also a popular area for squatters, although the attrition by death rate is pretty severe. A lot of the murky small businesses that manage to hold on there cater to squatters who can't afford to pay for housing, but if they want to stay alive have to pay for some warding. There are two kinds of cheap wards: the ones that don't work, and the ones that mess with what for want of a better phrase I'm going to call black magic. Which gives you the idea. The homeless are better off sleeping in the gutters in Old Town, but I admit that for Old Town's sake it's a good thing most of them don't.

It didn't take a combox or a kick in the head to tell anyone in New Arcadia that if they were looking for suckers to look west.

"I was pointing west," I said grudgingly. "Big deal."

"We don't know if it's a big deal yet or not," said Pat reasonably. "We won't know till we drive you out there."

"No," I said.

"It might be, for example," Pat continued unfazed, "that it isn't the west of New Arcadia at all; it could be somewhere a lot farther away—Springfield, Lucknow, Manchester." Manchester had a rep as a vampire city. "The globenet is the globenet; you never know where a specific piece of cosmail has come from."

"Unless you're SOF, and you track it down," I said.

There was a little silence. Jesse sighed. "It's not that easy. I mean, tracing something off the net is never easy—"

"There are all those boring laws about privacy," I said.

"—which even SOF has to make an effort to break," said Pat.

"—but a lot of the usual rules of, um, physics, don't work quite the same with Others as with humans," Jesse continued.

Yeah, I thought. How *does* a hundred-and-eighty-pound man turn into a ninety-pound wolf? Where does the leftover ninety go? Does he park it in the umbrella stand overnight?

"Geography and vampires is one of the worst. Where they are and where we are often doesn't seem to, uh, relate."

Vampire senses are different from human in a number of ways . . . It is not the distance that is crucial, but the uniformity. . . . Evidently this worked in both, um, directions. Einstein was wrong. I wondered if it was too late to give my skeggy old physics teacher a bad day.

"So even if we got a good read off a cosmail that we were sure was lobbed by a sucker we still might not know any more than we did before we wasted some of SOF's tax blinks cracking it. We can use all the help we can get."

"Which I think I said to you already not long ago," added Pat. "You might also keep in mind that the guys who don't want to be found usually have the edge on us guys who want to find them. Even the human ones, and they're usually easier. Sunshine, give us a break. We're not trying to ruin your life for fun, you know."

I stared into the bottom of my mug. Not Jesse or Pat's fault that I was bound to a vampire. I didn't think they'd be real open to the idea of making an exception for him. I wasn't happy about it myself. But I could hardly tell Pat that the reason SOF was so full of covert partbloods now made me feel worse, not better.

I was getting to a pretty bad place if I was beginning to wonder if maybe going bonkers and having to be bagged for my own good might be my best choice.

What if what I had pointed toward was *Con*?

No. The answer came almost at once. No. What I had pointed toward was something . . . something in itself sick-making, antithetical to humans. To anything warm and breathing. Betrayal would be a different sort of sick. I was sure.

I was pretty sure.

A human shouldn't be able to think in terms of betraying a vampire. It didn't work. Like those nonsense sentences they used to wake you up when you are supposed to be learning a foreign language. I eat the hat of my uncle. I sit upon the cat of my aunt. Depends on the cat of course.

It didn't work, like being able to see in the dark didn't work. The bottom of my mug was in shadow. I hadn't drunk the last swallow because it had a fine dust of tea leaves in it. Even they threw shadows, tiny shadows within the shadow, floating in the shadowy dark liquid. "Okay," I said.

It might have been Bo I'd found. That I'd felt through the globenet. That was about as sick-making a thought as I could have. Bo, that Con was supposed to be finding so we could go spoke his wheel before he spoked ours. Again. Permanently.

"Then you'll come with us?"

I thought about it. There wasn't much to think. "I have to be back at six," I said.

"You got it," said Pat.

IT WAS JUST Pat and Jesse and me. Aimil went back to the library. When we awkwardly said good-bye, her face was full of bright shadows I couldn't read. I looked at her, trying to resettle her in my mind as a partblood and a SOF. Did it take that much effort? I didn't know. It was taking me a lot of effort to be whatever I now was.

While Pat did some shifting-papers-around things and Jesse disappeared for a few minutes I moved over to the sunlight falling through the gray window of Pat's office. The sunlight felt thin, but it was sunlight. SOF windows were all gray because of the proofglass: proof against bullets, firebombs, kamikaze Weres, glass- and steel-cutting demon talons, spells, charms, almost everything but an armored division with howitzers. Proofglass had only come on the market about ten years ago, just after the Wars, which might have been a little less fatal if it had been invented a few years earlier. All high-risk businesses and the military and most other government departments, plus a lot of paranoids, both the kind with real enemies and the other kind, now had proofglass in their windows and their vehicles. Proofglass upgrader was a popular new career among young magic handlers. You didn't have to be a magic handler to get hired as an upgrader, but you'd probably live longer.

Nobody had figured out how to make it less gray though. Gray and depressing, like being in jail. Hadn't they done studies that humans really need sunlight? Not just light. Sunlight. And all humans, not just me. I hoped Charlie's wasn't going to have to put in proofglass.

I hoped I was still human.

Pat drove and put me in the front seat with him. "Can you still feel—whatever?"

I thought about it. Reluctantly. I poked around for that feeling of *Here*. I found it. It was like finding a dead rat in your living room. A large dead rat. "Yes," I said.

"West?"

"Yes."

We drove. Old county buildings quickly became Old Town, which turned almost as quickly into downtown and then rather more slowly into nothing-in-particular town, blocks of slightly shabby houses giving way to blocks of somewhat seedy shops and offices and back again. It wasn't a big city; we went over the line into what most of us called No Town far too soon. In the first place I didn't want to go there at all, in the second place I didn't like being reminded that it was so close. New Arcadia's only big bad spots are in No Town, which did compel a certain amount of evasive driving. Even a SOF car can only go where there are still roads, and urban bad spots get blocked off fast. But we weren't going nearly indirectly enough for me.

Here moved out of the back of my mind into the front, like Large Zombie Rat getting up off your living room floor and following you into the kitchen where you realize that it's bigger and uglier than you thought, and its teeth are longer, and while zombies are really, really stupid, they're also really, really vicious. They're also nearly as fast as vampires, and since they don't just happen, they're made for a purpose, if one is coming after you, that's probably its purpose, and you're in big trouble.

Here was getting worse. It was going to burst out of my skull and dance on the dashboard, and it wouldn't be anything anyone wanted to watch. "Stop," I said. Pat stopped. I tried to breathe. Zombie Rat seemed to be sitting on my chest, so I couldn't. I couldn't see it any more though—there didn't seem to be anything left but its little red eyes—no, its huge, drowning, no-color eyes—

"I—can't—any—more—turn—around," I think is what I said. I don't remember. I remember after Pat turned around and started driving back toward Old Town. After what felt like a long time I began breathing again. I was clammy with sweat and my head ached as if pieces of my skull had been broken and the edges were grinding together. But Zombie Rat was gone.

That had been far too much like the bad spot the SOF car hadn't protected us from, the day Jesse and Pat took me back out to the house on the lake. (Those no-color eyes . . . both mirror-flat and chasm-deep . . . if they were eyes. . . .) But we hadn't tried to drive through a bad spot. And this time it was just me. Pat and Jesse hadn't noticed anything. Except my little crisis.

I didn't know if I was angrier at their making me try to do— whatever—or at the fact that I'd failed. I'd been to No Town when I was a teenager. It wasn't like I had no idea. Any teenager with the slightest pretensions toward being stark, spartan, whatever, which I'm afraid I had had, will probably give it a try if it's offered, and it will be offered. And No Town is a rite of passage; quite sensible kids go at least once. I'd been there more than once. Some of the clubs were pretty spartan by anyone's standards. Kenny said (out of Mom's hearing) this was still true. And it was also still true (Kenny said) that you dared each other to climb farther in, over the rubble around the bad spots, although nobody got very far. But I hadn't got any less far than anyone else, when I was his age.

So had whatever-it-was moved there since my time, or was I just more sensitive now than I had been? No Town was actually a lot cleaner now than it had been when I was sixteen and seventeen, which was right after the Wars. Having been once captured by vampires, did I now overreact to their presence? If "overreact to vampires" wasn't a contradiction in terms.

Or was this another horrible, specific one-off, like my having heard the giggler when no one else could?

I didn't know if I wanted the answer to be yes or no. If it was no, then it might mean my sucker connection was general, which didn't bear thinking about. But if it was yes, then it meant I was picking up something to do with Bo. Which didn't bear thinking about.

Unless it was Con. Unless this had been his daylight wards, protecting him, protecting *us*, in the company of a couple of sucker-hating SOFs.

No. It wasn't Con. Whatever it was, it wasn't Con.

Pat drove around into the SOF back lot again. Neither of them had said any word of blame or failure or frustration to me, although I felt I could hear them both thinking. Words like "triangulation." I didn't know if they'd marked where I made them turn around. Prob-

ably. But neither of them mentioned it. Yet. "I'd take you straight to
Charlie's but I don't think you want the neighborhood seeing you
show up in a SOF car," Pat said, as offhand as if we'd been buying
groceries.

I started to shake my head—unmarked SOF cars were like SOFs
out of uniform; you still knew—but changed my mind. "Thanks." I
fumbled for the door handle.

"Do you want to come back in? You look a little . . . worn. There
are a few bedrooms in the back. They're pretty basic but they have
beds and they're quiet. Or I could run you home."

This time I did manage to shake my head. Carefully. "No. Thanks.
I'm going for a walk. Clear my head." The last thing I wanted to do
was lie down in a small dark room and try to go to sleep. I didn't want
to go home either. There might be a dead rat in the living room.

I got out of the car, lifted my face to the sunlight. It felt like a
good fairy's kiss. Except good fairies don't exist.

As I walked toward the exit Pat called after me, "Hey. Didn't you
want to tell us something? When you came in."

I looked at him, at the way the shadows fell across his face. He
was leaning on the roof of the car, which was unmarked-cop-car
blue. That was probably why the shadows in the hollows of his eyes,
his upper lip, his throat, looked blue. "I forget now," I said. "It'll
come back to me."

Pat smiled a little: a twitch of the lips. "Sorry, Sunshine."

I raised a hand and turned away again. He said softly, "See you."
He could have meant only that he'd see me at Charlie's, where we'd
seen each other for years. But I knew that wasn't what he meant.

I WENT FOR a long walk. I spiraled slowly through Old Town, from
the outside edge, where SOF headquarters and City Hall lie on the
boundary between Old Town and downtown, to the next circle
where the area library and the Other Museum and the older city
buildings are, through several small parks and down the long green
aisle of General Aster's Way (purple in autumn with michaelmas
daisies, some municipal gardener's idea of a joke), and then into the

back streets of Charlie's neighborhood, where everyone gets lost occasionally, even people who have lived there all their lives, like Charlie and Mary and Kyoko. I was used to getting lost. I didn't mind. I'd come to something I recognized eventually.

I wandered and thought about the latest thing I didn't want to think about. There seemed to be so many things I didn't want to think about lately.

I didn't want to think about my increasing sense that something had happened to Con.

And that it mattered.

There *is no fellowship* between humans and vampires. We are fire and water, heads and tails, north and south . . . day and night.

Maybe I was imagining the bond. Maybe it was a way of dealing with what had happened. Like post-traumatic thingummy.

Con himself said the bond existed, but he could be wrong too. Vampires are deadly, but no one says they're infallible.

I blinked my treacherous eyes, watching the things in the shadows slither and sparkle. I had plenty to worry about already. I didn't have to worry about vampires too. One vampire. The last thing I wanted to be doing was worrying about him.

No, the next to last thing. The last thing I wanted was to be bound to him.

I hadn't thought I had any—did I mean innocence?—to lose, after those two nights on the lake. I didn't know you could go on finding out you'd had stuff by losing it. This didn't seem like a very good method to me.

Over two months of being slowly poisoned probably hadn't been really good for me either. And the nightmares had been bad. But in a way they'd still been pure. I'd made a mistake—a mistake I'd paid dearly for—but it had been a *mistake*.

A month ago, I'd *called* on Con. Okay, I was at the end of my tether. But I'd still asked a vampire for help—not Mel, not a human doctor of human medicine. And he'd helped me. The nightmares I'd had since weren't pure at all.

My thought paused there, teetering on the edge of a precipice, and then fell over.

What if it *hadn't* been a mistake, driving out to the lake? What if I'd had to do it—if not that exact thing, then something similar. What if that restlessness I hadn't been able to name had caused exactly what it was meant to cause?

That question I hadn't asked Con, out by the lake, *is my dad another of your old enemies? Or your old friends?*

Between the dark thoughts inside my head and the leaping, glittery shadows my eyes saw, I had to stop. I was at the edge of Oldroy's Park. I groped my way to a bench and sat down.

I sat there, and stared at the tree opposite me, and the way the rough ridges of its bark seemed to *wiggle* where they lay in shade. My thoughts were stuck on that night at the lake. I never liked coincidence much, but I hated the sense I was making now.

I watched the wiggling bark. It occurred to me that this was new. I'd been seeing into shadows, but merely what was there, as if there was a rather erratic light on it. This was something else. Which gave me something I could bear to think about, so I thought about it. A few more minutes passed and it seemed to me it was as if I was watching the tree breathing. I found a leaf in shadow, and looked at it for a while; it twinkled, as if with tiny starbursts, but rather than thinking ugh—weird, I kept watching, till there seemed to be a pattern. I thought, it's as if I'm watching its pores opening and closing. I looked down at my hands. The shadows between the fingers gleamed like a banked fire. The tiny shadows laid by the veins on the backs of them were a tiny, flickering dark green edged with a tinier, even more flickering red. The daylight part of the veins looked as it always did. In the shadow places I could see the blood moving.

I was sitting in sunlight, not shade. I automatically chose sun if there was any sun to be had. I remembered the sun on my back the first morning at the lake, like the arm of a friend. I closed my eyes.

I heard the footsteps but I didn't expect them to pause.

"Pardon me," said a voice. "Are you all right?"

I opened my eyes. An old woman stood there, a little bent over, leaning on the handle of her two-wheeled shopping cart. "You look—tired," she said. "Can I fetch you anything? There is a shop on the corner. And it has a pay phone. Can I call someone for you?"

She had a nice face. She would be someone you would be glad to have as a neighbor, or as a regular at the coffeehouse you and your family ran. I looked at the shadows that fell half across her face and saw . . . I don't know how . . . that she was a partblood. And that something about my expression was maybe making her guess I might be going through finding that out about myself. And remembering how hard this was she was going to ask me, a total stranger, if I was all right.

I hauled myself back into the ordinary world, and the vision faded. The shadows that fell across her face reverted to being the usual, disorienting, see-through, funny-edged shadows I'd been seeing for a month. She smiled. "I'm sorry to disturb you. I—er—I thought you might perhaps—er—"

"Want to be disturbed?" I said. "Yes. Isn't it . . . silly . . . how . . . upsetting . . . just thinking can be?"

"It's not silly at all. The insides of our own minds are the scariest things there are."

Scarier than vampires? I thought. Scarier than an *affinity* for vampires? Well. That was what she'd said, wasn't it? What my mind contained was an affinity for vampires.

She was fishing around in her cart and pulled out a package of Fig Carousels and another of Chocolate Pinwheels. I laughed. She smiled at me again. "Which?" she said, holding them out toward me.

I hadn't had a Pinwheel in fifteen years, although the secret recipe for Sunshine's Killer Zebras was the later result of a three-pack-a-week pre-Charlie's childhood. I pointed to the Pinwheels. She tore open the packet, sat down, and offered it to me. "Thank you," I said. She took one too.

We sat in silence for a while, and did away with several more Pinwheels. "Thank you," I said again.

"Maud," she said. "I'm Maud. I live—there," and she pointed to one of the old townhouses that surrounded the little park. "I sit here often, in warm weather. I've found it's a good place for thinking; I like to believe Colonel Oldroy was a pleasant fellow, which is why the disagreeable thoughts seem to fall away if you sit here."

Colonel Oldroy had been one of those military scientist bozos who spent decades locked up in some huge secret underground maze because whatever they were doing was so superclassified that the existence of a lab to do it in was confidential information. It still wasn't public knowledge where his lab had been, but Oldroy got the credit, or the blame, for the blood test SOF still used on job applicants. Before Oldroy there was no reliable test for demon partbloods. (Remember that *demon* is a hodge-podge word. A Were can't be a partblood; you either are one or you aren't. Anything else, anything alive that is, may be called a demon, although things like peris and angels will probably protest.) Pretty much the first thing that Oldroy discovered was that *he* was a partblood. He'd retired before they had a chance to throw him out, and spent the last twenty years of his life breeding roses, and naming them things like Lucifer, Mammon, Beelzebub, and Belphegor. Belphegor, under the less controversial name Pure of Heart, was a big commercial success. Mom had a Pure of Heart in her back yard. Oldroy may not have had a very happy life, but it sounded like he'd had a sense of humor. I wondered if he'd had anything to do with synthesizing the drug that made partbloods piss green or blue-violet but pass his blood test, or with setting up the bootleg mentor system.

"Sometimes you have help," I said. "Sometimes people come along and offer you Chocolate Pinwheels."

"Sometimes," she said.

"I'm Rae," I said. "Do you know Charlie's Coffeehouse? It's about a quarter mile that way," I said, pointing.

"I don't get that far very often," she said.

"Well, some time, if you want to, you might like to try our Killer Zebras. There's a strong family resemblance. . . . Tell whoever serves you that Sunshine says you can have as many as you can carry away, to bring back to this park and eat. In the sunshine."

"Are you Sunshine then too?"

I sighed. "Yes. I guess. I'm Sunshine too."

"Good for you," she said, and patted my knee.

I GOT HOME that night at about nine-thirty and had a cup of cinnamon and rosehip tea and stared out at the dark and thought. There was at least one good result of my negative epiphany that afternoon in Oldroy Park: there seemed to me suddenly so many worse things that worrying about Con seemed clean and straightforward. He had saved my life, after all. Twice. Never mind the extenuating circumstances. I stood on my little balcony and remembered: *I could not come to you if you did not call me, but if you called I had to come.*

"Constantine," I said quietly, into the darkness. "Do you need me? You have to call me if you do. You told me the rules yourself."

He'd said Bo was after us. And that Bo would make a move soon. I rather thought that "soon" in this instance meant a definition of soon that humans and vampires could agree on. Con should have been back before now to tell me what was going on, what we were going to do. How far *he'd* got in tracing Bo. He hadn't.

There was something wrong.

I SLEPT BADLY that night, but this was getting to be so usual that it was an effort to try to decide if the nightmares I'd had were the kind I should pay attention to or not. I decided that they probably were, but I didn't know what kind of attention to pay, so I wasn't going to. I went in to work, turned my brain off, and started making cinnamon rolls, and garlic-rosemary buns for lunch. Then I made brown sugar brownies, Rocky Road Avalanche, Killer Zebras, and a lot of muffins, and then it was ten-thirty and I had the lunch shift free.

I had pulled my apron off and was about to untie my scarf when Mel's hand stopped me long enough for him to kiss the back of my neck. I shook my hair out and said "Yes" and we went back to his house together and spent some time on the roof. There's nothing nicer than making love outdoors on a warm sunny day, and this late in the year it felt like getting away with something too.

Mel used to laugh, sometimes, right after he came, in this gentle, surprised way, as if he'd never expected to be this happy, and then he'd kiss me, thoughtfully, and I'd hang on to him and hope that I was reading the signs right. That afternoon was one of those times. He'd wound up on top, which, I admit, I had slightly engineered, since there was a bit of an autumnal breeze snaking around and it was nice and warm under Mel's body. His breath smelled of coffee and cinnamon. We lay there some time afterward—I loved that butterfly-wings feeling of a hard-on getting unhard inside me—and while we lay there I was all right and the world was all right and everything that might not be all right was on hold. And it was *daylight* and with my treacherous eyes shut I could just lie there and feel the sunshine on my face.

After a comfortable, rather dreamy lunch he went downstairs to take apart or put together some motorcycle and I went off to the library. I wanted to talk to Aimil.

She looked up from her desk, smiled faintly and said, "I have a break in, uh, forty minutes," and went back to whatever she was doing.

I had a pass through the NEW shelves where there was a book hysterically titled *The Scourge of the Other.* It was a good two inches thick. I considered stealing it and putting it through the meat grinder at Charlie's, but the library would only buy another one and the detritus of ink and binding glue probably wouldn't do the quality of Charlie's meatloaf any good. I knew without picking it up that the chapters would have rabble-rousing headings like "The Demon Menace" and "The Curse of the Were." I wasn't going to guess what noun was desperate enough for vampires. Four months ago I would have just scowled. Today it gave me a hard-knot-in-pit-of-stomach feeling. It was turning out I had a lot of Other friends. And Con, of course, whatever he was. *Con, are you all right?*

My tea was already steeping when I went back to the tiny staff kitchen to find Aimil. "So, how did it happen?" I said.

She didn't bother to ask how did what happen. "I knew about your SOFs at Charlie's because you told me about them."

"I told you so you wouldn't stop speaking to me because I seemed to like some guys who wore khaki and navy blue."

"That they were SOF was supposed to help?"

"They told the best Other stories."

"I guess. I could have done without the one . . . never mind. Anyway, so I recognized them when they came here. One day Pat and Jesse asked if I'd come by the SOF office some day for a chat—I hadn't realized you could feel *surrounded* by two people, you know?—and what was I going to say, no? So I said yes. And then they asked me if I'd be interested in doing a little work for SOF and of course I said no, and then they started working around to telling me they weren't so interested that I was a reference librarian as they were interested in what I was doing with Otherwatch and Beware. They seemed to know what I was doing at home too, and before I totally freaked Pat held his breath and turned blue. I said, what's to prevent me reporting you? And he said, because you're another one . . . I have *no* idea how they found out." Aimil stopped, but she didn't stop like end-of-the-story stop.

"And?" I said.

She sighed. "Rae, I'm sorry. They also said, because you're a friend of Sunshine's."

There was no window in the little library staff kitchen. I wanted sunlight. What had my friendship to do with anything? She'd been working for SOF for almost two years. "And you didn't tell me."

Aimil walked over to the door and closed it gently. I didn't want anyone to hear us either, but my spine started prickling with claustrophobia, or dark-o-phobia anyway. "I'm sorry," said Aimil. "It's only been since I've been working for them that I've started . . . have been able to *start* thinking of myself as Other. As a partblood. The best way to pass is to believe in the role, you know? My parents know, of course, but they haven't made any attempt to find out where it comes from. None of my brothers had anything weird happen to them, and so far as I know they don't know about me. I haven't told my family I'm SOF, and I haven't—hadn't—told *anyone* I'm partblood. Who was I going to tell? Why? The only person who would have a right to know is the father of my children, and I'm not going to have children and pass this on. I hope none of my brothers' kids . . . well. Because I'd have to tell them then."

I didn't say anything right away. "When did you find out?"

"Yeah," said Aimil. "Right about the time I met you. You looked as lost as I felt. And then it turned out we got along, and . . ."

"Did everyone but my mother and me assume that who my dad was was public knowledge?"

"It wasn't quite that bad."

I looked at her.

She said reluctantly, "It was maybe worse during the Voodoo Wars but by then everyone knew you, and your mom had married Charlie, and Charlie's family has lived in Old Town forever, and you were normal by context, you know? And then you had two dead-normal little pests for brothers. Nobody ever, ever caught you doing anything weird at school—you seemed just as fascinated as the rest of us when some of the Ngus and Bloodaxes and so on talked about magic handling. I don't deny that a few people looked at you a little sideways."

I'd let my tea sit too long, but the bitterness in my mouth seemed appropriate.

"You were into *cooking*, Rae. And a generation or two ago the Blaises were top dog, sure—"

Were they, I thought. So many things my mother never told me. Although I couldn't really blame her for my avoiding reading globe-net articles that mentioned the Blaises. Could I? I'd *wanted* to be Rae Seddon.

"You still heard a little about them at the beginning of the Wars . . . but then it's like what was left of them disappeared. So maybe you were genuinely normal, you know? Most people say that magic handling runs out in families sooner or later."

"The SOFs didn't think so," I muttered. Disappeared. *Bo's lot brought me a Blaise. And not just a third cousin who can do card tricks and maybe write a ward sign that almost works, but Onyx Blaise's daughter.*

Onyx Blaise.

Whose mother taught his daughter to transmute. How did the people who were looking at me sideways count those one or two generations? What else could my gran do? Had she done?

Disappeared *how*?

"And nobody gets more normal than your mom."

True. I would think about how to thank her for my very well embedded normalcy later. It might be difficult to choose between cyanide and garrotting.

"Can we go outside?" I said.

The sun was behind a cloud but daylight is still better than indoors. "Aimil. I want to ask you a favor."

"Done."

"Okay. Thanks. It's what SOF wants me to do—try and get some location fix on one of your creepy cosmails. But I want to do it somewhere that isn't behind proofglass."

"In daylight," said Aimil. "Okay. We'll do it at my house. My next afternoon off is Thursday."

"I'll find someone to swap with."

"It's not only the proofglass, is it? It's also SOF. You don't want to do it just because SOF tells you to."

I nodded. "I know they're the good guys and everything, but . . ."

"I know. Once I found out they were watching me I changed the way I do some stuff. They are good guys and I do work for them and I don't mind—much. But it's all a little nomad for me. And I still have this silly idea that my life belongs to *me*."

There were good reasons Aimil and I were friends.

I WENT HOME that night and stood on the balcony again and said to the darkness, "Con, Constantine, are you all right? If you need me, *call me to you.*"

For a moment I felt . . . something. Like a twitch against your line when you're half asleep or thinking about something else. It may be a fish and it may be the current . . . but it *may* be a fish. (I'd learned to fish because Mel taught me, not because I longed to impale small invertebrates on barbed hooks and rip hell out of piscine oral cavities and smother fellow oxygen breathers in an alien medium.) The flicker itself made me think I was half asleep or thinking about something else, because I was straining after any sign whatsoever. And it was gone again at once.

THURSDAY AFTERNOON WASN'T flash ideal but I managed. Paulie was a little too not-sorry to change his single weekly four-thirty-in-the-morning shift for another afternoon that Thursday, and he hadn't made up the one he'd missed our last thirteen-day week yet either. I'd worry about just how not-sorry he was later. Meanwhile I got up at three A.M. to do a little extra baking like I had a point to make. As I drank the necessary pint-mug of blacker-than-the-pit-of-doom tea to get me going I stood on the balcony again, testing for quivers in the current. All I got was a stronger sense that there was something wrong; but I was good at feeling there was something wrong even when there wasn't—something I'd inherited from my mother—and there was nothing in this case but my own glangy unease to look at.

There are advantages to driving an old wreck instead of a modern car; wrecks bounce around and jerk at your hands on the wheel and help keep you awake. The charms in the glove compartment were more restless than usual too: I think they were objecting to the driving. By the time I got off work at noon I felt it had been several years since I'd had any sleep, and I had a nap instead of lunch. I brought sandwiches in a bag, and Aimil had a pot of tea waiting for me.

It was another gray day, but Aimil had pulled the combox table around so that the chair backed up against the window, which she had opened. What daylight there was fell on me as I sat there, and there was a little wind that stroked my hair.

"Where do you want to start?" said Aimil. "With the *bingo!* one from the other day, or do you want to start fresh?"

I hadn't thought about it. Good beginning. It was so hard to screw myself to do anything, the details got a bit lost. . . .

Who—or what—was I looking for? Con? Or Bo? Since I was doing it alone with Aimil I wasn't trying to make Pat and Jesse happy. So what was going to make me happy? Define *happy.*

But if I found something on the other side of the real globe that Pat and Jesse would get all tangled up in negotiations with their local SOF equivalents over, it might get them out of my hair.

Finding Bo wasn't going to make me *happy,* but I didn't want to look for Con with anyone else around, even Aimil. Which left Bo or the Unknown. The Unknown, at the moment, was unknown. Bo, on the other hand, was after me. Bo, then.

"Let's start with bingo."

Aimil brought up the file, highlighted the cosmail I wanted, and stepped back. I squinted at the screen. I could see the winking bar of highlighting, and the button was under my finger. I pressed.

It was like hands around my throat, a crushing, splintering weight on my breast; there was also a horrible, horrible pressure against my *eyes*, my poor dark-dazzled eyes . . . I was lost in the dark, I no longer knew which way was up and which down, I was vertiginous, I was going to be sick. . . .

No.

I steadied myself. I found an . . . alignment. Somewhere. Somewhere, reaching in the dark . . . I was . . . no, I wasn't standing. There didn't seem to be anything to stand on, and I wasn't sure there was any of me to stand *with*. If my feet had disappeared, then perhaps it wasn't surprising that my eyes—no, my sight—had disappeared too. This wasn't just darkness: this was what came after. This was the beyond-dark. And I could only see in the dark. My eyes were still there—or perhaps they were now my non-eyes—I couldn't see with them and blinking no longer seemed relevant, but the pressure was there. And why was it so difficult to breathe? Especially since at the same time breathing seemed as irrelevant as blinking. Why did I *want* to breathe?

Where was I? I was—*stretched*—along some intangible line; a compass needle. Compass needles don't mind the dark. Although I doubted I was pointing toward anything like a north that I'd recognize back in the real world. Maybe I'd found where Aimil's cosmail had come from. But where was here? And was there some clue I could take back with me to the world I knew?

If I could get back there.

I experimented with moving. Moving didn't seem to be an option. I was too much like nothing, here, in this nonplace, in the beyond-dark. Right, okay, next time I come I'll organize my question better going in. . . .

Next time, presupposing I get out of this time alive.

I was grateful for the pressure against my eyes, the difficulty breathing; it made me feel I still existed . . . somehow. Somewhere.

I was a magic handler, a stuff changer, a Blaise by blood, and lately, by practice. Not much practice but growing all the time.

I remembered another sense of alignment, when I had changed my little knife to a key. I reached for that sense. No, I reached for my knife. It shouldn't have been there, and I had no fingers to feel for it, but I was suddenly aware of it. I couldn't see it, but I knew that it was a light even in this darkness. And by its invisible light I could . . . see. See. Feel. Hear. Smell. Live. . . .

I heard a rustle, like leaves in a breeze. And for a moment I stood on four slender furred legs and I could feel and hear and smell as no human could.

And then I was back again, sitting in Aimil's living room, and her hand was reaching through my powerless fingers and pressing the button. The screen went dark. "That was *not* good," she said.

"What—happened?" I was amazed at the sense of my body sitting in the chair, of gravity, of sight (light; twinkly shadows), of fingers on a keyboard, feet against a floor. *Vampire senses are different from human in a number of ways.* Had I—? What had I—?

The leaves laid sun-dapples on my brown back as I stood at the edge of the woods with the golden field before me. I raised my black nose to the wind, cupped my big ears forward and back to listen.

Yeek. My human fingers closed on my knife. I was still in Aimil's living room.

"You were gone," said Aimil. "Not long—ten seconds or so—just long enough for me to take two steps and reach for the button. But your body didn't have *you* in it." She sat down, suddenly, on the floor. "Do you know where you went?" She bowed her head between her knees, and then tipped her face back and looked up at me. "Do you know?"

I shook my head. Experimenting with motion. I remembered the void, the alignment, the other senses—my little knife. My tree. My . . . doe. I wondered, when she had accepted the death she knew she could not escape, if she knew what her death was *for*, if that could have made any difference, if that was why she . . . I touched the knife-bulge in my pocket. It felt no different than it ever had. We sat in daylight; if I took it out it would look like any other pocket-knife. The second blade, which I rarely used, would be covered with pocket lint; the first blade, which I used all the time, would need sharpening. Folded up it was about the length of my middle finger, and a little wider and deeper; it was scraped and gouged by years in a series of pockets, sharing cramped quarters with things like loose change and car keys. And it glowed in the dark, even in the beyond-dark of the void. Glowed like a beacon that said, "Hold on. I've got you. Here."

I felt—carefully—after my experience of nowhere, of beyond-dark. Had I brought anything back after all, anything I could use?

Yes. But I didn't know what it was. It wasn't anything so straight-forward as a direction.

"Not caffeine after that," said Aimil, still on the floor. "Scotch." She got up on all fours and reached to the little cabinet next to her sofa. "And don't even ask me if you want to try again, because the answer is no."

I looked at her when she gave me a small heavy glass with a fin-ger's width of dark amber liquid in it, about the color of the thin wooden plates set into the sides of my little knife. "We won't try it again today," I said. "But we have to try again."

"No, *we* don't," she said. "Let SOF figure it out. It's what they're for."

"If they could figure it out they wouldn't be asking us."

"The Wars are over," she said.

"Not exactly," I said, after a pause. "Didn't Pat tell you—"

"Yes, he told me we'll all be under the dark in a hundred years!" she said angrily. "I know!"

I slid down to join her on the floor. I felt like a collection of old creaking hinges. I leaned over and put an arm around her. "I don't want to know either."

After a moment she said, "There have been two more dry guys in Old Town this last week. Have you heard about them?"

"Yes." It had been on the news a few days ago—great stuff to hear when you're driving alone in the dark—and Charlie and Liz had been talking about it when I brought the first tray of cinnamon rolls out front. They had fallen silent. I pretended I hadn't heard anything and toppled the first burning-hot roll onto a plate for Mrs. Bialosky. She patted my hand and said, "Don't you worry, sweetie, it's not your fault." Because she was Mrs. Bialosky I almost believed her, but I made the mistake of looking up, into her face, when I smiled at her, and saw the expression in her eyes. Oh. I almost patted her hand back and told her it wasn't her fault either, but it wouldn't have done any good. I guess I wasn't surprised to find out that Mrs. Bialosky wasn't only about litter and rats and flower beds.

"I wouldn't have joined SOF just because Pat can turn blue," Aimil said. "Working in a proofglassed room gives *me* asthma. Even part-time. Or maybe it's just all the guys in khaki."

I WENT BACK to Charlie's for the dinner shift, but Charlie took one look at me and said, "I'll find someone to cover for you. Go home."

"I'll go when you find someone," I said, and lasted two hours, by which time poor Paulie had agreed to give up the rest of his night off after being there all afternoon. Teach him to be glad to escape the four-thirty-in-the-morning shift. I was home by eight-thirty; it was just full dark. Charlie had sent me home with a bottle of champagne that had a glass and a half left in it: perfect. I stood on my balcony and drank it and looked into the darkness. The darkness danced.

I had had an idea. I didn't like it much, but I had to try it. I went back indoors and unplugged my combox. It's never quite dark under the sky, and I didn't have curtains for the balcony windows. I tucked the box under my arm, ducked into my closet, and closed the door. This was real darkness. There wasn't a lot of room in there, but I swept a few shoes aside and sat down. Turned the box on, listened to the resentful hum of the battery; it was an old box, and preferred to run off a wire. The screen came up and asked me if I wanted to enter the globenet. I sat there, staring at the glowing lettering. In the darkness, it didn't flicker at all, it didn't run away into millions of tiny skittish dwindling dimensions, like looking into a mirror with another one over your shoulder. I read it easily.

I liked it even less that my idea had worked. At least I didn't have to use a combox at Charlie's. It would have been difficult to explain why I needed a closet.

I brought the box back out of the closet and plugged it in on my desk. Not that I invited people home very often but I was touchy about looking normal even to myself now that I was behaving more like Onyx Blaise's daughter. Your combox on a desk is much more normal than your combox in a closet. Could my dad see in the dark? Could any of my dad's family? I couldn't remember any of them except my gran: the rest were tall blurry shapes from my earliest childhood. Aimil was right: the Blaises had disappeared during the Wars. But I hadn't noticed. I had been busy being my mother's daughter. Even if I wanted to contact them I had no idea how.

I could ask Pat or Jesse. Right after I told them I had a brand-new hotline to Vampire World the new horror theme park. It would blow the Ghoul Attack simulation at the Other Museum clean out of the water. It would make the Dragon Roller Coaster Ride at Monsterworld look like a merry-go-round. Just as soon as we get a few little details worked out, like how you get there. And how you get away again. Meanwhile I still hadn't told them that I could see in the dark. Would I have told them a few days ago, if Aimil hadn't been there? It was what I'd gone in to tell them.

I went back to the balcony. I felt for an alignment. I stood at the edge of the void, but I stood in my world, on my ordinary feet, looking at ordinary darkness with my . . . not quite ordinary eyes.

Constantine. Con, are you there?

This time I was sure I felt that tug on the line streaming in the dark ether—a coherent pinprick of something in the incoherent nothing. But I lost it again.

I was so tired I was having to prop myself against the railing to stay standing up.

So I went indoors and went to bed.

MEANWHILE ON OTHER fronts I was adapting. I usually hit it right the first time when I reached for the spoon or the flour sack or the oven control. I hadn't walked into a door in several days.

After the vision had risen like a tide and floated me off my grounding in Oldroy Park, after I'd seen what I'd seen in Maud's face—whether it was there or not, since I could hardly ask her—when the vision subsided and left me standing on solid earth again, some of the dizziness had subsided too. It was as if the dark was a kind of road map I'd been folding up wrong, and this time I'd got it right, and it would lie flat at last. Although road maps didn't generally keep unfolding themselves and flapping at you saying Here! Here! Pay attention, you blanker! I thought: it is a road map of sorts. But it was about a country I didn't know, labeled in a language I didn't understand. And it didn't *unfold* so much as *erupt*.

I didn't know if I'd seen what I'd seen in Mrs. Bialosky's face either, the morning she'd told me not to worry.

So, which did I like better: that my affinity was growing stronger, that it could pull me out of the human world into some dark alien space, or that I was merely going mad and/or had an inoperable brain tumor after all? Did I have a third choice?

I worked pretty well straight through that day and got home in time to have a cup of tea in the garden. Yolande's niece and her daughters had left after a two-week visit and it was none of my business but I was secretly delighted to have *our* garden to ourselves again. Yolande came out and joined me. I watched a few late roses do a kind of waltz with their shadows as a mild evening breeze played with them. Then I watched Yolande. I'd always liked watching her: I wished she could bottle that self-possession so I could have some. It was a little like Mel's, I thought, only without the tattoos. I was feeling tired and mellow and was enjoying this so much it took me a while to realize something strange.

The shadows lay quietly across Yolande's face.

I snapped out of being mellow and stared at her. She saw me looking and smiled. I jerked my eyes away hastily. What? How? Why? What could I ask her?

Nothing.

I looked at her again. The shadows on her face were quiet, but they went . . . down a long way. Like looking into the sky.

What did I know about her? She had inherited this house from some distant relative who had also been childless and felt the spinsters of the world needed to stick together. She'd moved here from Cold Harbor when she retired. I didn't recall she'd ever told me what

she retired from. She had that calm strong centeredness I thought of
as ex-teacher, ex-clergy, ex-healersister or midwife; I couldn't imagine her as someone in a power suit navigating a desk with a combox
screen the size of a tennis court and a swarm of hot young assistants
in an outer office whose haircuts were specially designed to look
chic wearing globenet headsets ten hours a day.

I couldn't ask. If she'd wanted to tell me it would have come up
long ago. It probably had nothing to do with what she'd done for a
living anyway. It was probably like having freckles or curly hair or
transmuting ability: you're born with it. But things like transmuting
ability tend to lead to other choices. . . . "I don't think you've ever
told me what you retired from," I blurted out.

"I was a wardskeeper," she said easily, as if she was commenting
on the pleasantness of the evening, as if my question wasn't entirely
rude.

Wardskeeper.

I wanted to laugh. No wonder her house wards were so good.
You didn't earn that title easily. There were hundreds of licensed
wardcrafters, first, second, and third class, for every wardskeeper.
The rank of wardskeeper granted an unrestricted authority to design and create any protection against any Others that any client
wished to hire you for. Even wardskeepers had specialties: large
business, small business, home, personal bodyguard, and the whole
murky business of watchering, which ranged from honest protective surveillance to downright spying. But you didn't get your wardskeeper insignia unless you could make a more than competent stab
at all of it.

Wardskeeper. She must then . . . her own house . . . but Con . . . I
realized I'd said the first word aloud—I hoped only the first word—
because she was answering me.

"No, I'm not your idea of a wardskeeper, am I?" she said. "I was
never anyone's idea. But once I was established, new business came
to me by word of mouth, and my prior clients usually had the good
sense to warn future clients that they were going to meet a drab little old lady—I have been old and drab since my teens, by the way—

who gave the impression of being hardly able to cross the road by herself." She looked at me, smiling. "I admit that crossing the road alone has never been one of my greater gifts. Cars move much too quickly to suit me, and frequently from unexpected directions. I was always a much better maker of wards."

I couldn't think how to ask my next question. I couldn't even summon up the spare attention to hoot at the idea of Yolande being *drab*.

"But then," she went on, almost as if she was reading my mind, "people often are not what one might expect them to be. I would not expect a young, likable, sensible—and sun-worshipping—human woman who works in her family's restaurant to have a friend who is a vampire."

Then I could say nothing at all.

"My dear," Yolande said, "I have now told you almost as much as I know about your private affairs. Yes, there are more wards about this house and garden than you are aware of, and the fact that you haven't been aware of them is perhaps an indication to me that I have not yet lost my skill. I knew, of course, that a vampire had been visiting, but I also knew that you had not merely invited him in, but that you were under no coercion to do so. A good ward, my dear, will also prevent a forced invitation from achieving its object. And my wards are good ones.

"It took no great effort of intellect to puzzle out some of what happened to you during the two days you were missing last spring, especially not with the reek of vampire on you. Sherlock Holmes—do young people still read him, I wonder?—made the famous statement that once you have eliminated the impossible, whatever remains, however improbable, must be the truth. This is a very useful precept for a maker of wards, and I am not, perhaps, wholly retired. Vampires, as vampires will, caused you harm; but in this case, very unusually, not terminal harm. This one particular vampire therefore can be assumed to have done you some service, and that service created some kind of bond between you. This wild theory, suggestive of someone farther into her dotage than she wishes to believe, has been lately fortified when he returned, not once, but twice.

"I know that your unlikely friend is a vampire, a male vampire, and that there is only the one of him whom you invite across your threshold. This I have found very reassuring, by the way. Had there been more than one, I think my determination to assume the best rather than the worst might have failed. Although I admit I have doubled the wards around my own part of the house. . . . I have nothing to indicate that he is *my* friend too, you understand, and the human revulsion toward vampires generally is well justified."

Yolande leaned forward to look into my face. "In the roundabout way of an old lady who perhaps spends too much of her time alone, I am offering you my support, in this impossibly difficult task you have taken on. The natural antipathy between vampires and humans means, I feel, that it *is* some task; I doubt either you or your friend is enjoying the situation. I don't suppose your new SOF colleagues know about either the task or the friend, do they?"

I managed to shake my head.

"I am not surprised. I doubt SOF is very . . . adaptable. Lack of adaptability is the root cause of much trouble in large organizations."

I thought of Pat turning blue and smiled a little. But only a little. She was right about their attitude toward vampires. She was right about the universal human attitude toward vampires.

"I had not planned to say anything to you. I had at first assumed that whatever happened four months ago was over. But the vampire taint on you remained: that wound in your breast was some vampire's handiwork, wasn't it?"

So much for the camouflage provided by high-necked shirts. I nodded.

"And then your friend came, and now there is no wound. The two events are related, are they not?"

I nodded again.

"That is as good a definition of friendship as I need. But . . . I will no longer call it a taint . . . the fleck, the fingerprint of the vampire is still upon you. I am afraid the metaphor that occurs to me is of the eater of arsenic. If you eat a very, very little of it, over time you can develop a limited immunity to it. I do not know why you should choose to . . . immunize yourself like this. Or why he should. . . . My dear, forgive me if I have been a hopeless busybody. But your inevitable and wholly justified dismay, confusion, and preoccupation of four months ago has changed, certainly, but it has not decreased. It has increased—alarmingly so."

She paused, as if she hoped for an answer, but I could say nothing.

"My dear, there is something else my wards have told me: that your nickname is more than an affectionate joke. I can believe no evil of someone who draws her strength from the light of day. If I can help you, I will."

The sense of a burden unexpectedly lifted was so profound it made me dizzy, not least that by its lifting I realized how heavy it was. I had assumed—I had *known*—that there was no one I would be able to tell about my *unlikely friend*—there was certainly no one I would have risked telling. And now Yolande had told me. There were two of us who knew.

Maybe that meant the task was not impossible after all.

Whatever the task was.

Well, wiping Bo out would be a service to all humankind, certainly, whether Con and I survived or not. But offhand I couldn't see how even having a wardskeeper on our side was going to be useful. Besides, I had a selfish desire to stay alive myself. Bag the future of humanity.

And Con was failing to show up to help me make plans. *He* was the one who had told me that time was short. The new dry guys in Old Town bore something of the same message.

But there was now another human who knew about Con and me—and hadn't freaked out. I felt better even if I shouldn't've.

"Thank you," I said.

"Don't thank me yet," said Yolande. "I haven't done anything yet, except pry into your private affairs. I would not have done so if I had felt I could risk not enquiring into them."

Well, thank the gods and the angels for nosy landladies. This nosy landlady.

"Is there such a thing as a—an—antiward? Something that attracts?" I said.

Yolande raised her eyebrows.

"My—unlikely friend. He should have come back, and he hasn't. And I don't know how to find him."

"And the binding between you?"

I shook my head. "It isn't strong enough, or—or it's like it crosses worlds. And I can't enter the vampire world." Or I can, I thought, but I don't know what to do when I get there. Like how to find anything. Like how to get out again.

"Then perhaps he has not called you."

Interesting that she should know he had to. "I think he is in trouble. I think he may be in enough trouble that he can't call me. Or he doesn't know how. Vampires don't call humans, do they?"

One eyebrow stayed up as she thought about this. "I see the difficulty." She sat silent for several minutes and I sat in that silence, half-remembering a thing called *peace*. I'd forgotten peace in the last four months. It said something about my state of mind that merely sharing the fact of Con's existence with someone else with a heartbeat made me remember it . . . in spite of the hard, dreadful knowledge of the existence of Bo.

She stood up and went inside. I gave myself another cup of tea and looked at the roses. Feeling at peace, however fragilely, made it easy to slip into the visionary end of the dark-sight. The rose shadows said that they loved the sun, but that they also loved the dark, where their roots grew through the lightless mystery of the earth. The roses said: *You do not have to choose.*

My tree said *yessssss.*

My doe stood at the edge of the forest shadows, looking into the sunlight, her back sun-dappled.

You do not have to choose.

I didn't believe it. Hey, how many hamburger eaters on the planet are haunted by *cows*?

When Yolande reappeared, her hands were full. "I can make something more connected for you, more like a—a loop in a rope; but here is something you can try straightaway." Two candles, and a little twist of strong-smelling herbs. "Put the candles on either side

of you, and the herbs before and behind you. Light them as well—do
you have smudge bowls? Wait a few minutes till the smoke from all
mingles. Then seek your friend."

I WAITED TILL full night dark, and then I settled on the floor inside
the open balcony door. I lit the candles and the herbs, and stubbed
the herbs out again. I waited for the smoke to mingle. It wasn't
exactly a pleasant smell, but it was interesting, and intense. A . . .
drawing sort of smell. It drew me into it.

I closed my eyes. *Con, damn you, where are you? I'm sure you're in
trouble.* **Call me to come to you, you stubborn bastard.**

I was back in the vampire space, but the smoke had come with
me, wrapped round and round me like an enormously long scarf,
streaming behind me into the human world, streaming before me
into the vampire beyond-dark. I lay, suspended, in between, but this
time I felt neither lost nor sick.

Sunshine, pay attention. I felt neither lost nor sick. It *wasn't* the
same space. It was some *other* weird Other void where no human
had any business. The big difference was that this one wasn't trying
to kill me. At least not at once. Was this the back way, the little country lane way, after the speed and roar of the superhighway had been
too much for me earlier? I still couldn't read the map.

Pity you couldn't just take a bus.

I wriggled a little where I lay—there was still the uncanny *pressure* of alien-space, the difficulty breathing, the blindness, the awk-
wardness, as if a human body was the wrong vehicle if you wanted
to travel here; but it lacked the malevolence of the nowhere I'd been
in that afternoon in Aimil's living room, and the smoke-scarf gave
me a little protection, as if against a bitter wind. If I were a car, then
I'd rolled my windows up. Okay. Here I was. I practiced breathing. A
little time went by, if time went by here. Till the strangeness, this
nonmalevolent strangeness, began to feel like . . . merely the medium I had to work with.

I was a painter who had been handed a dripping glob of clay, a singer who had been handed a clarinet . . . a baker of bread and cookies who had been handed a vampire.

I bent and turned, seeking the alignment I wanted. There . . . no. Almost.

There.

And then I heard his voice.

Sunshine.

Once. Only once. My name. *There.*

The shock of when I hit the exact bearing felt like putting my whole body in an electric socket. *Wow.* But then I was blazing along that line like an arrow from a burning bow. The smoke was stripped away by the speed of my going, my hair seemed to be peeling off my scalp, and the pressure was increasing . . . and increasing . . . I was being stretched—rolled like a ball of dough between palms to make bread-sticks, a fluff of sheep's wool twisted and squeezed to wind round a spindle—thinner and thinner and thinner, a bit of blunt thread crushed between huge fingers, poked painfully through the eye of a needle. . . .

Wham.

I dropped out of the darkness, the void, the Other-space, back into something like somewhere. Back into my body, if I had been out of it.

I fell a little distance, *smack*, onto something. Something rather chilly, and slightly yielding, but not very, and also curiously . . . lumpy. I would have slid right off it again.

Except that it wrapped its arms around me, rolled me over so that it was on top of me, pinning me securely with its weight, and buried its fangs in my neck.

I froze. Well, what are you going to do? And all this was happening *flickflickflick* like the frames of a movie, too fast to react to.

It was dark, black dark, as dark as the void I had so recently traveled, and while I could see in the dark, I didn't have much practice in this kind of darkness, and also . . . well there was this other stuff going on, you know? My chief awareness was centered on the feeling of teeth against my neck.

The teeth hadn't broken the skin. His teeth hadn't. His hair was in my face. I'd had his hair in my face once before, but he'd been bleeding on me that time. Maybe it was my chance to return the favor? He had said he wouldn't turn me—that he couldn't turn me. He'd also said that I could be killed, like any other human. Standard deaths of humans included being dry-guyed.

Maybe vampires didn't like drop-in visitors. Well, I'd tried to call ahead. Ha ha.

His teeth were still against my neck. Other than that he was motionless. I mean that. *Motionless.* Like being lain on by a stone. A stone with fangs, of course.

His hair smelled musty, damp. It wasn't an unpleasant smell—if it reminded me of anything it reminded me of spring water, wet earth and moss on the rocks around it—but it wasn't his usual vampire smell. Don't ask me how I knew it was him but I did. Besides the fact that I guess if it had been any other vampire he wouldn't have hesitated midway through the fang-burying action.

He was *cold*. Motionless and cold. Cold all the way down the length of him. . . .

There seemed to be a lot of skin contact going on here. I blinked against the dark. I shivered against his body. I felt, then, briefly, his lips against my neck, as they closed over the teeth. His face rested against the curve of my neck, a moment, two moments. Two of my heartbeats. He was growing less cold. I was used—sort of—to the lack of a heartbeat, but I was pretty sure he wasn't breathing either. What vampires call breathing. The fizziness I'd put my arms around when I'd discovered my car was gone, that day at the lake, that wasn't there either.

He raised his head. Another of my heartbeats, and another. He shifted his arms, so he was no longer holding me like a garage clamp holds a recalcitrant engine. I turned my head fractionally. I could see the gray gleam of his cheek and jaw in the blackness: my dark vision was adjusting. I felt my eyes *trying* to see, like when the eye doctor gives you one of those funny lenses to look through and everything is all wrong. It was disconcerting to see in what I knew was darkness like . . . burial; no, not a good metaphor. But wherever we were, it *felt* underground, and I didn't think that was just the darkness.

He raised his head a little farther and turned his head to look at me, and I saw the stagnant-pool color of his eyes change to bright emerald green again. I remembered that the first time I'd seen his eyes, the night at the lake, they had been stagnant-pool-colored; how had I not remembered that transformation? Probably because I hadn't seen it happen. That had been back in the days when I believed myself to be fully human, and when I couldn't look into a vampire's eyes.

He was also getting warmer. He was now no colder (say) than a hibernating lizard. This was still a little chilly from where I was though.

I felt his chest expand, and his first breath drifted across my face. I remembered being carried back from the lake, leaning against that chest, recognizing breathing, not recognizing any rhythm to it.

He'd taken his weight onto his elbows, so I could breathe more easily.

I remembered thinking, on the long walk in from the lake, that I wouldn't have been able to match my breathing to his. But he was matching his breathing to mine, now. I also abruptly realized that I was feeling his dick growing long and hard against my leg.

We were both naked.

I knew that vampire body temperature is at least somewhat under voluntary control, like circulation of the blood is. It is, perhaps, a bit variable, especially, perhaps, under stress. He'd gone from dead cold, you should pardon the expression, to what you might call normal human body heat, in about a minute. I'd known—I'd been pretty sure—he was in trouble; that's why I was here. Perhaps I'd—er—roused him too suddenly. Perhaps he was in what passes in vampire biological science for shock, and his control systems weren't responding.

That didn't explain the dick though. *It* was responding.

He was now suddenly hot, as hot as if he'd been in a kitchen baking cinnamon rolls in August. I already knew vampires could sweat, under certain conditions, like being chained to a wall of a house with sunlight coming in through the windows. He was sweating again now. Some of his sweat fell on me.

I've always rather liked sweat. On other occasions when I've had a naked, sweating male body up against mine, I've tended to feel that it meant he was getting into what was going on. This usually produces a similar enthusiasm in me. Not that there *was* anything going on . . . exactly. Yet. Remember how fast and suddenly this was all happening. And if he was in shock so was I. Maybe my brain hadn't fully come with me in that zap through the void, like my clothes manifestly hadn't. With a truly masterful erection now pressed against me I turned my head again and licked his sweating shoulder.

What happened next probably lasted about ten seconds. Maybe less.

I don't think I *heard* the sound he made; I think I only *felt* it. He moved his hands again, to tip my face toward him, and kissed me. I can't say I noticed any fangs. I had the lingering vestige of sense not to try anything clever with *my* teeth, which with a human lover I would have. But I was nonetheless busy with tongue and hands. I wriggled a little under him. I kissed him back as he tangled his fingers in my hair. I arched up off the floor a trifle to press myself more thoroughly against him. I was undoubtedly making some noises of my own. . . .

I always thought the earth was supposed to move when you arrived, not when you'd only started the journey.

One second I was raising my pelvis to meet him—and believe me, he was there—and the next second he had hurled himself off me and thrown me from him, and I was flying across the floor to fetch up with a bruising *whap* against the wall. He bounded to his feet and disappeared.

I lay there, considering. Point one: wherever the hell I was (and I hoped this was not too literal a remark), it had a smooth, glassily smooth, stone floor. The wall I had caromed into at a guess was the same material.

Point two: what the hell had *happened*?

Point three: where did I want to start counting?

I hoped I was going to have the opportunity to tell Yolande that she didn't have to make me anything special, that the herbs and candles had worked fine. If you wanted to call this fine.

I remembered, with an effort, that when I'd arrived—so to speak—Con had been cold and not breathing. But for all I knew this is merely the vampire equivalent of a nap. Lots of humans are cranky when they're woken unexpectedly. No. I didn't think his eyes would go stagnant-pond-colored for a nap. Okay. Maybe I had accomplished my mission—that he'd been in some kind of vampire trouble and I'd got him out of it.

I should have been embarrassed. I should have been paralyzed with embarrassment. I was sitting—no, I was crooked up—naked on a cold stone floor in the dark, having been cannoned off the wall by a . . . well, a creature . . . that I had been under the impression I was about to have an intimate encounter with. Maybe I should try to be grateful at having been spared intimacy with the most dangerous of the Others.

Gave a whole new meaning to the phrase *under the dark*.

I wasn't grateful. You want to talk cranky, coitus interruptus takes me well *beyond* cranky. My engorged labia felt like they were pressing on my brain—what there was of my brain—and if I didn't get to fuck someone, something, *now*—a vampire would do—I was going to fucking *explode*. My cunt ached like a bruise.

Beyond cranky, rather fortunately, doesn't transmute into embarrassment. It transmutes into fury. As my blood pressure began to re-arrange itself to a more standard unengorged pattern I was *seething*. I couldn't care less that I was also naked and alone in the dark of I had no idea where. Well, I couldn't care much. Not very much. Really.

It was a large room. Empty—except for me—and the ceiling was so high even my dark-sighted eyes couldn't make it out. No furniture. No windows. No anything. Funny sort of place for a nap. Or maybe for a solitary siege. But then I wasn't a vampire.

It was at least as dark as the inside of my closet. So nothing flickered when I looked at it. What there was to look at. Wow, what a bonus. I would try to control my euphoria.

He reappeared. He was wearing what I was beginning to think of as his standard get-up of long loose black shirt and black trousers. No shoes. I couldn't be sure but I didn't think I'd ever seen him in shoes. He was carrying something else, which he came close enough to hand over without looking at me. I unfolded it and discovered another long loose black shirt. When I had pulled it over my head it came nearly to my knees. *Gods bloody damn it all.* I was not in a good mood.

He was still not looking at me. I was still seething.

"I beg your pardon most profoundly," he said.

"Yeah," I said. "Nice to see you too."

He made one of those quick vampire gestures, too rapid for human eyes. My no-longer-quite-human eyes could about follow it: at any rate they registered frustration. Good. That made two of us. Although on second thought, or maybe semi-thought, I doubted he was indicating physical frustration. Uncomfortably I began to be glad of the long black shirt, which probably made me look like death, especially in this light, er, this no-light: black is not my color, any way you hang it. But then looking like death might be very attractive to a vampire. In which case there was even less to explain why. . . . My anger was subsiding. I didn't *want* it to subside. I needed the warmth. But he'd thrown me away, hadn't he? Whatever his dick said, *he* didn't want me. Anger was much better than misery. Misery approached. I wrapped my arms around myself and shivered.

Maybe he saw the shiver. "After your—" He paused. "You need food," he said. "I can't even feed you." He glanced down at himself as if perhaps he was expecting a peanut-butter sandwich to be suspended about his person. If he was contemplating opening a vein and offering it to me, the answer was *No.* If he was contemplating it, he rejected the notion. I wondered what he meant by can't *even* feed me.

"I must also thank you for . . . retrieving me," he said. Finally he looked at me.

Retrieving? Shiva *wept.*

"Any time," I said. "I'm sure I'll enjoy reviewing my assortment of *new* scars and recalling how I got them too. The ones from being slammed on my back and landed on like a sack of boulders, and the ones *a few seconds later* from being thrown across the room into a wall."

I saw him flinch. One for the human.

"Sunshine," he said. He made a move toward me, and I flinched away. One for the vampire.

I didn't mean to say it. I didn't mean to say anything about it. I was *determined* not to say anything about it. My voice came out high and strange, and sticky with wretchedness: "Why? I know about having to—*invite*—one of your kind." For about six months when you're thirteen or fourteen it's every teenage girl's favorite story: because it's about finding out that you have *power.* "Maybe I got the details wrong? Like you need it *engraved* RSVP—I suppose you prefer the black border to the narrow gold line—delivered to your door at least forty-eight hours before the moment? Maybe you need it printed in blood on—on vellum. And silly me, I couldn't find your *door* to deliver it." My voice was getting higher and higher and squeakier and squeakier. I shut up.

He stood there with his hands loose at his sides, staring at the floor. His hair flopped down over his forehead. I wanted to brush it back so I could see his eyes. . . . I wanted to do nothing of the kind. I would bite my own hand off before I voluntarily touched him again.

"I believe you were inviting more than you knew," he said at last.

I sighed. "Oh good. Cryptic vampire utterances. My fave. Now you're going to say something opaque and oracular about the bond between us, aren't you? That it got me here but let's not get carried away maybe?"

He moved so quickly I would not have stepped aside in time, but he stopped himself short and did not touch me. But he didn't stop very short. As it was he was standing so near it was hard not to touch him. I put my hands behind my back like a dieter offered a choice of Bitter Chocolate Death or Meringuamania. "I do not disturb you by choice," he said. "Can you not believe that?" He made another of those vampire noises: it went something like *urrrrr.* "Perhaps you cannot. This—our situation—is not made easier by thousands of years of my kind . . . disturbing your kind."

"Disturb is one word for it, I suppose," I said, nastily. I was still in a bad mood, still unhappy and wanting to cause unhappiness in return. And still half blasted out of my skull by events since I had found out that evening that my landlady knew I was jiving with a vampire. A lot had happened in a short space of time. Not just one particular thing out of a morbidly kinky soap opera.

"I too am disturbed," he said quietly.

I had my mouth open for my next uncharitable remark and changed my mind. I moved away from him, found the wall, and leaned back against it. I didn't want to sit on the floor—and have him looming over me—and there wasn't anything else to lean on. Except him, of course, and that wasn't an option right now. Disturbance: okay. If I could stop feeling mortally wounded in the ego for a moment I might begin to remember again what was going on here. He was a vampire. I was a human. We weren't supposed to have any bonds between us, except straightforward generic ones of murderous antagonism and so on. And, speaking of kinky soap opera, no one ever had an *affair* with a vampire, not even in *Blood Lore*, which was always getting prosecuted for one thing or another. The reason why, when you were thirteen or fourteen, you outgrew your fascination with the idea that a vampire couldn't do you unless you let him is that you began to take in the fact that shortly after you'd said, "Come and get me big boy," you *died*.

It was illegal to write stories and make movies about sex between vampires and humans. It was, in fact, one of the few mandates the global council really agreed on. The stories and movies got written and made anyway, but if the government caught you at it, they threw your ass in jail. For a long time.

Okay. He probably was disturbed too.

I looked at him, wondering if he was wondering how we'd wound up here, wherever here was. About why we'd been able to create this antithetical bond, and what exactly it consisted of. It probably was a good idea not to make it any more complicated—and intense—than we had to.

A small part of me whispered, "Oh, rats."

Another small part whispered, "Yeah, well, how come *he's* the one who managed to remember?"

Suddenly I was exhausted. "Truce?" I said, still leaning against the wall.

"Truce," he said.

I was only going to shut my eyes for a moment. . . .

I WOKE UP feeling rather comfortable. I was lying on something soft, but not too soft, and wrapped in something warm and furry. And there was a smell of apples. My stomach roared. I opened my eyes.

No, I didn't open my eyes, I only thought I had. I was having the most ridiculous dream of my life thus far—and I'd had some pretty ridiculous dreams in my day—something out of *Gormenghast* or *The Castle of Otranto* or *House of Tombs*. I wanted to say to my imagination, oh, come *on*.

But my stomach was still roaring (I often eat in my dreams, I know you're not supposed to) and the apples were sitting beside me with a loaf of bread, and a fantastic goblet hilariously in keeping with the general flamboyance of my immediate surroundings, so I sat up and reached for the nearest apple. And saw the silky black sleeve falling back from my arm.

I didn't hiss as well as he had, the night he discovered the wound in my breast, but I gave it a good shot. I was so used to my eyesight behaving strangely that the flitteriness of the lighting hadn't at first registered, but it did now: both that there was light, and that it wiggled. There was some heat source behind me; I turned around.

The fireplace, of course, was huge. It was shaped like some monster's roaring mouth; you could see the monster's eyes (well, two of them; I chose not to look for more) gleaming above the mantelpiece of its writhing lips (you might not think writhing lips would have any flat spots, but there were candelabra balanced up there, shaped like snakes' bodies and dismembered human arms); each eye was bigger than my head, and gleamed red, although that may have been the firelight. No, it wasn't the firelight.

Con, cross-legged on the floor, straight-backed, shirtless, barefoot, his head a little bowed, looked rather as he had the first time I saw him. Only not so bony. He was also less gray, washed in the ruddy firelight. And my heart beat faster when I looked at him for different reasons than it had that first time. He looked up as I turned;

our eyes met. I looked away first. I picked up the apple and bit into it. So, maybe he lived near an orchard (how long had I been asleep)? That didn't explain the bread. I wasn't going to ask. I wasn't going to ask about the bottle of wine on the floor next to the little table either (the table was a depressed-looking maiden in a very tight swathe of material with no visible means of support, holding the carrying surface at an implausible angle between her neck and one shoulder. Even more implausible was the angle of her breasts, which I don't think even cosmetic surgery could achieve), which was a straightforward local chardonnay. I'd have preferred a cup of tea. A glass or two of this on top of everything else that had been happening and I'd be off my chump. But hey, I was already. Off my chump, I mean. I poured some wine gingerly into the goblet. Pity to waste it: he'd already drawn the cork. Ever the polite host. The wine seemed to go a long way down before it hit bottom, like dropping pebbles in a well.

I ate a second apple and had a dubious sip of the wine. (It still tasted like straightforward local chardonnay, even from that histrionic beaker.) The damn goblet tingled in my hand. I *really* didn't want to get into some kind of communion with an overdressed tumbler. It was knobbly with what looked like gemstones. Oh please. I ate a third apple and started on the bread. Texture suggested cheating: additional gluten flour, probably, but the taste was not too bad; the baker must have the patience or the sense to let the sponge sit a while and ripen. Maybe I was just very hungry.

"Thank you," I said.

Con's shoulders rippled briefly: vampire shrug facsimile, maybe. "It is little enough," he said.

"How long did I sleep?"

"Four hours. It is four hours till dawn," he replied.

And Paulie had taken the early shift this morning. (He'd *offered*.) Okay.

My little excursion through nowheresville must have taken no time at all. One of the standard features of nowheresville, maybe, that made a kind of sense, but you didn't really expect your very own alarming out-of-this-world experiences to align with the science fiction you'd read as a kid. The science fiction you'd outgrown in favor of *Christabel* and *The Chalice of Death*. My eyes wandered involuntarily to the gem-festooned goblet. I had to admit my reading *had* sort of prepared me for an overheated fantasy like this room. About nowheresville I was on my own.

Con didn't look as if he'd suffered any ill effects from his coma, or whatever it had been. I wondered what passed for a near-death experience in a vampire? A slightly misplaced stake? He'd been able to go out foraging, anyway: the bread and the apples were both fresh.

"I wouldn't have expected you to . . . choose to sit next to a fire," I said, at random. Sitting next to a fire seemed like the sort of thing only silly, show-offy vampires would do. Like human kids playing chicken in No Town.

He didn't say anything. Oh, good, we're playing *that* game again. I ate another apple.

He raised his head and shook his hair back in an almost human gesture. Almost. "We do not need heat as you do," he said, and I expertly translated the "we" and "you" into "vampires" and "humans." "But we may enjoy it."

Enjoy. I didn't enjoy thinking about vampires enjoying things. The things they tended to enjoy.

"I enjoy it," he said, and, surprising me enormously, added, "it is the warmth of life and the heat of death."

Life as defined by warmth to a chilly vampire? Death by burning, death by the sun? Or the original death of being turned? Maybe he had been harmed by his coma: it was making him introspective. As being bounced off walls appeared to be doing to me.

I took a deep breath. "I—I have had a—a feeling that all was not well with you—for some time," I said. "I think it began the night you—healed me. But it took me a while to—to figure out that that was what I was picking up. If I was. If you follow me."

"Yes," he said.

He didn't say anything more for the length of time it took me to eat a fourth apple. Hey, they were small. Was it rude to eat, er, food, in front of a vampire? I'd done it before, of course. But if there was a future in congenial vampire-human relations there were grave (so to speak) etiquette questions to be addressed.

"Will you tell me what happened to you?" I said, half irritated at the need (apparently) to drag it out of him, half astonished at my own desire to know. What was this, friendship? Big irony alert. Here we're both agonizing over this carthaginian *bond* business and maybe it's only that we're learning to be friends. I could get into fireside sitting as the warmth of life too, probably. Hey, he was still a vampire and I was still a human and there was some other weird stuff, like transmuting and poisoned wounds and nowheresville. Not to mention going out in daylight.

But if we were supposed to be friends, I was going to have to get used to the fact that he wasn't the chatty type.

He said, musingly, as if he was listening to his own words as he spoke them, "I was more wearied by the effort to heal your wound than I realized at once. I had not, you see, ever attempted anything similar before. As I told you, I had to . . . invent certain aspects. Guess others. I am not accustomed to not knowing what I am doing."

One of the advantages of very long life. Lots of time for practice.

"I was careless after I left you. I permitted myself to be preoccupied. I was . . . sensed. By one of Bo's gang. I needed to escape, and not to let her trace you through me. Another maneuver I am unaccustomed to is protecting the whereabouts of a human."

I had the feeling he was saying something more than, "And they weren't going to get anything out of me other than my name, rank, and serial number." I wondered what a vampire address book would look like: would it have *alignments* rather than street numbers? What would an alignment index look like?

Could one vampire steal another vampire's address book?

"The first one called for assistance, of course; and they were very . . . persistent, when they caught the trace of you on me as well. I eluded them eventually. It was not easy. I came here. As you found me."

Naked in a dark empty stone room. Vampire convalescence gone wrong. "You mean you had been like that over a *month*? You schmuck, why didn't you call me *before*?"

He looked up at me, and there was undeniably a faint smile on his face. It looked a little grotesque, but not too bad, considering.

Nothing like as awful as his laugh, for example. "It never occurred to me."

I had said to Yolande: *Vampires don't call humans, do they?*

He looked back at the fire. "Even if it had, I do not think I would have done so. It would not have occurred to me that you could assist in any way."

"You called me. You called my name. Once. I wouldn't have found you if you hadn't."

"I heard you calling me. You asked me to answer you."

"I called you to call me."

"Yes. Sunshine, do you wish me to apologize again? I will if you desire it. I could not have rescued myself. I was . . . too far away. But I heard you, and I could still answer. You came and . . . brought the rest of me back with you. I am grateful. I thank you. That is not the way I would have chosen to . . . leave this existence. The balance between us has tipped again."

"Oh, the *hell* with the damn balance," I said. "What I'm thinking is, if you hadn't needed to protect me, it would have been a lot easier, right? I *weaken* you, don't I? Aside from your having got tired already bailing me out that night." With the blood of a doe.

There were times, like now, when the feel of light and warmth was . . . different too. Different like seeing in the dark was different— but differently different. Different in a way I knew didn't come from a vampire. Is this simple *nowness* of awareness some gift from her?

For a moment there were three of me: there was the human me. There was my tree-self. And my deer-self.

Surely we outnumbered the vampire-self?

"Weakened," he said thoughtfully. "I think your interpretation of weakness may be distorted. I am physically stronger than any human. I can go without sustenance for longer than any human. But you can derive sustenance from bread and apples, which I cannot. And you can walk under the sun, which I cannot. How do you define weakness?"

I was thinking about my experience of bringing the rest of him back. It was a little difficult *not* to think about comparative weakness when only one of you could fling the other one across a room and into a wall and you were the one that got flung. Okay, I was not going to pursue that line. I sighed. He had already told me he couldn't stand against Bo alone. Choosing me as an ally might have made more sense to me if getting calories out of bread and apples and going around in daylight had any discernable relevance to the issue. "Where am I?"

I thought he looked puzzled. Another of those vampire-senses-are-different moments, I suppose. "This is my . . . home," he said at last.

"You don't call it home," I said, interested.

"No. I might call it my . . . earth-place, perhaps. I spend my days here. I have done so for many years."

"Earth-place? Then we are underground?"

"Yes."

"What about the fireplace?"

He looked at me.

"Doesn't the smoke say 'Someone's here'?"

"The smoke is not detectable in the human world."

Oh. Vampires would hold a lot more than one-fifth of the global wealth if they patented a really good air filter. The cynical view of the Voodoo Wars is that the Others had done us humans a favor, by killing enough of us off and thus lowering the level of industrial commerce to a point that we hadn't managed to commit species suicide by pollution yet, which we otherwise might well have. Even if they looked at it this way, which I doubted, this would not have been pure philanthropy. Demons and Weres, whichever side of the alliance they'd been on, need most of the same things we do, and vampires . . . well. Maybe it depends on your definition of "philanthropy."

I looked around a little more. The only light was from the fire, and my dark vision was sort of half-confounded by something about this place, maybe just the thundering excess. Still, I could see a lot, and it was all pretty bizarre. The fur I was wrapped up in appeared to be real fur, long and silky, in jagged black and white stripes. I couldn't think what animal it might be. Something that didn't exist, perhaps, till a vampire killed it. With the slinky black shirt—and the bruises—I felt like something off the cover of this month's *Bondage and Discipline Exclusive*. All I needed was ankle bracelets and a better haircut. The buttons on the back of the sofa I was lying on were tiny gargoyle faces, sticking their tongues out or poking their fingers up their noses. Every now and then they weren't faces at all, but pairs of buttocks. The sofa itself was some kind of purple plush velvet . . . except that the shadows it laid were *lavender*. Well, if I could travel through nowheresville I suppose I shouldn't protest about shadows that were lighter than their source, or about furs from animals that didn't exist. My knowledge of natural history in black and white didn't extend much beyond skunks and zebras anyway. Maybe it did exist, whatever it was. The fur could have been dyed, but somehow this didn't suit my idea of vampire chic. Actually *Con* didn't suit my idea of vampire chic. This hectic Gothic sensibility was a surprise. "Interesting decorating principles," I said.

He glanced around briefly, as if reminding himself what was there. "My master had a sense of the dramatic."

I was riveted both by *my master* and *had*. As in used to have, as in dead, rather than undead? "Your master?" I said experimentally.

"This is his room."

Silence fell. Con returned to staring motionlessly at the fire. So much for leading questions. I sighed again.

Con, to my surprise, stirred. "Do you wish to hear about my master?" he said.

"Well, yes," I said.

There was a pause, while he, what? Organized his thoughts? Decided what to leave out? "He turned me," he said at last. "I was not . . . appreciative. But I was apt to his purpose. As there was no going back I agreed to do as he wished." Another pause, and he added, with one of those more-expressionless-than-expressionless expressions, like his more-than-stillness immobility: "A newly turned vampire is perhaps more vulnerable than you would guess. I was dependent on my master at first, whether I wished it or not, and

I . . . chose to let him teach me what I needed to know to survive. That was many years ago, when this was still the New World."

Eek, I thought. Three or four hundred years ago, give or take a few decades, and depending on which Old World explorers you are counting from. That can't be right: if he was that old, he shouldn't be able to go out in moonlight.

"He wished to rule here, when the Liberty Wars came, at least . . . unofficially."

The standard human slang was below ground and above ground. Unofficially would be below ground: being the biggest, nastiest junkyard dog of the dark side. Officially would still be pretty unofficial: control another two-fifths of the world economy, presumably, and make our global council into a bit of window-dressing.

"He might have succeeded, but he had bad luck, and a powerful and bitter enemy with better luck. There were not many of my master's soldiers left after the Liberty Wars. I was one. Much of my master's vitality left him with the ruin of his ambition. He turned collector instead. Those of his soldiers that had survived the Wars left or were destroyed, one by one, till only I remained. When my master also was destroyed, I was left alone."

I was glad of the warmth of the fire. Con's voice was low and, as ever, dispassionate, and I had no clue whether he'd been, you know, *fond* of his master in any way, maybe after he'd got over being unappreciative of having been turned. What purpose had Con been apt for? I was sure I didn't want to know. Good. One question that probably wouldn't get answered that I didn't have to ask. Why had Con stayed when everyone else left? I remembered him saying a month ago: *There are different ways of being what we are.* His master before the Liberty Wars sounded like your common or garden-variety world-takeover odin vampire thug, and a powerful one at that. So why had Con stayed? Con who didn't even run a gang now. More questions not to ask for fear he *would* answer.

But I didn't have much clue about the working range of vampire emotion. Blood lust. What else? (Other kinds of lust? Maybe it had been . . . life lust, earlier. No, I wasn't thinking about that.) Did Con

get over being unappreciative by getting over being *able* to feel appreciative? No—Con had just told me he was grateful for being rescued. But gratitude might be a human concept, applicable merely to
a situation that demanded some kind of courtesy, as pragmatically
meaningless as *thank you*. Well, at least he'd, hmm, *felt* that courtesy
was demanded.

And then there was Bo. The inconvenient bond between Con and
me that we were trying to, um, strengthen, without, um, intensity,
was because of Bo's threat to both of us. I did not like where this
thought was going.

"Your master's bitter enemy . . . was it Bo?"

"No. Bo's master."

Oh well *that* made it all better immediately. I stuffed a handful of
fur in my mouth to stop myself from whimpering.

Con looked up at me. Perhaps he thought the bread and apples
hadn't been enough and I was still hungry. "I destroyed his master.
It's only Bo now."

I bit down on the fur. Pardon me, I thought, if I don't find this
information overwhelmingly reassuring. *Only* Bo. And his gang,
which had chained Con up in a house by a lake not too long ago
from which he escaped only by a very curious chance. Con might not
fall for that one again but no doubt there were other possibilities.
Bo could be assumed to be the resourceful kind of evil fiend. Another
of those possibilities had almost got Con a month ago, for example.
Why didn't Con want to post an ad in the sucker personals—there
had to be hidden vampire zones on the globenet—asking for his old
comrades in arms to return for a bit and give him a hand? He could
pass out the contents of his master's old room as reward, since he
didn't seem too interested in them. If those were real gemstones in
my absurd goblet, it was probably worth the national debt of a
medium-sized country.

Why didn't he just run a gang, like a *normal* vampire of his age?
Who should have to because he couldn't go out in moonlight any
more.

There were so many questions I didn't want to know the answers to.

I pulled the fold of fur back out of my mouth again, and tried to smooth it down. Teethmarks, not to mention spit, probably lowered its value. I felt horribly tired, and alone, despite my companion. Especially because of my companion. I picked up the goblet again—it nearly took two hands; two hands would certainly have been easier, I was just resisting the idea of needing two hands—and teetered it toward my mouth. As it had seemed a long time before the wine hit the bottom pouring it in, it seemed rather a while before it touched my lips, tipping it back out. Drinking straight from the bottle, however, didn't seem like an option. Not in this room. In Con's room maybe—the empty one with no furniture. And no fire.

I wanted mountains of dough to turn into cinnamon rolls and bread, I wanted an unexpected tour group on a day we're short of kitchen staff, I wanted a big dinner party to ask for cherry tarts, I wanted to curl up on my balcony with a stack of books and a pot of tea, I wanted Mel's warm, tattooed arm around me and daylight on my face. I wanted to go home. I wanted my life back.

I had been here before. I had once had all that, and I drove out to the lake one night to get away from it.

"What *is* this thing, anyway?" I said, heaving the goblet up. I conceded, and used two hands. It could be a loving cup. First prize in vampire league sports. You didn't fill it with champagne, of course; you cut off the heads of the losing team and poured their blood in. Champagne later maybe when they ran out of the hard stuff.

"It is a Cup of Souls from the ceremony of gathering at Oranhallo."

"*What?*" I put it down hastily. Just *stop* asking questions, Sunshine. No wonder it goddam tingled against my goddam hand. Nobody knows where Oranhallo is. Well, nobody who knows is telling the rest of us. It's not a big issue on the Darkline but it is one of the things that keeps coming up. Among the people who think it exists somewhere you could describe by latitude and longitude, none of the plausible guesses are anywhere near New Arcadia. But there isn't any consensus on whether it is a geographic place or merely a part of the rite. It is a big magic handlers' rite, done by clan. The Blaises probably knew how (and where) to do it, but I didn't. I didn't know anything about cups of souls or ceremonies of gathering, but I didn't want to.

"It is one of the few articles in this room that my master was given," said Con. "Usually there was some constraint involved."

I bet there was. "Why would a magic-handler clan want to give something like this to a master vampire? Especially a master vampire."

"It was not freely given," Con said after another of his pauses. "But it was offered and accepted as payment for a task he had undertaken that was to their mutual benefit. There was some choice about the conclusion to this task. This reward was proposed as persuasion to make one choice instead of another. The Cup carries no taint that might distress you."

And your gracious dining accessories don't run to wineglasses from Boutique Central. "Then why does it buzz against my skin?" I said crossly.

"Perhaps because it was the Blaise clan that possessed it," said Con.

I jumped off the sofa, staggered, bumped into the little table, and heard the goblet crash to the floor as I ran off into the darkness. I didn't get far; Con's master had been a very enterprising collector, and I wasn't up to the weaving and zigzagging to make my way through the spoils. I collided with something that might have been an ottoman almost at once, and hit the floor even harder than the goblet had, although I didn't spill. Further note on vampire emotions, if any: don't expect a vampire to understand the turbulence of human family ties—including broken ones—or maybe it's that vampires don't get it about cowardice, and how a good sound human reaction to unwelcome news is to try and run away from it.

I picked myself up. More bruises. Oh good. It wasn't going to be a mere matter of high-necked T-shirts this time; I was going to need an all-over bodysuit plus a bag over my head. I turned around slowly, balancing myself against some great furled spasm of plaster that might have counted, in these surroundings, as an Ionic pillar. Con was standing up, facing me, his back to the fire, haloed by its light. Maybe it was my state of mind, but he suddenly looked far larger and more ominous than he had since before I knew his name. I couldn't see his face—maybe my dark vision had been further unsettled by my fall—but there was something *wrong* about his silhouette against the firelight; something wrong about him being surrounded by light at all. I remembered what I had thought that first time, by the lake: predatory. *Alien.* He wasn't Con, he was a vampire: inscrutable and deadly.

I made my way back toward the fire. I don't know if I wanted to reclaim Con as my ally, if not my friend, or if it was that there was no point in running away. I had to pass very close to him to reach the fire; there was only one gap among all the arcane bric-a-brac that would let me through. I knelt on the hearthrug—at least there was a hearthrug, even if the hairy fanged head at one end of it didn't bear close examination—and held my hands out toward the fire. It felt like a real fire. More important, it smelled like a real fire, and when I leaned too close the smoke made my eyes sting. It spat like a real fire too, and since there was no fireguard a spark fell onto the hearthrug. I glanced down; the hearthrug was unexpectedly unprepossessing, the fur short and brownish and patchy, having had sparks fly into it before. A few new burns wouldn't ruin its looks because it didn't have any. I felt hearthrugish. I'd never worried about my looks much; I had always had other things to worry about, like making cinnamon rolls and getting enough sleep. But I was beginning to feel rather too burn-marked. Like I'd been lying too near a fire with no fireguard.

Did I hear him sit down near me? You don't hear a vampire coming: I knew this by experience. But this wasn't any vampire; this was Con. I'd already promised to help him, if I could, because I needed his help. No. I hadn't promised. But it didn't matter. The bond was there. I hadn't ratified any contract, I'd woken up one morning to discover fine print and subclauses stamped all over my body. If I wanted a signature, it was the crescent scar on my breast. It meant I heard him coming even when I didn't hear him coming.

I waited a moment longer before I turned to look at him. Vampire. Dangerous. Unknowable. Seriously creepy. This one's name was Constantine. We'd met before.

Well.

"What do we do now?" I said.

"I take you home," said Con.

"Okay, that's today. What about tonight? Tomorrow?" I said.

"We must find Bo."

My stomach cramped. Maybe it was just the apples. I also had to learn that shilly-shallying was not a vampire gift. I wondered if I could teach him to say "perhaps" and "not before next week."

I knew this wasn't going to be a matter of loading up on apple-tree stakes (or table knives) and knocking on Bo's front door. "You don't know where he, uh, lives."

"No. I had only begun to search, since our meeting by the lake. He is well defended and well garrisoned."

I glanced up at the invisible ceiling. Given the furnishings the ceiling was probably phenomenal. Or antiphenomenal: like Medusa's head or the eye of a basilisk. "I hope you are better defended," I said.

"I hope so too."

I didn't like hearing a vampire talk about *hope*.

"My master specially collected things that defend, or could be turned to defense. He felt that his attempt to win what he desired by aggression had failed, and he wished his subsequent seclusion to be uninterrupted."

Gargoyles and tchotchkes: the vampire arsenal.

"I have always preferred solitude, and have improved on his arrangements. I have some reason to believe that if I never left this place no one would be able to come to me."

"You are forgetting the road through nowheresville," I said. Feelingly.

"I am not forgetting," he said. "I am assailable by you in a way I am assailable to no one and nothing else."

Assailable. An interesting choice of adjective. I looked up at him, and he looked down at me. I couldn't see into the shadows on his face. They remained shadows. They didn't wiggle or sparkle and they didn't have red edges. They didn't go down a long way. They were just shadows. Cute. The only person who still looked normal out of my eyes wasn't a person and wasn't normal.

The look between us lengthened. He might not be able to lure me to the same doom he almost had the second night at the lake, but it seemed to me it was still doom I saw in his eyes. I looked away. "Improvements," I said. "You mean some of this—this—" The phrases that occurred to me were not tactful: this tragic reproduction of William Beckford's front parlor, or perhaps Ludwig II's. "You mean some of this, er, stuff is, er, yours?"

"Nothing you may see, no. I do not like tying up my strength in objects. It was an old argument with my master. Physical shape has a certain durability that the less tangible lacks, but I feel it is a brittle durability. He believed otherwise."

And he's the one who got skegged, I thought. "Do you know what Bo's philosophy of, er, defense is?"

Pause. Finally he said: "He puts most of his energies into his gang. This will not help us locate him."

I sighed. "This is another of those vampire-senses-are-different things, isn't it?" I supposed I had to tell him what I'd found through the globenet—how I'd first found the bad nowheresville, the beyond-dark human-squishing space, and what else seemed to be in there. If "in" was the right preposition. Out? On? Up? With? After? Over? English has too many prepositions. Did I have to mention SOF?

I didn't have to tell him anything yet. He didn't seem to be in a big hurry to get me home. How close, in ordinary human-measured geography, was this *earth-place* to Yolande's house? Ally or no ally, I didn't like the idea of our being neighbors.

"Bo isn't his real name, is it?" I said. "It sounds like something you'd call a sheepdog."

"It is short for Beauregard."

I laughed. I hadn't known I had a laugh available. A vampire named Beauregard. It was too perfect. And he probably hadn't got it accidentally from his stepdad who ran a coffeehouse.

"How much time do we have?" I said. "Bo, I mean, not today's dawn."

I was beginning to learn when he was thinking and when he was merely thinking about what to say to me, a bumptious human. This time he was thinking.

"I have been out of context since we last met," he said. Yes, he said *context*. "I do not know. I will find out."

"Same time, same place," I murmured. "Not."

"I do not understand."

"We have to meet again, right?" I said. "And I have things to tell you too. I may have a—a kind of line on Bo myself."

He nodded. I didn't know whether to be flattered or outraged. Maybe he thought he'd chosen his confederate well. Equal partners with a vampire: an exhilarating concept. Supposing you lived long enough to enjoy the buzz. But I guess "Hey, well done, congratulations, wow" weren't in common vampire usage. Maybe I could teach him that too, with "probably" and "not before next week."

"I will come to you, if I may," he said.

"You would rather I didn't come here again." I hadn't meant to say that either, but it popped out.

A clear trace of surprise showed on his face for about a third of a second. I wouldn't have seen it if I hadn't been looking straight at him, but it was there. "You may come here if you wish. I . . ." He stopped. I could guess what he was thinking. It was the same thing I was thinking. Wasn't thinking. "Come. I will give you a token."

He slid easily through the gap in the impedimenta (sorry, this household brought out the worst in my vocabulary; it was like every bad novel and hyperbolic myth I'd ever read crowding round to haunt me in three dimensions) and made off into the dark. I had a sidelong peek at the overturned goblet as I passed it. My dark vision steadied if I kept it on Con's back, so I did, mostly, resisting the compelling desire to try to figure out what some of the more tortured blacknesses indicated by looking at them directly: hydras with interminable heads; Laocoön with several dozen sons and twice as many serpents; an infestation of triffids; the entire chariot race from *Ben-Hur*: all frozen in plaster or wood or stone. I hoped. Especially the triffids.

Con stopped at a cupboard. It had curlicues leaping out of its lid like a forest of satyrs' horns, and something—things—like satyrs themselves oiling down the edges. It *was* satyrs. Their hands were its handles. Ugh. Con, his own hand on one of the doors, glanced at me. "Why did the Cup distress you?"

I shrugged. How was I going to explain?

"My question is not an idle one," he said. "I do not wish to distress you."

Not till after we'd defeated Mr. Bo Jangles anyway. Oh, Sunshine, give a vampire a break. He probably thinks he's trying. "I'm not sure I can explain," I said. "I'm not sure I can explain to *me*. And vampires aren't much into family ties, are they?"

"No," he said.

I already knew vampires aren't great on irony.

"I . . . have got into this because of my inheritance on my father's side. I'm certainly alive to tell about it—so far—on account of that inheritance, right? But—" I looked into his face as I said this, and decided that the standard impassivity was at the soft, understanding end of the range, like marble is a little softer than adamant. "I'm a little twitchy about this bond thing with you, and the idea of—of—a kind of background to it—that your master had dealings with my dad's family—I don't like it." I didn't want to know that the monster that lived under your bed when you were a kid not only really is there but used to have a few beers with your dad. "And the only training I've ever had, if you want to call it training, was a few hours changing flowers into feathers and back with my gran fifteen years ago, and I feel a little . . . well, exposed. Unready." I could maybe have said, assailable.

"I see." Con stared at the ugly door for a moment as if making up his mind, and then opened it. Inside were rows and rows of tiny drawers. I could feel the—well, it wasn't heat, and it wasn't a smell, and it wasn't tiny voices, but it was a little like all three together. There were dozens of things in those drawers and not an inert one in the lot. They were all yelling/secreting/radiating a kind of ME! ME! ME! like the jock kids in school when the coach is choosing teams. I wondered what the cupboard was made of. I didn't feel like touching it myself and seeing if it might tell me anything. I didn't like the grins on the faces of the satyrs.

Con opened a drawer and lifted out a thin chain. The other voices/emissions subsided at once, some of them with a distinct grumble (or fart). The chain glimmered in the nonlight—the foxy-colored light of the fire didn't reach this far—it looked like opal, if there was a way to make flexible connecting loops out of opal. It was humming a kind of thin fey almost-tune; my mind, or my ear, kept trying to turn it into a melody, but it wouldn't quite go. Con poured it from one palm to the other—it looked fine as cobweb in his big hands—and then held it up again, spreading his fingers so that it hung in a near-circle. The almost-tune began to change. It would catch, like a tiny flaw tripping a recording, making it hesitate and skip; but each time it picked up again the tune had changed. It did this over and over as I listened, as Con held it up; and as I listened the strange, wavering nontune seemed to grow increasingly familiar, as if it were a noise like the purr of a refrigerator or the high faint whine of a TV with the sound turned off. Familiar: comfortable. Safe. I also felt, eerily, that the sound was becoming more familiar because it was somehow *trying* to become familiar: like the shape of a stranger at the other end of the street becomes your old friend so-and-so as it gets close enough for you to see their face and possibly that ratty old coat they should have thrown out years ago. This sibylline chain was *approaching* me . . . and dressing itself up as an old friend.

It knew its job. By the time it drifted off into silence I was reaching for it as if it belonged to me. Which maybe it did. Con dropped it over my hands and it seemed to stroke my skin as it slid down my fingers. I watched it gleaming for a moment—the gleam seemed to have a rhythm, like a heartbeat—and then I dropped it over my head. It disappeared under the collar of the black shirt, but I felt it lying against me, crossing the tips of the scar below my collarbones, resting in a curve over my heart.

"Thank you," I said, falteringly. I knew a powerful piece of magic when I saw it and hung it round my neck, but I had never heard of anything quite like this . . . *convergence*; usually you had to make a terrific effort to match things up even a quarter so well as this. Of course what I didn't know about magic handling would fill libraries.

Also, "thank you" seemed about as pathetic a response to such a marvel as anyone could make.

"I thought it would be glad to go to you."

"Er—didn't you—"

"No. My master was vexed when he discovered the necklet would not work for him nor any of our kind. This cupboard contains some of his other disappointments."

"There was a bit of a clamor, when you opened the doors," I said.

"Yes. These are human things, and they have seen no human since they were brought here." Pause. "They do not love being idle. Some of them are very powerful. I can restrain them, even if I cannot use them. I would offer them to you, if . . ."

"If there was any indication I wouldn't make a total botch," I interrupted, "which there isn't. To the contrary, if anything." The question of the existence of my demon taint, never far from the front of my mind these days despite serious competition from vampires and immediate death, resurfaced long enough to register that the "human things" had responded to me as human. Well, if they were comparing me to Con I was a shoo-in. I didn't know how long they'd been here, but a good guess was long enough to make them desperate. I touched the chain with my finger, and half-thought, half-imagined I heard a faint—the faintest of faint—hums. If I was going to say I'd heard it, I'd say it was a happy hum. But I wasn't going to say I'd heard it.

"The Cup was my mistake."

"Allow me to point out that it had been a rather tiring evening already," I said testily, "before I met the damn . . . *cauldron*. And I wasn't exactly prepared. Nor was I exactly *introduced*. Even a master handler—which I am not—can be caught off guard."

"The necklet will allow you to find your way back here," said Con. "You may, if you wish, investigate these things further, having prepared yourself."

I laughed a small dry croaking laugh. "That kind of preparation takes decades of apprenticeship. Ruthless, singleminded, hair-raising apprenticeship. It also requires someone to be apprenticed *to*, which in my case I have not got, besides being at least fifteen years too old to start." And possibly calamitously partblood.

After a pause, Con said, "I too had to . . . invent much of my apprenticeship. A master with whom you cannot agree is sometimes worse than no master."

Then why did you *stay*? I thought.

"There are few, I think, master handlers, who could have traveled the way you traveled this evening to come here, and lived."

My capacity for invention is flash hot stark, I thought. Sucker sunshade. Disembodied radar-reconnaissance. Not to mention Bitter Chocolate Death and Killer Zebras. Pity about the rest of me.

"If you will accept advice from me I would suggest you not come that way again, except in direst need."

"Happy to promise that one," I said. "But don't find yourself in direst need again either, okay? Or even plain old bland low-level semi-sub-dire need."

"Ah. No," said Con. "I will promise as well. To the extent it is within my mandate."

He closed the cupboard. I thought, if I do get back here, for my first trick I'm going to transfer all that stuff out of that deeply repulsive cupboard, which I'm sure isn't making any of it rest any easier. Supposing I can find anything more suitable in this baroque funhouse.

"We must be on our way. Dawn is a bare hour away."

"An *hour*?" I said. "You mean you're—this—is *that* close to—"

My dismay was hardly flattering, but Con answered with his usual detachment: "Not in human geography. But the fact that you are here at all—by the way you came—and the necklet you now wear—you will be able to walk some of my shorter ways."

My heart sank. "You just told me not to use nowheresville again."

Con said, "I cannot travel that road any more than I can walk under the sun. I do not take you that way."

"Oh," I said. "Well."

I DON'T KNOW how we came out above ground again, out into the ordinary night, with a little ordinary breeze and a few ordinary bats swooshing about. Bats. How quaint. I noticed they did not come from where we had come from, however. Wherever that was. I don't seem to recall coming out, like from a tunnel; the wilder, intenser darkness of Con's earth-place merely thinned and crumbled, and eventually we were walking on rough grass and turf. With bats skating overhead. I was uncomfortably reminded of my perfunctory clothing when the breeze showed a tendency to billow up inside the long black shirt, but I was so grateful to be breathing fresh air—and because I desperately wanted to be *home*—when Con took my hand I didn't instantly jerk it away from him again. At least he didn't offer to carry me. Even though I was barefoot again. It occurred to me that I had a pattern of being inappropriately dressed during my associations with Con.

His shorter way was a little like stepping on stepping stones while the torrent foamed around your feet—in this case the torrent of that conventional reality I was so eager to return to—and threatening at any moment to surge over the edge and sweep you away. I almost certainly would have lost my balance without his hand: you had to look down to see where to put your feet, and reality careering past at Mach hundred and twelve is seriously dizzy-making, plus some of the stepping stones were dangerously slick, disconcertingly like ordinary stones in an ordinary stream, although I didn't want to think what they were slick with, nor what the equivalent of getting soaking wet might be if I fell off. It was less unnerving than the way I'd gone earlier tonight, as that way was less unnerving than where Aimil's cosmail had taken me, but it was still unnerving. Very.

I wondered if traveling through nowheresville was part of the *You will begin, now, I think, to read those lines of . . . power, governance, sorcery, as I can read them,* that Con had predicted a month ago. But he'd said *read.* If this was reading I didn't want to know about doing.

Then the stones seemed to get bigger and bigger and the torrent slowed and grew calm, and we were at the edge of Yolande's garden.

I didn't notice him leave. I don't remember his dropping my hand. But as I recognized the shape of the house in the near-light of mundane night under the open sky, I realized I was alone.

I remembered as I staggered up the porch steps, trying to avoid the creakiest ones, that I didn't have the key to my apartment. Again.

At this rate I should start keeping a spare under a flowerpot for those nights I found myself doing something strange with Con while barefoot and unsuitably clothed. Maybe it was the necklet, but I put my hand over the keyhole and growled something, I don't know what, and *heard* the damn bolt click open. I also heard tiny ward voices chittering at me irritably, but they didn't try to stop me coming in. I rebolted the door tidily behind me.

I didn't take his shirt off. I fell onto my bed and was asleep instantly.

I HALF EXPECTED to wake up and find myself lying in a little pile of ashes, when the black vampire shirt disintegrated under the touch of the sun's rays; I more than half expected to wake up having had a long, labyrinthine dream about Con with a background to match—labyrinthine, I mean. No again. (Although I remembered when I'd last woken up in my bed and hoped that what I remembered about something-strange-with-Con had only been an embarrassing dream. It hadn't been a dream that time either—and the things-that-weren't-dreams were by this showing getting *more* embarrassing. Speaking of patterns I wanted to break *soon*.) I did wake stiff as a plank from all my new scrapes and bruises, and with a crick in my neck so severe I wasn't sure I was ever going to get my face facing frontward again. I looked over my shoulder at the little heap of abandoned clothing in front of the still-open balcony door as I stumbled into the bathroom and started running hot water for a bath. I'd been here before too, only last time it was the other vampires that had knocked me around.

Be fair, I thought. I'm in a lot better shape than I was when I got home four and a half months ago.

I didn't feel like being fair.

For just a *moment*—for fewer than the ten seconds it had lasted when it happened—I remembered his mouth on mine, his naked body hot and sweating against mine—

No. I put my head under the tap and let the water blast all such thoughts away. My hair needed shampooing anyway.

The shirt, although it needed a wash, still looked pretty glamorous in daylight. Good quality material. Nice drape. Even if black wasn't my color. Although at the moment a lot of me was dark blue and purple, and it coordinated very well with that. I scowled at the mirror. My own fault for looking. The chain round my neck gleamed in daylight too. It looked more like gold this morning, but if I stirred it with a finger it had a queer iridescent quality not at all like real gold, not that I had much acquaintance with the stuff. I had always favored plastic and rhinestones.

I took the shirt off carefully and put it with the other laundry. Was it natural fibers, I wondered, did it need to be dry-cleaned? I had somehow neglected to ask Con about these crucial details. Borrowing shirts from ordinary guys wasn't this complicated. For one thing, ordinary-guy shirts usually had washing instruction tags in them. This one didn't have any tags.

I took my bath and wondered if I was going to make it in to the coffeehouse for the lunch shift.

I wasn't anything like as bad off as I had been last spring. I was just sulky. I only took one bath. By the time the water had cooled from scalding to merely hot I could almost turn my head again.

I left the rainbow chain round my neck during my bath. I didn't want to take it off somehow, and I doubted that bubble bath was going to tarnish it. What I did do was introduce it to my other talismans. I hadn't a clue how to clean up after last night's magic—none of the words my gran had taught me seemed at all suitable, I felt kind of put off candles and herbs, and I wasn't in a very *thank you* mood. But I knew I should be doing something. This was a compromise.

As a solemn rite it wasn't much: I was cross-legged on the very rucked-up sheets of my bed, and still dripping from the bath, wrapped in an assortment of towels. I had pulled my little knife from the pants pocket of the trousers on the floor, and took the mysterious seal out of the bed-table drawer. I smoothed a bit of pillow and laid them there. Then, gently, I lifted the chain off over my head, and dropped it down around them.

I don't know what I was expecting. It just seemed like the thing to do. Knife, meet necklace. Seal, meet necklace. Necklace, meet knife and seal. I suspect we are going into some kind of fracas together, and that you are my co-conspirators—you and that underground guy—and I want to make sure you're all on speaking terms with one another before I ask you to guard my back.

Or something.

It was too late in the year for direct sunlight to touch my pillow at that time of day. So I don't know what happened. But there was a flash like—well, like a ray of sunshine, but it was some ray: like a golden sword, like a Christian saint's vision of glory. It landed on my talismans with an almost audible *whump*, like the king's grip had slipped and he'd clobbered the knight on the shoulder instead of merely tapping gently and dubbing him Sir Thing.

And the pillow caught fire.

I sat there with steam suddenly boiling off my wet towels, my mouth open, staring. And my brain had gone on vacation without advance warning, because I *reached into the fire, closed my hands around my three talismans, gathered them together, and pulled them out of the fire.*

The fire went out. The pillow lay there, charred and smoking.

My hands felt a little hot. No big deal. When I opened my hands, there were three overlapping red marks on the palms: one long thin almost rectangular oval, for the knife, one smaller shorter fatter oval for the seal, and a scarlet curl over the ball of one thumb, a slightly ragged thread-width stripe, for the chain. None of the objects themselves now felt any more than human-body-temperature warm. None of them looked a trace different than they had a minute before. Before they had been set on fire by persons or forces unknown.

"Oh," I said. My voice quavered. "Oh my."

I MADE IT in for the lunch shift all right. I didn't want to stay home alone with myself. I hung the chain round my neck again, and put the knife and the seal in two separate pockets. I didn't feel like leaving anything in the bed-table drawer any more. We'd bonded or something—speaking of weird bonds. Our affiliation had been confirmed by setting one pillow on fire. I put the pillow in the trash and the sheets in the washing machine. My sheets had never been so clean as they'd been in the last few months. I hardly got them on again before something else happened and I was feverishly ripping them off and stuffing them in the wash with double amounts of soap and all the "extra" buttons pushed: extra wash, extra rinse, extra water, extra spin, extra protection against things that go bump in the night. Unfortunately I never could find that last button. Some day soon I'd buy another pillow and a new set of pillowcases.

Turned out once I was dressed in long sleeves and a high neck and jeans you didn't see the bruises much. There was one on my jawline that was going to be visible as soon as I tied my hair back and a gouge down my forearm that I decided I had to put a bandage on even if this made it look worse than it was. Couldn't be helped. You can't ooze in a public bakery any more than you can cook anything without rolling your sleeves up first. I'd worry what to tell Mel later.

Paulie was glad to see me. It had been a busy morning, but then it was always a busy morning. "We're full up with SOFs," he said. I grunted. I'd seen them on the way in, glancing through the door to the front, having thoughtfully come in the side way for staff only (and hungry derelicts), just in case of things like SOFs. I put a clean apron on and tied my hair up at lightning speed (lightning bolt, golden sword, Mach hundred and twelve), threw a little flour in my face to camouflage the bruise on my jaw, and was up to my elbows in pastry by the time Pat had drifted apparently aimlessly into the bakery. I hadn't seen him on my way in; he'd been moving pretty fast himself if they'd called him over from HQ. "A word with you on your next break?" he said.

"I've only just got here," I said, smudging flour and butter and confectioner's sugar together briskly.

"Whenever," he said, loitering.

"It'll be a couple of hours," I said quellingly. I could feel Paulie raising his eyebrows behind my back: Pat was usually a friend with privileges. That had been before I'd found out my loyalties were not merely divided, they had hacked me in two and were disappearing over the horizon in opposite directions.

"Whatever you say, ma'am," he said, saluting, although not very convincingly. "I don't suppose there are any cinnamon rolls left?"

"No," I said.

"Walnut sticky bun?" said Paulie. "Blueberry muffin, pumpkin muffin, orange, carrot and oat muffin, pear gingerbread, honeycake?"

"One of each," said Pat, and disappeared.

Paulie hadn't been with us long enough yet to pretend to be impervious to the sincere flattery of people gorging themselves on the stuff you had made. He rubbed his face with a sugary hand to disguise the grin and went off to load up a plate and shout for Mary to take it out front.

I WAS TEMPTED not to admit when I went on break but I was having to do enough lying just plugging through my days—and nights—and didn't want to get too used to it. It was like I didn't want to forget the difference between daylight and nighttime: and both my funny eyes and my funny new life-and-undead style seemed to be prodding me relentlessly in that direction. Not funny.

My sunshine-self. My tree-self. My deer-self. Didn't we outnumber the dark self? My hands patted the two pockets that contained the knife and the seal, leaving two more smudges on my apron.

I took the apron off and washed my hands and made myself a cup of tea and went out front. Pat had either come back or was still there. Paulie's piled-up plate two and a half hours ago hadn't been enough; he was now eating Lemon Lust pastry bars and Killer Zebras. Any normal human ought to have a gut he'd have to carry around on a wheelbarrow, the way he ate. This had crossed my mind once or twice before, being many years acquainted with Pat's eating habits, but he was SOF, you know? So he got a lot of exercise and had a high metabolism rate. I wondered again what kind of demon he was. If he was a rubberfoot, which came in blue sometimes, he could walk up walls, for example, which must burn a *lot* of calories. I nodded to him and went out to sit on the wall of Mrs. Bialosky's flower bed. The sun was shining.

He followed me. "Listen to the news last night?" he said.

I was *making* it, I thought. I suppressed a shudder. "No."

"One killed and three missing in No Town," he said. "The one killed is confirmed sucker."

"You can't be sure this soon that the other three are anything but missing," I said. "Maybe they ran away."

Pat looked at me.

"They may have run away from something else," I said, "that had nothing to do with vampires."

"The moon may be one of Sunshine's Killer Zebras, but I doubt it," said Pat. "A lot of people saw these four hanging around together earlier in the evening."

I didn't say anything.

"Four is a lot for one night, even in No Town."

I still didn't say anything.

"We'd like you to come round this afternoon and have another stroll through a few cosmails," said Pat.

"I don't get off till ten tonight."

"We'll wait," Pat said grimly. "There's one little snag—Aimil doesn't want to do it. She says you tried it on your own a few days ago and it took you away somewhere. She said she thought you'd died. Now, why would you want to try it on your own, I wonder?"

"Why do you think?" I said, looking at him steadily. The shadows on his face lay plain and clean. I slid a little further into my strange seeing. These shadows had a slightly rough or textured quality I was beginning to guess meant partblood—I'd seen it in Maud's face first, but Aimil had it too—and in Pat's case this not-quite-human aspect was distinctly blue. But the shadows said there was no deceit beyond the basic subterfuge of passing for pureblood human. Pat was who he said he was, and believed what he said he believed. "I want to find these guys too," I said. "And SOF, begging your pardon, makes me nervous."

Pat sighed and rubbed his head with his hand, making his short SOF-norm hair stand on end. "Look, kiddo, I know all the usual complaints about SOF and I agree with most of them." He saw me looking at his hair and smiled a little. "So I don't happen to mind the hair and the uniform, that's not a crime, is it? But we can protect you better at SOF HQ than you can protect yourself anywhere else. What if what you were tracking had noticed you were searching for it the other day? You think you could have got back out fast enough for it not to follow you home? The fact that Aimil is still alive proves that it didn't notice. But I think that was dumb luck. Nobody has ever lived a long happy life depending on dumb luck, and depending on *any* kind of luck is as good as tearing your own throat out when you're messing with suckers. I don't care what extra powers you got, Sunshine."

I swallowed. "Did you say all that to Aimil?"

"You bet I did, babe, and more besides. She is, after all, on our payroll and subject to our rules. You aren't. Yet, although I've thought about it. But SOF doesn't pay so good and generally we have to blackmail people like you and Aimil, to put it bluntly, not to mention figuring out what the *official* description of what we wanted you for would be. I could probably tie you up in a big knot of top-secret intelligence bureaucracy—we've got powers to compel ordinary citizens in certain circumstances, did you know that? And we could make these the right kind of circumstances, never fear—but it would take too long and I suspect it would make you ornery. We need you too badly to risk pissing you off, if we can get you any other way. By the way, you *were* planning on coming to us with anything you found on the other end of Aimil's cosmails, weren't you? You don't have any noble, suicidal plans to take these suckers on by yourself, do you? Tell me you are not that stupid."

I said with perfect honesty, "I have no intention of trying to take these suckers on by myself, no."

Pat looked at me with a slight frown. "Why doesn't that sound as reassuring as it should?"

I gazed back at him as innocently as I could.

He sighed. "Never mind. We'll see you at ten tonight. In fact, I'll come by myself at closing."

"I'm not going to sneak out the back way and go home if I've told you I'll come," I said, annoyed.

"You haven't actually said you will come," said Pat calmly, "and I don't want you walking around by yourself at that hour, in case Bozo gets wise between now and then."

This was a little too near a little too much of the truth. "Bozo?" I said carefully. "Do you have a name?"

"Have we ever had a name?" said Pat. "You find 'em and you stake 'em and then you burn 'em to be sure. But we're obviously chasing a master vampire here, and it's easier if we call him something. Assuming it's a him, which they usually are. So we're calling him Bozo. So, are you saying you'll be waiting for me at ten tonight then?"

"But if Aimil—"

"I'll tell her you're coming anyway and we've got that cosmail saved and we can do it without her if we have to. She can either come be part of the safety net or sit at home waiting for really bad news *and* be hauled over the carpet and messily fired later on."

"What sweethearts you SOFs are," I said.

There was no humor at all in Pat's face when he replied: "Yeah. But we're real devoted to the idea of keeping the live alive. What did you do to your chin—and your arm? Is that from when you fell out of Aimil's chair?"

"Must be," I said. "I don't remember that well."

IT WAS A fairly ordinary day at the coffeehouse. We had one crazy wander in off the street who wanted to tell all of us that the end of the world was coming. He had an interesting variant of the standard format: in his reading the moon was going to be moved in front of the sun and kept there to create a permanent eclipse while the creatures of dark took over down here. The moon would be held in place by the something-o-meter invented by the creatures of dark and which they were presently perfecting. He said "creatures of dark," not "vampires." I suppose I was in a twitchy mood anyway, but I didn't like this. There are lots of creatures of the dark, but I would have said that except for vampires none of them is bright enough to invent a something-o-meter. So why didn't he say vampires? He did say eighteen months, tops, before the eclipse began.

It was a good thing he hadn't washed in a while and raved like a loony or some of us might have believed him. I told myself his story would make a good novel. It would sure make a better novel than it would a reality. Mel got rid of him. Mel goes all Good Old Boy amiable and eases them out the door, and the thing about it is that when Mel does it, they don't come back. The only times we've ever had to call the cops is when Mel hasn't been there. Ranting crazies make Charlie nervous. Because this is Old Town we get a fair number of crazies: hell, we feed most of them, out the side door, but not so many of them rant. Charlie can soothe a customer determined to pick a fight when Mel would just throw him out the first time he swore at one of the waitresses, and I'd back Mel against most brawlers, but taking them on their own terms isn't a good way to avoid calling the cops. Sometimes I think more throwing out would be a good thing—we have enough customers, we don't need to put up with the flaming assholes—but Charlie's is Charlie's because of Charlie, which is probably a good thing too. But Mel is the one who deals with the noisy nutters. If there's ever a Mel's it will be racier. And Charlie's will have to hire a bouncer with a degree in counseling.

This crazy came in during the lull between the late-afternoon muffin-and-scone crowd and the early supper eaters so there weren't too many people around. Mrs. Bialosky was there, and I didn't like the way she listened to him either: it seemed to me she was having some of the same thoughts I was. Maybe she was just thinking about full moons. The crazy hadn't mentioned what was going to happen about the moon's phases. He must not be a Were himself.

"Hey, a little live entertainment for slack time," Mel said to me. "This one missed the mark, okay, next time I'll get jugglers." I smiled, because he wanted me to, but I noticed he was rubbing one of his tattoos: the hourglass one, that you can't see which way the sand is running. It's a charm about not running out of time. He'd been listening to the crazy too.

I couldn't see into the shadows on Mel's face. They flickered less than some but the red edges were more dazzling as if to make up for this. I didn't know if I couldn't see past the dazzle because I *couldn't* couldn't, or because I didn't want to. If I didn't want to, what was it I was afraid I was going to be seeing?

By ten o'clock I was tired, and I wanted to go home and go to bed. I had a lot of sleep to catch up on. The last thing I wanted to do was slope off to SOF HQ and plug into another live socket and fry my brains some more, but when Kyoko came into the bakery to tell me Pat was in front waiting for me, I didn't duck out the back door—even though I hadn't promised. I may have given the cinnamon-roll sponge a few more vicious stirs than it needed, but then I threw my apron into the laundry, washed off the worst of the day's spatters and stains, and went to meet my fate.

I paused briefly under the doorway. A few days ago I'd tacked up a string over the lintel, so I could stuff some of Mom's charms up there. They balanced on the narrow lintel edge and were kept from pitching over by the string. She hadn't said anything, but then we'd never discussed the fact that she was coming into the bakery when I wasn't there (she rarely crossed the threshold when I was) and leaving charms round about. Well, so, the glove compartment was full. Or she was wearing me down. And they wouldn't last long trying to protect a doorway that had people coming and going through it all the time, but at least they could keep their eyes (so to speak) on me when I was there. And while they still had what in charms passes for eyes.

The funny thing was that I'd begun to feel them there, and kind of didn't mind. I've said that charms usually rub me up the wrong way, like a rash, or a colicky baby living in the spare bedroom whose mom sleeps deeper than you do. And when I stood under the doorway for a moment I felt their—well, their good will, I'm not sure it was any stronger than that—soaking in. I felt like a baba sucking up rum. Or possibly chopped piccalilli vegetables vinegar. I shook my head to make the opalescent chain swish over my skin and patted my pockets.

Pat and I walked over, to my surprise. "I kinda want to know if there's anyone close enough to make a pass at you," said Pat. "Hope you got a table knife in your pocket."

"Very funny," I said.

"Shouldn't be necessary," said Pat, unfazed. "I got a few of ours skulking in the shadows, ready to race to our rescue."

This was not comforting, not so much because a vampire could have struck in from nowhere and killed us both before any human defender had done any more than take a deep breath and wonder if there was a problem, but because of what SOF didn't know about my extracurricular activities. I didn't want SOF watching me that closely. And I didn't like their spending that kind of expensive human time on me. "You sound like you're taking this very seriously."

"You betcha."

"Why? You haven't got any proof yet that what Aimil and I are doing is anything but psycho doodling."

Pat was silent a moment, and then gave a heavy sigh. "You know, Sunshine, you're a pain to work with. You think too much. Have you read anything about the little black boxes that are supposed to register Other activity? Called tickers."

"Yeah. They don't work."

"Actually they work pretty well. The problem is that there is a larger number of unregistered partbloods in the general pop than anyone wants to talk about—well gosh isn't *that* surprising—and the tickers keep getting confused. Or, you know, sabotaged. It's been a real bad problem in SOF for some reason. Can't imagine why. There's ways around this problem, however, once you all know you're reading off the same page. So we got some tickers that give us pretty good readings, once we figured out how to set 'em up. And I'll tell you that a couple we got down in No Town about fused their chips when you did your locating trick for us a few days ago, and they did it again that afternoon when, it turns out, you were committing your felony with Aimil."

"Felony my *ass*," I said.

"Attempting to consort with an enemy alien is a felony, my pretty darling, and all Others are enemy aliens. It's not one of those rules anyone wants to pursue too close, but it has its uses. And trying to locate 'em is near enough to trying to consort with 'em for me. Anyway, we've never had readings like these readings. What you're up to may be psycho doodlings, all right, but they're great big strong psycho doodlings and we're beginning to hope you may be the best chance we've seen in years and not another one of my over-optimistic bad calls."

I considered having a nervous breakdown on the spot. I probably could have thrown a good one too, about how I couldn't take the strain, that my life had crashed and burned those two nights I went missing by the lake and all Pat and SOF were doing now was stamping out the ashes and oh by the way if you have an axe handy I'll run mad with it now and get it over with since my genes are being slower off the mark than I've been expecting since I figured it out two months or whatever ago, and by the way, that was SOF's doing too, you guys and your sidelong suggestive little chats. While half my brain was considering the nervous breakdown recourse the other half was considering whether maybe I could locate Bo well enough *and then let SOF handle it.* Con and I wouldn't have to go within miles (vampire miles or human miles) of No Town. We could sit at home drinking champagne and waiting for the headlines: NEW ARCADIA SOF DIVISION ELIMINATES MAJOR VAMPIRE LAIR AND DESTROYS ITS MASTER. Our correspondent, blah blah blah.

My imagination wanted MOST IMPORTANT STRIKE SINCE VOODOO WARS, but it wouldn't be. It felt global to me because it was my life on the line.

But it wasn't going to happen that way. I didn't even know why, not to be able to explain it. But I could feel it, like you feel a stomachache or a cold coming on, or somebody's eyes staring a hole in your back. SOF could go in and mess things up for a little while, stake a few young vampires and maybe wreck Bo's immediate plans. But . . . maybe this was something else I was learning to see in the shadows. Maybe it was from traveling through nowheresville or walking Con's short ways last night when I *was* somewhere else: watching my reality stream by, finding out there are other places with other rules. I was beginning to understand how the connections in the vampire world *really* aren't like our human connections in our human world.

I was tethered to Con as absolutely as he had been shackled to the wall of the house beside the lake. And he and Bo had a bond that required one of them to be the cause of the destruction of the other one. I guessed now that this was as natural a situation to a vampire as making cinnamon rolls was to me. I wondered what happened if a vampire involved in one of these lethal pacts did the vampire equivalent of falling under a bus: did the other one, foiled of catharsis, spin off into the void instead? The really nasty void, that is. Which could explain why it was so godsbloodyawful a place to visit.

He could have warned me, I thought. Con could have said something, that second morning by the lake. Would it have occurred to him? No. Besides, what was he going to say? "Die now or later"? That had been the choice all along. And as far as my situation now being the mere sad inevitable result of my being in the wrong place at the wrong time: grow up, Sunshine. Bo would be just a tiny bit irritated with me personally. Having not only escaped but taken his prize prisoner with me. What had kept me alive so far—my scorned and ignored magic-handling talent, my reluctant and harrowing alliance with Con—was also what was causing the bond. Ordinary mortals don't get bound up in ceremonial duels to the death with master vampires. But ordinary mortals don't survive introductory vampire encounters either.

I cast back to that second morning at the lake and thought, he *did* warn me—or remind me. I just didn't hear it. Why should I? And why should he think I needed warning? "*. . . That we are both gone will mean that something truly extraordinary has happened. And it almost certainly has something to do with you—as it does, does it not?—and that therefore something important about you was overlooked. And Bo will like that even less than he would have liked the straightforward escape of an ordinary human prisoner. He will order his folk to follow. We must not make it easy for them.*" I was the one who'd assumed the time limitations around Con's annotations of our predicament.

More recently Con had said, *I knew what happened at the lake would not be the end.* And it wasn't like I'd been surprised.

Okay, what if—just as a matter of keeping our position clear here—*what if* we managed to off Bo now? What new chains of vengeance and retaliation would we have forged instead?

I wanted to laugh, but I didn't want to come up with a likely story to explain to Pat what I was finding to laugh at. Unless I wanted to make the laughter hysterical, as a lead-in to my nervous breakdown.

But I didn't. I wanted to find Bo and get on with it. Whatever happened next. *Whatever.* I would think about whatever if there was a tomorrow to think about it in. Right now today was enough—like getting away from the lake alive had been enough. If Aimil's cosmail was Bo, and I could trace it, and SOF could offer some protection from being traced back, then I'd risk doing it with SOF. I *wanted* to find Bo. And hadn't I just been saying there was a bond between Bo and me as well? Big ugly mega yuck.

What I didn't want was to get sucked in again and maybe somehow this time pop out on top of *Bo*. As things I couldn't bear to think about went, this was very high on the list.

My sunshine-self, my tree-self, my deer-self. Didn't we outnumber the dark self?

What I had to figure out, fast, was if there was going to be a way I could make a mark, leave a clue, carry some bad-void token away with me that Con and I could follow or interpret better or faster than SOF could. There'd been kind of a lot going on and I hadn't sorted what I had found—or half found, or begun to find—in Aimil's living room. If sorting was a possibility. Aimil had been afraid I'd died . . .

No. I'd figure it out. I had to.

Did the tickers do anything but register activity, could they define it?

They'd pick up Con and me too, when we started going somewhere—wouldn't they? If. Supposing our rough human-world guesses were right, and what we all wanted was in No Town. But . . . if SOF was now going to start keeping a closer watch on me, were they going to plant a ticker near Yolande's house? Oh, gods. Could she disable a SOF ticker?

Aimil, looking subdued, was waiting in Pat's office, with Jesse and Theo. She got up from her chair and put her arms around me.

I hugged her back and we stared at each other a moment. "I guess these guys worked you over so the bruises don't show," I said.

"Which is more than can be said for you," said Aimil, touching my jaw gently.

"I got that doing chin-ups on the top oven," I said. "Let's get on with this, can we? I want to go home and go to bed. Four in the morning is already soon."

Pat's combox was on, and the saved cosmail winked at us as soon as he touched the screen. Even before plugging in to the live connection it looked evil to me; the flickering print seemed to have a kind of *bulgy* red edge, so that it looked like tiny scarlet mouths howling behind every letter of every word. "Ready?" said Pat.

I sat down and put my hands on the keyboard, like I was going to do some perfectly ordinary com thing, tap a few keys, see what the headlines were on the Darkline. "Ready," I said. He pressed the globenet button and the mail went live.

I was almost sucked in after all. Hey, I didn't know what I was doing. Was there an apprenticeship for this? The globenet hasn't been around all that long, but magic handlers adapt pretty fast—they have to. If I'd been apprenticed, could I have learned how to trace a cosmail? No. If this was something magic handlers now routinely did, SOF would have a division of magic handlers that did it. And they wouldn't be all over me like a cheap suit. I was going where no one had gone before. And I wasn't having a good time.

It was my talismans that held me together, and in this world. I felt them heat up, *wow*, like zero to a hundred in nothing flat with the throttle all the way open, like a cold inert vampire being brought back to undeadness by a surprise drop-in guest. I guessed there was a red hoop around my neck and over my breast now, and a red oval on each thigh. I hoped they wouldn't set my clothes on fire, which might be hard to explain as well as embarrassing.

It was pretty excruciating. It was like being dragged forward and hauled backward simultaneously: as if I was living the moment when my divided loyalties ripped me apart and took off with their riven halves. Other-space yawned, and while last night, with Con at the far end of the back-country-lane version, it had merely been remote and unearthly and nowhere I had any business being, tonight it was the bad one again, the shrieking maelstrom. If I went headfirst into this one I wouldn't come out, except in small messy pieces.

But I was frisking on the boundary of dangerous territory for a purpose. Dimly through the inaudible din, I thought, perhaps this is Bo's defense system. Okay, if I can find where the defense system is, presumably I can find where what it's defending is. Or is that too human a logic? I tried to orient myself, carefully, carefully, staying firmly seated on the chair in Pat's office, feeling my talismans burning their variously shaped holes into my flesh. I wasn't the compass needle myself this time—that would have been too far in—I was trying to angle for a view so I could see where the compass needle pointed. . . .

There.

And I was flung over backward, with the chair, and landed on the floor so hard the breath was knocked out of me. This was just as well, because Pat's combox exploded; droplets of superheated flying goo rained down on me as well as tiny fragments of gods-know-what, and larger pieces of plastic housing. There were a few half-muffled shouts of surprise and pain, and then there were a lot of alarm bells ringing. I was still struggling to get some breath back in my lungs when people started arriving. I had thought those were real alarm bells. They were.

What looked like everybody at SOF headquarters poured into Pat's room, and there were more of them than you'd think for ten-thirty at night. Once I could breathe again I could tell the medic I wasn't hurt. (There are medics on duty twenty-four-seven at SOF HQ: our tax blinks at work. Well, okay, lots of big corps have medics on duty, but few of them have combat patches. This one did.) My shirt had got a little torn, somehow, and the chain and the mark it made were visible; he gave me some burn cream for the latter, while he muttered something about the weird effects of a combox blowout. Fortunately it didn't seem to occur to him to suggest that there was something funny about my necklace and I shouldn't wear it.

I didn't mention the hot spots I could feel on my thighs. I was glad still to have thighs.

Pat had fared the worst; he needed stitches in one shoulder where he was hit by the biggest single chunk of flying combox, and had several inelegant burn marks on his face and one hand, although none of them serious. "Hey, I was an ugly bastard before," he said. "It's not gonna ruin my social life." Even Pat had been rattled, however, because the two guys who rushed in and sat down at the other combox in the room—one of them with a headset he kept muttering into—had been tapping away intently for several minutes before Pat noticed. I had been watching them as I lay on the floor, but I was pretty hazed out myself and hadn't managed to think about what they might be doing. I had half-noticed Jesse doing an ordinary startled-human stillness thing when those two came in, but I hadn't registered it. I did register Pat snapping into awareness and then exchanging a hard look with Jesse.

And then the woman came in and the tension level in the room went off the scale. I felt like we were in one of those old-fashioned movie rockets where the Gs of escape velocity crush you into the upholstery. Okay, so my metaphors had taken a wrong turn, but when I first looked at her there were no shadows on her at all: it was as if she was *glowing*, in great sick-making waves, like a walking nuclear reactor or something, if I had ever seen a nuclear reactor, which I have not. Instant headache. Instant wanting-to-be-out-of-here, wherever here was; hereness seemed to fade under the onslaught of her mere presence.

This had to be the goddess of pain. And I had thought that name was just a joke. Uh-oh.

She snapped a few undertone orders to one of the fellows with the headset; he was obviously not happy, and he shook his head. His partner in crime shrugged and spread his hands. "Your little stunt has just bombed HQ's entire com system," she said in a cold clear voice that was worse than any shouting. "What the *hell* are you doing?"

Pat, almost visibly pulling himself together, said, "I had clearance. Ask Sanchez."

"You didn't have clearance to close the regional HQ down, and you obviously didn't do your homework about safeguards," said the woman, not a split atom's worth mollified. "You still haven't told me what you were trying to do, and Sanchez isn't here."

One of the headset guys on the other combox barked something, and she listened to them briefly. When she turned to glare at Pat again he was a little more ready for her. "We were trying to trace an Other cosmail to a land source. We have been working with Aimil, here," nodding to her, "for some months. This is Rae Seddon, whom we had reason to believe might be able to help us. This is the second time she's tried to make a connection. As for safeguards, I . . ." and he ran off into a lot of technical jargon I didn't understand a syllable of, and didn't want to. I tuned out.

By this time I was breathing again, although my lungs felt sore. Not nearly as sore as my head, however. My eyeballs felt like they were embedded in glass splinters and my entire skull throbbed. I was now seeing a fat glaring red edge to everything, an erratic fat glaring red edge, sometimes as wide as a pocketknife, sometimes as narrow as an opalescent chain. It didn't need shadows. It looked like cracks in reality, opening into the chaos I'd seen protecting the way to Bo through nowheresville. I clung to the arms of the re-righted chair I'd been helped into once the medic was done with me.

"Hold *still*," he said. He was trying to put stitches in Pat's shoulder. I didn't want to look at the goddess of pain again; I knew it was my eyes, but there was something really *wrong* about her, and whatever it was, it made my headache worse.

I watched a couple of people gathering up pieces of combox. Another person appeared bearing a big bottle of some kind of, presumably, solvent, and was wiping up the littler gel blobs. Somebody else was flipping the bigger blobs into a bucket. I noticed that some of them left marks behind them. Jesse had minor burns on one forearm; Theo and Aimil hadn't been touched. It could have been a lot worse.

It was a lot worse. It just wasn't about being burned by combox gel. My red edges were, I thought, narrowing. Not fast enough.

I didn't notice the pause in the conversation till I heard my name being repeated. "Rae Seddon," the goddess was saying. I jerked my eyes up—and flinched: neither my eyes nor my head was ready for sudden movements—and equally unequal to meeting the goddess' eyes. "I heard about the incident a few weeks ago," she said, "with the vampire in Old Town."

I didn't say anything.

"I'd quite like to have a chat with you myself sometime," she said.

I still didn't say anything. I glanced at Pat. He was so poker-faced I knew he was worried. There was a big red halo around his head, and the shadows across his face were so blue I was surprised they weren't obvious to everyone. I hoped they weren't.

"I doubt I can help you," I said, not looking at her. "I think it was an accident."

"Some power residue from your experience at the lake?" she said. I didn't like having her so up on my history. I wondered what else she knew. "Yes, I agree that that is the most likely. But it is the first such incident I'm aware of in any of our records"—did this mean she was interested enough to have had research done on it?—"and I would like to know as much about it as possible. SOF is always interested in unusual and unique cases. We have to be." She smiled. I saw it out of the corner of my eye. It wasn't that she didn't mean it, exactly. It was that it was an official lubricant-on-the-sticky-gears-of-community smile. It suited her aura of poisonous gases. A toxic oil slick on the sea of society. I didn't like the smile. I found Pat's single-minded commitment to the total annihilation of vampires a little inopportune but I believed he was one of the good guys. I didn't believe she was.

I didn't smile back. I tried to look too beat up from what had happened to be able to smile. I wasn't. What I was was too beat up to make myself smile when I didn't want to.

"I assume that tonight's misguided attempt at a *connection* was also based on some faulty reading of that same residue?"

The tone of her voice could have made cinnamon rolls unroll, cakes fall, and Bitter Chocolate Death melt. I hoped cravenly that she was talking to Pat.

Pat said, "There's a precedent. Milenkovic—"

"You'll have to do better than that, Agent Velasquez," interrupted the goddess. "Milenkovic was a senile old woman."

Pat took a deep breath. "Ma'am, Milenkovic's field notes clearly record—"

Jesse was arguing with the guys at the backup combox. I wanted to hear what was going on there but I didn't want to appear interested in anything while the goddess was still staring at me. I didn't think she was listening to Pat's dogged description of poor Milenkovic's misfortunes. I concentrated on looking stunned and blank. And maybe stupid. I was a marginal high school grad who baked bread for a living. Intellect was not a big feature. Hold that thought. Behind the blank look I was testing the memory of what had happened while I was plugged in. Had I found anything, or had I been repelled before I could make a fix? I wasn't going to stand up and make a directional cast as I had done the last time in this office, not with the goddess watching. But it felt a little . . . directional. And I was afraid if I didn't try it soon I might lose it, if there was anything to lose.

Aimil moved into my line of vision. She was looking at me too, but her look said, *Can I help?*

I stood up slowly. I felt shaky anyway, but I made myself look shakier yet. Aimil rushed to take my elbow. As I moved, I felt it. . . .

Yes. I'd found something. And I hadn't lost it yet.

I think Aimil felt the shiver run through me, and she probably guessed why. "Rae's pretty knocked around," Aimil said, and I recognized her placate-the-inquisitor voice: one of the area library bosses got that voice, and when she was in residence at Aimil's branch library Aimil found special projects across town to attend to. "May I take her home?"

"Tell me, Rae," said the goddess. "Do you think you discovered anything useful this evening?"

"I don't know," I said carefully. "It was over pretty suddenly, and now I have a terrific headache."

"Usually," said the goddess, "the sooner the interview after the experience, the more information is obtained."

I tried to look as if I would like to be cooperative. "I'm sorry," I said. "It was like I was falling into chaos, and then I went over backward in the chair and the combox exploded."

The goddess' radar was telling her I was holding something back. With a great effort I raised my eyes again and met hers. There was no way I was going to try to read any shadows on her face: it was as much as I could do to look at her at all. What the *hell* was this? Some kind of wild personal warding system? I'd never met anything like it.

We stared at each other. She wasn't my boss—and she wasn't a vampire—and life with my mother had taught me not to intimidate easily, although this last took some effort, and my head was spinning even worse than . . . Uh. *What?* She was *trolling* me. . . .

This was strictly illegal: a violation of my personal rights, and anything an illegal fishing expedition found was automatically forfeit too, in theory, but once you know something you know it, don't you? There is a license you can get to do a mind search under certain circumstances but there is a list of prior requirements as long as the global council's charter—besides that, you need to be a magic handler particularly talented in etherfo interchange—and in practice there are only a few specialist cops and specialist lawyers who get one. And likely some SOFs: but if the goddess had the license, she was misusing it now.

"*Hey,*" I said, and put up my arm, as if to ward off a physical blow. Trolling isn't an exact science for even the best searcher, and the searchee has to hold still. Big police stations have a mind-search chair as standard equipment, and a medic standing by with a shot of stuff that on the street is called *delete*, which makes you hold still all right and you may not move real well again for a long time afterward.

I was pretty sure she hadn't had the chance to pull anything out of me but I sure didn't like her trying. I also thought I understood why those I disconcertingly found myself thinking of as my gang—Pat and Jesse and Aimil and Theo—looked so jumpy.

"I am so sorry," she said, not sorry at all. "I am accustomed to assisting recall in our agents. I did it automatically."

The hell you did, lady, I didn't say. You were hoping I wouldn't notice. I did say, "Good night. If I remember anything, I'll let you know."

She would have liked to stop me, but perhaps she didn't quite dare. I had noticed what she'd tried to do, and an accusation of illegal mind search would be embarrassing to SOF even if they denied it convincingly. It occurred to me that she must really, really want anything I could tell her, to have taken the chance. Was she that flash on vampires or was there something else going on? Silly me. Of course there was something else going on. If she was just megahot on vampires, she and Pat would be buddies, and they weren't.

It also occurred to me that she couldn't have pulled anything out of me, because if she had, she'd've found a way to hold me, and she was letting me go.

I turned very carefully to the door, wanting to get through it before she changed her mind. I also didn't want to shake my fix loose till I'd had a chance to explore it. I felt it swimming, the way a compass needle swims as you turn the casing.

Aimil clung solicitously to my elbow. "My car's in back," she said.

We were halfway down the final corridor when we heard someone running up behind us: Pat. "I've left Jesse trying to deal with the goddess," he said. "Sorry, Sunshine, can you move any faster? I want us all out of here before she thinks of a reason to yank us back in."

They hustled me along between them. Pat was holding his wounded arm pressed against his body, but his grasp on me was strong enough. Once I was outdoors I felt the fix run through me again. "I have to stop," I said. Pat didn't argue, but he glanced over his shoulder.

We stood at the top of the little flight of stairs into the parking lot. I took a deep breath and tried to settle myself, wait for the compass needle to stop waving back and forth. It didn't want to stop waving back and forth. A void needle will presumably be confused by moving around in ordinary reality, the way an ordinary compass needle will be confused by steel beams and magnetic fields.

I hoped there weren't any steel-beam and magnetic-field equivalents nearby. Settle, I told it. I haven't lost it, I thought, please don't tell me I've lost it. . . .

"Um," said Aimil. "I don't know if this might be of any help to you," and she pulled a bit of exploded combox from her pocket and offered it to me.

"You darling," I said. Sympathetic magic is never the best and is usually the crudest, but when you wanted grounding there is nothing better, and any damn fool with a drop of magic-handler blood six generations back can tap it. I held the scrap of plastic in both hands.

This time I didn't have to turn around. I felt it slamming in over my right shoulder—no, *through* it—toward my heart. Like a stake into a vampire.

I dropped the bit of combox and threw myself away from its line of flight. The chain round my neck and the knife and seal in my pockets blazed up again—and I seemed to have a friction burn across the front of my right shoulder where the whatever-it-was had grazed me in passing—it felt like someone had taken an electric sander to me.

Pat caught me, or I might have fallen down the steps onto the pavement. *"Wow,"* he said, and almost dropped me, as if he'd caught hold of something burning; but he was a true SOF, or he had his damsel-rescuing hat on that evening, or he was more worried about me than about the skin of his hands or the stitches in his shoulder. He flinched but his grip tightened.

"Sorry," I said. "That was a little of what blew the combox."

Aimil shook her head, slowly went to where the bit of broken combox was still rocking on its curved edge where it had landed, bent down even more slowly, and picked it up. Brave woman. But it wasn't the sort of clue we could afford to leave lying around: everybody knows about sympathetic magic, which would include all the goddess' spies.

Pat rubbed his hands down the sides of his legs. "Shiva wept," he said. "Sunshine, you okay?"

"Yeah," I said. "More or less." I looked in the direction that the invisible stake had come from. No Town again. I looked back. "Your stitches are bleeding."

"Did you get anything?"

"No Town. We knew that."

Pat expelled his breath in an angry sigh. "So we blew out the com system, destroyed a lot of equipment, *and* got the goddess of pain on our butts, and all we know is that it's No Town. Bloody hell."

I glanced at Aimil, who was valiantly not saying "I told you so."

"I'm sorry," I said.

"Not your fault, Sunshine. I'm sure we're on to something with you, we just have to figure out how to use it. Some day we're going to cruise you around and see if it is No Town at all, and if we can get some kind of angle on it."

I thought this sounded like trying to find the epicenter while you're falling into the cracks in the earth, but I didn't say anything.

"But that's the long way and I'm impatient. Damn. John's a com whiz. I should have asked him before. He could take on the goddess' little walters; I just thought Sanchez—well. It plays as it plays, and the goddess is going to be watching our every move now."

"Who is she?" I said.

"The goddess of pain? Sunshine, you're slipping. She's second in command here at div HQ, but we keep hoping she'll get promoted out of regional and out of our hair. Jack Demetrios—he's the boss—he's okay."

I did know that. But I didn't know how to ask about the goddess' weird vibes. "Does she have any—er—unconventional personal wards or anything?"

Pat looked at me in that too-alert way I didn't like. "You mean other than the fact that her walking into a room makes any sane person want to run out of it? You mean she's got that effect as a switch on her control board? Hey, Sunshine, what are you picking up?"

I shook my head. "Nothing. Too much happened tonight is all."

"She tried to troll you, didn't she?"

"Yes," I said.

"But you blocked her," said Pat. "Thank the listening gods. I'm glad you blocked her anyway, but I always like seeing the goddess screw up."

I HAD SOME trouble convincing them to let me drive myself home. I had a *lot* of trouble convincing them. Aimil knows me well enough to know to stop arguing eventually, but I left Pat scowling and furious. But he wasn't scowling and furious as hard as he should have been. That meant that they already had something planted out at Yolande's to check up on me. Hell.

The Wreck was in a good mood. We got home at a steady thirty-five mph and it didn't diesel for more than fifteen seconds after I turned the key off. I fumbled in the side pocket for something to write on and something to write with: all the usual glove compartment things had got crowded out of the glove compartment by charms. I scribbled, *Yolande, help. SOF is monitoring here for Other activity. S,* and stuck it under her door. I tried to listen for any tickers in the neighborhood but that wasn't in my job description and I didn't know what to listen for.

I dragged myself upstairs. I hadn't cleaned up all that well from last night, so it was easy to fish out a few wax chips from the candles Yolande had given me and dump them into a smudge bowl and light a candle under them. I waited till the chips began to grow soft, and I could smell, faintly, their aroma. Then I closed my eyes and aligned myself. . . .

I didn't want to go anywhere. I just wanted to leave a message. The chain around my neck began to feel warm. Only a little warm.

. . . *Sunshine?* . . .

. . . *Found* . . .

. . . *Tomorrow* . . .

. . . *Beware* . . . *SOF here* . . .

IT WAS A good thing my hands knew what to do because the rest of me was barely responsive to automatic pilot the next day, or anyway the gear assembly needed its chain tightened up several links. I got through the morning, the Wreck took me home, I fell asleep several steps from the top of the stairs but my feet carried me the rest of the way into my bedroom and I woke up at three, lying slantways across my unmade bed, my feet hanging over one end, my cheek painfully creased and my bruised jaw made sorer by a wad of bedspread. The sin of untidiness chastised.

"Oh, ow," I said, rolling over. Bath time. When in doubt, take a bath. My family (especially those of them who remembered clearly what it had been like to share a one-bathroom house with me) every year at Winter Solstice give me enough bubble bath to last me till next Winter Solstice. I wasn't going to make it this year though. I always got through a lot of bubble bath, but this year was in a category of its own.

When I was dressed I went out onto my balcony to brush my wet hair in the sunlight. Yolande was in the garden, cutting off dead-heads. She looked up at the sound of my doors opening. "Good afternoon," she said. "May I make you a cup of tea?"

"Love it," I said. "Give me five minutes."

When I came downstairs her door was open. I closed it behind me and made my way to her kitchen. My apartment was one of the attics; hers was the whole of the ground floor, and it was a big house. I didn't linger to stare, but I found myself looking around at everything I had seen before with the new idea that any of it might be possible secret wards; and it did seem to me that the shadows lay differently on certain things than on others, and some of those certain things were pretty unexpected. Could that faded, curling postcard that said *A Souvenir of Portland* leaning drunkenly against a candlestick be anything but a worthy candidate for a housecleaning purge?

Yolande was fitting the tea cozy over the pot when I came in. There were cups on the table. I knew where her cookie plates lived, so I got one down and put my offerings on it: chocolate chip hazelnut, Jamdandies, Cashew Turtles, plus butterscotch brownies and half a dozen muffins. (Fortunately I hadn't landed on the bakery bag when I fell asleep.) Technically we aren't supposed to take anything home from the coffeehouse till the end of the day, but I'd like to see anyone try and stop me.

"It is ironic," she said, "that SOF, our white knights against the darkness, are causing you such bother. But I think I can guarantee they will not notice your friend if he comes again. You will forgive me if I made my obstructions specific again to him only. Were you successful the other night?"

I didn't mean to laugh, but a sort of yelp escaped me. "Yes. If anything too successful."

Yolande said, "I'm afraid that is sometimes the inevitable result of the possession of real power. That it is stronger than you are, and not very biddable."

"I don't think it's my so-called power that's the problem," I said bleakly. "It's the trouble it gets me into."

Yolande pulled my cup toward her, settled the tiny silver sieve over it, and poured. Before I met her I had thought you made tea by throwing a tea bag in a mug and adding hot water. Four years ago I'd convinced Charlie to inaugurate loose tea in individual teapots at Charlie's. I told him that a coffeehouse that sold champagne by the glass could stretch to loose tea. Our postlunch afternoon crowd had instantly ballooned. Must be more Albion exiles in New Arcadia than we thought. Albion had been hit very badly by the Wars.

"I doubt your interpretation," said Yolande. "If I may be blunt, I don't think you'd still be alive if you were a mere pawn."

"I know this is pathetic of me, but sometimes I think I'd rather be a pawn. Okay, a live pawn."

Yolande was smiling. She had that inward remembering look. "Responsibility is always a burden," she said.

"Next you're going to tell me it doesn't get any easier."

"Quite right. But you do grow more accustomed to it."

"Wardskeepers have this whole rigorous training thing. So you aren't doing anything—stuff doesn't happen till you're ready for it."

She laughed, and it was a real laugh. "Only in theory. Tell me, what were your first cinnamon rolls like? And didn't the recipe look simple and pure and beautiful on the page? And the instructions your teacher gave you, before he left you to get on with it, were perfectly clear and covered everything?"

I smiled reminiscently, stirring sugar into my tea. "They were little round bricks. I still don't know how I did it. They got *heavier*.

They can't have weighed more than the flour I put into them, you know? But I swear they did. There's a family myth that Charlie used them in the wall he was building around Mom's rose garden. I wouldn't be surprised."

"The first time I cut a ward sign—cutting a sign is your first big step up from drawing all the basic ones, over and over and over, and you *long* for it—I managed to wreck the workshop. Fortunately my master believed my talent was going to be worth it. If we all survived my apprenticeship."

"I blew out the ovens once, but that wasn't entirely my fault. . . . Okay. Point taken. But I don't think anyone knows how to travel through nowheresville."

"Then I hope you are taking good notes, to make teaching your students easier."

"You are a hard woman," I said.

She leaned forward and lightly touched the chain around my neck. "That is a potent thing. You have others, I think, but this is new. It has a great sense of darkness around it, and yet it is a clear dark. Like a bit of jewelry in a black velvet case. A gift from your friend, I imagine."

I nodded, trying not to be unnerved by her perceptiveness.

"My master would be most interested, but he lives on the other side of the country."

"Your master?" I said, startled out of politeness. "But you're—"

"Old," she said composedly. "Yes. Older perhaps than you think. Magic handling has that effect. Surely you know that?"

"I thought it was a fairy tale. Like pots of gold and three wishes."

"It is not a very reliable effect, and ordinary ward- and spellcrafters won't notice much difference. But to those of us who soak ourselves deeply in a magical source, it can have profound consequences. This is not a chosen thing, you know. Or it chooses you, not the other way around."

"I always thought my grandmother looked very young," I said slowly. "I haven't seen her since I was ten. When I was in my teens I decided it was just that she had long dark hair and didn't look like other people's grandmothers."

"I never knew your grandmother, although I knew some of the

other Blaises at one time. But my guess is that she was much older than you had any idea of."

"Was," I said. "None of it got her through the Voodoo Wars. Or my father either."

"I'm sorry."

"I don't *know* they're dead. But I can't believe my gran wouldn't have let me know. . . ." My voice trailed off. "I . . . I have been my mother's family's kid all my life—even when we were still living with my dad, I think—till four months ago. Almost five months ago. It's a shock to the system."

She looked at me thoughtfully. "Consider the possibility that you had to be a certain age to bear it, when it finally came to you."

"There must have been an easier way."

She laughed again. "There is always a better way, in hindsight."

I said, trying to smile, "The cousins I know—my mother's sisters' kids—are married by the time they're my age. The younger ones do stuff like play varsity sports or collect stamps or dollhouse furniture. The two in college, Anne wants to be a marine biologist and William wants to teach primary school. It's like the Other side doesn't exist. Even Charlie, who you'd think of anyone would remember, says he'd almost forgotten who my dad was." I paused. "I don't even know how my parents met. It doesn't seem very likely, does it? That Miss Drastically Normal should fall for Mr. All That Creepy Stuff. All I know is that my mom worked at a florist's before she married my dad.

"What happened to the safety net, you know? If I was going to turn out this way, why didn't I get apprenticed? Why didn't my gran leave a codicil in her will asking someone to keep an eye on me? She taught me to transmute. She knew I'd inherited *something*."

Yolande didn't say anything for several minutes while I sat there trying not to be embarrassed for my outburst. "I don't believe in fate," she said at last. "But I do believe in . . . loopholes. I think a lot of what keeps the world going is the result of accidents—happy or otherwise—and taking advantage of these. Perhaps your gran guessed you might be one of those loopholes. Perhaps she left a codicil in her will saying to leave you alone at all costs. What if you'd been apprenticed, and learned that there is no way through no-wheresville?"

I COULDN'T SETTLE down to read that evening—anything about the Others made me twitchy, anything else was so irrelevant as to be maddening. *Child of Phantoms*, another favorite comfort-read for over a decade, failed to hold me. Reading was of course a problem with my dark vision getting in the way, but in fact flat black type on a flat white page was easier to deal with than almost anything else. I did pretty well so long as I remembered to keep my head and the page perfectly still; if I didn't, the print jumped sick-makingly into three dimensions. It was like the advertising about some latest thriller or other: *This story is so exciting it will leap off the page at you!* For me it did. This is disconcerting when you're reading *Professional Baking Quarterly*, which I usually tried to do. It made me feel I had some of the right attitude, and the letters page was always good for a laugh. Mom renewed my subscription every year as a supportive-maternal present. Surprise.

I did shut myself into the closet for half an hour with my combox. I had to screw up my courage to hit the "live" button. But nothing happened except what is supposed to happen. Whew. Perhaps the com cosmos isn't so homogenous after all. I knew that the official line is that the comcos is entirely a human creation, but then the official human line would be that, wouldn't it? And if there is a lot of vampire engineering in it, that would help to explain both where a lot of vampire money came from and why every authority on the planet—business, ecosyn, social service, governmental, all of them—is droolingly paranoid about vampires. However, if my combox was still in one piece and the comcos equivalent of the Big Ugly Thing That Ate Schenectady hadn't burst out of the screen and seized me, there must still be enough human input to the workings of the com-cos to keep it . . . heterogeneous.

So I glanced through my cosmail to make sure I wasn't missing anything important. The usual globenet come-ons: a ride on the space bus for only a hundred squillion blinks and the soul of your firstborn child. A plastic surgeon who guaranteed to make you look like Princess Helga or your money back. And your face back too? I wondered. Learn spellcasting at home in your spare time, earn zillions, and live forever. I'd always assumed the living forever was out of the same scam as the earning zillions. I wondered how old Yolande was—how old her master was. I doubted it was four hundred years.

I answered a few cosmails. My presence in various Other zones had faded in the last five months. I could have given definite answers to some of the pet topics (Has a human, once captured, ever escaped from a vampire? Have a human and a vampire ever had a conversation on any kind of equal terms? Have a human and a vampire ever had *any* conversation and parted with the human still alive?—Barring some of the media stuff, although another pet topic was whether any of the vampire interviews were real). I had no desire to do so. But it had only been since my first contact with Other-space that it had occurred to me perhaps it would be a good idea to continue to pretend that Cinnamon—my ether name for seven years—was an ordinary woman who hadn't had anything surprising happen to her lately.

When I came out of the closet it was barely twilight. I thought sunset was never coming. This might be the first day of my life I'd ever wanted darkness to come sooner. I always wanted daylight to last longer. I had a lot more trouble getting up at four A.M. in winter when it was still going to be dark for hours than in summer when it would be glimmering toward dawn by the time I got to Charlie's.

I took a cup of chamomile tea out on the balcony and waited, feeling the darkness falling as if it were something landing on my skin.

I heard him coming this time. I don't know why I thought of it as hearing, when it had nothing to do with my ears. I didn't see any shadows moving among the other shadows of the garden either, although I knew he was there. But it was more like hearing than it was like anything else, like seeing in the dark is more like seeing than it is like anything else.

"The way here has grown in complexity," he said.

"Oh—ah?" I said. "Oh. That will be Yolande's new wards. SOF has set up some tickers and I don't know what all."

"Tickers," said Con.

"You know," I said. "You must know. SOF uses them—they record any Others that come near them. Tick tick, back at HQ where they're watching the monitors."

"I have not had much contact with SOF."

The Lone Ranger of vampires. Did that make me Tonto? "Whatever. The point is SOF thinks they're protecting me. So I asked Yolande to disarm any SOF snoopers that would notice you."

"Yolande."

"My landlady."

"You have told her about me?"

I snorted. "*She* told *me*. Turns out she's known all along. And she's a wardskeeper. She's real useful to have on your side."

Con was silent. I felt sympathetic. I wouldn't have liked the idea that he'd brought a friend into our business either. I was so keyed up that I didn't think about our disastrous last meeting till I'd already taken his hand, and then it was too late. He came back from wherever he'd been, presumably thinking about having another human foisted on him, and looked at me. His fingers curled around mine. I had a Senssurround Dolby flash of The Ten Seconds That Didn't Go Anywhere, but I hit the mental censor button and it went poof.

"Listen," I said, although it was even less like listening than the nonsound of him moving toward me had been like listening. It was strangely easier too, doing it with him, showing him my new road map rather than trying to figure it out myself. He knew the language *and* the landscape. I had a great idea: next time Pat called me in to SOF for a little more technical mayhem, I'd bring Con. "Hi, I'd like you to meet my helpful vampire friend. Don't worry, my landlady is a retired—mostly retired—wardskeeper, and she says he's okay." Sure. Speaking of having more humans foisted. Pat would take some foisting.

But I stared into Con's green eyes, and *aligned* myself, or him, like you might take someone's shoulders and turn them round so they're facing the right direction, like you might point at a map once you've told your companion, see, it's those mountains you see right over there. . . .

For a very nasty moment I thought I'd somehow managed to re-make the live contact. That we weren't looking at a map of those mountains, but had been transported there, and the tigers were clos-ing in. I jerked back, but Con's hand held me, and the jerk was like the click-over of the kaleidoscope, and the colored bits fell into a new arrangement.

It was weirdly something like looking through an aquarium at a lot of fish. The fish were whizzing around like crazy—cannonball fish—but I could see them individually, a little, and they did look like distinct and specific little whizzings-around instead of like chaos. This was interesting, although it didn't really get me any farther; they were still moving too fast for me to track a pattern or make my way among them. But this wasn't as sick-making—or as terrifying—to watch or to think about. Presumably this was a good thing. But I remembered the quality of the terror, and wasn't sure that *not* being terrified was wise or sane.

What we were looking for was behind the whizzing things. And that was still just as sick-making, just as terrifying. I didn't like this animated three-dimensional map. *Here be dragons.* Much worse than any dragon, which are pretty straightforward—and straightfor-wardly alive—creatures that merely suffer that little character de-fect about liking to eat human flesh. *Here be horrors indescribable.* I barely sensed the dreadful loom of it—the differentiation of it from its manic pinball machine guard system—before I was repelled, re-pulsed, hurled away more violently than Con had thrown me the other night . . . except it was Con, this time, who caught me.

I was flopped against him, his arm round my waist, my ear pressed to his silent chest. I grabbed at his other arm, steadied my-self, balanced again on my own feet, which seemed very small and very far away. "Have I given us away? Con, was that *live?*" The world still spun. If there had been anything in my stomach but tea (the muffins were a long time ago) it might have come up. As it was, the tea sloshed vindictively a few times and subsided. The chain burned round my throat.

"No," said Con. "My Sunshine, you must learn moderation. This is not an enemy you can defeat by rushing his front gate."

I made a little choking noise that might have been third cousin twice removed to a laugh. "I had *no* intention of anything resembling gate-crashing. I thought I was just looking. Except it wasn't, um, looking."

"No," said Con. I could feel him thinking. "If you were a new—one of us—there are things I could teach you. I do not think I can teach a human these things."

I sighed. "I believe you. Like seeing in the dark probably doesn't bother you because you don't spend a lot of time seeing in the *light*, right?"

"I am sorry."

As partners we left a lot to be desired. "Was that him?"

Con's eyes blazed briefly. Vampire eyes catching sight of their chosen prey. Don't look. "Yes."

"Can you—can you track him any better from what I—sort of—showed you?"

Con's face arranged itself in one of its invisible-to-the-naked-human-eye almost-expressions. I guessed this one was irony. Note: existence of vampire irony. "I am not sure. It is certainly a signal we want to take heed of. How we take heed without jeopardizing ourselves unnecessarily I do not yet know. Remember that was not *live*, as you put it. It was only your memory—your exegesis—of what you saw."

I shivered.

"I believe you were in less danger, even last night, than you may fear. What this is is a little like . . . what are those machines with the strange radiance, which attract insects to their deaths?"

"Zappers? Bug zappers. Bug flies in—zap."

"You were zapped. The machine does not register the—bug. It merely zaps. I use these zappers also."

"Vampires don't use bug zappers?" I said, interested. There's nothing like an immediate death threat to make you crave a little superficial distraction. I'd observed this phenomenon before. "All that hanging around out of doors after dark you guys do?"

"No."

"Wrong kind of blood?"

"Vampires do not—er—register on insect radar."

"Oh." At last: a really good reason to want to be a vampire. I was one of those people you invite on your picnic or your hiking expedition, because the bugs will all crowd around me and leave everyone else alone.

Sunshine, get a grip. "Um. This isn't the first time I've been . . . well, let me tell you the rest of it." I did. "So last night was the third time and the worst. You don't think he might be using a sort of fancy zapper that says, 'Hey, boss, this bug keeps coming back'?"

"I think I will ask you not to go near that place again for the time being. Even if this Pat asks you to try."

"It's not Pat I'm so worried about," I said. "It's the goddess of pain."

"Ah." His expressionlessness took an ominous cast.

"Con," I said nervously.

His gaze came back from wherever it had been and he looked at me. "No," he said. I didn't ask what "no" meant. Vampires are a little like burglars, okay? If a bright, determined vampire really wants to get into *your* house, he's going to do it, and the best alarm system in the world and the electric moat and the sixteen genetically enhanced Rottweilers and the wards and the charms and the little household godlets blessed by the priests or pontifexes of the religion of your choice, and spellcast by the best sorcerers money can buy, aren't going to stop him. Or her. You really don't want to piss a vampire off, because it's a lot harder having all that plastic surgery and the hemo treatment to change your blood chemistry than it is to sell your house and go live in a small cabin with nothing in it to steal. Also, the hemo treatment not only costs a bomb, occasionally it kills you, although at least two of the global council members have had it done twice that anybody knows about, and are still here.

The usual, which is to say, expensive, drastic options aren't available to coffeehouse bakers. Having realized that my being alive geared Bo up, Con wasn't my best choice, he was my *only* choice.

But the problem with having a nonhuman as your ally was that a nonhuman might not be, you know, very *sentimental* about the odd human life here and there. Especially not a vampire nonhuman about a human who shows signs of reading the mind of the vampire's human ally. And fair is fair. I wasn't very sentimental about vampires as a group either, was I?

"I can say no to the goddess if I have to," I said, perhaps a little more loudly than necessary.

"I am certain you can, Sunshine," said Con.

He was gone a moment later. I didn't exactly see him go, but I didn't-hear him moving away from me, and didn't-see the shadow among the other shadows, after he was gone. I didn't pay a lot of attention, however, because I was preoccupied with the feeling on my mouth, as if he had kissed me before he left.

MORE HORRIBLE GRISLY marking time, wondering what was going on. Wondering what is going on behind my back, wondering what is about to leap out of the shadows at me. At my worst I could begin wondering if I'd imagined Con. Well, he was the part that didn't fit the pattern, wasn't he? Nice, helpful, if somewhat unreassuring-looking, vampire. Puhleez.

There was enough to remind me there was *something* going on—starting with the scar on my breast and moving through seeing in the dark and the spontaneous combustion of pillows and ending, perhaps, with the fact that there didn't ever *not* seem to be some SOF or other at Charlie's now, and that any time I walked in or out of the door, whoever-it-was's eyes fixed themselves on me. For a while I'd made a point of coming in by the side door any time the coffeehouse was open, but I decided this was making a bigger issue of something I couldn't do anything about, so on days I was feeling hardy I went through the front. Let 'em stare. It had taken Aimil's remark to make me notice that Mrs. Bialosky was occupying her table more than usual. But she'd nominated herself as one of my protectors in one very practical way: some mangled version of recent events meant that we still had gapers coming in to check out if I had three heads or spoke in tongues. They didn't stay long if Mrs. Bialosky rumbled them. Which kindly took the onus off our staff, which if they weren't getting as tired of my notoriety as I was, had every right to.

But it was all too much, and my overworked and exhausted brain started looking for things to call imaginary. Con was such a perfect choice. I sometimes felt if I could get rid of Con I could be rid of all the rest of it—Bo, my heritage and weird talents, SOF's suffocating interest, the lot. I knew it wasn't true. But . . .

I did have one nice surprise. One afternoon I came out of the bakery and discovered someone unfamiliar sitting at Mrs. Bialosky's table, and with whom Mrs. B was in deep conversation. I couldn't resist this, so I slid along behind the counter to get a look without walking up to the table and staring: not that my subterfuge worked, because Mrs. B immediately raised her head and looked back at me. But this made the other person turn to look at what Mrs. B was looking at. She broke into a smile when she saw me: it was Maud. I hadn't registered till then that there was a large plate on the table between them that presently contained a light sprinkling of crumbs and one single remaining Killer Zebra.

One of these mornings at four-thirty A.M. I was expecting to find a SOF lurking on a street corner too, and the fact that I didn't see one didn't convince me there wasn't one there somewhere. Pat had made an official offer to have me escorted to and from home, which I didn't let him finish before I refused. Other than that I hadn't seen much of him: damage control with the goddess, I assumed. I was interested myself that my desire for autonomy was still stronger than my fear of what might or was about to happen. My unfavoritest corner, when I arrived at Charlie's before dawn, wasn't the nearest one, where Mandelbaum met the main road, but across the square, at the mouth of one of the littlest and darkest alleys of Old Town. I pretended to fish for my keys and then made a big pantomime fuss about choosing the right one every morning as I scanned for shadows that didn't lie right. Shadows *never* lay right in that corner. I always felt watched, these days. It was just a question of watched by whom. Or what.

After I opened the door and went in, I relocked the door behind me before I turned off the alarm system. Used to be I didn't bother to relock the door. I'd asked Charlie to program an extra few seconds' delay to the bell so I could. He'd looked at me worriedly, but he'd done it. And he hadn't asked any questions. He wasn't going to say the "v" word if I wasn't.

We don't have a state-of-the-art alarm system at Charlie's—we can't afford it—but this is one of the ways having SOF friends is useful, and we do have some funny little gizmos that tell you if anything has been disturbed. Nothing went on being disturbed, except my mental state.

I was pulling maple cornbread out of the ovens at about eight one morning when Mary came in to say Theo wanted a word. I thought about it. "Okay," I said. "Time I had a break, I guess."

Theo sidled in like the reluctant bearer of unwelcome news. My private bakery kettle was beginning to hiss and burble. "Tea?"

He shook his head.

"Cornbread?"

He brightened immediately. I was as bad as Paulie, really, despite how long I'd been doing this. Someone wants to eat my food, they're automatically my friend. Someone who doesn't want to eat my food, they automatically aren't. This is an awkward attitude if you hang out a lot with a vampire.

Theo was an old enough hand in the kitchen—my kitchen anyway—to know to approach something fresh out of the oven with caution. He took the whacked-off still-squodgy-with-baking end of a loaf of maple cornbread gingerly and watched happily as the approximately quarter-pound of butter he put on it melted through. He would lick the plate when he was done. This was one of the advantages of eating out back: table manners weren't required. I'd been known to lick plates myself. Once when I was teasing Kyoko about him, I mentioned he was a plate-licker. She looked briefly interested. "Oh? Maybe he's human after all." Then she shook her head. "Nah. He's SOF." This was in hindsight a better joke than I'd realized.

"You'd better get it over with," I said, after he'd finished licking the plate.

He sighed. "Pat would like to see you this afternoon."

I'd decided in the predawn darkness of the morning after I'd met the goddess what I was going to say the next time Pat wanted to talk to me. "It won't do him any good. Something burned out the other night. *I* burned out. I woke up the next morning with a piece missing. It's still missing."

He looked surprised, worried, then thoughtful. Then, to my great surprise, hopeful. "He'll still want to see you."

"Why are you looking so pleased?"

He hesitated. "The goddess wants to take over. Take *you* over. She says it's because Pat destroyed government property, that he's bungled, that she wants to clean up the mess, that you're to be sent back where you came from after she's sure no security has been breached, that it was all glang anyway. But it's really because she's pissed off that someone may have thought of something or discovered something before she did. Something that might be important—something *she* might be able to use."

"And you think Pat'll think that merely blowing out the county HQ's com system on a bad call is *better* than the goddess finding out maybe it's a good call?"

"Yeah."

I thought of her walking-nuclear-reactor aura. "If I wasn't afraid of the goddess already, I would be now."

He smiled. It was a rickety sort of smile. "You don't know half. You don't want to know half. You want my advice, you stick to suckers. When do you get off today? Pat'll come by just before."

"Three," I said. His eyes were wandering to the muffin racks. There were bran raisin and oatmeal applesauce allspice waiting to go into the cases up front. "Have one for the road," I said.

"Thanks," he said. He took two.

PAT DRIFTED IN at a few minutes to three. I now knew that it would take a lot to make him look short of sleep, and he looked short of sleep. He looked worse than short of sleep. He raised hollow eyes and said, "Hey, Sunshine."

"You look like hell," I said. I was scraping out the last baking tin. Our Albion crowd would have to be really hungry today to get through this lot. And I'd made my special cream-cheese sauce to go with the triple-ginger gingerbread. I'd long felt that gingerbread, while excellent in itself, was still essentially an excuse to eat the sauce, so I'd always made twice as much per portion as the original recipe called for. Then it turned out that some of our customers were even more crazed than I was, so I'd started making three times as much, and we served it in little sauceboats. You got purists occasionally that didn't want any sauce, but the slack was taken up somehow.

"Thanks," he said.

"What's happening?"

He shrugged. His shoulder must be better. Maybe blue-demon blood made you heal fast too. "What Theo told you."

"You look like you've been let out of the dungeon. I thought thumbscrews were passé."

"The goddess doesn't need thumbscrews. She just looks at you and you feel your brains melting."

I thought of the other night. "I believe you."

"Theo says you've lost it."

"Yeah. I'm safe from the goddess. No brains left to melt."

"No one is ever safe from the goddess." The Pat I knew surfaced and he gave me a familiar look: shrewd, humorous, no nonsense. "How lost do you suppose it is?"

I pulled off my apron and untied my hair. "Lost enough for now. If I replace a fuse and the system starts working again, I'll let you know."

"Maybe you're just tired," said Pat.

"Maybe," I said amiably.

Pat ran his hand through what there was of his hair. "I don't like it when you agree with me, Sunshine. It's not your style. What aren't you telling me?"

"That I'm relieved not to have to try again," I said.

I knew he bought it: he sagged, suddenly looking smaller and older. I felt a fierce pang of guilt, but I reminded myself that he believed that the only good vampire was a staked, beheaded, and burned vampire. Briefly and wistfully I considered a scenario where Con and I had a SOF team with us when we . . . whatever . . . but I recognized this as a fantasy, like a scenario where the goddess of pain retired from SOF and opened a day care center.

"You look like a man who needs caffeine," I said. "I'll grab us something from the counter and meet you outside. Do you want privacy or comfort?" Comfort meant the nice little tables out front, overlooking the square and Mrs. Bialosky's flower bed, still doing its stuff with chrysanthemums and asters this late in the year.

"Privacy," he said.

He was sitting at one of the unsteady tables in the grim little courtyard behind the coffeehouse that by never doing anything with we could continue to avoid opening to customers. You got used to the roar of the kitchen fans and Mom had a couple of tough little evergreen shrubs in pots that could survive the cooking fumes. Pat and I didn't talk about anything much after all. He drank the coffee and engulfed the various buns and other edible objects I'd brought, but absentmindedly, like a refueling procedure. The fact that he didn't argue with me about trying again, about trying to find out the extent of the burnout—about whether or not there really was a burnout— made me feel more guilty.

Silence fell. Pat stared into nothing. "I'm sorry," I said.

He looked at me. "I believe you," he said. He stood up. "I'm not sure I believe the rest of it, but I believe you're sorry about it." He paused. "Makes my life easier in some ways." Another gleam of the normal Pat as he said: "Maybe by the time you've decided you're not burned out any more the goddess will have found someone else to crucify."

I didn't say anything. He rubbed both hands through his hair this time, and added, "I didn't say this. But watch your back, Sunshine." Then he left.

MEL WANDERED OUT a few minutes after Pat had left. I was staring into my teacup. I'd forgotten to bring a sieve out, so there were tea leaves in the bottom of it, but I couldn't read them. "You look like a woman who needs a good laugh," he said. "Have you heard the one about the were-pigeon and the streetcleaner?"

"Yes," I said. "Mel, d'you suppose *anyone* is exactly who they say they are?"

"Charlie, maybe," he answered, after a little pause, of surprise or consideration. "Can't think of anyone else. Hmm." I watched his hand lift off the table and rub one of his tattoos.

Maybe I should have been thinking about tattoos myself, but there's a real big drawback to them. Any charm can be turned against you, if you run into the thing it's supposed to be protecting you from, and the thing is enough stronger than the protection. A powerful enough demon adept or magic handler can overwhelm one too, although that's serious feud stuff and not common. A tattoo feeds itself on *you*, so tattoos do tend to be a lot more stable and longer-lived than the ordinary charms you set around and hang up, including the ones you wear next to your skin; but a charm that isn't living off you can be destroyed a lot more easily if it does go—or is sent—rogue. A rogue tattoo can eat you up. It happens occasionally. Before five months ago I didn't figure I needed any heavy warding. Now that I did, tattoos were the last thing I was going to try.

"Charlie," I said. "I can't think of anyone else either." Not Mel. Not me.

"Not Mrs. B," said Mel, smiling. "Sunshine, I don't like metaphysics unless I'm drunk, it's only three-thirty in the afternoon, and I'm working tonight. What's up?"

If Mel had really been trying to pass as a motorcycle hoodlum, his tattoos wouldn't be as beautiful or as elaborate. Lots of sorcerers go in for a superabundance of tattoos, but they mostly keep them hidden—they're harder to rogue that way. Hence the long enveloping robe and deep hood technique with inked-up sorcerers when they're actually handling magic. (For day-to-day, walking-the-dog, doing-the-shopping use, a lot of sorcerers disguise the real shape of their tattoos with cosmetics. Long sleeves and high collars are *hot* in the summer—and there are favorite sorcerer tattoos that go on your lips and cheeks and forehead too. But—I love this—magic can apparently be a bit perfunctory about certain things in the heat of a transaction. Any tattoo a sorcerer wants *working* while he or she handles magic can't be distorted with face paint or pancake foundation because it may turn out to be the *apparent* figure that performs. Or doesn't.)

My dad didn't have any tattoos. That I remembered. But I didn't remember my dad very well, and not all sorcerers have tattoos.

But sorcerers are sorcerers. Tattooists mostly make their livings punching charms in leather, not live skin, and they'll try to talk an ordinary member of the public out of it if you already have, say, three magic-bearing tattoos, even little boring ones, and they'll tell you why. In vivid detail. It isn't just the rogue possibility: a lot of magic-bearing tattoos can sort of *unbalance* you. You start not being quite sure where the real-world lines are with a lot of tattoos whispering in your dreams. Of course having lots of magic-bearing tattoos is one way of saying you're a tough guy—first because the implication is that you need all that charm and ward power, and second because you're hardy enough to bear the drain and the disorientation.

But there are better ways of showing you are a tough guy than having lots of tattoos, partly because no tattooist who wants to keep his or her license is likely to cooperate, and the ones who don't have licenses are too likely to make a mess of it. There is only one small secondary quarter-circle's difference between a ward against drunkenness and another one against eyestrain, for example, and the latter won't get you home safely with a load on. And that's one of the common, simple wards, and most of Mel's tattoos weren't common or simple. But they were magic bearers, not ornamental. You could smell it, like ozone when a storm is coming. And besides, nobody who had *any* pretensions to hanging out with a biker gang would dare have ornamental tattoos. Ornies are for wusses.

Mel couldn't be a sorcerer—sorcery isn't something you can successfully hide for long—but he did have a lot of tattoos. It was typical of him too that when he had come to talk to Charlie about a job the first time he had his sleeves rolled up above the elbows and his shirt open at the neck, in spite of the fact that it was January and *freezing*.

Although maybe he just had a good take on Charlie, who in his affable, openhearted way, enjoys Charlie's reputation as a place slightly on the edge.

I said, "Mel, who are you?"

Mel picked up both my hands and kissed them. His lips were warm. When he laid them back on the table he didn't let go. I watched the sunlight twinkle among the fine hairs on the backs of his hands, and the red and gold and black of the tattoos there. Both the hairs and the tattoos had an unusually bright red edge, as if there was firelight on them. Or in them. His hands were warm too. Human temperature. The temperature of the fire of human life. Speaking of metaphysics. "I'm your friend, Sunshine," he said. "Everything else is just static on the line."

I wondered if he'd heard what Pat had said. I wondered who had done his tattoos. Maybe what I thought I knew about magic-bearing tattoos was from the same script as the disquisition about how masturbating will make you blind and a cretin. (Even 'ubis don't damage your sight.) Maybe I should ask him. But then I'd have to tell him why I wanted to know.

Even if you could successfully hide being a sorcerer, Mel still couldn't be one. Sorcerers are loners—they don't do things like get jobs as cooks in coffeehouses, or jive with their old motorcycle gang— occasionally they hang with other sorcerers, but usually for some specific and time-limited purpose. Sorcerers are too paranoid to have ordinary human friends and too competitive to have sorcerer friends. The street version about sorcerers is that they are basically not to be trusted: humans aren't meant to be that mixed up with magic. Not even magic-handling humans.

Where did *sorcerers* get their tattoos?

Maybe I didn't know anything any more.

I DROVE HOME thinking about that *Watch your back*. I was already watching my back, and Pat knew it. Was he warning me to watch my back against *SOF*? Was a loyal—if partblood—member of SOF warning me that SOF itself was not to be trusted? Okay, lately I'd heard about partbloods needing to stick together for mutual defense, and I'd heard a long time ago about the goddess of pain, and I knew none of our SOFs liked her; but I thought—I assumed—this was only because she was a hardass bitch who was more concerned with her own career path than with making humanity safe from the Others. Was Pat suggesting something more ominous? And if he was, was he suggesting it about one overambitious gorgon with skewed priorities, or about a treacherous vein, you should forgive the term, running through all of SOF?

Gods and angels, wasn't Bo *enough*?

At a stoplight I flipped open the glove compartment and looked at the clutter. A few of the charms twitched. Poor Mom. At least she was trying. I realized that I was grateful for the useless tangle, even if it was useless. Because she was doing *something*. She hadn't averted her eyes from the fact that I needed help. She merely had no clue how much help, or what kind. Only Con really knew, only he didn't know, because he wasn't human, so he didn't know what he knew. Or something.

When I got home I sat staring at the shadows the leaves from the trees threw on the driveway. They glinted and did strange things with perspective like all shadows did now, but they were beautiful and they didn't mean anything. They were what happened when light fell on leaves. It wasn't late summer any more; it was autumn, and the leaves were beginning to turn. A pale yellow one like a big flat blanched almond skittered across the hood of the Wreck.

I opened my knapsack and swept the thatch of charms into it, including one spark plug, quite a lot of string, and a few rubber bands, from back in the days when the glove compartment performed the usual function. I was pretty sure I felt a tiny penetrating buzz when my skin connected with one of the charms, but I had no idea which one. Then I went and knocked on Yolande's front door.

She opened it almost at once. "Come in," she said. "I have spoken to my old master."

I sighed. I followed her in. She took me to a room I had not been in before, next to the kitchen, also overlooking the garden. I knew at once that not many people came here—first because if she wished no one to know that she had been a wardskeeper, or at least to believe she was a retired wardskeeper, this room would give the show away; second because the *privateness* of it radiated from everything in it, like heat or light. I brushed one hand across my face, as if it was a veil I had difficulty breathing through.

She noticed this and said, "Oh! Pardon," and lifted something down from over the door we'd come in. The sense of private space invaded lessened—sank—like water. I looked down, bemused. The shadows on the floor were very active.

She laid the thing she had moved down on the desk. I sat in the chair in front of it, I leaned forward, held a hand over it: *something* beat at my palm. It wasn't heat any more than my dark vision had to do with my eyes, but it was perhaps related to heat, and it manifested itself a bit like heat against the skin. I moved my hand and looked at the thing. It was a tiny round piece of what looked like stained glass. I could see the leading of it, but I could not see if the fragments made up a picture, or if any of the bits were painted. The shadows swam in it very strangely.

Wardskeeper. It sounded so . . . solid. Even if you blew up the occasional workshop, at least you knew you were in training, and for what. Your master told you what to do, what to do next.

Yolande, watching my face, said, "I'm sorry, my dear. I know this is one of the last things you want to hear, but I think you are in over your head in exactly what you are best suited to be in over your head in—my grammar grows confused—and you are doing very well."

She was getting almost as bad as Con. What happened to random chat? I wanted to say, "All I wanted was to bake cinnamon rolls for the rest of my life," but I knew it wasn't true, and besides, I was tired of whining. So I didn't say it. I picked up my knapsack, out of the seething not-wetness still roaming about the floor, and set it on her desk. As I lifted it I had felt the charm-thatch inside it *scrambling* to stay away from the not-wetness; as I set it down, it seemed to be trying to escape contact with the top of the desk. Well, I thought, I guess at least one of them is live.

Her eyes widened, and then she frowned. "Lift it up again, if you would," she said. I did, and she took something out of a drawer, and spread it out, and then gestured for me to put the knapsack on it. I did. Whatever was going on subsided.

"What have you brought me to look at?" she said.

I opened the knapsack, but had a sudden reluctance to touch the charms. "Wait," she said, and brought something else out of another drawer: a pair of wooden tongs. They had symbols scrawled up their flat sides. I groped around, grasped an end of the tangle, and hauled it out. It seemed to have half-unraveled itself: it came out looking like crochet gone very, very wrong. As it came free of the knapsack one end snaked around as if seeking something, and then began climbing up one arm of the tongs. Toward my hand.

"*Drop it,*" said Yolande sharply. I dropped. It landed on the desk; there was a hiss and a bad smell—a *really* bad smell—and then there was a forlorn little heap of bad crochet work (plus one spark plug) with a torn-out hole in it, edged by a purply brown stain. The stain writhed.

"Ugh," I said.

"Ugh indeed," Yolande said mildly. "That was no ward; that was a fetch. Where was it?"

"In the W—in my car," I said.

"Do you keep your car locked?"

"Not here," I said, cold needling up my spine.

"No," she said. "If whatever had placed this had come here, I would have known it."

"Then it—they—someone—something can get into a locked car," I said, the coldness continuing to climb. *Something,* I thought. No, wait—vampires didn't do fetches. Did they?

"Where do these other items come from?"

"Oh—since I was missing those two days, my mother has taken to buying charms for me. They're supposed to be wards. It occurred to me to ask you if any of them was, um, live."

"Have you no wards on your car at all?"

"Only standard issue—the axles, the steering wheel." Every car manufacturer in the world had a ward sign worked into its logo, and every car company in the world stamped the center of its steering wheels with its logo. "I did have the door locks warded by the guy who sold it to me, but I guess it didn't work." I scowled. Oh well. Dave had never claimed to be a ward specialist: he only promised the Wreck would run. "And the car is fifteen years old—they hadn't invented the alloy yet." Which enabled car manufacturers to ward almost everything. There was a big difference in used car prices pre- and post-alloy. Some of us, including Mel, Dave, and me, thought that the alloy was the latest vehicular version of those skin creams that *guarantee* no wrinkles, those diet plans that *guarantee* a figure like this year's reigning vidstar in thirty days.

Lately the commercial labs were working on a ward that would dissolve in paint, like salt in water, and make every painted surface warded too. When they got it there would be a huge advertising campaign, but it wouldn't be that useful really. Like salt water. If you needed to melt some triffids it was great, but there hadn't been a trif- fid outbreak in generations. If you had mouth ulcers or a sore throat you were better off with alum or aspirin. If you had vampires the paint on your car might give them a few friction burns, but it wasn't going to stop them breaking the windscreen and dragging you out.

Your best traveling ward unfortunately was still the motion of traveling itself. I didn't like it that Yolande wasn't saying the usual things about the warding power of motion, not to worry, etc., etc. Well: but we'd just proved there was something to worry about. That fetch sure hadn't been undone by riding around in a car.

Yolande had picked up something that looked a lot like a knitting needle—it even had a tiny hook on the end—and was poking at the mess of crochet. There was one pale blue bead that still had a bit of glimmer to it. "I think some of these were live quite recently," she said. "I think what they have warded is the usefulness of the fetch, which has worn them out. You don't have any idea when you ac- quired it, I don't suppose? How long have you been stuffing charms into—?"

"The glove compartment," I said absently. A fetch was usually roughly the shape of the thing to be fetched—something that was trying to find or fetch a person was often a sort of elongated star shape, with a bead or a crystal or a chip at its center for the heart, and smaller beads or crystals or chips for the head, hands, and feet. I was sure I would have noticed my mother giving me a fetch . . . and besides, she wasn't that stupid. Eight years with my dad had made her less easy to fool than most ordinary people about anything to do with magic, and she was constitutionally hard to fool about anything anyway.

When had I noticed that the clutter, including eight or a dozen loose charms, in the glove compartment had turned into a matted snarl? I'd opened it—when?—to look at a map. I'd been sitting in the driver's seat. Several things had plopped out onto the floor. I'd heard them rustling around, the way charms will, and, still looking at my map, I'd groped around on the floor for them. I picked up one or two, but I could still hear the rustling. They were creeping across the floor under the passenger seat, humping themselves over the drive shaft, and one or two of them had made it under the driver's seat, which was fast moving for charms. I still hadn't paid a lot of attention. I'd scavenged around under the driver's seat and pulled out anything that squirmed, and shoved the whole lot back into the glove compartment without looking at any of it.

But if there'd been a fetch under the driver's seat, then the wards would have mobbed and then tried to disable it.

That had been a day or two or three after I'd taken that inconclusive ride to No Town with Pat and Jesse.

Watch your back, Pat had said.

"SOF," I said in disbelief. No, in what I wished was disbelief. In a belief that made me feel like I'd been dropped down an elevator shaft into icy water. "Someone in SOF did this to me. In *SOF.*" And whoever it was wasn't going to like it at all that it hadn't worked. No genuinely innocent member of the human public should be able to denature a fetch.

"My dear," said Yolande. "Large organizations are inevitably corrupt. The more powerful the organization, the more dangerous the corruption. When I was young I wanted to belong to one of the big wardcraft corporations—Zammit, or Drusilla, if I proved skillful enough. Several of my master's apprentices went to such places, and he was always gloomy and preoccupied for weeks—months—after he'd 'lost' one of us. That was always how he'd describe it—that he'd lost Benedict, he'd lost Ancilla. I was lucky; I was a slow learner. By the time I was ready to choose how I would pursue my vocation, I was ready to stay where I was, and go on working with my master. There were only three of us for many years: Chrysogon, Hippolyte, and myself, other than our master, and a few apprentices who came and went."

Note, I thought, the next time I meet someone with a really strange name, ask them if they're a wardskeeper.

"It is still better that SOF exist than it not exist. One must also earn a living; there is no equivalent in the SOF world for my master's small group of wardskeepers."

She was right there. The Sentinel Guild are pretty sad and the Vindicators are worse.

"The SOF fellow who came here once: he is your friend."

"Pat," I said. "Is he?"

"He is not perfect," she said. "But nor am I. Nor are you. Nor is your dark companion. But yes, he is your friend. He wishes the defeat of the evil of the dark, as do we all."

Depends, I thought, on what you mean by the evil of the dark. Or maybe by "we."

"Pat is not only interested in—in what you can do for SOF. Or for his career."

"Don't forget my cinnamon rolls, which make strong men weak and strong women run from the bus station in high heels over our cobblestones to get to Charlie's in time. If you know all that, can you tell me who planted the fetch?"

"No, I'm afraid not. I know about Pat because he sat in one place waiting for you for twenty minutes once, and that place happens to lie under the remit of one of my more ambitious wardings, and it went on taking—er—notes as long as he sat there."

I doubted I could persuade the goddess to come sit quietly under the oak at the end of Yolande's drive for twenty minutes.

"I told you I had spoken to my master about you. I also spoke to Chrysogon. We believe we can create something for you but it would be better, stronger, if—"

"You want blood," I said, resignedly. Most wardcrafters made do with something like a dirty apron, which I was sure was what my mother had been using. A few of the more determined or well-established ones will ask for hair or fingernail clippings. But there's an *enormous* black market in things like hair and fingernail clippings and the more you're likely to want a charm the less safe you're going to feel passing out bits of yourself. Blood's the worst. Not only is it blood, which is by far the most powerful bit you can hand over for all sorts of purposes, but any concept that contains "magic" and "blood" together makes the majority of the human population think "vampires" and freak out. This is actually totally stupid, since vampires aren't interested in teeny wardcrafter vials of blood, and a vampire that wipes out a wardcrafter's shop isn't going to jones for you because they've had this tiny hit like an ice cream stand flavor-of-the-month sample and cross continents till they've found you and had the rest of you. But the paranoia behind the general principle is valid.

"Yes," said Yolande.

I'd never met a wardskeeper, though, let alone had one do up a personalized ward for me. And as concepts go, one that contains "Yolande" and "black market" is going to disintegrate on contact. So that should be fine, right? Except I have this thing about blood, and Con's little healing number on me hadn't helped it.

"Um," I said.

Yolande was smiling. "You may close your eyes," she said.

"Okay."

"If you would hold out your hands palm up, and extend both fore-fingers, and then I am going to prick the center of your forehead."

The chain round my neck had begun to warm up before I closed my eyes, and I could feel a gentle warmth against both legs as well. Oh, gods, guys, I said to my talismans, isn't this *way* below your dignity? I flinched at the sting in my forehead, but the fingers were easy, even for me.

I touched the warm chain with one hand, and fished in my pocket with the other. "Maybe you can translate something else for me. I found this at the bottom of a crumbly box of old books at a garage sale."

"Well! How extraordinary. This is a—a Straight Way: very clear and plain. Clean and—old—very untainted for a ward so old. It represents the forces of day, of daylight. The sun itself is at the top, then an animal, then a tree. Interesting—the animal is a deer, I think; usually it is a fierce creature, a lion is the most common. This is not only a deer, it has no antlers, and is therefore perhaps a doe. And then round it, round the edge of the seal, do you see the thin wavy line? That is water. With these things you can resist the forces of darkness, or they cannot defeat you. Of course this is only a ward."

"The peanut-butter sandwich you throw over your shoulder at the ogre," I said. "So maybe you'll make it over the fence if he stops to eat it."

"But this found you. That is important. The forces of day is not a very uncommon ward, but this is simply and exquisitely done and—it found you. Keep it near you and keep it safe. My heart lifts that this thing found you. It is good news."

Don't tell me how much I need some good news, I thought. "When do you think your, um, ward will be ready?"

"Soon. Please—please ask your dark ally to wait till it is ready. It will not be more than a day or two."

Back to the bad news. Yolande and her wardskeeper friends thought Con and I were going to face Bo that soon. Well, I suppose I thought so too.

LATER. UPSTAIRS. THE balcony door open; candles burning; I sat cross-legged, hands on knees. I wasn't going anywhere. I just wanted a word.

How soon.

Not tonight. Not. . . . next night. Then . . .

No sooner. Yolande . . . ward . . . me

It was going to take a lot of work before this alignment business replaced the telephone. But I wouldn't be around to see it, since it looked like I had two days to live.

And I'd been complaining about waiting.

So, WHAT DO you do when you know you have two days to live? Wait a minute, haven't I been here before? No. I was only pretending, last time. I hadn't known that I was sure Con would save me, last time, till this time, when I knew he wouldn't. But I had been here before: I was still finding out I had more stuff to lose by losing it. And I already knew I thought this was a triple carthaginian hell of a system.

So, where was I? Right. What you do when you know you have two days to live. Not a lot different than if you didn't know. Six months you could do something with. Two days? Hmph. Eat an *entire* Bitter Chocolate Death all by yourself. (Actually I bombed on this. Mel had to eat the last slab. A pan of Bitter Chocolate Death isn't very large, but it is *intense*.) Reread your favorite novel, the one you only let yourself read any more when you're sick in bed. I might have enjoyed this more, since I'm never sick, if death didn't seem like a very bad trade-off. Buy eight dozen roses from the best florist in town—the super expensive ones, the ones that smell like roses rather than merely looking like them—and put them all over your apartment. I bought five dozen red and three dozen white. I have one vase and one iced tea pitcher, which has regularly spent more of its time holding cut flowers than iced tea. After I used these, and the two twinkly-gold-flecked tumblers and two cheap champagne flutes plus the best of my limited and motley collection of water and wine glasses, I emptied out my shampoo bottle—which was tall and rather a nice shape, even if it was plastic—into a jam jar, and put a few in it. I cut most of the rest of them off at the base of the flower and floated them in whatever else I had that would hold water, including the bathtub. I decided this had been one of my better ideas. The last three—two red, one white—I tied together and hung upside down from the rearview mirror of the Wreck. Better than fuzzy dice.

Take a good long look at everyone you love—everyone local; you've only got two days. And don't tell anybody. You don't need to be surrounded by a lot of depressed people; you're already depressed enough for everybody.

Of course in my case I couldn't tell anybody because either they wouldn't believe me or they'd try to stop me.

I thought about being rude to Mr. Cagney. It was something I had been longing to do for years, and I somehow managed to be behind the counter on the second morning when he needed someone to complain to. But I looked at his scrunched-up, petulant face and decided, rather regretfully, that I had better things to do with my last morning on earth. So I said "mm-hmm" a few times, refilled his coffee cup (which he changed tack to tell me was cold: okay, I'm not Mary, but it was *not* cold) and left him to Charlie, who didn't know it was my last morning on earth, and was hastening over from cranking down the awning to stop me from being rude.

Other things I didn't do included waste any time trying to find out who'd planted that fetch on me. Yolande did a sweep on the Wreck for me and didn't find anything but two new wards tucked under the front bumper and a ticker behind the rear license plate. She was quite taken with the wards, saying she was falling behind on research faster than she knew, that they were a whole new design of traveling ward and by far the most effective she'd seen. They had to be SOF too. An example of a large corrupt organization getting it right. She left all of them alone.

I had been hoping to see Pat. I could promise anything he liked for tomorrow or the day after that. But he didn't show up, as he mostly hadn't been showing up since the night we blew out HQ. He must be getting his cinnamon roll fix by white bakery bag. In a world where I was less and less sure of anything, I was sure that that jones was real. I was sorry not to have a chance to say good-bye, except of course I wouldn't have said good-bye. When Mary came into the bakery to ask if there was anything hot out of the oven she didn't know about to tell Jesse and Theo I said, carelessly, "Oh, I'll bring it: I'll try my new whatever-these-are on them." I liked the idea of inventing a new recipe on my last day on earth, and I've always liked to see my guinea pigs' faces when they first bite down. I said, "So, say hi to Pat for me," and they both looked at me as if there was a hidden message, which there was, although I doubted they were going to guess it. They were distracted quickly enough by the whatever-these-were: I'd have to do the unthinkable and write out the recipe, so Paulie could have it. And maybe Aimil would come up with a good name. Sunshine's Eschatology. Hey, my eschatology *would* have butter, heavy cream, pecans, and three kinds of chocolate in it.

I'd miss feeding my SOFs: they were good eaters.

I'd miss being alive.

I had been due to work through the early-supper split shift but I decided I wanted to see the sun set from my balcony once more so I wheeled Emmy into it. Didn't want her to lose all her bakery skills just because she'd been made assistant cook next door—Paulie was going to need her. I'd already bent Paulie's arm into a pretzel till he'd agreed to take the dawn shift tomorrow. The Thursday morning system had broken down so completely I no longer remembered if I owed him some four A.M.s or he owed me some. The confusion was probably good for him. He was about to have to learn to be chief baker real fast.

There were some people it was too difficult to say good-bye to, so I didn't try. Mom, of course. If I'd made a point of going into the office to say good-bye to her that day, however casually, she'd've been calling the cops and the hospital before I got the words out of my mouth. Once a mother, always a mother, and I'd have to have some spectacular reason for breaking the awkward but practical truce that we never spoke to each other unless on specific coffeehouse business. Kenny was bussing tables; we exchanged "Hey"s. I'd never said good-bye to Kenny and this wasn't the time to start. I had seen Billy for about two-thirds of a second earlier in the afternoon, when he blasted into Charlie's long enough to fling over his shoulder at the nearest parent the information that he was spending the rest of the day with the equally hyperactive friend accompanying him. He did not acknowledge me; I was part of the family backdrop. What was to acknowledge? My importance lay in the availability of the eight muffins and two-each-from-every-bin-and-four-if-they-were-chocolate-cookies they took with them as they blasted out again.

Mary and Kyoko I said "See you" to. I waved to Emmy, who was in the main kitchen looking harassed, but I was beginning to suspect that her harassed look was covering up the fact that she was having a really good time and didn't quite believe her luck. I always checked out with Charlie, to make sure there weren't any last-minute gaps I might be able to fill, to make sure our schedules for tomorrow matched. I'd told him about the swap with Paulie; I only said I was tired, and I know I looked it. We didn't say good-bye either. Our ritual went, "See you tomorrow, Sunshine," and "Yeah." I said "Yeah," as usual. Even on days off he said "See you tomorrow" because even on days off he usually did.

I hadn't realized that I never said good-bye to anyone about anything.

Mel. He was on break when I left, and he wasn't jiving with some guy or guys in greasy denim about overhead cam shifts through hot pastrami or meatloaf sandwiches—or for that matter discussing world news with one of our more coherent derelicts. Mel was leaning against the corner of the building drinking coffee and muttering to himself. I knew what he was muttering about: he'd given up smoking ten years ago but he still wanted a cigarette every time he drank coffee, and he drank a lot of coffee. Sometimes his fingers twitched, not from the caffeine jag but from the memory of doing his own roll-ups. This made him drink more coffee. One day he was going to wake up and discover he'd turned into a coffee plantation, and then Charlie's would have its own fresh home-grown beans even if we had to replace our chief cook. There are worse things to wake up and discover you've turned into. A vampire, for example. Although the books say you'll know it's coming.

Mel looked up and saw me, and his face eased into his good-old-boy smile. Mel used his charm as deliberately as laying an ace on the table, so you could see exactly what it was. It was one of the good things about him. Whatever he might not be telling you, what he did tell you was the truth. *I'm your friend, Sunshine.* He still looked like someone who should be wearing greasy denims rather than an apron, although the tattoos confused the issue: greasy denims and a long hooded cloak? Hmm. I wondered if sorcerers ever used food splotches instead of cosmetics.

"Hey Sunshine."

"Hey."

"We still on for Friday afternoon?"

I nodded, probably too vigorously, because his smile faded. "Something wrong?"

Nothing that wasn't wrong the last time you asked me that question, I thought, only it's got wronger faster than maybe I was expecting. I shook my head, trying to be less vigorous. "No. Thanks."

He swallowed the last of his coffee, put the mug down on the ground, and came over to me. "Sure?"

"Sure. Yeah." I put my arms around him, leaned my face against his shoulder (my forehead against the oak tree that was visible beneath the torn-off sleeve of his T-shirt), and sighed. He smelled of food and daylight. I could feel his heart beating. He put his arms around me. "Probably just lingering indigestion from eleven-twelfths of a Bitter Chocolate Death yesterday," I said. I felt the small kick of his diaphragm as he laughed—he had a sort of furry-chuckle laugh—but he knew me too well. "Try again, Sunshine," he said. "Do blue whales OD guzzling all that sea water? Your veins *run* chocolate—finest dark semisweet—not blood."

Pity it looked red, then. It gave vampires ideas. I didn't say anything.

"You can tell me about it on Friday, okay?" he said.

I nodded. "Okay." If I said any more I would probably burst into tears.

I DROVE HOME slowly. I thought of going by the library, but decided Aimil came into the "too difficult" category, and she might conceivably make some kind of guess what I was feeling so gloomy about and I didn't want to take the risk. What a really awful reason not to see someone for the last time. But I was so *tired*.

I sat in the car again at home and watched the leaves turning. It seemed to me a lot of autumn had happened in the last two days.

I thought of the two days out of time I'd had after Con had diagnosed me and before he was supposed to come back and cure me. I'd known I was dying, but it kind of hadn't mattered. It wasn't only that I believed Con would find a way to heal me. It was that there wasn't anything I could do. I didn't have that luxury this time. I was going to have to go through with it, whatever it was. I'd always scorned the stories where the princesses hung around waiting to be rescued: Sleeping Beauty, spare me. Tell the stupid little wuss to wake up and sort out the wicked fairy herself. I found myself thinking that sleeping through it sounded pretty good after all.

Yolande was looking out for me, and her door was open before I'd climbed out of the Wreck. I walked draggingly up to her. I didn't even know that it was going to be tonight. I remembered those extra nights I'd waited for Con, with death lying on my breast like a lover. What a long time ago that seemed. I tried to make this a hopeful thought, but it refused to work. It was like trying to blow up a popped balloon. Hello, Death, *you* again. Just can't keep away, can you?

Saints and damnation. Mostly damnation.

Yolande drew me into her workroom. There was a little heap of . . . sunlight on her desk. What? I blinked. It looked like . . . as if there was a chink in the blind, letting a single ray in to make a pool there: except it wasn't a pool, it was a *heap*, and there was no ray of sun. I could feel my eyes fizzing back and forth like a camera's automatic lens, trying to find the right setting and failing. The heap cast no shadows. It was a small domed hummock of pure golden light.

I had stopped to stare, and Yolande went to her desk and picked it up. It seemed to flow over her hands, slowly, like rivulets of warm honey, or small friendly sleepy snakes. It was, I thought, as it separated itself over her fingers, a latticework of some variety. The filaments met and parted in some kind of pattern, and the filaments themselves seemed to carry a pattern, like scales on a snake's back. It moved slowly, but it moved; it curled round Yolande's wrists. My strange sense of it—them—being friendly but half asleep remained. "It will wake up when it touches you," she said, as if reading my mind. "We had to put it together in great haste, and it's not yet used to being—manifest."

She came toward me, stretching the light-net gently between her hands like a cat's cradle, and—threw it over me.

For a moment I was surrounded by twinkling lights; and then I felt it—them—settling gently against my skin, delicate as snowflakes, but warm. Bemusedly I held one arm out to watch the process. You know how if you watch, if you concentrate, you can feel when snowflakes land on you, feel the chill of them, almost individually at first, till your face or hand or arm begins to numb with the cold, and then they melt against your skin and disappear. So it was with these tiny lightflakes: I saw them as they floated down, shimmering down, felt them when they touched me, lighter than feathers or gossamer, and over all of me, for clothes were insubstantial to them. But they were not merely warm, a few of them were uncomfortably hot, and left tiny pinprick red marks; and while they dissolved on contact like snowflakes, they appeared to sink through the surface of my skin, leaving nothing behind, no dampness, no stickiness, no shed scales. . . . After they'd all vanished, if I turned my arm sharply back and forth I could just see the webwork of light, like veins, only golden, not blue. I itched faintly, especially where belt and bra straps rubbed.

Yolande let out a long slow breath. I looked at her inquiringly. "I wasn't sure it was going to work. I told you we had to put this together very quickly."

"What—is it?"

Yolande paused. "I'm not sure how to explain it to you. It is not a ward, or only indirectly so. It is a form of comehither, but generally only sorcerers ever use anything like it. It—it gathers your strength to you. It taps into the source of your strength, more strongly than you can unaided.

"Most magic handlers have a talent for one thing or another, and it is drawn from one area of this world or another. A foreseer with a principal rapport with trees may see visions in a burl of her favorite wood, for example, rather than in the traditional crystal ball. A sorcerer whose strongest relationship is with water will be much likelier to drown his or her enemy than to meet them in battle, although one with an affinity for metal would forge a sword."

"Affinity," I said bitterly. "My *affinity* is for vampires."

"No," said Yolande. "Why do you say that?"

"Pat. SOF. That's why they want me. Because I'm a m-magic handler"—I could hardly get the phrase out; *handling* seemed far from the correct term in my case—"with an affinity for vampires."

Yolande shook her head. "The hierarchies of magic handling are no particular study of mine. But your principal affinity is for sunlight: your element, as it were. It is usually one of the standard four: earth, air, water, fire. Sometimes it is metal, sometimes wood. I have never heard of one for sunlight before, but there are—are tests for these things. Yours is neither fire nor air, but a bit of both, and something else. While I was doing the tests and coming up nowhere, I thought of sunlight because of all the days I have seen you lying in the sun like a cat or a dog—I have only ever seen you truly relaxed like that, lying motionless in sunlight. And you told me once about the year you were ill, when you lived in a basement flat, and how you cured yourself by lying in front of the sunny windows when you moved upstairs. I thought of your nickname—how I myself had relied on your nickname to tell me the real truth about you, after the vampire visited you. . . .

"As for your—let us call it counteraffinity: your counteraffinity may be for vampires. I have never heard of this either, but I do know it is often a magic handler with a principal affinity for water who can cross a desert most easily; a handler with a principal affinity for air who can hold her breath the longest, someone with an affinity for earth who flies most easily. It is the strength of the element in you that makes you more able to resist—and simultaneously embrace—its opposite. You are not consumed by the dark because you are full of light."

I didn't feel full of light. I felt full of stomach acid and cold phlegm. I knew about the four elements, of course; I even knew a little about this counteraffinity thing. Magic handlers with a principal fire element never get hired by the fire service; fires tend to be harder to put out with them around. But an Air or a Water is a shoo-in for the Fire Corps because Airs never seem to suffer smoke inhalation and water seems to go farther with a Water. A lot of lives have been saved by the Airs and the Waters in the Fire Corps. I'd never thought of it as having to do with counteraffinities though.

But then I had never thought a lot about magic handling. I had always been too busy being fascinated by stories of the Others.

"I can see in the dark—er—now," I said, not wanting to get into how it happened, "but it makes me kind of nuts. In the dark it's okay. But I see in—through—the shadows in daylight too. But I see through them—strangely. I mostly can't make sense of what I'm seeing." Or if I can I don't know if I'm imagining it, to *make* it make sense. "And most of them wiggle."

Yolande looked interested. "Perhaps you will tell me more about that some time. I may be able to help."

Some time, I thought. Yeah. "The shadows on you don't wiggle though. They just lie there, like all shadows used to."

"Ah. That will perhaps be the purification process of wardskeeping. If you become a master, as I eventually did, you go through a series of trials that are to make you what you are as intensely as possible. You would not be able to do what a master does without this. I imagine you will see other masters of their craft as you see me."

I still hadn't decided if the shadows that fell on Con moved around or not. Dark shadows were different from light shadows. So to speak. If they didn't, did that make him a master vampire? What *is* a master vampire? SOF used the term for someone who ran a gang.

I held both arms out and admired the faint twinkly gold, felt the faint prickly itch. I pulled a handful of my hair forward where I could look at it and it too was laced and daubed with gold. Maybe Yolande could sell the process to a hairdresser: bet you didn't have to touch it up every few weeks.

Pity I wouldn't be around to demonstrate.

The sun was near setting.

I dropped my arms. "Thank you," I said. "That is so feeble. But—thank you very much."

"You're very welcome, my dear," said Yolande.

"I must go now, I think."

"Yes. But I hope you will come back and tell me about it."

I met her eyes and saw with a shock that she *did* know. I tried to smile. "I hope I will too."

I SAT JUST inside the open doors of the balcony, cross-legged, hands on knees. I didn't bother to try to align, to ask him anything, to tell him anything. He would be here soon enough. He would be here. This time what was doomed to happen wasn't going to be put off. It would begin tonight. And, probably, end there too.

The sun reddened the autumn colors on the trees. The shadows darkened and lengthened.

PART FOUR

PERHAPS THE FLAKES of light had settled in my eyes too when Yolande's web had fallen around me. Sitting still and waiting, watching the sun set, I hadn't thought much about the way the shadows fell and moved; it was always easier when I was motionless myself. But I saw him clearly, this time. I saw him, and not merely by a process of elimination, one wiggly shadow moving in a specific direction. He was a dark figure, human-shaped. Vampire-shaped. He was Con.

A dark figure: dark with glints of gold, as if lightflakes fell on him, sparked like struck matches, and fell away.

Did I hear him or not? I don't know. I had a feeling like sound of him, as I had a feeling like sight. I saw him disappear around the corner of the house. He would be coming up the stairs now; I felt his presence there. He would be opening my door—hmm, did he open doors to walk through them? No, wait. Vampires couldn't disintegrate themselves—I didn't think. A few sorcerers could, but they were the really crazy ones. If you've invited a vampire across your threshold, maybe the door simply didn't exist for him any more? Or anyway why did the front door always *whoosh* gently when I opened it but not when he did?

And I knew when he was standing behind me. It wasn't that I heard him breathing. But the vampire-in-the-room thing was unmistakable.

I stood up and turned around.

He looked different. It might have been the lightflakes but I don't think so. I probably looked different too. If you're going into what you know is your final battle maybe the preliminary loin-girding always is visible. My experience is limited. I don't know that I would necessarily have identified the way Con looked as a vampire prepared for his last battle, but as a thumbnail description it would do.

I was always surprised at how big he was. That's probably something about the way vampires move—the boneless gliding, that human-spine-unhinging creepy grace. You didn't believe it, so you made the vampire smaller in your memory to make it a little more plausible. (Uh. I don't know about the generic *you* in this case. So far as I knew I was the only human, so far, who'd had the opportunity. Or the need.) It's funny, vampires have been a fact of human existence since before history began, and yet in our heart of hearts I don't think we really *believe* in them. Every time one of us meets up with one of them we don't believe in them all over again. Of course in most cases a human meeting up with a vampire is looking at their immediate death and so not believing it is the last forlorn hope—but I'm here to say that being acquainted with one doesn't lessen the feeling much. I didn't believe in Con.

Tricky.

I believed in my own death more.

I stretched my hand out and put it on his chest, where no heart beat. He was wearing another one of his long black shirts. It might have been the one I had worn a few nights ago, except that that one was hanging in the back of my closet with the cranberry-red dress. My vampire wardrobe.

I let my hand drop.

But he reached out and picked it up. There was a fizz, a shock, as his skin met mine. I felt him twitch—ever so slightly—but he didn't loose my hand. He turned it over instead, and then laid it gently, as if it had no volition of its own, in the palm of his other hand. The invisible spark happened again, but he didn't startle this time. My back was to the fading twilight, but in the shadow of my body the occasional gold glints of the web were just visible.

"What is this?" he said.

"Yolande gave it to me. She said it would help me draw on the source of my strength."

"Daylight," he said.

"Yes. Does it hurt you?"

"No."

I thought about that *no*. It sounded a little like the "no" of the kid playing so-called touch football who has just had the three biggest kids in the neighborhood tag her by knocking her down and sitting on her. They asked me after they let me up if I was hurt. I said no. I was lying. "Let me rephrase that."

A small shiver in his breath. Really quite a human noise: audible breath with a catch in it, like a muted laugh. "When you are a little too hot, a little too cold, does it hurt?"

Old Mr. Temperature Control, I thought. What do *you* know about too hot and too cold? No, I *still* wasn't thinking about any of that. Delete that thought.

"Or if you pick up something a little too heavy for you, does it hurt? It is only a little pressure on the understood boundaries of yourself."

I liked that: a little pressure on the understood boundaries of yourself. Sounded like something out of a self-awareness class, probably with yoga. See what kind of a pretzel you can tie yourself into and press on the understood. . . .

I was raving, if only to myself. I took a deep breath. Okay. My new light-web was to Con no worse than hauling an overfull sheet of cinnamon rolls out of the oven and making a run for the countertop before I dropped them was to me.

I looked into his face, dully lit by the last of the twilight, and realized, with a shock, that I had no doubt: the shadows there lay quietly too.

"Ready?" he said.

I smiled involuntarily. Are you joking? "Yes," I said.

"I have taken what you showed me and . . . measured it, by the ways I know. I believe that between us we shall . . . attain our goal."

Our goal, I thought. I didn't translate this into practical terms.

"We do not travel in your nowheresville, but I fear the way we are going is nonetheless . . . unpleasant. I will need your assistance. It will not be easy both to travel that way and to guard our presence from too-early detection."

I closed my eyes—*hurling* myself into this, to stop myself from thinking about it—took a firmer grip on his hand, and began to search for the alignment. This was very different from the fuzzy non-telephone line I had used to talk to Con; for that I could just go to the edge of whatever it was that was out there, and grope. This was more like walking through a snake pit with a forked stick, hoping you could sneak up behind the snake you wanted and nail it with the stick before it nailed you. Meanwhile hoping that none of the other snakes saw you first.

I glanced apologetically at the ever-so-slightly-like-the-back-of-a-snake pattern glinting faint gold against—*in*—my skin. I said one of my gran's words: it was only a little word, a little word of thanks and of settling, settling down, settling in, but I thought the light-web might like it. Then I closed my eyes again.

There.

This may have been the light-web too, or it may have been that I'd now done my compass needle maneuver several times and was getting the hang of it, or it may have been Con. Some of it was Con; I could feel the faint scritchy buzz of connection through our palms. There seemed to be a variety of paths laid out before us: there was the totally evisceratingly worst, the slightly less worst but worst enough, the still really bad, the only basic deadly dire, and probably a few others. I was looking at the Catherine-wheel glitter of the way that had blown out SOF HQ and at the looming thing that was our destination as Con arranged us on the boundary of one of the other, the quite-awful-enough-thanks ways. The looming thing and its guardians didn't look so much like an aquarium this time—or if it did, those fish were *sick*—more like the special effects in one of those postholocaust movies. Any moment now the ghastly mutants would come lurching on screen and wave their deviant limbs at us.

I wished it was a movie.

"Come," said Con, and we stepped forward together.

By the time we'd walked off the edge of the balcony we were firmly—if that's quite the word I want—into Other-space. Vampires probably can bound lightly down from third stories, but I didn't want to try it. As it was I was immediately having a precarious time keeping my feet; there didn't seem to be any up or down—although this is a good thing when you've just walked off a balcony—or sideways or backward or forward for that matter, other than the fact that *we* had backs and fronts and our faces were on one side of us rather than another. This path, whatever it was, was a lot worse than Con's short way home the other night. At least I had feet, which was an improvement on nowheresville.

Hey, not only did I have feet, I got to keep my clothes on.

I could still see the looming thing that was what we were aiming for, and since I didn't know anything about the protective detail I assumed that my function was to keep watching it. Con propelled us. Presumably forward. He seemed to know up from down and sideways from sideways. I felt *things* whiz past me occasionally, and while I couldn't've told you what they were, I could guess they weren't friendly. Every time I set my foot down it seemed to resolve the place I was in a little more, as if my invading three-dimensionality was making my surroundings coagulate, and little by little there seemed to be another sort of stepping-stone system after all, although rather than the ordinary world sluicing by between the stones it seemed to boil *up*, and become part of the no-up-no-down-no-anything-else. I felt as if I would like to be sick, but fortunately my stomach couldn't figure out which was up either, so it stayed where it was.

After some kind of time there began to be half-recognizable ordinary things in the careening entropy: a street lamp. A corner of a dilapidated building with a revolving door, one of whose panes was broken. A stop sign.

A road sign: Garrison Street.

We were in No Town.

As we went on ("on" still used advisedly), we flickered more clearly into No Town. Sometimes we took a step or two on broken pavement as if we were actually there. Maybe we were.

There were now other people sporadically present also. I didn't like the look of any of them. We passed several nightclubs with people wandering in and out. There were bouncers at the doors of some of them, but that mostly wasn't the style in No Town. If you could walk, you could walk where you wanted to. Even the seriously flash spartan clubs, the places where people who lived in downtown high-rises went when they wanted to feel like they were slumming but were still willing to pay thirty blinks for a short glass of wine to prove they were slumming only because they wanted to, had more subtle ways of getting rid of you.

Meanwhile, outdoors, if you fell down, you lay there, and people still ambulatory stepped over you: horizontal bodies were part of the ambience. Maybe you got rolled, while you were lying there being ambient. Maybe you got taken home for dinner. To be dinner. It wasn't a good place to linger in for anyone—anyone alive, that is—but there was another myth, that if you were high enough, the suckers would leave you alone, because your blood would screw *them* up. I don't think this is something I'd want to rely on myself. There are ne'er-do-wells among the Others like there are among us humans, and my guess is there are suckers who have developed a taste for screwed-up blood. Also, if you're hungry enough, you'll eat anything, right? And a still-breathing body facedown in a gutter is real easy to, you know, catch.

I was having trouble staying upright as we winked back and forth between worlds. If when visible I was staggering a little, I would fit right in.

I was a little afraid I might see someone I knew. Gods and angels, never underestimate the power of social conditioning; even under the circumstances, when I was fully expecting never having to face or explain anything to anyone again after the next few minutes or hours or time-fragments splintered by chaos-space, I was worried about this, that I might see Kenny, or his friends, or some of the younger, dumber regulars at Charlie's; or even what remained of a few of the guys my age I knew who hadn't got back out of drugs again. What was I afraid of? That they might see me too—holding hands with a vampire? That I would look as if I was merely under the dark and going to the usual fate of a human seen in the company of a vampire? I was supposed to *care*?

I didn't know what any humans might be making of us. But I began to see vampires looking back at us. I didn't have any trouble recognizing them. I didn't know if this was because they weren't bothering to try to pass, or if I just knew a vampire when I saw one these days.

I didn't notice when the first one did more than look, when the first one came at us. I didn't notice till Con had . . . never mind. He did it with his other hand, and with the hand that held mine, jerked us back into chaos-space. He wiped the splatter of blood off his face with his forearm, except there was blood on his arm too. I was afraid I'd see him lick his lips. I didn't. Maybe I didn't watch long enough. Maybe, you know, *used* blood isn't of much interest. My hand trembled in his: in the hand of my lethal vampire companion.

I was alive, human, with a beating heart. I was all alone.

The next time there were several of them. This time Con jerked us out of chaos-space, because he then had to let go of my hand. I was glad I didn't have to find out what would happen if I got left there alone without him. I wasn't glad for very long.

I didn't know what I was supposed to do: note to myself, in my next life, get some martial arts training—get a *lot* of martial arts training—just in case. Again, as with the first vampire who attacked us, something happened—quicker than I could follow—quicker than I wanted to follow, and I yanked my gaze away, afraid of what my dark vision might make out for me. There was blood, again, but there was also at least one vampire left over while Con was otherwise engaged, and he was looking at me. I looked at him, not thinking about anything but my own terror, my eyes wide open, open so wide that they hurt. He met that gaze—hey, he knew a human when he saw one, and he knew he was a vampire—and I *saw him falter*, and then Con had turned from whatever he was doing and . . . took care of that one too, too fast for me to look away. I think I probably cried out. Jesse wasn't going to rescue me, this time. I wasn't going to come to myself with human arms around me and a human voice shouting in my ear, *It's all over. You're all right.*

There was now quite a lot of blood, and . . . bits and pieces. I had blood on me too. Con seized my hand again, and said sharply, *Come.* I didn't dare look in his face. There would be no comfort, no reassurance, in the face of any vampire. When I took a running step to keep up with him, my shoes slipped. In the blood. There was so much blood on our hands that as it dried, our fingers stuck together. The *meaty* smell was a miasma, a poison gas.

We didn't duck back into the chaos-space. I had half-forgotten my alignment, but it was now as if it was *tied* to me—or I was tied to it. It was pulling us along, through these dark broken streets where the shadows lay twisted and crumpled like dead bodies, pulling as if we were on a leash. I wanted to untie it, but I couldn't, I mustn't—I wanted to—no, it was too late; even if I had funked it now, at the last minute, after the last minute, all it would do now is get us killed. Sooner.

I could hear them—someone—keeping pace with us—why didn't they close in, cut us off, attack us? Con said quietly, as if there was no urgency whatsoever, "Bo will not be able to say your name. Either of your names."

What? Sunshine. Rae. Daylight names. Old vampires can't say daylight words either? The very old vampires that can't go out in the moonlight that is only faint reflected sunlight? The academics would have said Con counted as very old, and he didn't even wait for full dark: twilight was good enough for him. And he called me Sunshine. *There are different ways of being what we are.* Apparently Bo hadn't aged so well. Something to talk to the academics about. Variability of Aging Among Vampires. Usage of Certain Words Pertaining to Daylight by Aged Vampires. Maybe I could get my pass into the Other Museum's library after all. No, wait. I was about to die.

I didn't immediately see what good Bo's not being able to say my name was going to do me. Bo wasn't going to need to say—or know— my name to kill me.

Okay. Names are power. We'd had that back at the lake. Big deal. Fangs are more power. We'd had that at the lake too. Con had chosen to let me go. Bo wasn't going to.

Why *had* I agreed to this anyway?

"You feel the pull strongly?" Con went on in that infuriatingly calm voice. "Bo has connected to our presence here. If we are separated, go on. Follow that connection to its end. Leave me. I will catch up with you when I can."

Oh good. I was so glad he would make the effort to catch up with me later. Although I wished he'd used the word *goal* or *aim* rather than *end*.

"I recommend—" he added, dispassionate as ever—I was trying to remind myself that he always sounded unbothered, not to say dead. Or maybe that it was a good sign he sounded so unflapped now, as if this was still all part of the normal range of vampire activities. I almost didn't hear the rest of what he was saying: "—you do not attempt to retreat into any Other-space, including the way I have brought us both. You would only draw some of Bo's creatures after you, and their advantage there would be greater than yours."

Right. Like it wasn't greater than mine *everywhere*.

I realized that while we were no longer in the chaos-space, we weren't exactly in No Town either. Or at least I hoped it wasn't No Town, because if it was, our human world was in even more trouble than most of us knew about . . . than I knew about . . . again the thought came to me: What did I know? Pat said a hundred years, tops, before . . . And the people who came to No Town for thrills weren't likely to notice that the whole scene was sliding over the edge of normal reality into. . . .

I felt the pull strongly all right, like a hand around my throat that was slowly tightening. If I was a dog on a lead, I was wearing a choke collar, and my master didn't like me much. Maybe it was that sense of pressure that made my vision go funny; but then, my vision had been funny for two months now, and I was kind of used to funniness. But this was a new kind of funniness, where things seemed to dance in and out of existence, rather than merely in and out of light and darkness.

There were streetlights where we were—some of them still worked—and great swathes of darkness. There was the uneven pavement under our feet, the potholed roads, the crumbling curbs. Once I stepped unawares on a manhole cover and the sound this made, even in this night of horrors, made my heart leap into my throat. There were tall buildings that seemed to prowl among the shadows; a few of them had dim lights burning that gave the old peeling posters on their walls an undesirable life: huge painted eyes winked at me, fingers as long as my legs beckoned to me. The way the clubs leaped out of the night with their noise and bewildering lighting, stabbing and erratic, rhythmic and dazzling, rainbow-colored or this week's fashion match, heightened that sense of *Other-where*: hey, I wanted to say to some of the humans we passed, you don't need drugs, let me tell you, there are spaces between worlds, there are master vampires that loop invisible ropes around your neck and drag you to your doom. . . .

We are running through No Town. I hear our footsteps—no, I hear my footsteps, and the kind of unmatched echo that chills your blood, because you know it means you're not alone, and what you're not alone with isn't human. I remember when hearing and seeing were simple, it had to do with sound and light and the manageable equations they taught you in school. I am wondering if anyone notices us; the only kind of running that goes on here is the furtive kind, no joggers out to burn off last night's burger and fries or reach the buzz of an endorphin high. No one, hearing running footsteps—especially running footsteps with an unmatched echo—is going to look up if they can help it. I guess I can stop worrying about seeing someone I know. . . .

A few people do look up, though: bad consciences, old habits, a momentary—or drug-induced—forgetfulness about who or where they are? I think I meet the eyes of one young woman: I see her take me in, take Con in, disbelieve us both . . . and then we're past her, running out of the light-surf, back into the ocean of darkness.

Into a fresh seethe of vampires. They didn't want to connect with me. Lucky me. I winced and twitched out of the way of anything I saw, anything I half-saw; I stopped trying to *see* anything, and let my instinct—whatever instinct this was—keep me moving. Where was Con? No, I still knew him from the rest of them. For one thing, he was the center of the seethe. If there's only one guy on your team, he's the one everybody else is jumping on.

It went on in a horrible almost-silence.

There was a hot circlet around my neck and across my breast; there were two small fires burning in my two front jeans pockets. Apparently they'd learned their lesson that first time, when the sunsword had hit the pillow; they didn't set my clothes on fire this time either. And it wasn't because they weren't really putting it out: they were. The evening we'd blown SOF HQ wasn't even a dress rehearsal for what was going on now.

Even with my talismans going full throttle my luck didn't hold for long. Something—some*one*—crashed into me, tore me away from Con, out of the seethe; it was taking me somewhere. It was, in fact, the same direction I was being dragged by my invisible leash, but I didn't feel I wanted any help getting there sooner; besides, whatever Con had said about going on without him, I'd rather not, thanks.

I saw a *shape*, and ducked away from it. It seemed a little uncertain of its own bearings; it missed its grab, and teeth ground down my arm, strangely fumbling, if teeth can fumble. Hey, my jugular is up this way. I wished for a nice apple-tree stake, well impregnated with mistletoe, except I didn't know how to use it; staking takes training. The table knife had been a one-off. . . . I put my right hand in my pocket, braced the butt end of my hot little knife against my palm, and pointed it up between my fingers: not with the blade open, just the hard blunt end of it, like a single fat brass knuckle. I saw it momentarily, shining like a tiny moon, like a slightly misaligned gemstone in a ring.

Then I swung it, with my paltry human strength, up in the general direction of where the base of the breastbone that belonged to the teeth in my other arm might be.

I connected. The wide blunt end of my knife . . . *sank in*. As it did it blazed up, no longer moonlike but sunlike, golden, shining, a tongue of flame, and in its light I saw a golden lattice extending up my arm.

I had just time to remember what had happened in an alley when I had used a table knife.

The noise was different. There were no narrow alley walls for the gobbets to smack against. Instead I heard the thick heavy *splat*,

like loathsome rain, as they fell around me. I'd forgotten the smell—
the smell of something long dead and rotten. I thought, they're not
even a little human any more when they explode: they shatter so
easily, like throwing an overripe melon against a fence. No melon
ever *smelled* like this. . . .

Con rematerialized from wherever he had been, from whatever
he had been doing. I just managed not to wince out of his way too.
The problem was he looked like a vampire, and at the moment he
looked a lot more like a vampire than he looked like Con. One of the
even-more-comforting-than-usual stories about vampires is that
sometimes, during vampire gang wars for example, they go into
berserker furies and tear anything they can get their hands on apart,
not only their enemies but their comrades, the guys on their own
side. Supposedly the berserker fit can last quite a while, and if a particularly effective dismemberer gets to the end of the bodies around
it before the fit wears off, it will tear *itself* to shreds too.

Maybe this is a consoling story when you're at home with a book
or reading it off your combox screen: the idea that there are that many
fewer vampires in the world, that they had done each other in while
we humans cowered safely behind closed doors with a *hell* of a lot of
wards nailed over them. (If you find yourself so unlucky as to be living
somewhere there is a sucker gang war going on, you pin *a lot* of wards
around your house, and you do *not* go out after dark or before dawn
for *any* reason.) I didn't know what a vampire running amok looked
like, but it might have looked like Con. It wasn't just . . . it wasn't. . . .
Look, if you ever have the opportunity to choose between being eaten
by a tiger and bitten by an enraged vampire, take the tiger.

I was probably off in my feeble little human she's-in-shock-wrap-
her-in-a-blanket-and-get-out-the-whisky space. Humans don't deal
with extreme situations very well. Our pathetic bodies freak out.
We freeze, and our blood pressure falls, and we can't think, and all
that. I stood there, staring, while Con snarled and showed me his
teeth, and didn't offer me the blanket or the whisky or the hot sweet
tea. Then—maybe he remembered I was his ally, maybe he'd remembered that but had momentarily forgotten, seeing me as soaked

in blood and sprinkled with the remains of a mutilated enemy as he, that I was a mere human. Maybe the snarl was the vampire equivalent of "Hot damn! Well done!"

Whatever. He stopped snarling, and . . . drew his face together. When he seized my slimy hand and pulled me along after him again I didn't gibber, I didn't collapse, and I didn't throw up. I stuffed my knife back into my pocket, and went.

I wish I could forget how it feels, your hair stuck to your skull with blood, foul blood running gummily down inside your clothes, invading your privacy, your decency, your *humanity*, till it chafes you with every breath, every movement, the tug of it as it dries on your skin feeling like some kind of snare. Blood in your mouth, that you cannot spit the vile taste of away. I think I must have gone into some kind of berserker fury myself. There are things you don't want to know you can do, aren't there? But if you're lucky you never find them out. I found out too many of them, all at once. I, who had to leave the kitchen at Charlie's when they were whacking up meat into joints or putting slabs of drippy pulpy maroony-red stuff through the grinder.

Blood stings when it gets in your eyes. And it's *viscous*, so it's hard to blink out again. It may not only be because the blood stings that you're weeping.

I have always been afraid of more things than I can remember at one time. Mom, when I was younger, and still admitted to some of them, said that it was the price of having a good imagination, and suggested I stop reading the *Blood Lore* series (which was past thirty volumes even then) and maybe retiring *Immortal Death* and *Below Hell Keep* from the top bookshelf for a while. I didn't, but it wouldn't have done any good if I had. Reading scary books is weirdly reassuring, most of the time: it means at least one other person—the author—has imagined things as awful as you have. What's bad is when the author comes up with stuff you hadn't thought of yet.

I'd thought it was bad when I was just *reading* stuff I hadn't thought of.

And even then I'd known that sometimes it's worse when the author leaves it to your imagination.

I stopped using my knife. I found out I didn't have to. I found out I could do it with my hands.

It was still mostly Con, that we got through. Even warded up the wazoo and covered in bright gold cobweb I was still only human. I was still slower and weaker than any vampire. But I had Con. And I *was* warded and webbed, and the vampires didn't like tangling with me. They kept choosing to tangle with Con, even though they could see—graphically—what had happened to the last vampire or twelve or twenty-seven or four thousand and eight vampires that had tangled with Con. If we ever got to the end of all this, ha ha and so on, and wanted to find our way back out of the maze, it wasn't a thread we would have to follow but a path paved with undead body parts.

Maybe they thought they'd wear him out or something.

I still got a few. You'd think offing a few vampires would feel like doing a community service, wouldn't you? It doesn't. Not even when they don't explode. That's why I started doing it with my hands. They didn't explode, I discovered, if I merely jammed my fingers in under their breastbones and pulled.

My vampire affinity.

I lost track. There was gore and gruesomeness and then more of it and I hated all of it, and was ready to be killed, just to get away from it, if someone would promise me, *cross their heart and hope to die,* very very funny, that I wouldn't rise again. In any semblance. I still wasn't sure about the mechanics of turning and it seemed to me that dying in the present circumstances probably wasn't the best recipe for staying quietly in my grave afterward. Supposing someone found enough of me to bury.

I would have liked to give up. I *meant* to give up. But I couldn't. Like I couldn't stay at home and hide under the bed, I guess. Maybe it was promising Con to stick around as long as I could. *Stick* seemed the right verb under the circumstances. Every time I lifted one of my blood-clotted shoes there was a sticky, ripping noise.

And then everything went quiet, at least except for the noise I was making. Mostly it was just breathing. Maybe bleating a little.

One of the things that had happened during the business of savaging our way through Bo's army was that I'd begun to know where

Con was, like I knew where my right hand or my left leg was. It was a bit like unwrapping something from swathes of tissue paper, or following an idea through its development to a conclusion. You have an inkling of something, some shape or concept, and it gets clearer and stronger till you know what it is. It happened while the occasional shrieks and dead-flesh noises went on, all those near-misses with my own death. I understood that I was crazy, crazy to be still alive, crazy to be doing what I was doing to stay alive, crazy to be trying to stay alive. This knowingness about Con was a strange island in a strange ocean.

That sense of Con's presence, of his precise location, had undoubtedly saved my life several times in the carnage, if it hadn't done much for my sanity. But it meant that when things suddenly went quiet and I felt someone—some vampire—coming noiselessly up behind me, I knew it was Con.

Well well, said a silent voice from an invisible speaker. *This meeting has been much more amusing than I anticipated.*

I didn't have to hear Con snort. He didn't, of course. Vampires don't snort, even with derision. But I knew as Con knew that the voice was lying when it said *amusing.*

I also knew who this was. Bo. Mr. Beauregard. The fellow who had got us in all this. The fellow we were here to have the final meeting with. Him or us. I was pretty sure things had only started to get *amusing,* even if they hadn't gone quite as Bo had expected so far. And while I knew vampires didn't get tired, exactly, I knew that they could come to the end of their strength. I'd seen Con coming to the end of his, out at the lake. I didn't know how one evening of tearing up your fellow vampires limb from limb matched against having been chained to the wall of a house with a ward sign eating into your ankle and the sun creeping after you through the windows every day, day after day, but I doubted Con was feeling bright-eyed and bushy-tailed now. I sure wasn't. I was missing my nice sympathetic human emergency room tech saying, "There's nothing really wrong with you, we're giving you a sedative and you can go home." I was also so tired that the weirdness of my dark vision was starting to bother me again, like new shoes that aren't quite broken in yet that you've been wearing too long. I couldn't tell how much of what I seemed to be seeing was happening, and how much of it was my overstressed brain playing tricks on my eyes.

I stared around, trying to make sense of what I was . . . okay, *not* seeing, it was dark in here, wherever it was. When had it become *in here*? We'd started out on the streets of No Town, more or less. Well, we weren't there any more. Given the . . . mess . . . I was glad no humans were likely to stumble across us. I tried to settle down, settle back into my skin—except I didn't want to be in my skin any more. I didn't want to be me. I didn't want to *know* me.

But the animal body was overriding the conscious brain, the brain that ground out concepts like *worthwhile* and *not worthwhile*. My medulla oblongata was determined to stay alive, whatever my cerebrum said. For a moment I seemed to be floating up above myself, looking down at the bloody wreckage, at the two figures still standing, Con and me, standing next to each other, facing in the same direction.

When Bo spoke again, I *snapped* back together, body and mind. I could almost hear the clunk, as the bolts slotted into place, trapping me with myself again. I may have hated and feared myself now, but I hated and feared Beauregard worse.

Welcome, welcome. Do come in. Welcome between us, Connie, has been a curious affair for some years now, eh? I imagine you haven't been too surprised. Perhaps you explained it to your companion. I hope so, Connie. It would have been rude of you to omit explanation, I feel, and you have always been the soul of courtesy, haven't you? Your little human, Connie, is very enterprising. She has been nosing around me for some little while. I'm surprised, Connie, that you would allow a human to do your, shall I say, dirty work? You must have found your experience a few months ago more debilitating than I realized. Or perhaps more corrupting.

And I had thought Con's laugh was horrible. I blanked out when Bo laughed, like you blank out when you're conked on the head. It's not a voluntary response.

Maybe I should have been insulted that I was being ignored. I wasn't. I didn't want him to say anything to me. The mere experience—I won't call it sound—of his voice was like having the skin peeled off me—the skin I hadn't wanted to fit myself back inside a few moments ago. Very, very distantly it occurred to me that if I was feeling a little brighter I might find it funny that Bo seemed to be accusing me of being a bad influence. On a vampire. But I wasn't feeling brighter.

Oh yes, I am here, waiting for you. Do keep coming on. After all, you have worked quite hard to progress so far, have you not? It would be a pity to waste all that effort. And I really don't feel I could let you go now without paying your respects to me personally. It would be so rude. And wasn't I just saying, Connie, that you are the soul of courtesy?

The voice itself was flaying me alive. What was left of my mind and will were addled with the effort to remain—myself. Slowly, painfully, I moved my right hand, slid it stickily into my pocket, and closed my gummy and aching fingers around my little knife. It wasn't hot any more, but the painful pressure of the voice eased a little. I dropped my eyes and through the smeary muck on my forearms I could see the occasional gleam of golden webbing.

Do walk on. Please.

That *please* seemed to last a century.

Walking on being precisely what he was trying to prevent us from doing, by the nonsound of his voice. I squeezed my knife till I could feel it grinding into my palm, and took a step forward. So did Con. He didn't take my hand again, but as we moved, his shoulder brushed mine. I realized it was important not to appear to be struggling. Con could probably have moved faster without me, but he didn't; he waited. So I raised my other foot and took another step. And another. Con matched me, and with every step we touched, briefly, shoulder or arm or back of hand. There was a sort of quiver against my breast, as if the chain that hung there was rearranging itself.

You must be tired, said the voice. *You are walking so slowly.*

But I heard it too. He was losing this round, as he had lost the first one, because we weren't paralyzed and helpless. Because I wasn't dying under the scourge of his voice.

I wondered how much worse it would be if he said my name.

It became easier as we went on; he'd withdrawn, I guess, plotting his next move. We didn't get rushed by any minions trying to kill us either. I kept my hand wrapped around my knife, and I felt the little hard lump that was the seal against my other leg. The chain felt stretched across my breast like a rock-climber spread-eagled across a particularly tricky slope. I pretended I was going forward *bravely*, ready for the next challenge. But I'd been wounded by that voice: the bitter burning of acid. My body throbbed with it, despite the talismans, despite the light-web. Every step blew a little gust of pain through me. I tried not to shiver, which would only make it worse; and besides, pathetically, I didn't want Con to despise me. As our shoulders brushed, I felt him helping me, offering me his strength. I forgot again that he was a vampire, that I was afraid of him too, that I hated what he could do and had done, tonight, hated him for making me find out what I could do. He was also all I had. He was my ally and if I was going to let him down, which I probably was, at least let me not do it because I just *lost* it.

The silvery luminescence that began eerily to come up around us was genuine light of some sort, light that a human eye could respond to. But there was nothing here I wanted to see, that I wouldn't rather be able to trick myself into half-believing I wasn't seeing, that my human neurons were confused by the vampire thing I was infected with.

We were in a huge room. There were enormous pipes, and the remains of scaffolding, and machinery, all round the walls, and more overhead. Some kind of derelict factory; No Town was full of them. This one had been renovated, in a way; the sickly wash of marsh-light gleamed off knobs and rivets, dials and gadgetry that no human had ever invented, let alone put together. I wondered, dimly, if there was any purpose to them, or if they were merely backdrop, window dressing, the latest vampire version of Bram Stoker's febrile fantasy of ruined castles and earth-filled coffins. Big or important vampire gangs always had a headquarters, and headquarters usually contained some accommodations for those nights they wanted a change from eating out, and they felt like throwing a dinner party at home. Such a space would be suitably decorated to inspire further adrenaline panic in their visitors, and the word was that techno degeneracy had been the staging of choice since the Wars, although how anyone found this out to report it on the globenet was a mystery. Stoker and his coffins had always been nonsense, but the vampires had borrowed the idea for a century or two as a mise-en-scène because it worked. The lack of scarlet-lined black capes and funny accents tonight wasn't making me happy.

I knew immediately that I didn't like techno degeneracy either, but I wouldn't have liked earth-filled coffins any better. If there was any surprise, it was that I had any energy left to dislike anything.

I was much better off disliking the décor, and trying to convince myself I wasn't seeing it anyway. At the far end of the big room there was a dais, and on that dais sat Bo.

I felt his eyes on me. *Look at me,* they said. It wasn't a voice this time, or even a compulsion, like the drag like a rope round my neck I had felt earlier. *Not* looking into his eyes felt like trying to prevent my heart from beating. But I didn't look, and my heart continued to beat.

The dais was a tall one, and on the steps up to it lounged several more vampires. They were all watching us with interest. I could see the glitter of eyes. I wondered if vampire eyes really do glitter, or if it was something to do with the marsh-light, or with my dark vision, or with the fact that I'd gone crazy and hadn't figured this out yet. So, okay, chances were I wasn't going to stay alive long enough to do any figuring, but I was still alive at the moment, and I was . . . it seemed ridiculous even as it occurred to me, but I was *angry.* I'd had my life ruined by this disgusting, undead monster. I had nothing to lose. All the best stuff in the books—and sometimes in history too—gets done by people who have nothing left to lose and so aren't always looking over their shoulders for the way out after it was over. I thought, wistfully, that I'd rather be looking over my shoulder for the way out. But I wasn't. I was about to die. But if I could take him—the Bo-thing—with me, it would have been worth it.

The thought flamed up in me, like the sun coming up over the horizon. Yes. *It will be worth it.* I took my hand out of my pocket.

Now all I had to do was *do* it.

We reached the bottom of the dais. Those eyes were still pulling at me. Deliberately, consciously, voluntarily, I lifted my own eyes and met them.

Monster didn't begin to cover it. Ironically the greeting we'd had from his guard corps had done me a service; I think if I hadn't already been shocked beyond my capacity to handle it I wouldn't have survived the initial blow of looking into the eyes of the master. Maybe it was a good thing I'd already lost my soul, that I was already half out of my body, my mind, my life. Because it meant I wasn't *there* to meet the full force of Bo's gaze.

It was bad enough anyway. The distillation of hundreds of years of evil shimmering in those eyes, and his enjoyment of my looking at it.

But he also expected me to crack, to disintegrate, immediately. He thought that as soon as I looked into his eyes it would be all over. Never mind that I could, apparently, look into ordinary vampires' eyes. That happened occasionally. (I saw this in his eyes too, and thought, it did? Remember this. The part of me that was looking forward to finishing dying said, *What for?*) Bo was a master vampire. He could destroy *vampires* with his glare. A mere human would incinerate on the spot.

Oh, and his eyes were colorless. Did I say that? I hadn't thought of evil as being without color but it is. Once you get past plain everyday wickedness, the color is squeezed right out of it. Evil is a kind of oblivion, having destroyed everything on its way there.

I did go up in flames. But they weren't the flames he had anticipated. The light-web blazed up, like a lit fuse running back to the detonator, the bomb, snaking along the ground as it had been laid out: a slender tongue of fire began in a curl on the back of each of my hands. They ran up my arms, licking along the lines of the lattice, across my breast—the chain around my neck flared—into my scalp; I could feel my hair rising, waving in the fire, or perhaps it became fire itself; running down my back, my belly, my legs. The lighting of that fuse was looking into Bo's eyes.

I was on fire. I put one flaming foot on the first stair of the dais, and stepped up. I was still staring into Bo's eyes.

I felt, rather than saw, the vampires on the dais slither together and descend on Con. I don't know if they saw me burst into flames or not; I don't know if they were the sort of flames that anyone sees, even vampires. If they did see the light-web ignite, presumably they thought it was to do with their master having me well in hand, and they could afford to concentrate on Con. But Bo gave me another gift, as I toiled up the dais stairs toward him, letting me see, briefly, out of his eyes, to the bottom of the dais, behind me. I saw the other vampires pull Con down. The vampires around Bo's dais would be the elite, of course, as the welcoming committee had been the cannon fodder; and as I say, I'm not sure that vampires get tired, exactly, but they can come to the end of their strength. I thought now, as I flamed (I seemed to hear the roaring of flame too) that Con might have given me more of his remaining strength than I had realized, to get me this far. More than he could spare.

Which meant I *had* to . . .

I saw one of the vampires bend over him, as they pinned him down, its mouth open, fangs shining: it buried its face in his throat. I saw him jerk and heave, but they had him fast. I saw another vampire delicately unbutton the remains of his shirt, stroke his chest. . . .

I saw its fingers reaching under Con's breastbone for his heart.

It wasn't anything so clear and noble as a decision that since I could do nothing for him I might as well get on with what I was doing. That Con was dying in a good cause if I could finish it before I died too. It wasn't a meeting of my strength against Bo's either, because Bo was still the stronger. He was going to stop me before I reached him.

I was two steps from the summit, the crown where Bo sat enthroned, and I couldn't go any farther.

But I still couldn't watch Con die. I *couldn't*.

Think about cinnamon rolls. Think about the bakery at Charlie's. Feel the dough under your hands and the heat of the ovens. Think about Charlie cranking down the awning, Mom going into the office and flicking on her combox before she takes off her coat.

Think about Mel in the kitchen next door. Think about Pat and Jesse sitting at their table, eating everything that Mary puts in front of them; think about Mary pouring hot coffee.

Think about Mrs. Bialosky sitting at her table, and Maud sitting across from her.

. . . And for a moment I saw them, Mrs. B and Maud. They were holding hands across the table, and their faces looked haggard and strained and awful, as if they were waiting to hear the news of someone's death. News they were expecting. And then Mrs. B looked up, straight at me, as she had the day I had been watching her from behind the counter, and Maud looked up too, over her shoulder, as Mrs. B was looking. Their eyes met mine.

Standing behind them I seemed to see Mel. He held out his arms toward me, and flames leaped from his skin, as if his tattoos were a light-web.

I took the last two steps. I was standing in front of Bo.

But I couldn't bring myself to touch him—to try to touch him. I said that *monster* doesn't cover it. There is no word for a several-hundred-year-old vampire who has performed every available wickedness over and over till he has to invent unavailable ones because he'd worn the others out. His flesh was not flesh; it was a viscous ooze, held together by malice. His voice was a manifestation of malignancy, for he had no tongue, no larynx; his eyes were the purest *imagination* of evil: flawless in a way that flesh could never be.

I knew that if I touched him I would be re-created into such as he was.

The scar on my breast burst apart, and my poisoned blood ran down.

I stopped. I stopped *trying.*

But Bo made a mistake. He laughed.

I reached into my left-hand pocket, and took out the daylight charm. I didn't look at it, but I felt the tiny sun spin and blaze, the tree shake its leaves—*yesssss*—the deer raise her head, acknowledging her own death, watching it come toward her. I felt the moving line of the water-barrier around its edge. As Bo laughed, I threw the charm down the noisome hole that indicated his mouth. A little tracery of fire followed it, like an arrow carrying a rope across a chasm. The mouth-hole closed with a *sucking* sound—something an ear could hear. What there was that was left of him in the real world wavered and became vulnerable to reality again, as the force and concentration of his will faltered in surprise.

Surprise and pain. The fire—my fire—ran up his face; his eyes

No no I can't say

But he had been strong and evil and undead for such a long time, and I had been alive and human for such a short time. My little fire wavered, and began to ebb. His face writhed: he was about to speak.

Sssssss

A hiss? I'd heard Con hiss—vampires did hiss. The giggler had hissed. It was a horrible noise even from a . . . an everyday, an everynight vampire. It was much worse from Bo, as everything about Bo was worse. But was it a hiss? Or was it his attempt to say my name?

I was back at the lake, where it all began. The sun flamed outside the house. The lake water lapped at the shore. For that first time I heard my tree: *Yesssss*. Perhaps there had been a doe standing in that forest, looking through the trees at the house, on her way home, to some dappled place where she would doze till sunset.

Beauregard! I shouted. *I destroy you!*

And I put my hands into the mire of his chest, and wrenched out his heart.

THE SKY WAS falling. Ah. Okay. Skies don't fall; therefore I was dead. I'd kind of expected to be dead. I felt rather comfortable, really. Relieved. Did that mean I'd succeeded? Succeeded in what? There'd been something I'd been desperate to do before I checked out for the last time . . . couldn't quite remember . . .

Sunshine

Why can't you leave me alone? There is a lot of noise. Shouldn't be able to hear anyone saying my name. So, I'm not hearing someone saying my name. So go away, damn it. *I don't want to be here, shivering in this polluted body.* My hands . . . my hands . . . touched . . . *I won't remember.*

I'm not dead yet, I thought composedly, but I am dying. Good. I don't want to spend the rest of my life being careful not to remember.

I hope I did whatever it was I wanted to do first.

Maybe I could go back just long enough to find out.

Sunshine

Con, on his hands and knees, crouched over me. The floor shook under us, and there was a lot of . . . stuff . . . falling down and flying around. Not a good place to be, unless you were dying, which I was. Con, I wanted to say, don't bother. Let one of these flying chunks of something or other finish the job. I'm tired, and I don't want to hang around. My hands . . .

"Sunshine," he said. "We have to get out of here. Listen to me. You have undone Bo; he cannot put himself back together. You have succeeded. This is your victory. But there is much of his—his animus—released by the final destruction of his body. This place is being pulled to pieces. I cannot carry you through this. Sunshine, *listen* to me. . . ."

I was drifting off again. I paused in the drift, momentarily caught by the sound of Con's voice. He sounded positively . . . emotional. I wanted to laugh, but I didn't have the energy. I began to drift again.

I felt him lift me up—I wanted to struggle; leave me *alone*—but I didn't have the energy for that either. He rearranged me, leaning against him, one arm around me, the other hand cradling my head, tipping it toward his body. . . .

Blood. Blood in my mouth.

Again.

No

I wanted to struggle: I did want to. I could have not swallowed. I could have let it run back out of my mouth again: Con's blood. This wasn't the blood of a deer, this time, a mortal creature, killed for me, killed because she was like me, more like me than a vampire. Less like me than a vampire, perhaps, by the fact of her death, by the fact that the recently life-warm blood of her had saved my life. That had been a long time ago. I hadn't known what was going on, that time. I knew well enough this time. This was Con's heart's blood. The heart's blood of a vampire.

When did I cross the irrevocable line: when I drove out to the lake, when I tucked my little knife into my bra, when I transmuted it into a key, when I unlocked my shackle, when I unlocked Con's?

When I took him into the daylight, and stopped it from burning him?

When he saved my life by the death of a doe?

When I discovered I could destroy a vampire with my hands?

When I destroyed Bo with those hands?

Or when I agreed to live, by drinking Con's heart's blood?

I don't know what happened at the foot of the dais, when Bo's crack troop set on Con while I was climbing the stairs. I don't know if what I saw was entirely some mirage of Bo's, to confound and weaken me, or whether something like it did happen. I would rather think that some of it did happen. That the wound in his chest was already there when he pressed my mouth against it. This was no mere flesh wound, this time, no tiny slash from a tiny blade. I did not want to think of him sinking his own fingers, tearing his own . . .

I lifted my head with a gasp, and began to struggle to my feet. He eeled up beside me: still that vampire fluency, even after everything that had happened. Even with that wound in his chest.

He took my hand again, and we ran.

It takes some coordination, running while holding someone's hand, but if you can get it right, every time your linked hands swing forward you get a little extra force for that stride. Some of that was the vampire cocktail I had just swallowed; it coursed through me, giving me a strength I knew didn't belong to me, *shouldn't* belong to me—shouldn't be letting me keep struggling, letting me run, letting me use my poisoned hands. Clinging to his hand too, or perhaps his clinging to mine, let me stop thinking about what my hands had recently been doing.

So, would it have been better to die?

Too much has happened since my last sunset. Con may be right that I cannot be turned, and that it won't be the daylight that kills me, but the touch of the real world will, whatever the sun is doing.

I missed the little hot lump of the seal against my leg. The chain swept back and forth across my breast in time with my running footsteps, but slowly, weighted by the thick poisoned blood of the reopened scar.

My sun-self, my tree-self, my deer-self. Don't they outweigh the dark self?

Not any more.

We ran, and a wind like the end of the world howled around us, and huge fragments of machinery, having crumbled apart and fallen, were yanked up again and tossed like bits of paper. I think the roof was caving in as well; it was a little hard to differentiate. There was no trail to follow, of dismembered vampire remains or anything else; I don't know how Con knew which way to run, but he seemed to, and I ran because he was running, because it seems like a good thing to do when hunks of flying metal the size of small buses are razoring through the air around you, even though I suppose you're as likely to run *into* the wrong place at the wrong time as you are to have lingered in the wrong place at the wrong time if you were moving more slowly.

For the moment, for just this moment of running, I seemed to be committed to the idea of trying to stay alive.

Then we were actually running down something that looked like a corridor, toward something that looked like double swinging doors. We put our unlinked hands forward to push through, and for a miracle the doors swung back, like normal doors in the real world are supposed to do. We were outside, *outside*, in No Town, under a night sky, breathing real air.

Maybe I didn't have time to die, when I ran back into the real world. Or maybe I was too surprised.

We ran straight into the arms of a division of SOF.

In a way I was lucky: they recognized me almost immediately. I was hysterical; this was definitely one thing too many, and when I got grabbed by three guys I did one of them some damage before the other two got a bind on me. I couldn't *bear* the touch of—well, of flesh—against mine, especially against my hands, so it's a good thing they had a bind ready, rather than the old-fashioned routine of spread out on the ground with my hands twisted up behind my back. The bind should have stopped me cold, but I was still full of adrenaline, or dark blood, or the remains of the strength the light-web had gathered for me, or poison, or whatever you like, and I thrashed and squirmed like someone having a fit for a minute or two before it stopped me. By which time I'd heard a half-familiar voice say, "Wait a minute, isn't that—that's Rae, from Charlie's, remember, she—"

You have to hand it to the SOF training drill. A madwoman covered in blood runs out of nowhere, promptly tries to maim one of your teammates, and then goes off in fits, and this guy had enough presence of mind to make an ID. And then a completely familiar voice, now kneeling beside me as I panted inside the fully expanded bind, saying, "Sunshine. *Sunshine.* Can you hear me?"

I could. Just. His voice sounded like it was coming through a filter, or a bad phone connection, which might have been the bind. I don't think it was, but it might have been.

The person saying "Sunshine, can you hear me?" was Pat.

I nodded. I wasn't ready to try and say anything. I'm not sure a nod from a person in a bind is very recognizable, but Pat got it.

"I can let you out of the bind if you promise—if you're okay now."

I thought about it. I was lying on the ground. A good bind will prevent you hurting yourself as well as hurting anyone else, and I didn't seem a whole lot worse than I'd been before SOF grabbed me. And from inside a bind you don't have any responsibilities. Did I want to be let out?

Gods and angels, what was happening to Con? SOF knew me; they might listen to me. I couldn't do Con any good foaming at the mouth and being a loony. Couldn't afford to die yet either. First I owed it to him to get him out of this. If they hadn't staked him already. Urgency shot through me, tying some of the scattered bits of my personality and will together again. Granny knots probably, but hey.

I said as calmly as I could, "Yes. Okay. I'm a little—dizzy."

Pat patted the bind where my shoulder was, and then pulled its plug. It *fwumped* and collapsed. He made to take my arm, help me to stand up, but I flinched away, saying, "Please don't touch me." He nodded, but I could see he was worried—the way I must look would worry anyone—and the way the little ring of SOFs around us moved, they were ready to drop me again at the first sign of new trouble.

I turned slowly around—I *was* dizzy, and I didn't want anyone alarmed into doing something I would regret—and looked for Con. He'd apparently taken capture more quietly. He was standing, watching me. They had handcuffs on him. *Handcuffs.* You don't handcuff a vampire—well, there are sucker cuffs, but these were ordinary ones. From where I stood I didn't think there were even any ward signs on them. A vampire could break out of ordinary cuffs like a human might break out of a doughnut.

I'm not usually a very good liar. Whatever I'm thinking shows on my face. I hoped it wasn't on my face *Hey you halfwits you've put cuffs on a vampire.* I hope I only looked confused and dizzy. I certainly felt confused and dizzy. "You okay?" I managed.

Con nodded. He looked a little peculiar, but it had been a peculiar evening.

"Friend of yours?" Pat asked neutrally.

I nodded. They must have seen us running. . . .

I turned to look at what—where—whatever we had run from. I'd registered that we were in No Town.

We were in what remained of somewhere in No Town. A lot of it seemed to be lying in pieces on the ground around us. The doors we'd run through led from a building that ended in a jagged diagonal rake of broken wall about eight feet above the doors at its lowest point; there was no roof. Neither of the buildings on each side had any roof left either. One of them still had some of its front wall standing, which was nearly as tall as I was; the other one had a bit of side wall still in one piece. Not a very large piece.

I turned back to Pat. "What—happened?"

He almost smiled. "I was hoping you might be able to tell me. Since you're—er—here. We got a report that it was raining—um—body parts, in No Town. Really freaked some of the clubbers. We sent out a car to take a look and they were radioing for help before they arrived. By the time we got here it was raining exploded buildings as well. And more body parts. The—er—body parts appear to be vampire. Ex-vampire, as you might say. The ones we've had a closer look at."

I nodded. I glanced again at Con. My brain was slowly beginning to function. I realized that the reason Con looked peculiar was because he was *passing*. Don't ask me how he was doing it. But SOF thought he was human.

"I can take the cuffs off your friend too, if you say you know him," Pat said, a little too neutrally. "He was a little—upset, when you, er—"

"Went nuts," I supplied. "Sorry."

Pat looked at me. I saw it registering with him that the way I looked, whatever had caused it, I had reason to be a little on edge. He looked away again, and nodded, and someone stepped forward and released Con. He joined Pat and me. The circle of SOFs unobtrusively rearranged itself again to keep us under guard. Pat the lion tamer, in with the lions. Con moved a little stiffly, like a man who'd had a hard night. Or like a vampire trying to look human.

He looked a lot better than he had the afternoon we'd had to walk back from the lake. He didn't look like anyone you'd want to take home to meet the family, but he didn't look like a mad junkie either. Or a vampire. And *I* didn't look like anyone you'd want to take home to meet the family. We were both beat up, ragged, blood-saturated, and filthy, and my nose was as stunned as the rest of me, but I guess we stank. Con's black shirt stuck to his body in such a way I couldn't see the wound in his chest. If it was still there. My own breast ached and burned, but if I was still bleeding, it had slowed to an ooze.

I crossed my arms, but with my elbows well in front of my body, so that my hands hung loosely from my wrists out to either side, without touching any of the rest of me. I wasn't remembering any more of what had happened than I had to, but I knew there was something wrong with my hands.

I wondered where Con had picked up passing for human in the last five months. Was that one of the things I had given him, the night he had given me dark sight? Or was he taking his cue off our jailers somehow? Not that anybody had said they were our jailers.

Yet. I didn't want to say anything like, can we go home now?, in case they did. Besides, I didn't know that I wanted to go home. I didn't know that I wanted to do anything. My pulse seemed to throb in my hands.

There was a tinny buzzing from someone's radiowire: Pat's. I saw his expression get grimmer, and it had been pretty grim already. "Yeah. Okay. No, my guess is things are going to stay quiet now. Yeah, I'll leave a few to keep an eye out, and you can send any clean-up crew you can find. Yeah." He looked at me. "Deputy exec Jain wants to debrief you."

My heart sank. The goddess of pain. And you don't debrief civilians.

"You and Mr.—" Pat turned politely to Con.

"Connor," Con replied.

"Mr. Connor. You and Sunshine can ride back in my car, and Sunshine can tell you a little about our Depex Jain."

I almost managed to be amused. The intrusive presence of the goddess had just put Pat on our side. I guessed we'd need him there. The effort to be amused faded, leaving cold exhaustion.

PAT DID THE best he could for us. The goddess wasn't going to wait for us to have showers, let alone food and sleep. (I would have liked to see Con in one of their fuzzy khaki jammy suits though.) Pat radioed ahead from the car, and Theo and John met us with blankets and tea. (I wondered who got to hose down the inside of the car.) We were also offered the opportunity to have a pee. Such magnanimity. I accepted. Con did not. Don't vampires *pee*? It had been one thing on the walk back from the lake, when he'd been on short rations for a long time. Okay, do they *have* a digestive system? Maybe it all goes straight into . . . never mind. At least I could wash my hands, although I felt the soap only slide over what I most needed to scour away. I cleaned my face with a paper towel, so my hands never touched anything but paper.

Con hesitated no more than a moment when offered tea or coffee, and chose tea. He wrapped the blanket around himself. It was yellow, and didn't help his complexion. He was impressive as a vampire but mostly just ugly as a human. There was a kind of *threateningness* to his ugliness but you couldn't have said why. There was a study once about whether ugly or good-looking people are more imposing. Generally the uglier you are the less imposing, till you reach a sort of nadir of ugliness and then you get *really* imposing. I thought Con just missed the nadir. Just. He was also shorter as a human. I didn't get this at all. But if it meant the goddess would underestimate him that would be expedient. Possibly even life-saving. Although I wasn't sure how I felt about going on having my life repeatedly saved. My thoughts were moving slowly and indistinctly, and they stumbled a lot. I'd had to take the tea mug into my hands to drink from it, but I kept my fingers well away from the brim where my lips would touch. They offered us food, but I refused; it would be sandwiches, something you'd have to touch with your hands. And my refusal made Con's look less odd, maybe.

When Pat took us up to the goddess' office, there were seven of us. Pat, Con and me, Theo and John and two people I didn't know beyond occasionally seeing them at Charlie's: Kate and Mike. The goddess wanted to dismiss everyone but Con and me—she had her own people present, of course—but Pat, going all formal, declined to be dismissed, and began reeling off some directive or other. I'd heard him asking for some SOF reg book and seen him poring over it in the little turnaround time between the car and the goddess' office, but I hadn't thought about it. He was now proving that since he'd nabbed us in the field, he was responsible for us, even in the presence of a superior officer, because he was a field specialist and she wasn't, and the situation was insecure.

One for Pat. But the lines around the goddess' mouth got harder, and her mouth more pinched. And we were all going to pay for it.

Mainly she went for Con. Because she knew there was something wrong about him? Or because he was the stranger? If she hadn't done it before I skegged the HQ com system, she would have read any available file on me after, which wasn't a happy thought, especially the presumption that it would get fatter as a result of her interest. I wondered if Yolande could make a ward against SOF 'fo-collecting techniques. A ward that didn't proclaim itself as a ward, that only made me look boring. Because my natural boring-ness would have taken a fatal injury tonight. Nobody—certainly not Pat or the goddess—was going waste any more time believing my story about having blown myself out the night I blew out their com system.

But there I went again, planning as if I had a future, and I hadn't decided about that yet. The future would be difficult without usable hands, and the old wound on my breast. . . . But I wanted to get Con out of here. His future was his business.

There were more voices. The goddess' voice made my head ache. I had to listen, to pay attention, and I had to *think*, to be careful, to be ready . . . ready. . . . The effort was making me start to disintegrate again. . . . I was drifting, it was so much easier to drift. . . .

What is your name? asked the goddess.

Connor, Con replied.

First name?

Malcolm.

And you live?

I have only recently come to this area, and have not yet decided if I am staying. I rather think that I am not.

But your local address?

I am renting a house by the lake.

Loud intake of breath from everyone except me and Con.

No one lives by the lake any more, said the goddess, as if she had caught him out in a lie.

Con shrugged gently. Yes: my rent is very reasonable, and I like the solitude.

There was a momentary pause. It was true that nobody lived by the lake any more, but there wasn't a good reason why not. There were bad spots, but there were bad spots everywhere, and there were perfectly good *not* bad spots by the lake too. The goddess might think no human could bear the hauntedness of the lake, but she couldn't nail him as an unregistered partblood or illegal Other on it. Let alone a vampire. And my little trouble five months ago had been the first of its kind in years. Con's choice of location would bring that trouble to mind, of course, but there wasn't any way that my presence in the middle of whatever had happened tonight wasn't going to bring that trouble back to center focus in everyone's mind. Maybe Con even had a plan. Which was a lot more than I had. I wanted to rub my aching head but I didn't want to use my hands.

Who is your landlord?

I do not know. I pay the rent to a post office box in Raindance. The rental was arranged through an agent.

What agent?

I do not remember; the papers are at home.

You could produce the papers.

Yes.

What brought you to this area?

Its natural beauty.

That stopped her for a moment. She wasn't a trees and sunsets sort of person. I wondered vaguely where she lived. She wasn't a downtown high-rise sort of person either. Nor could I see her in grotty unorthodox Old Town. I couldn't see her redoing one of the houses in Whiteout. I couldn't see her as a person with a life. I imagined her spending her off-duty hours folded up in a drawer. If she had any off-duty hours.

What do you do for a living?

I am fortunate in not having to work for a living.

This startled her—well, he hadn't been found in circumstances conducive to guessing he was a member of the independently wealthy—but you could see her shift her view to relishing despising this already-suspicious character now revealed as a parasite on the body of society. A mosquito or a leech or something bloodsucking. Ha.

And how then do you support yourself?

My father left me comfortably off.

And your father was?

He dealt in rare and valuable objects.

She was hoping she'd got him, or soon would. What kind of rare and valuable objects?

Con shrugged again, gently. Anything he could buy and sell.

Jewelry, bric-a-brac, other ornaments. Small things mostly. Sometimes paintings, sculpture, larger furniture. He was very clever at it.

I thought of his earth-place, and wondered if he was plugging in
his master in the necessary role of human father. I wondered if his
earth-place was anywhere near the lake. I wondered if vampires also
felt that the best lies stick as near to the truth as possible, because it'll
be easier remembering later what you said. I wondered if vampires
really shrugged, or if this was verisimilitude, like having a father.
He did it pretty well.

The cross-examination went on. I wondered how much Con
knew about human law; he could protest being held without explanation, he could protest the questioning. Perhaps he didn't want to.
Perhaps staying human was enough of an effort, and he wasn't going
to make waves. Perhaps he didn't *mind*. He certainly gave no impression of minding. I told myself that he was a vampire, and vampires
don't give the impression of minding things, perhaps even when
they are pretending to be human.

It didn't occur to me that *I* might protest being held without explanation. I didn't want to encourage them to think about why they
might want to hold me. It seemed to me they had too many good
choices.

But with a sudden cold drench of antidisintegration fear I wondered what time it was. How long had we been—occupied with Bo
and his gang? It had still been deep dark when we'd run through
those doors and straight into the SOF div waiting, presumably inad-
vertently, for us; but which end of the night was that deep dark? And
how long had we been here?

When was sunrise?

When the goddess started asking me questions I had to come
back a long way to focus on her words, to try to answer her. I was
too shattered to be frightened at the same time as I was too shattered
to be anything *but* frightened: to be able to think of a story to tell
her, since I couldn't tell her the truth. In theory I had a lot less to lose
than Con, but it didn't feel like it. I mean, all I'd done was destroy
some vampires. Maybe I hadn't gone through the proper channels,

but nailing vampires is always a plus. She should pin a medal on me. I didn't think she was going to.

Watch your back, Sunshine.

When Con and I had planned our confrontation with Bo, we hadn't thought about what happened after. Well, he may have, but if he had, he hadn't let me in on it. He wasn't a big talker. Also, after Bo, assuming that there *was* an after Bo, our reason for alliance was over; he probably hadn't thought there was anything to discuss.

I sure hadn't thought about needing a good cover story. Who investigates the extermination of *vampires*? If we escaped, we'd've escaped, and it'd be over with. Of course we hadn't planned on blowing up No Town.

The thought returned: after Bo, if there was an after Bo, there would be no reason for Con and me to have anything more to do with each other.

The goddess was talking to me.

Yes, Mr. Connor and I had met five months ago, during my—our—involuntary incarceration at the lake. No, I hadn't mentioned him before. Yes, perhaps I should have: but I had wanted to forget everything about that time, and I had not guessed I would meet him again. No, our meeting tonight was not planned, but no doubt it had something to do with our being drawn back, together, by the vampire we had escaped from those months ago.

With crushing scorn the goddess declared, People don't escape from vampires.

I had my one great moment then. I said that I guessed the vampire must have planned for us to escape, because it wanted to pull us back again later, after we thought we were safe.

Even the goddess had to pause. I didn't think vampires played cat and mouse with their victims to such an extent as to let them run around loose for several months before putting a paw over them again, but vampires are indisputably unpredictable. And it maybe made a sort of teeny sense out of my com-system-exploding habits.

Then how, she said between her teeth, do you explain how you escaped *this* time?

All due respect, ma'am, said Pat, crisp and formal, not sounding like Pat at all, Some big sucker gang war, obviously. These two in the wrong place at the wrong time. Might explain how they got away last time too; some kind of sting, maybe.

And why didn't we know about a gang war important enough to raze better than a third of No Town? snarled the goddess.

Don't know, ma'am, said Pat, but we're going to find out.

The goddess' next few questions to me were positively gentle. No, I couldn't remember how I—how we'd—escaped, five months ago. I didn't precisely remember that we'd escaped at all. The entire experience was very blurred in my memory. Shock no doubt. Ask Pat. I'd told him as much as I remembered. I guessed I remembered even less now.

She didn't ask Pat. She'd read the file.

She didn't mention the other night, and the circumstances under which I'd met her the first time. This should have felt like a respite. It didn't.

She turned back to Con. What did he remember of the two days he'd spent chained up in the house by the lake? Or perhaps it had been more than two days in his case?

No, he didn't remember it very well either. He thought it might have been longer than two days. He thought he remembered the young lady being brought in after him. He had been hiking, and had planned to be away from home for some time anyway. No, he didn't remember precisely how long he was gone. He had spent several days after he returned in something of a daze. He lived alone and had, thanks to his father's bequest, few responsibilities. No one had missed him. He had contacted no one after his ordeal. No, he apologized, it had not occurred to him to make a report to SOF either. He understood he should have. He would be happy to make a full report now, yes, but there wasn't much report to give. He remembered so little. No, it hadn't put him off living by the lake. He lived by a different part of the lake.

And where was that again?

On the southwest side.

Near No Town.

Not very near.

The goddess let this pass, maybe because it was true. But then she began on this evening's events. Con was very sorry, but he didn't remember them clearly either. The notorious vampire glamour, he suggested, had confused him.

He must remember something.

He remembered standing at his front door, breathing the autumn-scented air, and watching the sun set.

He must remember more than that.

Con paused and looked thoughtful. He did this very well: understated but clear. Like the tone of his voice: not inscrutable vampire but reserved human male. Reticent as opposed to undead. He could have a great future in the theater, so long as no one expected him to do matinees.

He remembered a great deal of confusion, and fear, and pain, and er—blood. He touched his blood-stiffened hair apologetically. And explosions. At some point he discovered Miss Seddon there with him amid the—er—uproar. He did not remember any other humans present, but he had not been looking for them. He had been looking for a way out, as had Miss Seddon. Naturally.

Con closed his eyes momentarily at this point. I almost wanted to tell him not to overdo it.

Naturally, said the goddess dryly. Mr. Connor, you seem to be taking all the *uproar*, as you put it, very calmly.

Con spread his hands, and smiled faintly. He *smiled*. Really.

It is over now, he said. What would you have me do?

I would have you tell me the truth! she shouted.

I jumped in my seat. I hadn't been watching her. I'd been watching Con, and the window blind. It was hard to see much; the blind was closed, the proofglass behind it would dull any light trying to come through it, and the goddess' office was brightly lit. But I was pretty sure the corners of the windows were a paler gray than they'd been when we came in.

I looked at the goddess. I tried to look into the glaring shadows on her face, but I was very tired, and the shadows were layers thick. I could see nothing through them except more shadows. My head throbbed.

But I could see her eyes. I didn't like what I saw. She couldn't have guessed, could she? She *couldn't*.

What was there in some secret SOF archive? About vampires? About vampire-human alliances?

Watch your back, Sunshine.

Why would she be watching me? What was there in my file that had caught her eye? Something important enough to lay a fetch on me for?

Something she had, after all, picked up during her illegal troll of me the night we met?

Was she trolling me now? My head hurt so much I couldn't tell how much of it was her godsawful aura and how much was . . . just the way I was feeling. Had she tried to troll *Con*? If she had—no, wait, she couldn't've or he'd be staked and beheaded by now—okay, even if he had blocked her—what might the *block* tell her? Wouldn't a vampire block look—taste, smell, whatever—different than a human one? Or did Con's passing include the shape of his mind to a mind search?

But being able to block a mind search was illegal too. Ordinary humans couldn't do it. Which meant anyone who did wasn't an ordinary human. And if you know something, you know it, even if you got that knowledge by proscribed means. Like by trolling without authority.

It wasn't my back that needed watching at this moment. It was Con's. As well as his front, sides, top, bottom, and any other attached bits.

I stared at the window. In the lower corner nearer me there was a tiny gap where the blind didn't fit true. I was sure I could see light coming in.

The goddess had her back to the window. She had a huge desk—of course—that sprawled in front of it, but it was a big room, and there was plenty of space for her minions and Pat and his lot plus Con and me. Her desk was empty. Even her com gear was all shut away in a wall closet; I knew this because one of her vassals folded the doors back and sat down in front of it. There was a lot of it; it looked like it would take up the entire wall if the doors were pushed back all the way. I was glad I wasn't a techie. If I'd understood any of what I could see, I would have been even more jittery than I already was.

There were now fifteen of us. She'd only had three flunkies when we entered, but when it turned out she wasn't going to be able to get rid of Pat one of them muttered into her wire and four more people had entered almost as soon as she'd finished speaking, marching nearly in lockstep. The goddess must keep them in a cupboard right outside her door for those moments when she needed to oppress a situation quickly. Maybe she chose people who wanted to spend their off-duty hours folded up in a drawer too, the better for rapid retrieval.

We faced each other over her desk, them and us. Con and I sat in two chairs about six feet apart. Pat, keeping up the pretense that we were under defensive surveillance, had a pair of people behind each of our chairs. He leaned against the wall behind us, but off to one side, nearer Con; I could see him out of the corner of my eye without turning my head. His wire squeaked at him periodically; occasionally he muttered back. Once I saw him jerk his head up and stare at us—Con or me, I couldn't tell—after some very agitated squeaking. I wondered what his field people might be telling him about what they were finding in the remains of No Town. I wasn't used to seeing Pat wearing a wire. He hadn't any time I'd seen him at Charlie's. He hadn't when I visited his office downstairs here. He hadn't even when we drove out to the lake. The wire made him look a lot more threatening. More like a regular member of SOF, the huge national agency dedicated to protecting humans against the Other threat, which as one of its minor local operations had planted an illegal fetch on me.

Even with a wire, Pat wasn't nearly as threatening as a vampire.

Or as the goddess.

Several of the flunkies' wires squeaked at them too. I saw them glancing at each other worriedly. Perhaps they always looked worried. Being the goddess' flunky can't have been an easy job, even if you have the personality for it.

The goddess paraded up and down behind her desk, occasionally leaning on it for emphasis, occasionally coming round to the front to sit on the edge and stare at us. She ignored everyone else.

I thought I saw her glance at the window too. Okay, I could make a dive for Con the moment she touched the blind, but that would give two things away simultaneously: what he was. And what I could do.

The air in the room seemed to press against my skull like a tightening vise. Maybe it was just the goddess. I looked at my hands. I thought I could see tiny filaments of green or black running up the backs of them, running up my arms, like gangrene spreading from the site of infection. I couldn't see any sign of the golden web, even though the blanket wrapped around me had rubbed a lot of the blood off. I could see only green and black. Death as an infection. The infection had begun five months ago. Maybe I'd already died back at Bo's headquarters—perhaps when the scar on my breast reopened—and it hadn't quite caught up with me yet. Maybe Con had delayed the inevitable by making me—offering me his blood to drink. Undead blood was used to keeping dead people moving, after all. So maybe it didn't matter if I gave myself away. I was worm fodder as soon as the green and black filaments reached my beating heart.

It did matter. I would be giving Con away too.

I'm very sorry, Con was saying to the goddess. I know how thin my story sounds. But there is nothing else to tell you. It was all very baffling to me—to Miss Seddon and me—too.

There was a little silence. I set my tea mug down on the floor, and groped in my pocket for my little knife, the knife that glowed with daylight even in the dark, the knife that burned Con if he touched it. I held it a moment before I pulled it out, wondering if I was dead—not undead, Con promised me I couldn't be turned, just dead, a new form of zombie perhaps, which would explain why my brain was refusing to work properly, why nothing seemed quite real, not even my fear. A zombie's brain always goes first, while sometimes their hearts go on beating. If I was dead, perhaps I couldn't save Con from the daylight any more either. The knife was warm in my hand. Body heat. But zombies are usually cool. Like all the undead. My knife was warm like the touch of a friend, against my gangrenous hand. Suddenly there were tears in my eyes. Do zombies weep?

I pulled the knife out. I made all the effort I was capable of, to be here, to be *present*, in this room, with Con and Pat and the goddess of pain.

"Pardon me," I said. "I want to return your knife before I—er—forget." I should have said something about why I was remembering now rather than at some other moment, why I had Mr. Connor's knife in the first place, but I couldn't think of anything. I was at the end of my thinking. It was taking all my energy to be here.

And I didn't know that it would work. It was merely the only thing I could imagine to try.

Con turned toward me. He almost forgot to be human. When I tossed him the knife his hand moved toward where it was going to be. . . . I *felt* him check himself. He plucked the knife out of the air a little too neatly, but not impossibly so. Not inhumanly. He caught it, and closed his fingers around it, rested his hand on his knee. The knife had disappeared. If there was anything to see as it burned him, if it burned him, if it was still full of daylight—of my sunshine—no one in the room would see. He set his tea mug down, so he still had one hand free. "Thank you," he said, and turned back to the goddess as if for her next question.

We had our one bit of luck then. There was a wire-squeak so momentous, apparently, that one of the goddess' minions risked whispering it to her, and she was distracted, perhaps, from this curious business of Mr. Connor's knife. She wasn't very happy about whatever news the minion gave her, whatever it was.

Then she sighed, elaborately, as if releasing tension. As if asking everyone in the room to relax. I didn't relax. Con didn't, but then he was never relaxed, any more than he was ever tense. He was just there. Pat didn't relax. I couldn't see any of the rest of us. The minions didn't relax. I'm sure there is a regulation in their contract that forbids them to relax. The goddess looked around at us and smiled. It wasn't a very good smile. If I had to choose, I would say Con did it better.

"Well," she said. "It has been a long night and everyone will be better for a rest. And you two warriors"—she tried to make this sound unironical, but she failed—"according to the latest report, have been a part of the destruction of a major vampire sanctum—perhaps an instrumental part of that destruction. You must forgive what may appear to be my excessive zeal here tonight; but occurrences like this are rare, and SOF *must* know as much as possible about any event concerning the Others, especially the darkest of the Others, to be as effective as we can be. And we have found, over and over again, that the sooner we speak to any and all witnesses, the better.

"I would appreciate it if you would return, later, when you are rested, and fill out formal statements, which we can keep on file. I would also appreciate it if you would make yourselves available for further discussion, at some future time. Occasionally it has happened that witnesses do remember later what they were too shaken to comprehend at the time; perhaps as we learn more about what happened, some detail we can describe to you will loosen something in your memories, something we can use.

"You must see that to the extent it is possible you had a crucial role in tonight's events we *must* discover what that role was.

"And in the meanwhile, perhaps"—she was moving as she spoke—"after the night that has passed, the light of morning will make us all feel better."

With *better* she pulled the blind. Daylight, filtered by proofglass but unmistakably, undeniably daylight, fell full on Con.

How long after sunlight touches him before a vampire burns? The stories say immediately, but what is immediately? One second? Ten? I sat still, rigidly still, my nerves shrieking. Con, of course, looked as he always looked: neither tense nor calm. Twenty seconds. Thirty. Surely thirty seconds was longer than *immediately*?

What is the algebra of how long one live person with an affinity can protect one vampire from the effects of sunlight as compared to one small inanimate daylight-charged pocketknife? Supposing that the person is still alive and the affinity is still functioning, the pocketknife still charged, and the fact that the vampire was presently passing for human didn't morph the process so that Con was about to collapse in a little heap of cold ashes with no gruesome intermediate stages.

Forty seconds. Fifty.

Sixty.

That's good enough.

I burst into tears, and Con was up off his chair at once—as immediately as the fire that hadn't come—and kneeling beside mine, one hand on my shoulder. My blanket had fallen off. I felt my affinity yank itself from wherever it lived—somewhere around my heart apparently—and *throw* itself toward the shoulder he was touching. It was still there. Still live. I heard a rustle, like a sigh of leaves.

Trees are impervious to dark magic.

The hand that held my knife still hung by his side.

It seemed to me that as a performance it wasn't too unlikely that he'd put his hand on my shoulder, after whatever it was that we'd been through together. Maybe we were calling each other Mr. Connor and Miss Seddon, but we'd come out of whatever it was holding hands. I turned my head and stared at him, into his leaf-green eyes, into the face of the monster I had saved, and been saved by, probably too many times to count, now, any more, even by what he had called *that which binds*. Perhaps that was why I could feel my affinity working its way through his body, through the vessels that carried his blood, a special little squad of it racing down to his burned hand. I put both my hands—my contaminated hands—on his shoulders, and leaned my head against him, and wept and wept, and the warmth, the human-seeming warmth of his body through the tattered, filthy shirt against the palms of my hands felt the way my knife had felt: like the touch of a friend. The healing touch of a friend.

I had meant to burst into tears, to break the scene, to give Con a chance to move, and to put up his sun parasol sitting in the next chair, but it had been easy—too easy, and it was hard to stop crying, once I'd begun. It took me several minutes to get to the gulping and hiccupping stage, by which time all of Pat's people were rushing around holding boxes of tissues and bringing damp towels to wipe my face with and brandishing fresh cups of tea. The goddess and her people hadn't moved at all. She looked like a naturalist observing faulty ritual behavior: not at all what she had been led to believe was the norm for this species, but was therefore interesting precisely for that reason, and how could she turn it to her advantage? I didn't like it, but I'd worry about it later.

Her people stood and sat around looking stuffed. Working for the goddess didn't encourage the acquisition of damp-towel-fetching skills.

I would worry about it all later. I was getting used to the idea that I might have a later to worry about it in. Maybe. I was so *tired*.

I had dropped my hands from Con's shoulders to juggle tea and towels and tissues. I looked at them, my hands, going about their usual business of grasping and manipulating. I couldn't see the green and the black any more. But I couldn't see the gold either. I knew the seal was gone forever, and the chain—I couldn't feel the chain against my breast any more, although the reopened wound had stopped aching. Had I heard the rustle of leaves when Con touched my shoulder? *Sun-self, tree-self, deer-self. Don't they outweigh the dark self? Not any more.* I would worry about me later too. About my hands. I would ask Con. . . . I hoped I would have a chance to ask Con. Because after I got him out of this daylight, our alliance was over.

Con. He still knelt beside me. An ordinary man might have looked silly, doing nothing, but even as a relatively successful human-facsimile he looked so . . . unconventional? Unsomething. Silly didn't come into it. Or maybe that was just how I saw him. It was day again, and Con was my responsibility, and we were surrounded by people who must continue to believe he was human. I looked at him. He'd dropped the yellow blanket when he left his chair. He looked better without it, even blood-mottled and with his clothes hanging off him in sodden-and-dried-stiff rags.

"Pardon me, Miss Seddon, but I think I must beg you to keep my knife for me a little longer. I don't believe any of my pockets have survived the night's encounters." He held it out to me, turning and opening his hand: the palm was unmarked. I felt that my affinity emergency-squad was dancing around in some little-used synapse somewhere, giving each other teeny microscopic high-fives.

I put down a towel and accepted the knife, slipping it awkwardly back into the pocket it had come out of. I was careful not to look at the goddess as I did this: as if it was just a little jackknife. I wondered if vampire clothing had pockets. What would vampires keep in pockets? Handkerchiefs? House keys? Charms against being grilled (so to speak) by angry, high-ranking SOF officers?

I'd managed to move my chair a little during the commotion after I burst into tears. Con was safe for the moment, in shadow. I stood up and looked at the goddess. She was taller than I was, of course. There are spells to make you appear taller than whoever you are talking to, but they are expensive, and all but the best have a nasty habit of revealing you as your real height the minute you turn your attention to someone else. I guessed the goddess was just tall. "I apologize for making a fuss," I said, as respectfully as I could. Maybe she was so accustomed to reeking hostility from most of her colleagues and interviewees that she didn't register it any more. Maybe she would assume I didn't like her because she'd intimidated me successfully. Well, she had.

"May we leave now, please?" I continued, holding my poisonous hands out placatingly, palms up. "I will come back whenever you like, but I'm so tired I can't think. And I want a bath." Several baths. And what I was wearing—the remains of what I was wearing—would go into the trash. No, the bonfire. I would start running out of clothing soon if I wasn't careful. If I had a future it would have to include some shopping.

She made gracious-cooperation noises that were about as sincere as my respectfulness, and we were allowed to leave—Con and I, and Pat and John and Theo and Kate and Mike. In the windowless hallway Con and I drifted nonchalantly apart. I was trying to remember if there were any unexpected windows around blind corners. I hadn't been at my best when we'd come through the first time. I wasn't at my best now, but against all odds, I was improving.

Pat expelled a long noisy breath. "Well held, you guys," he said. He glanced at Con. I could guess he was torn between wanting to celebrate a partial victory against the goddess and wanting to know who and what the hell my apparent ally really was. He caught my eyes and I watched him decide to trust me. I watched him watching me watching him decide to trust me. It was true: I owed him. That was something else I'd have to figure out later.

"Can I give you a ride home, Sunshine?" he said casually.

"That would be great," I said feelingly. Even supposing I had bus fare in my pocket, which I didn't, I didn't yearn for the experience of getting Con and me anywhere in public. Any sane bus driver would refuse to let us on board, the way we looked, not to mention the nearest stop was a mile and a half from Yolande's and I didn't think I could walk that far.

I doubted that any nowheresville way was available in—from—daylight. And if I was too tired to walk from the bus stop I was way beyond too tired to deal with any nowheresvilles.

And turning up at Charlie's, looking like this *and* with Con in tow, wasn't an option.

"John, you want to take Mr. Connor—"

"He can come with me," I said firmly. "We have to—talk."

"I bet you do," said Pat. "Okay, Sunshine, I won't ask, but take notes, okay? I'm not going to do my heavy SOF guy trick and make you do your talking here because you've already had that from the goddess, and besides, if she found out I'd taken you to my office and got more out of you than she did she'd bust my ass back to Tinker Bell patrol."

There is a legion of little old ladies (of assorted ages and sexes) who manage to believe that the Others are mostly small and cute and harmless, and live under toadstools, and wear harebells as hats. A lot of them ring up their local SOF div to report sightings, because that is the citizenly thing to do, and since there are a few ill-tempered Others who sometimes pretend to be small and cute and harmless—I'd never heard of any of them wearing harebells, however—these have to be checked out. But it is not a popular job.

"I've been getting reports from No Town right along, you know," continued Pat, "and I want to know what you guys *did*. And I want it in triplicate, you got that? But I'm a patient man and I'll wait. I won't even tell the goddess I took you home together."

"He's lost his house keys anyway," I said glibly, "and we can call a locksmith from my house."

"He keep a fresh change of clothes at your house too?" said Pat. "Does Mel know? I didn't say that."

No windows yet. The other SOFs went their own ways, and it was just Pat and Con and me. Down a few more corridors, and now we were walking toward the glass doors into the parking lot. Con unobtrusively moved near me again and I tucked my arm under his arm and pretended to lean against him. It didn't take a lot of pretending, any more than my tears for the goddess had.

Pat's glance flicked over us again and I realized he was having to make an effort not to go all, well, *male*. He wanted badly to try to put Con in his place and thus find out what his place was. He wanted this as a pretty high-ranking SOF officer, he wanted this as my friend and self-designated semiprotector and semiexploiter, and he probably even wanted this for Mel, who he was at least sure was genuinely human, although ordinarily he would consider my private life strictly my own business. And he'd be having mixed feelings about suspecting Con as some kind of freaky partblood for the obvious reasons. But I recognized the signs in this (comparatively) respectable middle-aged SOF agent from the staring and grunting contests we got occasionally at Charlie's, and from some of the biker bars I'd been to with Mel. I had a sudden frivolous desire to laugh . . . as we walked through the swinging doors and out into the morning.

The sun was still low but the sunshine on my face felt like the best thing that had ever happened to me. I couldn't help it: I stopped, and raised my face to it. Con stopped with me of course. "Sunshine for Sunshine," Pat said mildly. "I'll get the car," and he went on, running his hands over his head as if smoothing down feathers from his frustrated dominance display. I hadn't picked up any response from Con—I could always feel Mel *not* responding—but then Con didn't noticeably respond to much of anything. And it wasn't that vampires didn't have their own shoving competitions—we had, after all, just survived a particularly extravagant one of these. I didn't feel like laughing any more.

I put Con's arm around my waist so I could raise both hands to the sun, as if an extra twenty inches of extended arm was going to make a big difference to its curative properties. I didn't care. I held them, palm up, till I saw Pat's car coming toward us, and Con handed me carefully into the back seat, and slid in after me.

I curled up and pretended to go to sleep on Con's shoulder so we didn't have to make conversation and Pat wouldn't try. This really was pretense: I couldn't go to sleep, at least not yet, and was afraid to try. Even keeping my eyes closed was an effort, but I listened intently to all the normal noises of morning in the city, smelled gas fumes and early coffee bars, and felt Con's arm around me—and his spiky hair occasionally brushing my face—and managed to keep the sights of the night before from replaying themselves against my eyelids. The smell of coffee—penetrating even through the smell of *us*—reminded me of Charlie's, and there was one of those weird bits of mental slippage that trauma produces: I thought, oh, what a good thing I'm not dead, I never did write that recipe down for Paulie. . . .

It felt like a long drive, although it wasn't, still well before rush hour, and in a real car instead of the Wreck. "Check in as soon as you can," was all Pat said when he dropped us off.

"Thanks," I said.

"Thank you," said Con.

Again that flick of gaze to one, then the other of us. "Yeah," said Pat, and drove away.

I HAD AVOIDED losing my house key by not taking it with me. I fished it out from under the pot of pansies and the crack in the porch floor and opened the door, half-watching my hands still, as if they might turn on me and try to tear my own heart out. Con followed me up the dark stairs. My apartment was full of roses. I'd forgotten about the roses. None of them was more than half open. It felt like some kind of miracle: it felt like centuries since I'd bought them, two days ago. I was supposed to be dead. I would be going to *work* tomorrow. Cinnamon rolls. Roses. They were from another world. The human world.

I glanced at my hands again. Hands that earned their living making human food. There isn't much that is a lot more nakedly hands-on than kneading dough.

The ward wrapped around the length of the balcony railing had a big charred hole in the middle of it. When we'd walked through it last night, into Other-space, presumably. The poor thing: it had probably felt like a garage mechanic presented with a lame elephant: wait just a sec here, I never said I did *all* forms of transport. It had been a good ward, and it had survived my smoke-borne passage on my way to find Con. I'd find out later if it could be patched up or if it was blown (or squashed) for good.

I left Con in the middle of the shadowy floor and went out into the daylight again, holding my hands out in front of me like sacrifices or discards. Con moved forward till he was standing at the edge of the shadow. "There is nothing wrong with your hands," he said.

I shook my head, but I lowered my hands till they rested on the balcony railing. There were scorch marks on the railing. On their backs, with the fingers curled up, my hands looked dead.

"Tell me," he said.

"I had to—touch him," I said in a low voice. "I tried not to, but he was too strong. He was winning. I put my hands . . . I *touched* him. Bo." As I said it all the other things I was trying not to remember about the night before came racing back, bludgeoning their way into my mind. I felt myself begin to fragment again. When I'd been facing the goddess, I'd known what I was doing for a little while. Now that there was no immediate threat to organize myself around. . . . I shivered, even in the daylight. Thin, cool, autumn sunlight, with winter to come, with its shorter, colder days, before the baking heat of summer returned. Autumn daylight wasn't going to heal my hands.

Or the reopened wound on my breast. I hadn't had to look at it yet, accept its reappearance yet, while all of me was covered with crusted blood.

"Sunshine," said Con gently. "He had no power to hurt you physically. He had had no such power for many years. His strength was in his will, and in the physical strength of those he controlled by his will. If his creatures—his acolytes—had not hurt you, he could not."

I wanted to say, he *did* hurt me—his creatures *did* hurt me—they taught me what I could do. I would never have done what I did to Bo, if I had not already done it to his followers. "He almost killed me!" I said at last, aloud, feebly. This was an unendurably anticlimactic way of describing what had happened. Merely dying seemed like a minor difficulty, like an alarm clock that had failed to go off or a car that wouldn't start. Maybe I had been hanging out with vampires too much.

"Yes. By sheer force of evil. Only that."

"*Only* that," I said. "*Only* that."

"Yes."

I turned my head to look at him, leaving my hands awkwardly where they were. The Mr. Connor of the goddess' office had gone; my Con was back. There was a vampire in the room. He looked tired, almost as a human might look tired, as well as ragged and filthy. My vampire looked tired. I took my hands off the railing so I could go back into the shadows to Con. I reached out to touch him, twisted my hands away from him at the last moment. But he took my hands by the wrists, and kissed the back of each fist, turned them over and waited, patiently, till the fingers relaxed, and kissed each palm. It was a strange sensation. It felt less like being kissed than it felt like a doctor applying a salve. Or a priest last rites. "There is nothing wrong with your hands," he said. "The touch of evil poisons by the idea of it. Reject the idea and you have rejected the evil."

I was being lectured in morality by a vampire. I wanted to laugh. The problem was that he was wrong. If he'd been right maybe I could have laughed. "My hands feel—they've been—changed. I can feel this. They—they don't belong to me any more. They are only—attached. They feel as if they may be—have become—evil."

"Bo's evil was a very powerful idea."

"I thought I was coming to pieces. I am not sure I'm not. My hands—my hands are two fragments of what is left of me." Two ruined fragments.

There was a pause. "Yes," said Con.

"How do you know?" I whispered.

I waited for him to drop my hands, to move away from me. The pleading whine of my voice set my own teeth on edge. He was only still with me because the sun trapped him here till sunset.

He didn't move away. He said, "I see it in your eyes."

This was so unexpected I gaped at him. *"What—"*

"No. I cannot read your secrets. But I can read your fears. My kind are adept at reading fear. And you look into my eyes as no other human ever has."

I looked away from him. *War and Peace,* my fears. All fifty-odd volumes of the *Blood Lore* series. The complete globenet directory. For sheer length and inclusiveness my fears were right up there. I hoped he was a speed reader.

He dropped my hands then, but only to put a finger under my chin. "Look at me."

I let him raise my chin. Hey, he was a vampire. He could break my neck if he wanted to. This way he didn't have to.

"You are not afraid of everything," he said.

"Nearly," I said. "I am afraid of you. I am afraid of *me.*"

"Yes," he said.

There was a curious comfort in that "yes." I had definitely been hanging out with vampires too long. This vampire.

I remembered standing in the sunlight in my kitchen window, the morning after my return from the lake. That moment when I first began to feel I might recover, from whatever it was that had happened.

The splinters that my peace of mind had been smashed into—if not, perhaps, after all, my sanity—were sending little scouting filaments across the gaps, looking for other pieces, whether I'd sent them out to look or not. Where the scout-filaments met, they'd start winding themselves together again, knitting themselves back into rows. . . . They were probably building on those first granny knots from when I'd agreed to be let out of the SOF bind and be responsible for my behavior.

No: from the first granny knots of the morning after Con had brought me home from the lake.

I was going to have some more scars and the texture of the final weave was going to change. Was changing. It was going to be *lumpier*, and there were going to be some pretty weird holes. I never had been able to learn to knit. I don't do uniformity and consistency. Even my cinnamon rolls tend to have individual personality. I could probably cope with a few more wodgy bits in my own makeup.

Maybe my medulla oblongata was refusing to take any crap from my cerebrum again. *Shut up and get on with the reconstruction. If you can't find the right piece, use the wrong one.*

I took a step backward, still facing Con, still within reach of him, but so that the sunlight touched me.

There was something struggling out of the murk here, trying to make me think it: If good is going to triumph over evil, good has to stay sane.

Say what? Oh, *please*. I'm still thinking about *breathing*. Now I'm supposed to start in flogging myself to go on fighting for the forces of . . . well, "good" is some freaking mouthful. It sounds like some Anglo-Saxon geek with a big square jaw and a blazing sword, any vestigial sense of humor surgically removed years before when he was conditionally accepted to Hero School.

But that was kind of where I'd wound up, even if I'd missed out on the jaw and the training. Because I was definitely against evil. Definitely. In my lumpy, erratic way. And I knew what I was talking about, because I'd now met evil. That was precisely the point.

I'd touched it.

And I was going to have to remember for the rest of my life that I'd touched it. That these hands had grasped, *pulled* . . .

But us anti-evil guys have to stay sane. Lumpy and holey, maybe, but sane. Listen, Sunshine: Bo was *gone*. He wasn't going to get the last word now.

I hoped.

At least not until later this morning.

"I'm going to run a bath. I'll flip you for who goes first." I had a jar on my desk, next to the balcony, that held loose change.

"Flip?" Vampires. They don't know anything.

I won. I was almost sorry. I felt obliged to have only one bath, and a fast one, but I made it count. If I rubbed my palms a little rawer than I needed to for an *idea*, at least my hands felt like my hands while I was doing it. Perhaps the touch of the rose petals, when I'd had to move all the floating roses out of the bath so I could get me into it instead, had helped.

There was no wound on my breast. I hadn't believed it at first. I kept rubbing the soap all over my front, from throat to pubic line, as if maybe I'd *mislaid* it somehow. But it wasn't there. The scar was. I thought it looked a little . . . wider, shinier, than it had, the day after Con had closed it the first time. But it was a scar.

But my chain was gone too, and there was a new scar, which dipped over the old one, in the shape of a chain hanging around my neck. Together they looked like some new rune, but I couldn't read it.

There was no sign of the golden web, no matter how hard I scrubbed.

. . . *What* had I been saying about *going on* fighting for the forces of good? In that mad little moment right after Con had said something *comforting*? That a vampire had seemed to say something comforting should have told me I was having a crazy moment, not a returning-sanity-and-hope moment.

Going on doing anything like what I'd been doing these last five months—horribly culminating in what I had done last night—was approximately the *last* thing I wanted.

Especially when it meant bearing the knowledge of what I'd done. And that going on doing it would mean bearing more of doing and more of knowing.

But Pat had said we had less than a hundred years left. Us humans. No, not us *humans*. Us-on-the-right-side. And there aren't enough of us.

Okay, here's the irony: if I went on with this heavy magic-handling shtick I was likely to be around in a hundred years.

I pulled the plug and started toweling myself dry. I rubbed violently at my hair like I was trying to friction-burn undesirable thoughts out of my head. I washed and dried my little knife tenderly, however, and put it back in my fresh, clean, dry pocket. I was dressed in the first thing out of the top cupboard in the bathroom, where all my oldest, rattiest clothes lived. Then I started another bath and called Con.

I found a one-size-fits-all kimono in the back of my closet that Con could get into, or rather that would go round him; at least it was black. I could give him the shirt in the back of my closet but it wouldn't be long enough on him.

Right. I was clean. Con had something to wear. On to the next thing. Food. I didn't have to think any more long-view thoughts yet. I still had small immediate things to organize myself around.

I was frying eggs when he came out, looking very exotic in the kimono. I stood there holding a skillet with three beautifully fried eggs in it and said miserably, "I can't even *feed* you." How I'd organized my entire life: feeding other people. I heard what I was saying—or what I was saying it to—a moment after the words came out, but his gaze did not waver.

"I do not eat often. I do not need food."

I shook my head. I'd narrowly avoided mental breakdown as a result of facing ancient all-consuming evil, and now I was about to lose it over giving a vampire breakfast. I felt tears pricking at my eyes. This was ridiculous. "I can't eat in front of you. It's so . . . I feed people for a *living*. If I don't do it I'm a failure. I *identify* as a feeder of . . ."

"People," said Con. "I am not a person."

I'd just been having this conversation with myself in the bathroom. "Yes you are," I said. "You're just not, you know, human."

"Your food grows cold," said Con. "It is better hot, yes?"

I shook my head mutinously. He was right, though, it was a pity to ruin such ravishing eggs.

"I will drink with you," said Con.

"Orange juice?" I said hopefully. It had to have calories in it. Water didn't count.

"Very well. Orange juice."

I moved three white roses out of one of my nice glasses, gave it a quick wash, and poured orange juice in it. It was one of the tall ones with gold flecks. Silly thing to drink juice out of. I didn't see him drink—it occurred to me I hadn't seen him drink his tea in the goddess' office either—but nearly half a gallon of orange juice disappeared while I ate my eggs and two toasted muffins and a scone. (What a good thing that it hadn't occurred to me to empty my refrigerator before I died.) Did that mean he liked it, or was this his demanding standard of courtesy again?

"What does it taste like?" I asked.

"It tastes like orange juice," he said, at his most enigmatic.

How was I planning on defining us-on-the-right-side, anyway? Con had been on the right side as compared to Bo. Con was still a vampire. He still . . .

I did the dishes in silence while Con sat in his chair. The kimono made him look very zen, sitting still doing nothing. I'd seen it first at the lake, that capacity for sitting still doing nothing with perfect grace: although that wasn't how I'd thought of it when we were chained to the wall together. And it was interesting that he retained it when he wasn't under the prospect of immediate elimination with no way out, which might be expected to focus the mind. If it didn't blow it to smithereens.

I did the dishes slowly. We'd done washing and eating. There wasn't anything to come except to figure out sleeping arrangements. Con had acknowledged that vampires did something like sleep during the day. And my body had to have sleep soon or I was going to fall down where I stood. But my mind couldn't deal with it. I'd tried to convince myself to haul some laundry downstairs but I couldn't face the effort: *stairs*: the assault on Everest, and where were my Sherpas? I rescued Con's trousers from where he had rinsed and wrung them out and draped them over the towel rack (you don't think of vampires in domestic-chore terms, but I suppose even vampires have to come to some arrangement about getting their clothes washed), and hung them on the balcony for the sun and wind to dry them; at least they were still trousers, if a trifle ravaged by events, which was more than could be said for the remains of his shirt. I scuffled around in my closet again—at some peril to life and limb, since my com gear tended increasingly to get left in there—and pulled the spare shirt out, and left it on the closet doorknob.

Every utensil was scoured within an inch of its life and dried and put away too soon.

Sleep. No way.

At least, being this tired, and still half-watching my hands for renegade moves, I wasn't interested in—or maybe I should say I wasn't capable of brooding about—what else might happen in a bed-type situation. Or could happen. Or wasn't going to happen.

I was capable of brooding about being afraid to be alone. Afraid to sleep.

"You'll have to have the bed," I said. "There are no curtains for the balcony, and the sun gets pretty much all round the living room over the course of the day. I'll sleep on the sofa."

He was silent for a moment, and I thought he might argue. I'm not sure I wasn't waiting hopefully for an argument. But all he said finally was, "Very well."

OF COURSE I couldn't sleep. I would have liked to pretend—even to try to pretend—that it was because I wasn't used to sleeping during the day, but with the hours I sometimes kept at the coffeehouse I had to have learned to take naps during the day or die, and I had learned to take naps. Up until five months ago "something or other or die" had always seemed like a plain choice in favor of the something or other.

Sleep was no friend today. Every time my heavy, aching eyes closed, some scene from the night before shot onto my private inner-eye movie screen, and I prized them open again and lay, dismally, in the soft golden sunlight of early autumn, surrounded by the smell of roses.

I don't know how long I lay there. I turned on my side so I could watch the sunlight lengthen across the tawny floor as the sun rose higher, as the light reached out to pat my piles of books, embrace the desk, stroke the sofa, draw its fingers tenderly across my face. I was comfortable, and safe: safer than I'd been since before the night I drove out to the lake, and met Con. Bo was gone, Bo and Bo's gang. But I couldn't take it in. Or I couldn't take it in without . . . taking in everything it had involved. We'd done it, Con and I. We'd done what we set out to do, and, furthermore, what we'd known, going in, we wouldn't be able to do. Or I had known we wouldn't be able to do it. What I hadn't known was that I'd been *counting* on not being able to do it. And I'd been wrong. We'd *done* it. *Done* is a very thumping sort of word. I felt like I was hitting myself with a club.

I didn't feel safe. I felt as if I was still waiting for something awful to happen. No. I felt as if the thing I most dreaded had arrived, and it wasn't death after all. It was me. *I'm afraid of you. I'm afraid of* me.

As little as three months ago I'd thought that finding out I might be a partblood, and might as a result go permanently round the twist once the demon gene met up properly with the magic-handling gene, was the worst thing that could happen. It was the worst thing I could imagine. I'd pulled the little paper protector of disuse off the baking-soda packet of my father's heritage and dropped it into the vinegar of my mother's. The resultant fizz and seethe, I'd believed, was going to blow the top of my head off. Now those fears seemed about as powerful as the kitchen bomb every kid has to make once or twice to fire popcorn at her friends. I felt as if mere ordinary madness would have been a reprieve. I'd known about the bad odds against partbloods with human magic-handling in their background. I hadn't known anything about Bo. About what a thing like Bo could be.

Black humor alert. And I still didn't know if my genes *were* getting ready to blow the top of my head off. Although it seemed to me they'd had the best opportunity any bad-gene act could possibly have wanted, and had let it pass them by.

I wrapped the blanket closer around me and stood up and went into the bedroom. I'd drawn the curtains tightly together and the bed was in heavy shadow and I wasn't paying attention, so it took me a moment to realize he wasn't in it.

He couldn't have *left*. It was *daylight* out there. Panic rose up in me. I would have guaranteed I didn't have the energy for panic. One more thing to be wrong about. And what was I panicking about anyway? Being left alone with myself? I'd rather have a vampire around?

Well. Yes.

I didn't have time to finish panicking. He stood up—or more like unfolded, like a particularly well-jointed extending ladder or something: *stood up* doesn't really describe it—from the far side of the bed. "What are you doing on the *floor*?"

He just looked at me, and I remembered the room I had once found him in. The room that wasn't his master's. At least he was still wearing the kimono.

"I'm sorry," I said. "I can't sleep."

"Nor I," he said.

"So you do sleep," I said. "I mean, vampires sleep."

"We rest. We become . . . differently conscious than when we are . . . awake. I am not sure it is what you would call sleep."

No, and orange juice probably doesn't taste like orange juice to you either, I thought.

I couldn't sleep, but I was too tired to stand up. I sat down on the bed. "I—we did it, you know?" I said. "But I don't feel like we did it. I feel like we failed. I feel like everything is worse now than it was before. Or that I am."

He was still standing. "Yes," he said.

"Does it feel like that to you too?"

He turned his head as if he was looking out the window. Maybe he was. If I could see in the dark, maybe a vampire could see through curtains. Maybe it was something you learned to do after the first hundred years or so. One of those mysterious powers old vampires develop. "I do not think in terms of better and worse."

He paused so long I thought he wasn't going to say any more. It's probably an occupational hazard, becoming a fatalist, if you're a vampire.

But he went on finally. "What happened last night has changed us. Yes. Inevitably. You have lived—what? One quarter of one century? I have existed many times that. Experience is less to me than it is to you, for I have endured much more of it. And yet last night troubles me too. I can—a little—guess how much more it must trouble you."

I looked down, partly so he couldn't read anything in my eyes, although he probably already had. Maybe that was why he had been looking through the curtains. Vampire courtesy. Previously observed.

Troubled, I thought. Okay.

"Sunshine," he said. "You are not *worse*."

I looked up at him, remembered what I saw him do. Remembered what I had seen myself do. Remembered Bo.

Tried to remember that we were the victors.

Failed. If this was victory. . . .

I was so tired.

"I will do anything it is in my power to do for you," he said. "Command me."

A vampire, standing on the far side of my bed, wearing my kimono, telling me he'd do anything I asked. Steady, Sunshine.

I sighed. I wasn't up to it. "I don't want to feel alone," I said. "Lie down on the bed and let me lie down beside you, and put your arms around me. I know you can't do anything about the heartbeat, but I know you can breathe like a human if you want to, so will you please?"

I looked at his face in the shadows—the shadows that lay motionless and fathomless across it—but it was expressionless, of course. He lay down, and I lay down, and he put his arms around me. (Note: do vampire limbs get pins and needles?) And breathed like a human. More or less. It was a little hard to ignore the lack of heartbeat that close—no, you may not *think* you're aware of a pulse in the body lying next to you, barring your actual head on an actual chest, but, trust me, you are—but he was the right temperature and that helped. And somehow the solidity of him, the fact that my open eyes could see nothing but his throat above the folds of the kimono and his jaw above that, felt strangely as if he was protecting me, as if he could protect me from what I had brought back with me, had roused to consciousness within me, the previous night. I curled my deceitful hands under my chin. And I found myself falling asleep after all.

I dreamed, of course. Again Con and I were in Bo's lair, and there were vampires coming at us from all directions, flame-eyed, deadly, horrible. Again I saw Con do the things I would rather not have seen anyone do; again I did things myself I would rather not have done nor know that I had done. It does not matter if it is them or us, after a certain point. It does not matter. There are some things you cannot live with: with having done. Even to survive.

Again my hands touched Bo's chest. Plunged within it. Grasped his heart, and tore it free. Watched it burn. Watched it deliquesce.

And again.

And again.

I felt the poison of that contact sinking through my skin. It did not matter if it was *only* the poison of evil, the poison of an idea: it was corruption, and it corrupted me. I felt the fire of the golden web rise up in me: through me: and lift away.

I wept in my sleep.

When Bo caught fire and burned, I too burned: my tears left little runnels of fire down my face, not water. They dripped on my breast, where the wound had reopened. They burned especially terribly there. My tears and the light-web burned me, and then left me.

For a little while after this I blew on the wind as if I were no more than ash. But I was blown eventually out of darkness into light, and as the light touched me I began to take shape again. I struggled against this—I was fragments, bits of ash. I was nothing and no one, I had no self and no responsibilities. I did not want to be put back together again, to face everything I was and had done, and could do again. *Another hundred years, tops, and the suckers are going to be running the show. The Wars were just a distraction.*

I did not want to feel the poison eating through me again, to see those gangrenous lines crawling up my arms where the golden web had once run, toward my still-beating heart; to see myself rotting. . . . I would rather be ash, dry and weightless, without duty or care. Or memory.

Or severed loyalties.

Here was a memory: I was sitting on the porch of the cabin by the lake. It was night. I could hear behind me the ping of my car's engine as it cooled. It was a beautiful night; I was glad I had come.

But my life was about to change irreversibly. Irreparably.

My death was about to begin.

I listened for the vampires, knowing I would not hear them. It was too soon in the story of my death for me to hear them.

Instead I heard a light, human step rustle in the grass, in last year's half-crumbled leaves. I turned in amazement.

My grandmother walked up the steps to the porch, and sat down beside me. There was more gray in her hair than there had been fifteen years ago. She looked worn and discouraged, but she smiled at me as I stared at her disbelievingly.

"I do not have much time, my dear," she said. "Forgive me. But I had to come when I heard you weeping. When I understood what you wept for." She picked up my hands—in a gesture very like Con's—and then held them together, as she had done long ago, when she had taught me to change a flower into a feather. "Constantine is telling the truth," she said. "There is nothing wrong with your hands. There is nothing wrong with *you*. Except, perhaps, that you came into your strength too quickly, and all alone, which is not how it should happen—if it is any comfort, this is not the first time it has happened this way to someone, and it will not be the last—and yet if it had not happened that way to you, you might not have done what you did, partly because you would have known it could not be done. And so you would have died."

"Would that have been so bad?" I said, trying to keep my voice level. "Mel would have mourned, and Aimil, and Mom and Charlie and Kenny and Billy . . . even Pat, maybe. Even Mrs. Bialosky. But—would it have been so bad?"

My grandmother turned her head to look out at the lake, and again I was reminded of Con, of the way he turned his head to look through the curtains. She was still holding my hands. "Would it have been so bad?" she said, musingly. "I am not the one to answer that, for I am your grandmother, and I love you. But yes, I think it would have been so bad. What we can do, we must do: we must use what we are given, and we must use it the best we can, however much or little help we have for the task. What you have been given is a hard thing—a very hard thing—or you would not have to ask if your failure and early death would be so bad a thing to happen instead. But my darling, what if there were no one who could do the difficult things?"

"Which difficult things?" I said bitterly. "There are so many of them. Right now it feels as if they're all difficult things."

I waited for her to tell me to pull myself together and stop feeling sorry for myself, but she said: "Yes, there are many difficult things, and they have been almost too much for you—too much for you to have to bear all at once. Remember what Constantine told you: that he too is shaken, for all that he is older and stronger than you are."

"Con is a *vampire*," I said. "He's one of the *difficult things*."

"Yes," she said. "I'm sorry."

"Pat says that we have less than a hundred years left," I said.

And for a third time she reminded me of Con, in the quality of the silence before her answer. But she sighed like a human. "Pat is perhaps a little pessimistic," she said.

"A little!" I said. "*A little!*"

She said nothing.

We sat there, her warm hands still holding mine. I was waiting for her to tell me everything was all right, that I would be better soon, that it would all go away, that I would be fine. That I would never have to look at another vampire again. That we had all the time we needed, and it wasn't my battle anyway. She didn't. I heard the little noises that the lake water made. I felt the pieces of my severed loyalties grinding together. Of the fragments of me.

I thought about the simplicity of dying.

At last I said, and surprised myself by the saying: "I would be sorry never to see the sun again." I paused, and realized this was true. "I would be sorry . . . never to make cinnamon rolls again, or brownies or muffins or—Sunshine's Eschatology. I would be sorry never to work twenty hours straight on a hot day in August and tear off my apron at midnight and swear I was going to get a job in a factory. I would be sorry never to leave my stomach behind when Mel opens the throttle on this week's rehab project. I would be sorry never to tell Mom to mind her own damn business again, never to have Charlie wander into the bakery and ask me if everything is okay when I'm in rabid-bitch mode, not to make it to Kenny and Billy's high school graduations, supposing either of them manages to graduate. I would be sorry never to reread *Child of Phantoms* again, never to argue with Aimil about Le Fanu and M.R. James, never to lie in Yolande's garden at high summer. . . ." Wonderingly I said, "I'd be sorry never to hear the latest SOF scuttlebutt from Pat again."

I paused again, longer this time. I almost didn't say it. I whispered: "I would be sorry never to see Con again. Even if he is one of the difficult things."

I woke with tears on my face and Con's hair in my mouth. I don't think any of me moved but my eyelids, but he raised his head immediately. I sat up, releasing him from dreadful servitude. He rolled to his feet at once, and drew the curtains back. Night had fallen.

"It's dark out," I said unnecessarily.

"Yes," he said. I didn't see him shed the kimono or walk out of the room, but suddenly he wasn't there, and the kimono was a black puddle on the dark floor. When he reappeared he was wearing his own clothes. The black shirt looked much better on him than it had on me. The trousers looked pretty bad, but they were better than nothing. They had to be damp still, but I told myself he could raise his body temperature to steam them dry if he wanted to. Another of those little perks to being undead.

He hadn't buttoned the shirt.

There was no wound on his chest.

I'd been here before.

But there was a scar.

I climbed off the bed—standing up, a little dizzy—went to him, touched it. "That's new," I said.

"Yes," he said.

I wanted to know why: what would scar a vampire? Another vampire's try for your heart? Or the touch of live human lips on such a wound? But I didn't ask.

"You slept," he said.

I nodded.

"It is over. Last night is over," he said. "And Bo is gone forever."

I looked up at him. There was no expression on that alien, gray-skinned face. If it wasn't for the eyes, he could be a statue. One carved by a particularly lugubrious sculptor.

Ludicrous, I thought. Insane, grotesque, impossible.

I looked away, so he couldn't read my eyes. But he'd said he could only read my fears, not my secrets.

I would be sorry never to see Con again.

"It is beginning to be over," I said. "Last night is beginning to be over. I dreamed—I dreamed of my grandmother."

"She who taught you to transmute."

"Yes."

He nodded—as an articulated statue might nod—as if this made perfect sense. And as if this were the last, perfect stroke, and the story—or the statue—was complete.

I wasn't going to cry. I *wasn't*.

"We are still bound, you and I," he said. "If you call me, I will come."

I shook my head, but he didn't say any more. "You could call me," I said. Spectres of the sort of black Bakelite phone fantasy that Con's master might have tucked away in a corner gyrated briefly across my mind's eye.

"Yes," he said.

I touched the new scar on my neck, the one that crossed the old scar, the one in the shape of a necklace. "I have lost the chain you gave me. I'm sorry. I couldn't find the way, even if you did call me."

"You have not lost it," he said. There was a pause. "The necklet is still there."

"Oh," I said blankly. I suppose if a pocketknife can be transmuted into a key a chain can be transmuted into a scar. Maybe on the same grounds as that it's hard to leave your head behind because it's screwed on. Although it had been as well for Con a little earlier that my pocketknife was still detachable. Carefully I said, "I would not want to call you if you did not want to come."

Another pause. I bit my lip.

"I would want to come," he said.

"Oh," I said again.

Pause.

"Would I . . . do I need to be in danger of dying?" I said.

"No," he said. But he turned his head, and looked through the window, as if he was longing to be gone.

I stepped back. I took a deep breath. I thought of cinnamon rolls. And Mel. I thought of trying to help save the world in less than a hundred years, doing it Pat's way. "I'm sorry," I said. "I'm trying to turn this into some kind of human good-bye thing, you know? You're free to go."

"I am not human," he said. "I am not free."

"I am not some kind of trap—or jail cell!" I said angrily. "I am not a rope around your neck or—or a shackle around your ankle! So—so go away!"

Perhaps it was the wind of my anger. I heard a rustle of leaves.

He looked again at the window. I wrapped my arms around my body and leaned back against the end of the bed, and stared at the floor, waiting for him to vanish.

"When do you again make—cinnamon rolls?"

Gaping at him was getting to be a bad habit. So was saying, *What?* I gaped at him. I said, *"What?"*

Patiently he repeated, "When do you go again to your work of feeding humans?"

"Er—tomorrow morning, I guess. What time is it?"

"It will be midnight in two hours."

"Six hours then. I leave here a little after four."

Slowly, as if he were an archaeologist deciphering a fragment of a long-dead language, he said, "You could come with me. Tonight. I would return you here in time for your leaving to go to the preparation of cinnamon rolls. If you are sufficiently rested. If you . . . wished to come."

What does a vampire actually *do* at night? Go for long invigorating walks? Research the habits of badgers and owls and—er—I wasn't very up on my nocturnal wildlife. "Aren't you—er—hungry?"

Another pause. Time enough for me to decide I'd imagined what he'd just said.

"I am hungry," he said. "I am not so hungry that I cannot wait six hours."

I thought of how totally, horribly difficult tomorrow was going to be. I thought of all the stories I was going to have to tell. I thought of all the truth I was going to have to *not* tell. I thought of lying to Charlie, to Mel, to Mom. To Mrs. Bialosky and Maud. To Aimil, even to Yolande. I thought of facing Pat again. I thought of having to talk to the goddess again—among other things about the disappearance of Mr. Connor, whose address would turn out to be false. I thought of how much easier all these things would be if Con vanished into the night, now, forever. They wouldn't be easy—nothing was ever going to be completely easy again, after last night. And I hated lying. I had been lying so much lately.

Almost everything would be easier, if Con went away forever.

Con said, "I would rather bear you company a few more hours than slake my hunger."

I didn't make up my mind. I heard my voice say, "I'll get dressed." I turned—like a walking statue, a badly made puppet—and went to the closet. I managed to turn the knob and open the door before my brain caught up with me. By that time the decision had already been made.

Since my living room closet was now full of com gear, my bedroom closet was impassable. Where, or for that matter when, had I last seen my black jeans? As I say, I don't do black, and my wardrobe isn't based on the concept of dematerializing into the shadows. "This may take a minute," I said. I hoped I didn't sound like I was begging.

"I will not leave without you," he said.

His voice was still expressionless, and I could not see him now, as I was, on my knees on the floor of my closet, fumbling through a pile of laundry that might have stayed folded if it had had a shelf to go on, but it didn't and it hadn't. Maybe it was because I was thinking about self-unfolding laundry that made it so easy to hear that he was telling the truth. *I will not leave without you.* I looked at my hands, the hands that had touched Bo and held his heart while it melted and ran stinking down my wrists and dripped sizzling to the disintegrating floor, and which were now efficiently sorting wrinkled laundry. I saw my hands clearly, although it was dark, because I could see in the dark, and they did not look wrong or strange or corrupt to me; they looked like my hands. Deeper in the closet—where *were* those damned jeans—where it was really very dark, and while I was thinking about jeans, I saw the faintest glimmer of gold on the backs of them, on the backs of my hands, and on my forearms. I had not lost the light-web either.

This was now my life: Cinnamon rolls, Sunshine's Eschatology, seeing in the dark, charms that burned into my flesh where I could not lose them. A special relationship with the Special Other Forces, where not everybody was on the same side. A landlady who's a wardskeeper. Untidy closets. Vampires.

Get used to it, Sunshine.

I came out of the closet wearing black jeans and a charcoal gray T-shirt I had always hated. And red sneakers. Hey, red turns gray in the dark faster than any other color.

He held out his hand. "Come then," he said.

I went with him into the night.

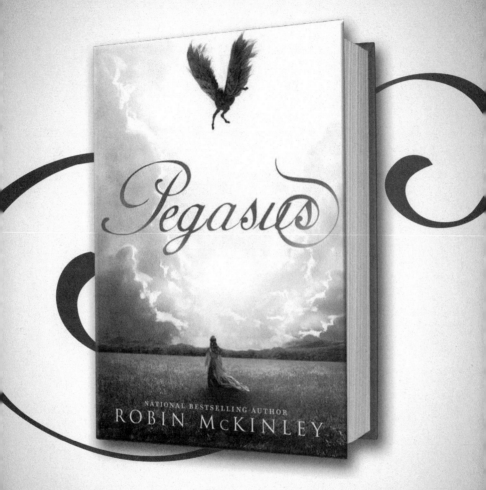